SAVAGE JUSTICE

SAVAGE JUSTICE

A NOVEL

Ron Handberg

A Birch Lane Press Book
Published by Carol Publishing Group

A Birch Lane Press Book
Published by Carol Publishing Group
Birch Lane Press is a registered trademark of Carol Communications, Inc.

Editorial Offices: 600 Madison Avenue, New York, N.Y. 10022
Sales & Distribution Offices: 120 Enterprise Avenue, Secaucus, N.J. 07094

In Canada: Canadian Manda Group, P.O. Box 920, Station U, Toronto, Ontario M8Z 5P9.

Queries regarding rights and permission should be addressed to Carol Publishing Group, 600 Madison Avenue, New York, N.Y. 10022

Carol Publishing Group books are available at special discounts for bulk purchases, for sales promotions, fund raising, or educational purposes. Special editions can be created to specificatons. For details, contact: Special Sales Department, Carol Publishing Group, 120 Enterprise Avenue, Secaucus, N.J. 07094
Manufactured in the United States of America
10 9 8 7 6 5 4 3 2 1

Library of Congress Cataloging-in-Publication Data
Handberg, Ron.
    Savage justice / by Ron Handberg.
      p.   cm.
    "A Birch Lane Press book."
    ISBN 1-55972-116-2
    I. Title.
  PS3558.A6425S28   1992
  813'.54—dc20   91-41397
                       CIP

To Carol, with love always

Acknowledgments

My deepest thanks to my wife, Carol, and my children, Deborah, Greg, and Melinda, for sharing and believing in my dream; to my friends Nancy Mate, Al Austin, Carol Ellingson, David Tripp, and the late Joe Bartelme for their faith, encouragement, and criticism; to sexual-abuse therapist Bill Seals, for his information and expertise; to Paul Hannah, for his legal counsel; to Jack Caravela, my agent and friend, who first helped me to revise the book and then to sell it; to my editor, Gail Kinn, for her patience and insights; and finally, to all of my friends and colleagues, past and present, at WCCO Television in the Twin Cities.

Savage Justice is a work
of imaginative fiction.
Any resemblance to any persons,
living or dead,
or to actual events
is coincidental,
a reflection
of the way the world is
in reality.

SAVAGE JUSTICE

One

The darkened street was quiet, save for the wind.

Desolate and cold. Eye-watering cold.

On a Friday or Saturday night, in the summer, the sidewalks would have been jammed, the stream of cars on the street unending. Bumper to tailpipe, windows down, tunes blaring, filled front seat and back with the young in search of a quick piece or a quick fix.

Or the old in search of the young.

But this was a Tuesday night in November.

The sidewalks were barren. Tattered pieces of newspaper cartwheeled in the wind, the flickering neon lights of the bars and all-night cafés attracting only those in search of warmth.

A few cars passed, and now and then a bus, windows fogged, closed tight against the cold, its occupants in a hurry to be home.

One car was in no hurry.

It hugged the curb, moving slowly, its right signal indicator flashing, forgotten in the succession of turns around the block. The windows of the Continental were almost as dark as its glistening black finish.

"Where the fuck is he?" said a voice from within.

The figure behind the wheel was indistinguishable, a shadow framed only by the glare of passing headlights or silhouetted

1

against the windows of a lighted storefront. The car was still moving, circling, always moving, but barely. Searching. Prowling.

Rick watched from the deep shadows of the doorway. His skin was numbed by the cold, and his nose was filled with the pungent smell of the steam rising from the sewer manhole just beyond the sidewalk. His eyes strained but failed to penetrate the darkened windows of the Continental as it moved slowly toward him and finally stopped opposite the darkened doorway.

There was no movement, no sound except the deep gurgle of the car's engine. Minutes passed, and nothing stirred. Even the wind had diminished from a whistle to a whisper.

Rick saw no one on the street but an old woman huddled on a bench a half block away, scarf tight around her face, a shopping bag clutched to her body for warmth and security—waiting for a bus to rescue her from the cold and take her home.

Rick knew she could not have seen him emerge from the doorway. Hesitantly, warily. Hands deep in the pockets of his old Navy pea jacket, colored the same deep blue as the stocking cap on his head. Making him seem a part of the darkness.

Nor could she have heard the hum of the car's automatic window descending.

Rick sauntered slowly toward the idling Continental, casually glancing again up and down the street. Only when he was certain he was unobserved did he lean forward and look into the window of the car.

"Rick?" The shadow inside the car spoke.

"Right," the figure responded. "Russell?"

The answer came with the unsnapping of the door locks.

"Climb in back," the shadow said.

It was only after he opened the door and was sliding in that Rick realized Russell had a friend, huddled on the far side of the backseat. Face averted, pressed against the opposite window.

It was hot inside the Continental, the rear heater pouring out warm air as the defroster worked to keep the windows clear. Rick sank into the soft leather cushions and loosened the top button of his jacket. He rubbed his hands together, hoping to hasten the warming. He tried to look more closely at his companions, but they remained mostly hidden in the dimly lit interior, the glow of the instruments on the dashboard providing the only clue: Russell had a hawk nose, which neither the darkness nor his raised collar could completely hide.

As the Continental slowly pulled away from the curb, Rick felt the first touch of . . . what? *Fear?* No, not fear. Not now, anyway. *Uncertainty?* Maybe. Who wouldn't? Strange car, strange men, unknown destination.

"How old are you, kid?" Russell's voice demanded from the front seat.

"What's the difference?" Rick replied.

"Just wondering."

"Old enough. How's that?"

Russell grunted.

The car picked up speed, quickly passing all of Rick's familiar haunts. It had been on this same street three nights before that another stranger had sidled up to Rick as he stood in the shadows.

"You're Rick, right?"

Rick had been holding a half-eaten piece of pizza, his first food in two days. Bought with three quarters he'd scavenged from the return slots of pay phones at the bus depot. He'd had no job in weeks and had refused to join the bums in the food lines.

"Who are you?" Rick had asked the man.

"Never mind. You don't want to know."

"How do you know me?"

"You don't want to know that either."

Rick had studied the man. He was well dressed, in a double-breasted overcoat that hugged his body, polished loafers with gold pins, a hat low over his eyes.

"Want to make some easy money?" the man had asked.

"Doing what?"

"I think you know, kid. But not in the front seat of some car."

"With you?"

"No."

"Who then?"

"Never mind who. You'll never know."

"What are you talking about? When? Where?"

"Soon. In a nice place. Real nice. Plush."

Rick had taken another bite of pizza, his eyes narrowing suspiciously. "You a cop?"

The man had let out a harsh laugh. "Hardly," he'd said.

"What do I have to do?"

"Get checked out by a doctor. Then wait."

"Checked out?"

"Routine," the man had replied. "We have to make sure there's no VD, no AIDS. Don't want to take any chances, you know."

"How much are we talking about here?" Rick had asked.

"More than you've ever seen in one night."

"No, man, I don't think so," Rick had said as he turned to leave. "I sure as hell need the bucks, but this sounds far out."

The man had grabbed his arm, pushing his face close to Rick's. His eyes were glittery. Piercing. Like the arrowheads Rick had once collected and polished as a boy.

"I wouldn't walk away from this, kid. My friend doesn't like to be turned down."

Rick *had* felt fear then, looking into those eyes. And now, settled into the warm comfort of the Continental, he wondered if he should have kept right on walking.

Two

"Alex, quick! Get back on the set."

Alex Collier was walking across the newsroom, still rubbing away the last of his makeup with a grubby handkerchief, when Cody Strothers caught up with him.

"Where the hell have you been?" Cody shrieked.

"Taking my face off, Cody. What the hell's going on?"

"We've got a jet in the water off LaGuardia. It could be a Northwest flight headed home to Minneapolis," he replied, almost exulting.

Cody was dragging Alex back toward the studio, tugging on his arm while searching frantically for Barbara Miller, Collier's co-anchor.

"I can walk, for Christ's sake," Alex barked, shaking free of his grasp.

They had just signed off the late news, and Alex was once again exhausted, in no mood to be pushed around by another agitated young producer in blue jeans and a button-down shirt. It had happened too many times before.

"Barbara!" Cody shouted, his acne scars reddening in the excitement. "Where the hell's Barbara?"

"Across the hall in the john," Derek sniped.

"Well, get her out here, *now*! And get the crew back into the studio. We may have to go with a bulletin any second."

Derek Glover was slumped insolently against the wall, unshaven and smirking, his straight black hair hanging to his shoulders. He had long since tired of the floor director's job, taking orders from college-boy pricks like Strothers.

"She says she just took her makeup off and isn't getting back on the goddamned set until she gets it back on. That's a quote."

Cody was livid. "You deliver a quote from me to her, okay? Tell her to forget her fuckin' makeup. She's a news anchor, not a beauty queen. Go tell her, Derek, go! Move your lazy ass."

Derek glared at him, not certain whether to report the insult to the union steward now or later. When he saw Cody's anger, he decided to act first and bitch later—and hurried off to the green room in search of Barbara.

The studio crew was scurrying to get the lights on and the cameras back into position as Alex nonchalantly took his place at the anchor desk. He was plugging his earpiece in and checking the microphone when a newsroom assistant rushed into the studio with a piece of wire copy for Cody.

"*Shit!*" Cody shouted, waving the paper in the air. "*Goddamn it!* It's a United flight bound for Denver. Son of a bitch! I thought we might have a good local story for once. Stand down, everybody. The crisis is over."

The words had no sooner left his lips than Barbara Miller, every viewer's girl-next-door, rushed into the studio—blouse hanging out of her skirt, lipstick smudged, blond hair askew. She was obviously ignorant of the new developments, and certainly not ready to go on the air.

Derek was behind her, panting, his eyes frantically searching for the steward.

Alex would later regret it, but at the moment, he couldn't resist the temptation. He only hoped everyone else in the studio would catch on quickly.

"*Barbara, hurry!*" Alex shouted, fighting to hide his roguish grin from her. "*We're waiting.*"

Cody Strothers stopped in his tracks halfway across the studio, and the crew did an about-face, returning to their positions. They looked puzzled at first, but caught on quickly.

Only Barbara and Derek were unaware of what was happening,

and both were too befuddled to notice anything awry. Barbara struggled into her anchor chair, looking wildly for microphone and earpiece.

"What's happening, Alex?" she panted, still struggling with her earpiece. "What are we doing?"

"Don't bother with that," Alex said, hardly believing the ruse was working. "I'll cue you and fill you in as we go along. It'll have to be ad lib."

Another floor director, Phil Jenkins, began the make-believe countdown, hiding his smile behind cupped hands. "Five, four . . ."

Cody joined the charade, whispering urgently from the side of the set: "We don't know how many dead yet, Barb, but plenty, we think."

". . . three . . . two . . . one, cue!"

No camera red light went on, but Barbara didn't notice.

Alex began his mock narration. "We have just learned that a Northwest Airlines jetliner has plunged off the end of the runway at New York's LaGuardia Airport. Barbara Miller has the very latest details. Barbara?"

She was stricken, staring at Alex with pleading eyes, her lips moving silently. Alex was sure she was praying.

"Barbara?" he repeated.

She looked at the camera, back at Alex, back at the camera. She cleared her throat and plunged ahead.

"Well, as you know, Alex, details are still quite sketchy. We know very little, in fact." Then, remembering Cody's whispers, she took a chance. "We don't know how many passengers or crew were killed or injured, but preliminary reports indicate there may be many fatalities."

"Really?" Alex said with all of the seriousness he could muster. "What was the source of those reports?"

"Eyewitnesses, I believe," Barbara said, searching for Cody in the darkness beyond the set.

"Well, I know you've been monitoring the situation very closely, Barbara," Alex intoned, "and I'm sure the viewers would be interested in your personal assessment . . ."

By then, the stifled giggles from the crew behind the cameras became open laughter. The truth slowly dawned on Barbara, and her confusion and embarrassment turned to sudden and violent anger.

"You asshole!" she hissed at Alex. "You bastard!" She would have hit him, but her hand got tangled in the microphone cord.

"Damn right!" It was Derek, walking menacingly toward the set. "That was bullshit. You made us look like asses." Alex ignored him, but would not forget the venom in his voice.

"Calm down, Barbara," Alex said as soothingly as he could. "It was just a joke."

She was seething. "Is that your idea of a joke?" she demanded, still trying to untangle herself from the cord. "Making other people look like jerks. Maybe it is where you come from, but I'd say it's malicious, not funny."

"Cool off, for Christ's sake," Alex said.

"Shove it," she replied, pushing past him.

Alex walked alone from the studio back to his little cubicle in the newsroom, watching Barbara stride angrily ahead, chagrined now at what he'd done. Not exactly the way to win friends for the new kid on the block, he knew.

Alex had the head-turning good looks of a major anchorman. Except for a razor-thin scar along his left jawbone, which was easily covered by makeup, his face was without flaw: perhaps not as rugged as it once was, with the years beginning to show, but handsome by anyone's definition.

A serious face, straight and smooth, still tanned from the California sun—which he had abandoned to join WCKT in the Twin Cities.

His eyes were a deep brown, and deeply set, his eyebrows touched by the same sprinkle of gray as his hair. *Was it more than a sprinkle now?*

In most television stations, an anchorman of Alex's stature and salary would have had a private office. But not here, not in George Barclay's newsroom.

"We don't play favorites around here," Barclay had told Alex when he arrived. "You may be a star and make a lot more money than the rest of these people, but you'll have no frills, no perks in *my* newsroom."

Alex hadn't argued, admitting it made a certain amount of sense, and not wanting to do battle with Barclay. Not yet.

Barclay was the news director, the man who had hired Alex, a man with a big body and a booming voice. He'd heard stories of Barclay's gruff manner and rigid rules, but he also knew he was a hell of a news director, respected by his peers in the business and by those who worked for him.

At times like this, when the day was done, Alex craved being able to close the door to his own office and retreat to a little privacy. Instead, he sat down in his cramped cubicle, surrounded by a tackboard covered with fragments from his too well traveled career as a journalist, anchorman, and husband.

He stretched his legs as far as he could and surveyed the life displayed before him.

Among the tattered mementos was a picture of his ex-wife, Jan, and their two kids, Jennifer and Christopher, six and eight now, a thousand miles away with their mother in Philadelphia. Only slightly smaller was a shot of the stringer of bass he and Chris had caught the year before in northern Michigan. In some ways, he remembered the bass more clearly than he remembered Chris.

It had been four months since Alex had seen his family—the four months since he had started this job, his third in five years. Not a great work record, he thought, but not all that unusual in this business. *No, that was crap.* Three jobs in five years was strange, even in television. He knew it said more about him than about the business.

Jan had known it, too, although it took her several years to recognize that he would never be satisfied in one place for very long. By then they had moved four times, the last two moves with the babies in tow.

"It's a transient business," he had told her. A hundred times. But she knew differently. She saw others doing his same job but staying put in one place for at least a few years. She eventually came to realize it was he, not the business, that was transient.

And she finally said no. No to the moving, and no to the marriage. So Alex had moved on, minus his wife and children. To Sacramento, to San Jose, and, finally, to the Twin Cities.

At each stop the city was a little larger, the money a little better, the visibility a little greater. A year here, two years there, with never a contract without an out-clause for a larger market or for dollars that couldn't or wouldn't be matched. Never an attachment. Just read the goddamned news.

Alex knew that rumors followed him wherever he went, whispers of newsroom squabbles and management money battles, along with vague stories of a libel lawsuit in the distant past that had once cost him his job.

The truth about Alex Collier was elusive, and he wanted to keep it that way.

It had worked so far, and his goal of a top-ten television market wasn't that far off. And then, who knows, maybe a network anchor?

His life was rolling past as quickly as the words on the Tele-PrompTer. And with about as much meaning. He was alone again, a stranger in another newsroom in another city.

As Alex walked out to get a cup of coffee, he heard loud voices in the hallway just outside the newsroom. Curious, he edged closer to the door.

"He's like all the rest of those high-paid assholes. Thinks he's King Shit. Sits on his ass and collects a fat check. I know the type."

It was Derek. Alex could not see him, but he could hear Barbara's hissed response. "Cool it, Derek. It's over. Forget it."

"Fuck, no, I don't forget things like that," Derek shouted. "He's a real smartass."

"Pipe down," Barbara snapped. "Put a plug in."

Alex walked to the doorway. "Got a problem, Derek?"

The floor director turned quickly, showing surprise but no embarrassment or fear. "You're the problem, Collier," he growled.

"Want to tell me to my face?" Alex said, stepping through the door, challenging him.

Barbara quickly intervened, sliding her body between them. "Hold on, you two," she said. "We don't need this. It's stupid."

"I think this is between Derek and me," Alex said, starting to move past her.

People had begun to gather in the hall.

"We're leaving," Barbara said, pulling Derek with her. "Let's get a drink and cool off."

Derek resisted for a moment, but then followed—glowering over his shoulder. Alex returned his stare.

As he watched them leave, the paging system echoed in the building. "Alex Collier, please pick up two-five-o-four. Alex Collier, *please.*" Impatient Norm Schmaeder, the security guard at the back entrance.

Who the hell could that be? Alex wondered. The guards at the switchboard had strict orders not to bother the anchors with viewer calls after the newscast. Especially angry viewers or kooks. Alex wondered how many weirdos he'd talked to over the years. Too many.

"Alex Collier, two-five-o-four, please!"

Screw you, Norm, I'm moving as fast as I can, he thought as he crossed toward the blinking light on a nearby desk. Can't forget to give Norm the finger on the way out.

"This is Alex Collier," he said in his best newscaster tones.

He could hear a sharp intake of breath at the other end, but no words.

"Hello? Who is this?" he asked irritably, unable to disguise his annoyance at the late-night interruption.

"Alex?" The voice was tentative, distant. "I'm terribly sorry to bother you."

He pushed the phone tighter against his ear. The words were hushed and indistinct.

"Alex, are you there?"

He knew the voice, but before her name reached his lips, she rushed ahead. "Alex, this is Pat, Pat Shaw."

"I know," he said.

His mind tumbled back to college twenty years before. *Beautiful Patty Shaw. It's Patty.*

"It's actually Pat Hodges now . . ."

Her voice shocked him out of his momentary reverie.

"Where are you?" he asked hesitantly.

"Here. In Minneapolis. I know it's terribly late, and I know I shouldn't be disturbing you, but—"

"What is it?" He sat on the edge of the desk, surprised at the wobble in his knees. *C'mon, Alex, settle down. It was twenty fucking years ago.* "What are you doing in Minneapolis?" he asked, at a sudden loss for anything else to say.

"We live here. We have for a long time."

The years peeled away. His mind was flooded with memories. He had walked away from her without a word. He'd sent her a note, but it must have seemed like gibberish to her. *Too young, feeling trapped, must move on and make a career. You won't understand. I've got to do something with my life.*

Sophomore words, chicken-shit words.

"It's been a long time, Pat."

"I know," she said simply.

Then silence. Each waited for the other to speak.

"I can't believe it's actually you," he said at last. "When can I see you?"

"Soon, I hope. That's why I called. I need to see you, to talk to you . . . about a story."

The disappointment was as sharp as an arrow to the heart.

"A story?"

"I wasn't going to call, Alex. Not to renew old friendships. I didn't think you'd want that. But I've been watching you on the news, and I finally decided I had to call."

"Pat, I appreciate your thinking of me, and I'd like to see you, but I'm not a reporter, not anymore. I just read the news, I don't report it. We have other people around here who do that."

He felt guilty saying it, especially to her, but it was true. And had been for many years. Only the tattered awards on his tackboard were testimony to the fact it hadn't *always* been so. "I'd be happy to put you in touch with one of them," he added.

"I don't know *them*, Alex. I know you. At least I used to."

He detected a touch of urgency in her voice. "Please, Alex. I know you're busy, and I know this must seem strange. You owe me nothing, but I thought I could still ask a favor. It's important, maybe crucial. I don't know who else to talk to, who else to trust."

She seemed to be edging toward a mild hysteria.

"I owe you a lot, Pat, and I hear you. Settle down. We'll get together. But I'm not sure I can help. I'm new around here, and I'm supposed to just look pretty and read the news."

"Thank you, Alex. I won't forget it." Her relief was evident.

Alex suggested they meet the next day at Le Café, a small out-of-the-way restaurant in the warehouse district of downtown Minneapolis.

Only after he'd hung up did Alex realize he'd been too shaken to ask Pat anything about her present life, to say nothing of the past twenty years. She must be married. "*We live here,*" she'd said. *Kids? Job?* He knew nothing except that she was in Minneapolis and in a near panic over some kind of story.

And that he had never been able to forget her.

Three

Rick had never been in a car quite like this. It seemed to float. He could see the buildings, the streetlights, and other cars slip by, but there was no sensation of movement within. No bumps, no rattles, just the soft whirr of the heater and the muted melodies from the stereo speaker behind him. He had no idea where they were going, and he knew better than to ask.

The men in the car remained silent, apparently lost in thought, paying little attention to him. He rested his head on the seat cushion, closed his eyes, and wondered where and when this trip would end. He needed the money, that was for sure, and there was little in his young life he hadn't done for money. But this gig seemed so elaborate, so out of the movies, that he wondered what the final payoff would be. Wait and see, he told himself.

They had been driving for what Rick guessed to be ten minutes when his backseat companion reached into a small compartment at his feet and pulled out a bottle of Chivas Regal. He poured a finger of the whiskey into a glass and handed it to Rick, then helped himself.

"Go ahead, drink up. We're going to have to put the blindfold on before long." They were the first words he had spoken, and they were said gently, almost kindly. Rick did as he was told.

Rick sipped the liquor, feeling the warmth of it spread through his body, matching the heat of the car. They wound their way around the lakes of south Minneapolis, past the Calhoun Towers, the bandstand on Lake Harriet, the grand homes along Lake of the Isles. There seemed to be no destination, just a meandering path that eventually led them alongside Minnehaha Creek. Rick felt as if he ought to say something, to make conversation, to fill the void. Instead, he just sipped, watched, and waited.

Forty-five minutes after beginning its aimless excursion, the Continental stopped, parking in a picnic area along the Mississippi River, its engine still idling. Rick was asked politely to turn his head, and the darkness became total. The blindfold was tied securely behind his head, causing him uneasiness but no panic. He had been told to expect it, and was relieved when Russell said he wouldn't have to wear it for long. They were expected at their destination soon.

Rick was in a vacuum, seeing nothing because of the blindfold, feeling nothing because of the flying-carpet ride of the Continental. He occasionally sensed a sway of the car and guessed they were navigating a curve. But he found it was impossible to estimate their speed or direction or even to keep track of the passage of time.

The crunch of the tires on gravel and the slowing of the car told him they must have arrived. The front door opened and closed, then the other rear door. He could hear low conversation outside before his door opened, before he felt a gentle tug on his arm.

"Out. We're here."

Rick was led, still blindfolded, up a gentle incline, the gravel now beneath his feet. Steps, five of them. Doorbell chimes in the distance, behind a wall. A door opening, a rush of warm air from the inside.

"Ahhh, let's see what you've brought me." A new voice, husky, almost breathless.

"His name is Rick," Russell said. "He's clean. All checked out."

He must be talking about the medical report, Rick thought, remembering his visit to the doctor's office. The exam had been so quick he couldn't even remember the doctor's name. A few questions, a chest X ray, a blood test, and he was out the door. But apparently he'd passed the test.

Rick felt a hand on his, pulling him into the warmth. The skin on the hand was parched and had the feel of sandpaper.

"Come in, my boy." The husky voice, too, was parched, like the skin. "Let's look you over in the light."

It may have been light to them, but Rick was still deep in the darkness.

Rick sensed he and the husky voice were now alone in the house. There had been no farewells from the men who had brought him, but he guessed they had quietly slipped away after delivering their package.

The blindfold remained in place, and so did Rick. Not seeing, but *knowing* he was being examined closely. He wasn't surprised when he was politely asked to remove his coat and hat.

"You'll have to excuse the mystery," his host said, "but I must take proper precautions."

God, Rick wondered, have I heard that voice before?

Rick felt the sandpaper hand once again on his, leading him around furniture and through the house. He could smell and hear the crackle of a fireplace and almost tripped in the depth of the carpeting.

Fancy place, he guessed. Not what I'm used to, for sure.

The hand stopped him, and Rick heard a door open immediately in front of him.

"When the door is shut and locked behind you, you may remove your blindfold," Rick was told. "You will find yourself in a very comfortable room with everything you may need. Please refresh yourself at the bar, bathe, and relax in a robe you'll find in the closet. Please don't try to leave until you're summoned."

He was pushed gently ahead. The door closed and the lock snapped behind him.

The lights made him wince as he took off the blindfold. The room was not that bright. In fact, it was quite dim, but it took his eyes a moment to recover from the imposed darkness.

The room was more than comfortable. It was breathtaking, almost as large as the entire house Rick had grown up in, and much more expensively and elegantly decorated. Two sofas, an easy chair, a king-sized bed, all covered in what looked like the finest fabric, all resting on the same luxuriously cushioned carpeting he had felt on his way through the house.

The leather-covered bar in one corner of the room, fronted by two matching stools, was stocked with an imposing array of bottles of varying sizes and shapes and contents. Across from the bar, a large television screen and stereo system covered almost an entire wall.

Rick had trouble taking it all in. He had never been anywhere quite as impressive; it was worlds apart from his sidewalk and shelter existence of the past couple of years. Galaxies apart.

He walked to the bar, poured a shot of Johnny Walker Black Label into an etched glass, added some ice, and peered into the adjoining bathroom. Bigger than our old kitchen, he thought. Every wall was mirrored, floor to ceiling, and a sunken tub seemed the size of a small swimming pool. It came complete with gold handles, and the faucet itself was a golden figure of a young boy, whose penis was the spout.

It was only then he noticed the absence of windows. He was in an airtight box, unexposed to the outside world.

The painting of a fierce-looking Siberian tiger hung above the bed. Rick studied it from across the room: the gaping, drooling mouth, the bared fangs, and the glittering eyes. Rick turned away, not realizing his every move was followed by a button-sized camera lens in one of the tiger's eyes.

Four

Still puzzled and slightly uneasy from Pat's phone call, Alex threw on his coat and scarf and walked out of the station ready to meet the November chill. It *was* cold in Minnesota, in the mid-twenties, if he remembered correctly. And windy.

This is only November, he told himself, as he tightened the scarf around his neck. Just wait till January and February.

Alex had spent the past hour reviewing a tape of the late newscast, critiquing his own performance, watching for small flaws and imperfections in his delivery. Over the years, it had become a nightly ritual.

Sadly, Alex had again seen what the years and the monotony of reading the news had done to him: he'd lost his edge. It was hard to spot, but the intensity was gone; he was reading by rote, performing as an actor might who was doing the same play for the thousandth time. His heart was not in it.

As he headed toward the parking ramp, Alex saw Barbara walking alone ahead of him. She must have left the others at the bar, he thought. He wasn't particularly anxious to talk to her, but she heard his footsteps and slowed her pace, allowing him to fall in beside her.

They said nothing until they neared the ramp. Then Barbara stopped and took a deep breath. "I'm sorry about the scene back there," she said. "I overreacted in the studio, and I'm afraid that got Derek going."

"What's his problem?" Alex asked.

"He's a jerk. I don't think he has a real friend in the place. He tries to intimidate people. I'd stay clear of him if I were you. He has a nasty temper."

"So I see. Why do you put up with him?"

"He doesn't bother me," she said. "Must be because I'm a woman and he doesn't see me as a threat to his macho image."

Alex paused as they reached the elevator door. It creaked in the cold as it opened and closed on them. "May I ask you something else?" he said.

"Sure."

"I know you've been around for a while, and I was wondering if you happen to know of a Patricia Hodges. The name mean anything to you?"

Barbara leaned against the back of the elevator and thought for a moment. "The only Hodges I know . . . and I don't really *know* him . . . is Judge Nathaniel Hodges. He's on the Hennepin County bench. And quite a power hereabouts."

"What about his wife?"

"I can't remember her name, if I ever knew it. But I do know she's a lawyer. Why the interest?"

"A Pat Hodges called me tonight—after you'd left. She's an old college . . . friend who wants to talk to me about a story. She sounded so uptight it was a little unsettling."

The elevator stopped on the third floor, and the door opened reluctantly.

"More than likely she wants to tell you about a Junior League benefit or some bazaar," Barbara said with a sarcasm that seemed too advanced for her age. "She probably thought she had to add a little drama, a little mystery, to get your attention."

Alex knew she was wrong, but said nothing.

"Don't worry about it," Barbara added. "Maybe she's just hot for your body."

Alex feigned a small laugh. "I doubt that," he said. Once maybe, but not now. Not after what he'd done.

As Alex left the ramp, Pat Hodges was standing in her darkened living room, half a city away, listening as the wind wrapped itself around the house, the gusts pushing against the panes of the big bay window. A loose shingle flapped on the roof somewhere above her, and she could see—in the glow of the yard light—the last of the fallen leaves skittering across the lawn, tumbling and then taking flight in a windswept ballet.

She wasn't sure how long she had been there in the gloomy quiet, reliving her conversation with Alex. An hour? Had she made a mistake calling him? Perhaps. How strange it must have seemed to him to hear her voice suddenly emerge from nowhere with a muddled appeal for help. She could still hear his puzzled hesitation, the pauses more telling than words.

Pat's thoughts were interrupted by the lights of a car swinging into the driveway. She could hear the garage door open and knew her husband, Nathanial, was home. She hurried to the bedroom, crawled beneath the bedcovers, and propped an open book on her stomach.

"Up so late?" Nathaniel asked, as he walked into the bedroom. "That's not like you."

"I couldn't sleep," she said. "So I just kept on reading."

He slipped off his suitcoat and searched for a hanger in the closet. His body was as erect and lean as the day she married him, ten years before.

"How about you?" Pat asked. "I expected you hours ago."

"The meeting took longer than I expected. You know how judges love to talk. Then we all went out to dinner."

"I would have appreciated a call," Pat said.

"I *did* try to call, but the phone was busy."

Pat kept her eyes on the book, avoiding his questioning glance.

"So who was it?" he asked.

"Huh? What? Oh, the phone call. It was just a client wanting some late-night advice."

"I hope you bill him for it," Nathanial said lightly as he walked into the bathroom.

Why had she lied to him? she asked herself.

His question had caught her off guard, but it was more than that. She knew that if she'd told him the truth about the call, she'd have had to explain the reason for it. And she wasn't ready to do that, not yet anyway.

She put the book aside and turned out the light.

The next morning, Alex was awakened not by his alarm clock or by the warm body lock of a beautiful woman, but by the gentle nudges of Seuss the Cat, anxious to be fed and freed to roam.

The sky was beginning to lighten as Alex stumbled from the bedroom to the kitchen, retrieving the cat food from the cupboard as Seuss rubbed against and around his legs.

Seuss was one of the few things Alex had kept from his marriage. Not because Jan or the kids had wanted to give the cat up, but because their allergies had proved so strong that Seuss had to go — just like Alex.

So they'd traveled the country together in Alex's old TR4, the roving anchorman and his alley-cat companion.

Alex knew he ought to go back to bed if he was going to be fresh for the late shift. But sleep was gone as surely as the night, and he decided he ought to face the day.

He was about to let the cat outside when the phone rang.

"Awake?" It was Barbara Miller.

"Barely."

"Alone?"

"Except for the cat, yes."

"You have a cat?"

Alex, still half asleep, had difficulty hiding his annoyance. "C'mon, Barbara, what's up?"

"Well," she said, "I managed to get some information for you about the mystery lady. The one from college?"

She waited for a response, but Alex said nothing.

"Judge Hodges's wife *is* named Patricia, she *is* from Kansas, she *is* a lawyer. Met her husband while she worked for the public defender's office and he worked for the county attorney. That's all I know, except that she's supposed to be quite attractive."

"That seems to fit," Alex said. "You found out all of that before eight o'clock in the morning?"

"I have my sources," she replied.

"Sources you call in the middle of the night?" Then he remembered she was dating a Minneapolis detective.

"Are *you* alone?" he asked.

"I am now." Emphasis on the now. Alex suddenly understood how she had got the information, but he couldn't understand why she was so anxious to help. *What was in it for her?*

"You didn't tell him who wanted to know, did you?"

"Tell who?" she asked innocently.

"You know who."

"I never tell my sources anything I don't have to."

"Okay," he said. "Thanks. I'll let you know what happens."

He regretted that he'd asked Barbara to help. He had wanted to keep a distance between them, but now he'd allowed her to become a part of this little mystery, a part of his past.

He knew little about Barbara, despite sitting next to her on the news set for four months. That's the way he wanted it. He was suspicious of anyone so young who had come so far so fast. Shit, he thought, she can't be more than twenty-five or so. Hardly old enough to know what Vietnam was or who the Kennedys were. What is somebody like *her* doing reading the news?

Keep a distance, he told himself as he picked up the cat and carried him to the front door—opening it to the cold air and the first flakes of snow settling softly to the ground.

Five

Alex had no trouble picking Pat Hodges out. He would have recognized her immediately, anywhere, in any crowd. Twenty years had not changed that. Even across the room, there was no escaping her eyes.

She was alone in a corner of the café, looking uncomfortable.

He didn't blame her. He certainly felt strange himself: excited but cautious, eager but nervous. Like the teenagers they once were. Funny how that feeling comes right back, he thought.

He remembered her with a windswept, prairie kind of beauty — dark hair always tousled, dark eyes both innocent and sensuous, her smile open and inviting.

But as he approached her now, Alex was struck by the sharpness of her features and the severity of her dress. She wore little makeup, a minimum of jewelry, and a carefully cut but stark black business suit — offset by precious little color in the blouse or scarf.

The first impression, he had to admit, was of mourning, as though she had just walked away from somebody's funeral. She was trying to smile but finding it difficult.

She's as nervous as I am, he thought.

But Alex had no trouble smiling. He was in the acting business. His face had to light up every night on television.

"Alex, how nice to see you." Her hand was outstretched and the smile seemed easier now. "You haven't changed that much, have you? Then again, I've been watching you on the news."

Her hand was cool, her expression guarded. Her voice was warm but detached. Controlled. As though she were greeting a friend she hadn't seen for a few weeks, not a young love to whom she had once sworn everlasting devotion.

Alex sat down across from her. "You haven't changed much, either," he said, studying her closely. "As beautiful as ever." Actually, she had changed. No less attractive, he decided, but thinner . . . and what? Tighter? As though the years had somehow sapped the spontaneous good spirits from her.

Pat's hair was up, skintight across the cheekbones, blouse collar buttoned securely at the neck. Like a schoolmarm in an old Western flick, he thought. She looked all business, and Alex wondered now—as he had so often twenty years before—what she'd look like just out of the shower, hair wet and mussed, skin shiny with a steamy mist, wrapping a soft towel around her body.

He liked that picture a lot better.

"How have you been?" he asked. "We've got a lot of catching up to do."

"I'm fine," she said, "but I don't want to bore you with my life story. Not now."

"I wouldn't be bored."

"I would be. It's really not very interesting. I'm a lawyer, married to a judge . . ."

Barbara Miller had been right. It was the same Pat Hodges.

". . . living a quiet, dull, suburban life. That's about it. It wouldn't make a Hollywood thriller."

"Any kids?" he asked.

"No, sorry to say. There never seemed to be time. I regret that now, but I don't think Nathaniel—that's my husband—does. He's content with things as they are."

A few other people, probably tourists, had filtered into the restaurant, but they were seated several tables away. Alex saw two women across the room discreetly point toward him and exchange whispered giggles, but he ignored them.

"How about you?" she asked. "You've become a TV star."

"Hardly. But it's a living. I've made a lot of stops since Kansas."

"You're very good at the news. I enjoy watching you."

"And you're very kind," he replied, feeling the strain of the awkward conversation, sensing that she did, too.

"You have a family?" she asked.

"Well, I have an ex-wife and two children who live in Philadelphia. I don't see them very often."

"I'm sorry," she said.

"No need to be," he said, knowing it was not the full truth. "I'm doing all right."

The waiter appeared, and although each seemed relieved at the interruption, Alex could not ignore one piece of unfinished business. "You know," he said after they'd ordered, "I owe you an apology, twenty years overdue. I never dreamed I'd have the chance."

"Please, Alex, that's not why I came here. Let's forget it."

"How can I forget it? I was a jerk."

"We were kids, Alex. Just kids."

"Even kids deserve an explanation."

She looked away, making it clear to Alex that she had little appetite for discussing more of the past. Other things were on her mind, things more urgent than an unhappy history.

Leave it alone, he told himself. She's right. We were just kids. Get on with it.

"You mentioned a story on the phone . . . said that it was important . . . crucial . . . I think you called it. You sounded upset."

"It *is* important, almost life and death."

"That's pretty dramatic, Pat," he said.

She paused for a moment, studying him carefully. "Alex, I know this will sound mysterious, but I can't tell you anything unless you promise to keep me out of it. Completely."

He was wary. "I'm not sure that's possible. You're the lawyer, and I'm certainly not up on that part of the law. I do know you can only protect confidential sources so far. Then you can go to jail, maybe for a long time."

"I suppose that could happen," she said, "but with the First Amendment and all—"

"Don't tell me about the First Amendment," Alex said sharply, remembering all too vividly his own painful experience with the courts.

"Still," she said nervously, "it could be horrible for me if I was ever tied to this story."

"Worse than my going to jail?" he asked. "Like what?"

"Like the end of my career. My husband's career. Maybe a lot more. I just don't know all the damage it could do."

This is ludicrous, he thought. We're sitting here discussing confidential sources, and jail, and ruined careers, and I don't even know what story we're talking about.

"Pat, believe me, I want to be helpful. I'm more than a little curious, but as I told you on the phone, I'm not a reporter anymore. I'm not paid to be. I'm not sure I'd still recognize a good story if it fell into my lap."

"Well," she smiled, "this one *is* falling into your lap."

"How can I tell if it's a good story," he asked, his frustration showing, "if you can't tell me anything about it without the promise of total confidentiality?"

"What if I confide in you," she countered, "and you decide it *is* a good story, and then drag me into it?"

"I can't picture myself dragging you into it unless I'm being hauled off to jail on some contempt charge."

The conversation was going nowhere, and they both realized it. She lit a cigarette and spoke to him through the haze. "You wouldn't be willing to go to jail for an important story that needs to be told? That *has* to be told?"

"Maybe in the old days," he said, "when I was younger and still had all those big ideals. But now? I don't know."

"Even if kids' lives were at stake?"

"Kids' lives? What the hell are you talking about?"

"Just what I said. I can't tell you more without some guarantee of protection, but it does involve kids, and it does involve their lives and futures."

Alex's face showed all the skepticism he felt. "What more can you tell me? I've got to know more if I'm going to ask my boss to grant this confidentiality request."

"Your *boss*?" She was visibly alarmed. "Why does he have to know?"

As Alex was about to reply, the waiter arrived with their lunch. Pat ignored the food, intent on Alex across the table.

"He doesn't have to know about *you*," Alex said, finally, "but he does have to know that somebody is requesting unrestricted confidentiality. And he has to agree to it. After all, it's going to be the station's lawyers and their money if this thing, whatever it is, blows up in my face."

"Will you have to tell him my name?"

"I don't think so, but remember, this isn't my normal turf. I'm new at this place. I don't know what their policies are. I do know this: he's going to laugh me out of his office with what you've told me so far. I'll need a lot more."

She continued to watch him, apparently debating whether to go on with her mission.

She's obviously no stranger to deals, Alex thought. She's probably copped enough pleas as a public defender to make her a veteran negotiator.

"Okay," she said, finally. "I'll tell you this much more, but that's it. The story involves a well-respected, highly placed public official who is committing felonies almost every day and getting away with it. Because some people are afraid and others are looking the other way."

Before he could say anything, she added: "But you can't tell your boss even that if he insists on knowing who your source is. He's going to have to trust you, as I'm trusting you."

What the hell am I doing here? he asked himself. Why did I answer the goddamned phone? Life was complicated enough already.

"Deal?" she asked, interrupting his thoughts.

"I don't know what to say, Pat. This is way out of my league. Have you gone to the newspapers or anybody else with this thing? Somebody who knows what the hell they're doing? You must have other contacts."

"I haven't told anybody. I've met lots of reporters over the years, but I don't know any of them very well. I just don't know who to trust. Then I saw you on the news. It's taken me weeks to work up my nerve, but I knew I had to try."

If he could have disappeared in a wisp of her cigarette smoke, he would have. But there was no escape from those eyes.

"So I take all the risk," he said, "and you take none."

"I'm taking a risk even being here with you. And I'm willing to help. That's no small risk, believe me."

"Okay," he said, anxious to resolve the matter. "Let's do this. I'll talk to the news director, tell him what you've told me. I won't identify you, and if he says go ahead, I will. But I make no promises."

She nodded, and smiled, relieved.

He paid the check and helped her on with her coat. His hands lingered on her shoulders, but only for a moment. If she noticed, she gave no indication. He could have been a stranger.

"I'll call you," he said.

As he watched her walk away without a backward glance, Alex wondered if the qualms he felt came from the bomb she may have just dropped into his lap, or the one that had been ticking away in his mind for twenty years.

Six

Alex found the door to the news director's office closed, but he rapped lightly and heard a loud "C'mon in" from the other side.

George Barclay was talking on the telephone. He pointed to one of the swivel chairs. Alex took a seat.

"You think that's bad," Barclay was saying into the phone, "I was at a place a few years ago where the newsroom was so bad, they had their own saying: 'If it's news, it's news to us.' Honest to God. Now *that's* bad!" He laughed uproariously.

Barclay's body occupied much of the office. He was Orson Wellesian in dimension, his girth spilling out on all sides of the armchair. His neck overflowed his shirt collar like a waterfall of flesh, and his belly cascaded over his belt, the shirt and suit barely able to contain it all.

A full beard, more gray than black now, matched his overgrown eyebrows. His eyes seemed to peer out of a forest, but they were alive and sparkled with intelligence.

Barclay may not have been the picture of physical perfection, but Alex knew he was one of the best television newsmen in the country.

"He has the journalistic balls of an elephant!" one of Alex's former bosses had once said of Barclay. "He's big, he's fat, he can

28

barely waddle around the newsroom, but you give him a big story to cover and nobody in TV is better."

Barclay was still on the phone. "Oh, yeah, I remember him. Some reporter once asked him if he was interested in covering a birthday party for a hundred-year-old lady. 'Only if she's pregnant,' he said."

Another laugh. George enjoyed his own stories.

"Okay, well, you take care of yourself. If I hear about anything, I'll let you know."

He hung up and turned to Alex. "Another news director bites the dust. They're going fast these days. I don't know where the hell he's going to find another job."

"Sorry to hear it."

"What's up, Alex?"

"I need to talk."

"I heard about your little prank in the studio last night," Barclay said, a small smile on his lips.

"Really?"

"Sounded like fun, but not at all like you."

Alex fell silent, embarrassed now that he had allowed his fatigue and boredom to turn to the foolishness in the studio.

"How are you feeling?" Barclay asked.

"Okay, I guess. Why?"

"You seem tired on the air lately, almost uninterested. Like you can't wait for the newscast to end."

You might fool some people, but not George Barclay.

"Is it that evident?" Alex asked.

"To me it is. What's the problem?"

"I don't know, George. Sometimes I think I've lost it. Everything we do seems so pointless. Russia's coming apart at the seams, Eastern Europe's getting reborn, the Middle East is in turmoil after the Gulf war, and we're talking about a little nepotism at the Capitol or the latest cold front blowing in. I'm just tired of the same old shit, I guess."

"What's it been, Alex? Three stations in five years? That's a pretty fast track for anyone. No wonder you're feeling blitzed. Isn't it time you settled down awhile?"

"I've been hearing that for a long time now," Alex admitted, "from a lot of people. But I'm not getting any younger, and anchoring's a young man's business."

"At the rate you're going," Barclay warned, "you're going to age *before* your time. Slow down. Ease up. The world will await your fucking brilliance. Give it time. I've seen too many good people burn out in the heat of their own afterburners."

Alex paid attention to the advice because Barclay was his boss, and because he had come to respect him. But he still didn't know him that well.

"You've got a lot going for you, Alex. Good looks, good voice, authority, credibility, commanding presence. One of the best in the business. That's why we hired you, why we're paying you so damned much money. I can't have you dozing on the air. I hope you can snap out of it."

Barclay stroked his beard before continuing. The forest moved, but the eyes didn't waver. "Down deep, I think you want some respect. That's why you're so jumpy . . . why reading the news isn't enough for you. It's the choice you made, and it's a little late to turn back now."

It was the longest speech Alex could remember hearing George Barclay deliver.

"Thanks for the advice," Alex said. "I hear what you're saying, and I do appreciate it. Which brings me back to the reason I'm here. I need your advice on something else."

"What's that?" Barclay asked.

"I've got to be careful how I ask this," Alex said, glancing down at his notes, "so bear with me. I have a source who claims to know of, quote, a well-respected, highly placed public official, unquote, who is, quote, committing felonies almost every day, unquote. And getting away with it. Something about threatening kids' lives.

"This source," he continued, "will only give me the story if" — careful now, he told himself, no using he or she—"the source is promised absolute confidentiality. I can't tell anybody the name . . . not you, not anybody."

"What the hell are you talking about?" Barclay shouted, his wattles quivering. "Absolute confidentiality? Bullshit. We wouldn't have given that to the Mother Mary herself if she'd come in here to tell us about a virgin birth."

"That's what I told . . . the source," Alex said. "But he she is adamant. No promise, no story. And he she says it could be *very* big," adding his own emphasis.

"Why did this source happen to come to you?" Barclay asked, unable to disguise his curiosity or his disbelief.

"I can't tell you that, either. Except to say the source knows me and trusts me. It's me or nobody. Period."

"I'll be dipped in shit," Barclay muttered. He never ceased to express his disgust and disappointment with the same obscene phrase.

"So what do we do?" Alex asked, fearing already that Barclay's answer would be no. And not sure himself that he wouldn't be right.

"I'd like to walk away from it, Alex. We hired you because we needed you on the news, not off chasing phantom stories. And, frankly, I don't like the risk—not with that old libel suit hanging around your neck."

Alex shrank back from the reminder.

"Do you really want to get into the middle of this?"

"It sounds like a story to me, George. This source is an old friend. I don't want to walk away from this one."

The news director continued to stroke his beard, curling one strand of whiskers between his thumb and index finger like a piece of twine. He was trying to come up with a more suitable answer.

"Well, all right," Barclay grumbled, "but it's got to be on our terms. Tell this source to give you what he or she knows, and we'll pursue it as best we can. If it turns out to be a story, we won't run it until the source gives us the okay, or until we can guarantee that we can keep the source out of it."

"In short, you're putting this person in an impossible position," Alex said, thinking of Pat's intense eyes. And her fears.

"It won't be too comfortable, that's for sure," Barclay admitted. "But what is he or she doing to you right now? Same thing. What's the difference?" He paused. "And why don't you at least tell me whether this source is a man or a woman? I'm getting tired of saying 'he or she' or 'him or her' all the time. It pisses me off."

"You're a tough man to say no to," Alex smiled, raising a rakish eyebrow, "but I've made a promise that I'd better keep."

Barclay heaved himself out of his chair, obviously intent on ending the conversation. "Spend some time on this, Alex. Check it out, but don't be too disappointed if it doesn't develop. These things seldom do. But watch your step. Every step."

Barbara saw Alex leave Barclay's office and thought again of the epithets she had hurled at him the night before. *Asshole? Filthy bastard?* Had those words come out of her mouth? Indeed. Like lightning. A flash, an explosion. An unthinking thunderstorm, a torrent so vulgar she felt only embarrassment.

My God, she thought, what is happening to me?

It had been only four years before that she made her first visit to the station, a college graduate in search of her first internship. A farm girl in the big city, alone, awed, lost in a swirl of events and people. Confused by the skyways, dwarfed by the buildings, feeling as insignificant as a speck on the sidewalk.

She had met with a man who was then the news director of the station, carrying with her the audition tape she had made in her senior year.

"Tell me about yourself," he'd said, ignoring the tape, his eyes fastened on her.

The stare was familiar. It happened all the time.

"I grew up on a dairy farm near Willmar. My grandparents homesteaded it many years ago, and my folks built it up and kept it going. They're almost ready to retire, and one of my brothers plans to take it over."

The office was hot, and Barbara had felt the perspiration begin beneath her arms and on the back of her neck.

"Where'd you go to school?" he had asked.

Why don't they ever look at the résumés? she'd wondered. She'd spent a bundle getting them printed just right.

"I went to high school in Willmar and college at Southwest State. Majoring in journalism. I just got out last month."

He had finally glanced at the résumé and at the picture attached to it. Then back at her, comparing the picture to what he saw in person.

Both were strikingly attractive. Barbara knew it, and had come to accept the benefits her beauty had brought her over the years: better grades than she deserved, more dates than she wanted, more honors than she earned, more job interviews than her college record merited.

She had learned long ago that men still ran most of the world, at least the world she wanted, and that they appreciated a beautiful woman. Why not use what she had?

"I see you were Princess Kay of the Milky Way?" the news director had said, knowing the dairy industry bestowed the title each year on a deserving and beautiful farm girl.

"Yes, a couple of years ago. It was fun, but being a beauty queen was not the highlight of my life. I traveled a bit and met a lot of nice people. Got comfortable in public. But it also took a lot of time away from my studies."

She'd hoped that would help explain her mediocre grade point average, but he had paid no attention to that.

"So what do you want to do?" he'd asked.

"Whatever you have for me to do. Anything. I just want to learn. Eventually, I'd like to be a reporter and maybe an anchor, but I know that takes a long time and a lot of hard work. I just want to get started."

"You know an internship doesn't mean a permanent job here," he had warned. "We normally require two or three years of reporting experience in smaller markets before we hire anyone."

"I know that, but I've got to start somewhere. I've got to begin getting that experience."

The news director had agreed to take her on for a three-month internship, probably thinking she'd spruce up the place and maybe keep some of the younger male reporters happy. Fresh meat on the newsroom hook.

He never would have guessed that, four years later, he'd be gone and she'd still be there, sharing the top anchor position, still sailing on the wings of her looks, aided by an uncanny comfort in front of the camera.

The dairy princess was fast becoming a television queen, but now she found herself spouting four-letter words like a longshoreman. She didn't like what was happening to her.

The ringing phone brought Barbara back, and she hurried to pick it up.

It was another of George Barclay's newsroom rules: answer the fucking telephone, immediately and politely. Barclay couldn't tolerate ringing phones; he kept thinking of all the news stories they could be missing, that could be going to the competition—where they *did* answer the goddamned phones.

"Barbara?"

"Hi, Phil." It was Phil Tinsley, Detective Phil Tinsley, the Minneapolis cop she'd been seeing. "What's up?"

"Last night was great, Barb, really great. I just wanted you to know that."

"It *was* nice, Phil," Barbara said, thinking the conversation was sounding like dialogue from a Grade-B movie. "*Was it as good for you as it was for me? Ohhh yes . . .*"

Actually, it hadn't been *that* great for Barbara. Phil was an attentive lover when they started early enough in the evening, but when it was late, when he was worried about making the early shift on time, he rushed through the preliminaries.

"Phil, you're not calling just to compliment me, are you?"

"Now that you mention it, I *was* going to ask you about something," he said, as though it just occurred to him. "Remember asking me about Judge Hodges's wife?"

"Sure I do. Why?"

"Well, while I certainly didn't mention anything to anybody about our conversation, I did ask our lieutenant if there were any problems with any of our judges."

"You did *what?*" Barbara asked, astonished. "Why would you do that?"

"I was curious. You don't ask me questions like that without a reason, you being in the news business and all. I thought something might be up. That this woman, or the judge, could be in some kind of trouble."

"Phil, I can't believe you! I thought we could have a relationship and keep our jobs separate . . . that I could trust you to have some discretion." She neglected to mention that she had used their relationship by asking the questions in the first place.

"I'm sorry," he said, "I apologize, okay? But I thought you might be interested in the lieutenant's reaction."

"Reaction to what?"

"To my question," he said impatiently. "He got all huffy. Said nothing was going on that he knew about. That I had enough cases on my docket without worrying about any judges. It was strange."

"What? That he got pissed off?"

"*Real* pissed off," he said. "And I thought you'd like to know. For what it's worth."

"All right, then. Thanks. I don't know what it means, either. But it is interesting."

"Will I see you tonight?" he asked. "I'm off tomorrow."

"I can't, Phil, not tonight. I've got to cut some promos after the newscast, and I don't know when I'll be out of here."

That was a lie, but at the moment Barbara was more interested in giving Alex this new information than she was in cavorting with Phil.

Even if he didn't have to make the early shift.

Seven

Alex stood with his back braced against the November wind, watching the sleet swirl around his feet. The tiny white pellets stung his neck as he pulled the collar of his coat up around his ears and looked for cover.

He had walked eight blocks from the station to the Hennepin County Government Center, but he'd stayed inside the city's elaborate skyway system most of the way, escaping the onslaught of the weather until now. He was still without any kind of winter wear, but it was clear he could not afford to wait much longer.

He paused, shivering, on the corner, trying to decide which of several doors to enter. He finally opted for one downwind and hurried toward it.

Alex had seen the building from a distance, but this was his first visit. Surrounded by an open plaza, the Government Center stood on the edge of downtown, its red granite façade arching some twenty-four stories high, covering most of two city blocks. Its breadth spanned one city street, allowing traffic to flow below while the governmental employees worked in the maze above.

Alex had been told that construction of the building some fifteen years before had raised a storm of public protest, fed by reports of massive cost overruns and opulent quarters for the county officials and judges housed inside. The outcry had lasted for a few

months but had faded when the next scandal took over the newspaper front pages and the television screens.

Then the bureaucrats had moved happily into their swanky new
home.

As Alex was swept inside by the gusts, he was struck by the
soaring open expanse of the interior. The atrium, half as large as
a football field, rose the height of the building.

At first, he'd heard, the atrium was open at every floor. But after
several people committed suicide by leaping from the open floors,
county officials had become so embarrassed that they'd replaced
the railings with windows.

Alex had come there partly on a whim, partly out of genuine
curiosity. He'd told the newsroom assignment editor that he'd be
gone for a while, checking out a story. The editor, not accustomed
to anchormen doing anything but reading the news, had given Alex
a quizzical look, then reminded him not to be late for the early
newscast.

In a way, Alex's pretext was true. George Barclay *had* told him
to spend some time on the mystery story, to check it out. And
Alex had decided the first thing he ought to do was to get a look
at Pat Hodges's husband, the judge whose career she said could
be threatened as well as her own.

But if the full truth were known, he was curious to see the man
she'd married, in person. When he discovered that Judge Hodges
was currently presiding over a trial, the urge to see him at his job
became irresistible.

So he found himself standing at the elevator, slightly embarrassed, more than a little puzzled at himself, but determined to go
ahead.

There were about fifty judges in Hennepin County, and their
courtrooms and chambers were spread between the twelfth and
sixteenth floors of the Government Center.

Assignments were rotated, and on this particular week, Judge
Hodges was delegated to criminal matters, handling the trial of a
three-time loser named Lonnie, who was up on burglary charges
for the sixteenth time. Lonnie had demanded a jury trial because
he knew that while he had very little to gain, he had absolutely
nothing to lose.

Judge Hodges had cajoled and then all but clubbed the attorneys
and the defendant into arriving at a plea bargain, but the defense

was adamant: no deal without a guarantee from the judge of a sentence of no more than three to five years.

Judge Hodges knew that if he gave Lonnie so little time he'd run the risk of a permanent assignment to the drudgery of the criminal bench.

So the trial went on, a caricature of American justice. It was now in its third day, and concluding arguments were about to begin as Alex squeezed as quietly as he could through the courtroom door, careful not to disturb the proceedings.

But there was no big news here, and this hadn't been a heavily visited trial, even by the habitual courtroom gawkers. So all heads turned as the door squeaked shut and Alex slid into one of the rear bench seats.

Several of the women jurors whispered among themselves, nodding toward the newcomer and smiling sweetly in recognition. Even Lonnie-the-loser gave Alex a small wave. The others in the courtroom seemed to take little notice, and closing arguments began.

The evidence was so overwhelming it took the prosecutor only fifteen minutes to summarize the testimony of the parade of witnesses and to urge the jury to get the defendant off the streets once and for all. The public defender did the best she could, but her closing argument was more of a search for sympathy than a plea for acquittal. It looked as though Lonnie was about to become a four-time loser.

But Alex was less interested in the trial than he was in Judge Nathaniel Hodges.

For some reason, Alex had come expecting to find something of an intellectual wimp, spectacled and robed, hair thinning and Adam's apple bobbing. Ichabod Crane on the bench. Maybe that's what he had *hoped* he'd find.

Instead, he saw a man who could have been born to the movie role of a judge: erect, solid, athletic, deeply tanned, with graying hair, handsome in a Warren Burger way, only much younger. He wore the judicial robe with a sense of confidence and pride.

When the closing arguments in the trial were over, Judge Hodges announced he would instruct the jury the next morning and allow deliberations to begin. Then he left the bench, the others in the courtroom rising in deference to his departure.

Alex was about to leave, too, when the bailiff walked over with a note from the judge, asking Alex to join him in his chambers.

The bailiff led the way through the back of the courtroom and down a short hallway, where a secretary and a court clerk were working at word processors, too busy even to glance up.

The bailiff knocked lightly at the judge's door and then opened it and stepped aside for Alex. Judge Hodges had removed his robe and was sitting in shirtsleeves behind his desk. There was a broad smile on his face as he rose and came around the desk.

"Come on in, Alex," the judge said. "I recognized you from television and wanted to say hello. Pat has told me about you . . . said you went to school together back in Kansas."

"That's true," Alex said, "more years ago than I'd like to admit."

Face to face, the judge was even more imposing than he was on the bench. Although he was no taller than Alex, he seemed to loom over him. He had that kind of physical presence. His handshake had the strength of someone who worked out with weights, and his voice carried the same kind of authority.

"So what brings you here?" Hodges asked. "It's not often we get celebrity anchormen in our courtrooms. It certainly can't be today's trial. Lonnie wouldn't make the back page of the weekly shopper, let alone the ten o'clock news."

Alex chose his words carefully. "I happened to run into Pat, and we recognized one another from our days in Kansas." Not exactly a lie, but close. "We brought each other up to date, and she happened to mention that you were a judge."

Hodges was still smiling, listening with interest.

"Since I had never been to the Government Center, and since I happened to be in the area, I thought I'd stop by and see Pat's husband in action. Good background for a new newsguy in town."

It sounded plausible enough, and the judge seemed satisfied.

"I'm glad you did. Let me show you around."

"I have just a few minutes," Alex said, glancing at his watch. "I have to get back for the early show."

The chambers were as lavish as Alex had been led to believe they'd be. There was a huge desk of well-polished mahogany and a large leather sofa and two easy chairs to match, dark brown to complement the desk. Quality reproductions of a Chagall and two Matisse masterworks hung on the walls. Opposite them a huge window provided a panoramic view of the city.

There was soft carpeting everywhere except in the adjoining bathroom, which was all glass and brass, complete with a shower and changing area.

Alex could understand the taxpayers' anger. The judges lived better than the CEOs of some Fortune 500 firms.

"Pretty impressive" was all he could manage to say as they wandered through the judge's quarters.

"It might seem a bit much," Hodges acknowledged, "but we spend a lot of time here, and the county board—in all its wisdom—decided we should be comfortable. God knows, our salaries are nothing compared to what private law firms pay, so maybe we deserve it."

He sounds a little defensive to me, Alex thought, but maybe I'm just jealous of the space he has. Alex's own little cubicle could easily have fit into one corner of the judge's chambers.

Unlike his cubicle, however, Hodges's office was bereft of any personal touches. There were no pictures of his wife, or anyone else for that matter, except one of Hodges as a young man with the late Senator Hubert Humphrey. It's as if he has no life outside these chambers, Alex thought.

"I really do have to get going," Alex said, surprised to find how much time had passed, "or I'm going to be late for the newscast." As he hurried to leave the office, he promised to stay in touch and agreed that, yes, perhaps they could have dinner some night soon.

Riding down the elevator, Alex tried to sort through what he had seen and heard. One thing seemed clear: If Judge Hodges shared any of the tension Pat was feeling, he did a pretty good job of hiding it.

Barbara was already at the anchor desk when Alex rushed back into the newsroom.

"There you are!" she said. "People were starting to panic. We've only got five minutes till the news."

"Sorry. I got delayed."

"Where have you been?"

"Out," he replied tersely. He wanted to tell her to mind her own business. "Checking something out."

"Anything to do with your lady friend from Kansas?"

Alex looked at her, surprised. "Forget about her, okay? Forget I even mentioned her. It's nothing."

"I wouldn't be so sure," Barbara said, adjusting the tiny microphone on her blouse.

"What do you mean?"

"I talked to my source again. Something funny's going on."

"Stand by! One minute to air! Mike check!" It was Derek, shouting despite his standing only two feet in front of them.

"Barbara, do me a favor and—"

"Listen up! Mike check!" Derek again, a foot away now.

"Okay, okay, cool it, Derek," Alex said. "Testing, one, two, three, four . . . This is microphone position two . . ."

"Testing, testing, one, two, three . . ." Barbara chimed in. "Microphone position one . . ."

Derek stepped back behind the camera. *"Thirty seconds to air! Stand by!"*

"Can we get together after the late news?" Barbara asked. "I'll tell you more then."

Alex nodded as he watched the final ten seconds being counted down on Derek's fingers. When the red light above the camera came on, the middle finger of Derek's right hand was still extended.

After the early newscast the anchors were allowed a couple of hours off to eat and to rest up before returning to the station for the late show. Alex almost always used the free time to drive home and feed Seuss and, in nicer weather, to stroll down to the lake for a few casts to the waiting bass.

As his TR4 grudgingly pulled up in front of the house, Alex noticed a strange car, a black BMW, parked in the driveway. And as he walked up the sloping sidewalk, he saw a huddled figure perched on the doorstep, a parka hood over its head, the cat cuddled in its lap.

What's going on? he wondered. Who the hell is that? Seuss never allows anybody but me to hold him.

The answer came a moment later as Pat Hodges stood up, pulled the hood away from her head, and handed Seuss to Alex.

"How can you leave a cat out in this kind of weather?" she demanded. "It's shivering, and it's miserable. Do you want it to freeze to death, for God's sake?"

Before Alex could answer, Seuss bit him on the hand. *Son of a bitch!* So much for loyalty.

"I didn't know it was going to snow," he answered lamely. "Besides, he'd go crazy in the house all day. I don't know what I'm going to do with the damned thing."

He realized he was answering her questions before asking a few of his own. Like, what was she doing on his front porch, holding his cat, and then chewing him out? But she wasn't done yet.

"Why did you go see my husband today?" she demanded.

Even in the dark Alex could see the anger in her eyes.

"What?"

"My husband said you stopped by to see him today. I'd like to know why? I thought we had an understanding."

"Why don't we get inside first?" Alex said, fumbling with the key while trying to keep Seuss at bay.

Alex took Pat's parka, shook the snow off, and hung it on the bannister.

"Well?" she asked, trailing him into the house.

"Give me a minute, huh?" he said, with some annoyance. *What was she doing here, anyway*? "How about a drink? Gin, bourbon, scotch, Perrier?"

"I'll have a bourbon and water, thanks." Then, almost without pause: "Do you live here all by yourself?"

"Just Seuss and I. Or is it Seuss and *me*? I never could get that straight," he said, lightening up a bit.

"Seuss?"

"The kids named him. He was born in a hat in a neighbor's closet."

She followed him to the kitchen. "Isn't the house a little large?" she asked.

"Yeah. I don't use much of it. But it'll handle my kids if they come to visit."

As Pat stood in the kitchen doorway, Alex saw again that the years had done little to erode her beauty. She was wearing a heavy knit turtleneck sweater, which covered but could not hide the fullness of her breasts. Her hair had fallen around her shoulders, and despite her agitation, her features were relaxed, the skin no longer tight across her face. More like the girl he remembered, and quite a contrast to the lady he'd met at the restaurant.

He took a pizza from the freezer and put it into the microwave, then poured himself a Perrier.

"You don't drink?" she asked.

"Never before a newscast. I get drowsy enough as it is."

Pat walked to the living room and was standing, drink in hand, when Alex joined her.

"Don't you want to sit down?" he asked.

"I don't have much time," she replied, but she sat on the edge of the couch.

Alex touched a match to the kindling in the fireplace and flipped a switch on the stereo. The birch in the grate began to crackle and spit sparks like little Chinese firecrackers. He sat across from her, feeling again the intensity of her eyes and the spreading warmth of the fire.

"Your husband doesn't have a picture of you in his office," Alex said abruptly.

"What did you say?"

"Your husband. He doesn't have a picture of you in his office. I thought that was strange."

"You're very observant," she said, her eyes leaving his for the first time.

"He's a good-looking guy," Alex added. "Seems smart, too. Impressed me. You make a handsome couple."

"Why were you there in the first place?"

"Back to that, huh? I'm not sure. I was curious. I thought I should know a little bit about what I might be getting into here. I know I shouldn't have gone. I guess I wanted to see the man you married. To size him up, perhaps."

"You could have spoiled it, you know." Her voice was now more troubled than angry. "He didn't know I was going to talk to you. He only knew we went to school together back in Kansas."

"I think I covered that all right," Alex said. "I told him we just happened to run into each other. Nothing about lunch."

"I know. He told me that before I got caught in a lie."

"Look, Pat, what do you expect? Let's be honest. I wanted to see who you've been living with for ten years."

She said nothing, but watched as he fed more wood to the fire.

"Besides," he added, "I am worried. I don't know who you are now. People change."

"Alex, it's been twenty years!"

"And I haven't forgotten it, Pat. But you talked about your career and his being threatened if you ever got tied to this story of yours.

I wanted to see if your husband seemed as uptight as you did. He didn't, Pat."

"That's because he doesn't know what I'm doing, and I want to keep it that way."

Alex glanced at his watch. He had to be back at the station in an hour. "Want some pizza?" he asked. "I have to eat something."

"No, thanks, but I'll have another drink. Then I've got to go."

She was staring at the fire when he returned from the kitchen. She didn't seem to hear or notice him, and he couldn't guess where her mind was.

"I did talk to my boss," he said, anxious to bring her back. "He may have a solution to our problem."

"What's that?" she asked, her eyes back on him.

"We guarantee you confidentiality until we find out if there's a story or not. Until it's ready for air. Then it will be up to you. If you want us to run it, fine, but you'll have to take the same risks we're taking. If you don't want to take the risks, we won't run the story. At least not until we can guarantee you absolute confidentiality."

She was out of the chair, pacing again. "What kind of solution is that? That's nonsense."

"Wait a minute," he countered, getting up to face her, trying to remember George Barclay's reasoning. "Think about it. It just puts you in the same position we'll be in. If the story is important, and if it's true, then we should both have the guts to go with it. Regardless of the risks. You'll always have the fail-safe of backing out."

"But what if I say no and you still decide to put it on the air? How can I stop you? How can I avoid being dragged into it?"

"You could always deny any connection," he ventured.

"And commit perjury?"

"I guess you'll just have to take our word for it. We can't very well sign a contract. And, you know, we are taking *your* word at this point."

"I'll have to think about this," Pat said. "There's too much at stake."

"Look, Pat. I didn't ask for any of this. You called me, remember? You asked me for help. You came here tonight on your own. I didn't drag you. I still don't know what's going on."

"I know. I'm sorry."

"When can we talk again?" he asked, more casually than he felt.

She was putting on her coat. "Soon. Maybe tomorrow."

As Alex was about to open the door, she turned to him. "I want to talk about the past, Alex. I want to know what happened. I haven't forgotten."

She pulled his face to hers. Her mouth was on his. Her tongue was caressing his. Slowly. Sweetly. Tauntingly.

"What am I doing?" she whispered.

Then she was gone, a shadow moving through the falling snow, leaving Alex surprised and confused—and uncomfortably excited.

Eight

Rick took his time finishing the drink, then began peeling off his clothes. Following the instructions. He'd been wearing the same shirt and jeans for days, and he could barely stand the sight and smell of them. That's what happens when you sleep on cardboard in culverts or under bridges, he thought.

He was eagerly looking forward to the bath; warm water hadn't touched his body for days, not since he'd crept into the YMCA and sneaked a shower.

As the steaming water filled the sunken tub, Rick was surrounded by the mirror images of his body. Lean, from his spartan diet, yet muscular from years of lifting weights as a young kid. Before he left home, before he took to the streets.

Behind the tiger's eye, a new tape was fed into the recorder.

He stepped into the tub and watched the hot water cover his body to the neck, instantly turning his skin as red as a lobster in a pot. He moved his arms slowly beneath the surface, back and forth like the fins of a fish, creating small waves which lapped beneath his chin.

He closed his eyes, and his thoughts drifted with his body, bobbing in and out of wakefulness. *His mother's mittened hand as wrapped around his, the other holding a rope on the sled, tugging it behind them. A Flexible Flyer, the only one on the block. With varnished wood that glistened in the sun and a red stripe that ran down the center. Sleek. And could it fly! The snow would buffet his face, icy on his cheeks, blinding him in a blur of white. He could still hear his mother's laughing shrieks from the top of the hill.*

That's when they were still a family. Before his dad went away without a goodbye, before the smiles on his mother's face disappeared. Rick remembered so little of his dad. *Why couldn't he remember more?* There were so few pictures, so few memories, and his mother would never speak of him again.

Only her eyes spoke. And then they closed, too. Forever.

Rick slowly opened his eyes. *How long had he slept?* His skin was no longer red, but wrinkled. He quickly scrubbed his body, then stepped out of the water and wrapped himself in a thick towel which had been left hanging neatly next to the tub.

The mirrors were still steamed over, but he found a razor, wiped a space clear with his hand, and shaved away the four-day stubble. He didn't know what time it was; there was no clock in the room, and he had no watch. He felt disoriented, relaxed, and refreshed from the warmth of the water, but slightly dizzy from the drinks.

But time didn't matter, anyway. He had nowhere to go.

He poured himself another drink, wishing for a beer instead, and walked to the closet in search of the promised robe.

He no sooner had slipped out of the towel and into the robe than the lights dimmed and the door began to open.

He knew the fun was about over, the work about to begin.

Rick stood, drink in hand, as the door swung slowly open. He expected to see someone matching the husky, gravelly voice he had heard when he entered the house. Instead, he was looking at a young man not much older than himself, thin, clad in a bulky sweater and tight-fitting jeans, wearing sandals, and with a gold earring in his left ear.

They looked at each other, saying nothing, but understanding immediately they were not strangers. They had known the same darkened streets, the same dingy doorways, the same smoky bars. The same humiliations. All in the name of survival.

"I'm Roger," he said, his voice so soft it was almost lost in the large room. "Follow me, please. You can bring your drink, if you'd like." Rick followed in his ankle-length robe, feeling a little like a prizefighter being led to the ring.

In the corridor, dimly lighted by bluish bulbs sunk in the ceiling, the carpeting absorbed their footsteps. There was no sound except for the distant and muted rhythms of a blues band, the melody indiscernible, the beat more felt than heard. Rick extended both arms, brushing the walls with his fingertips, reaffirming this wasn't a dream. There would be no mother's whispers of comfort and reassurance.

"Wait here, please." Roger, five paces ahead, stopped outside a door, his knock no more audible than his voice.

Her breath had always held the sweet smell of mint, her voice the soft tinge of her Irish homeland.

"We're here." Roger was speaking into a small box next to the door. There was a click, and the door swung open.

There would be no more scent of mint. No more tender lilt of the voice. No more gentle arms. Only a grave on a slope of grassy ground, shaded by a maple sapling, slightly indented by the falling rain and the settling soil.

"Show him in, please."

The gravelly voice sounded harsher than Rick remembered.

Nine

The taste of Pat's kiss was still in his mind when Alex returned to the newsroom. Still preoccupied, he was relieved to find no crises waiting.

"Half hour to air. Makeup everybody!" Derek was again prowling the studio.

It was a fairly routine news night. Peace efforts in the Middle East were still floundering, the Democrats were searching for someone to run against George Bush, and the debate over the national debt had rekindled in Congress.

Locally, there was a tax protest at the state capitol, a house fire in a western suburb, the opening of a new play at the Guthrie Theater. Not much new to report, mostly rehashed stories from the early newscast.

That was fairly usual, and it only increased the pressure on the anchors to make the old news seem fresh and important. To make the audience *think* they were seeing something new.

That was the art of anchoring.

Alex knew almost any anchor could look good sitting in the middle of a breaking news story, like the Gulf war, surrounded by news bulletins and network interruptions. You could *feel* the excitement then; it permeated the newsroom and the news set and was easy to share with the audience.

No trouble getting up on those nights.

But they were the exception. Most newscasts were like this one: predictable and unexciting. It was up to the anchors to add punch, to keep the audience interested by the vitality of their performance.

That's why the good anchors were in such demand, why they were paid such enormous salaries. On many nights, they did more acting than anchoring.

Alex would have no trouble acting his role on this night, routine or not. George Barclay's warning was etched in his mind, but he knew it was more than that. Was it Pat Hodges? Maybe. Or the secret story she claimed to possess? Alex wasn't sure, but the feeling was back in his body and brain, the edge had returned. For the moment, at least.

"Are we still on for tonight?" Barbara asked during a commercial break.

"I guess so," Alex replied, "although I don't know what it's all about."

"I don't think it'll be a waste of your time," Barbara said.

The newscast went well. Barclay must have talked to the producers, Alex decided, because they'd spent more time on real news and less time on the frivolous bullshit.

Alex and Barbara quickly reviewed a tape of the program afterward, then ducked out of the station and walked a few blocks to a small bar in the Radisson Hotel. The bar was built for privacy, tucked away off the lobby and furnished with small groupings of large, deeply cushioned chairs of a red velvet velour.

They sat quietly until the drinks were delivered. Even in the shadows of the bar, Alex marveled at Barbara's made-for-television beauty. She was a natural blonde whose hair clung seductively to her face, giving her pale skin a golden glow that was only accentuated by the lights of the studio.

By now, it was clear to Alex that Barbara was a child of the medium. She had learned to play the television camera, keenly aware of every nuance of makeup and lighting, of every pose and posture.

But there was no posturing now.

"I don't know what's going on, Alex, but whatever that lady friend of yours knows may be worth listening to."

"What are you talking about, Barbara? She just wanted to renew old acquaintances, that's all."

"I think that's bullshit," she snapped. "I don't understand why you're being so secretive."

She crossed one leg over the other, her skirt riding up over her knee, exposing the shiny, stockinged underside of her thigh. Alex's eyes followed, even though he was listening to every word.

"What makes you think that?" he asked. "What'd your source say?"

"You know perfectly well who the source is, so we don't have to play games. Phil called me this afternoon. He said he'd made his lieutenant real nervous by asking some pointed questions about judges."

"Why would he ask his lieutenant about judges?"

"Because he wondered why I was asking *him* questions about the judge and his wife," she said. "He shouldn't have done it . . . and he's sorry he did. But that's what happened."

"What did he mean, he made his lieutenant real nervous?"

"Those are my words, not his," Barbara said. "Phil said that the lieutenant 'got real pissed off' when he asked if anything was going on with any of the judges. Told him to mind his own business."

This doesn't make any sense, Alex thought.

"Barbara, no games. I don't know what's going on. And that's the honest-to-God truth. There may be a story out there, and it may be about judges, and it may be big, but it may also be nothing."

Barbara looked suspicious, and he didn't blame her.

"I won't know anything until this lady decides to talk to me. That could be tomorrow, or it could be never. If she does talk, she wants her identity protected. . . . That's why you've got to forget about her."

"Easier said than done," Barbara replied. "It sounds as though it might be a good story. I know you think I'm a goddamned Girl Scout, but maybe we could call a truce for a while, and I could give you a hand with it."

Alex studied her. Her stare was steady. Unwavering. God, she *is* young, he thought. Can you really trust anybody that young? And somebody who sleeps with a cop?

"I appreciate the offer," he said finally, "but until I know more, I'm going to go it alone."

Barbara decided not to argue further. "Just don't forget I'm around," she said. "It's not often I get a chance to work on a good story, and I don't want to let it pass."

Good story? he wondered. Who knows what the hell we're getting into here?

"We'll see, Barbara," he murmured as they got up. "We'll see."

The sharp ringing of the telephone the next morning awakened both Alex and the cat, and it was hard to tell which was the more startled. But Seuss was the quicker out of bed, leaping atop the dresser and cowering behind a picture of Jan and the children.

It took Alex a moment longer to clamber from beneath the covers and cross the room to the phone. Fucking floors are freezing, he thought, remembering too late that his slippers were still beneath the bed.

"Hello." His voice was still groggy.

"Hi, Daddy!" The sound brought the picture on the dresser to life. It was Jennifer, his six-year-old daughter, obviously wide-awake in Pennsylvania.

"Hi, Jennie. How'ya doing? You're a real early bird, aren't you?"

Then he remembered: It's an hour later out there, and she's probably all ready for school.

"It's not *that* early, Daddy. Were you still sleeping? How's Seuss? Is it snowing there yet?"

"Hey, slow down, kiddo. Give me a second to wake up." He shook his head quickly. "Yes, I was still sleeping. Yes, Seuss is just fine. And yes, it's started to snow, but not too much yet."

Alex loved to hear their voices, to try and visualize exactly what they were wearing, the expressions on their faces. He missed them sorely, but he worried that by now he might have forgotten how to be a father. It takes practice to be a good parent, he knew, and he wondered if he still had the patience. Maybe he never did. Maybe Jan had realized that, too.

His son, Chris, was now on the phone, sounding more adult than his eight years entitled him to be. He asked about fishing, about a Vikings-Eagles game coming up in a couple of weeks, and, finally, if Alex would like to come to Pennsylvania for Thanksgiving.

"Does your mother know you're asking?"

"Sure, she's right here. Mom?"

"Alex?" The voice was tentative, almost shy. Different.

"Hello, Jan. Are you okay?"

"I'm fine, Alex. Just a bit weary from getting them ready for school."

At that moment, there was a click on the line. Call Waiting. Alex hated the invention, but the phone came equipped with it.

"Hold on, Jan. Another call. I'll be right back."

It was Pat Hodges, sounding as alertly awake as Jennifer.

"Are you busy?" she asked.

"I'm on the other line at the moment," he said.

"Are you decent? I'm just ten minutes away."

"Come over," he said, "but make it fifteen."

Back to Jan on the other line.

"Sorry about that. You sound as though things are getting to you. Anything I can do?"

"Not unless you want to take a couple of kids for a while."

Alex felt a flash of guilt. It was not a new feeling. "I'd love to, Jan, but I'm afraid that's not possible right now."

There was silence at the other end of the line.

"What's this about Thanksgiving?" he finally asked.

"Chris and Jennie would like you to come," she said. "To try and be a family again for the holiday."

"What about you?" he asked. "What would *you* like?"

There was another pause. He understood her hesitation.

"I don't honestly know," she said, finally. "Maybe enough time has passed, and I *would* like to do it for the kids."

"Well, let me think about it," he said. "We'll still be in the November rating book, and I'm not sure I can get the time off."

They left it at that, with Alex promising to get back to them in a week or so.

He quickly showered, and was pulling on his pants when the doorbell rang. He was still shoeless, his shirttail hanging out and his hair wet, as he headed toward the door.

He was toweling his hair dry as Pat stepped inside the door.

"I should have said twenty minutes," he explained with a grin.

Gone were the turtleneck sweater and slacks, replaced by a heather-gray wool jersey dress—the pleated skirt swinging as she walked, the top clinging to her body, outlining in detail what the sweater had only hinted at the night before.

Gone, too, was any vestige of her distance or timidity. She

walked in alive and radiant, grinning girlishly at his dangling shirt-tail and bare feet.

Alex could only stand and smile, caught up in her contagious good humor. "What the hell's gotten into you?" he asked.

She picked up Seuss and walked past Alex into the kitchen, still laughing. "Get dressed, will you," she said over her shoulder. "Then we'll talk."

When he returned to the kitchen, he found her sipping coffee, Seuss cuddled contentedly in her lap. "Now, what's up?" he asked.

"I've been doing a lot of thinking since yesterday," she said. "It's stupid to play games. I'll never forget or forgive what you did to me. But what's past is past. I'd like to get on with things, start over."

"In what way?" he asked.

"As friends, Alex."

"Because you think I can help you?"

"That's part of it, I suppose. I do need you now. But you must know I've never stopped wondering about you, not in all these years. We've both grown up now and there's no reason not to be friends again."

"It may not be that simple," he said.

"I'm the one who should be telling you that," she said. "You'll never know what you did to me. I had to leave school for a semester to get myself together. When I got back, no one seemed to know what had happened to you."

Alex shifted uncomfortably, then tried to change the tone of their talk. "How did you get to Minnesota?" he asked.

"After KU, I went to the Harvard Law School and managed to graduate near the top of my class. But I had trouble finding a job."

"How so?" he asked.

"Young women lawyers weren't in quite the demand they are today. Even the bright ones. The big law firms were paying lip service to equal-opportunity hiring, but, really, a lot of them were just 'old boys' clubs uncomfortable with the idea of too many women around. If you didn't play golf on Friday afternoon, or drink Jack Daniels after work, you didn't quite fit in."

There was no bitterness in her voice, simply resignation.

"When I got no irresistible offers from the big New York or Washington or L.A. firms, I decided to flush the idea of corporate law. It was too stuffy anyway. I opted for criminal law, and happened to hear of an opening in the public defender's office here in Minneapolis. I had to start somewhere.

"Then I met Nathaniel. He was working for the county attorney, and we faced one another in some petty little case, I don't remember what. We started going out. He was smart, considerate, good-looking, and a good lover, so we got married."

"That's it?" Alex asked. "Just like that?"

"Well, it was a little more involved, but you don't want to hear about it."

"After that?"

"After that, my husband became very active in politics, got into campaign work, helped elect some important politicians, and got himself appointed as a judge."

"And you?"

"I stayed with the public defender's office longer than I should have. I got burned out, fed up with a system where the quality of justice seemed to depend on how much money you had. Too often, the rich ones went free; my clients went to prison. When I finally quit, I joined a small criminal law office where the hours and pay were better and where the frustration wasn't as great."

"Your husband?" Alex asked. "What's he like?"

"Not an easy question. I'm not sure myself sometimes. Nathaniel's changed. Early on, it seemed like a perfect marriage. Lots of friends, lots of fun. Always on the go. Then we started to drift apart. I don't know why exactly. Maybe it was his job, maybe it was me. We started spending less and less time together. He was consumed by his work; I was distressed by mine. We don't argue or anything. We just don't talk much anymore."

They walked to the living room and sat together on the sofa, in the sun. She slipped her shoes off and tucked her legs beneath her, cradling the coffee cup in her lap. She leaned forward and touched the thin scar on his jaw. "I hadn't noticed that before," she said.

"It's hard to see," he admitted.

"When did you get that?"

"Years ago," he replied vaguely.

"How?"

He hesitated. She waited.

"It got cut by somebody who didn't like a story I was doing," he said, finally, his hand touching his throat. "Two inches lower and I wouldn't be here today."

"Jesus," she breathed. "Is that why you quit reporting?"

"Eventually, I guess. I not only got cut, but burned, on the same story. People don't let you forget."

"Burned?" she repeated.

"Figuratively, Pat." His expression showed it was not a subject he wanted to discuss. "I was set up."

She paid no heed. "Is that why you're so hesitant about this story?"

"Maybe so. I've tried to stay away from that kind of thing for years now."

Alex tried to steer the conversation in a new direction, but Pat persisted. "How'd you get into the news business, anyway?"

He shifted positions, uncomfortable talking about his past. "By accident, really. Just after I left you, I bummed around Europe for a while, working where I could, mooching where I couldn't. Staying in hostels or with friends I'd meet along the way.

"For a couple of months, I did some gofer work for the CBS bureau in Rome—running film to and from the airport, lugging gear, that kind of thing. Wasn't very glamorous, but I liked it. Those were pretty exciting days, if you remember. Vietnam and the protests, Nixon and Agnew, the first man on the moon. I wanted to feel part of it.

"So when I got back to the States, I went back to school. Dreamed of being another Scotty Reston or Ed Murrow. It didn't work out that way, of course. I spent a few years at small newspapers, learning the trade, covering a lot of little stories, always looking for the next job, more money, a bigger byline. I finally got out of newspapering and into television, which seemed a lot more appealing at the time."

Pat leaned forward, not wanting to interrupt.

"I met my wife . . . her name's Jan . . . while I was working at a small newspaper in Illinois." He paused, hesitant, but Pat's gaze urged him on. "She's a terrific lady, bright and fun and a great mother to the kids. Almost everything anyone could want in a wife."

"Then why the divorce?" Pat could not resist the question.

"Because I wasn't a great husband, I guess. It turned out we wanted different things. She wanted stability, a home to raise the

kids in, friends, neighbors . . . all of the things most people want
in a marriage. I wanted to keep moving, to get to the big time.
She finally ran out of patience and we parted ways."

Alex looked away, afraid to show the pain. "Leaving those kids
was maybe the hardest thing in my life. It's like losing an arm or
a leg. You can learn to live without it, but you always know it's
not there. You never stop missing it. I never stop missing the kids,
but I've tried to learn to live without them."

"Would you do it again?" Pat asked quietly.

"You mean make the same choice? I don't know. Life certainly
hasn't been much fun since the divorce. Lots of lonely days and
nights. But I'm not sure I was capable of making another choice.
It's a moot question, anyway."

The sun had warmed the living room, and they sat quietly, absorbing what they had learned about one another.

"Well," Alex finally said, "enough life history. What have you
decided about the story? What do you want me to do?"

She studied him carefully before replying. "I've decided to take
your word. I don't think I have much choice. I have to trust somebody."

"Not the greatest endorsement I've ever heard," he said, "but
I'll do everything I can to protect you, if it comes to that. However,
we both understand there are limits, right?"

"I understand, but I shudder to think about them."

"So what *is* the story?" he asked.

She hesitated, apparently not sure where to begin. Then the
words rushed out; they'd been held back too long.

"What would you say if you knew the chief judge of Hennepin
County, one of the most respected jurists in the state, and the
most likely next chief justice of the Minnesota Supreme Court, is
screwing young boys. Teenagers. And making movies of it. Maybe
more."

He caught his breath. "I'd say that's a hell of a story."

"I thought you would," she said, with a slight smirk.

"How in the world do you know this?"

"Ah, that will take time to explain," she said. "You'll just have
to take my word for it now."

"Can you prove it?"

"Of course I can't prove it. Not yet. That's why I called you."

"Wait a minute," he said, raising his hand. "Take a step back. I don't even know who the chief judge is. Tell me about him, and then tell me how you know all of this."

She put the coffee cup down, leaned back, and stared at the ceiling. The earlier exhuberance was gone; she seemed very tired.

"His name is Emmett Steele. He's about sixty years old, and he's been on the bench forever. He's a political power, he's rich, and practically everybody who's anybody in the state is beholden to him. He rules the courthouse with an iron fist. He's no one to fool around with."

"Is he gay?" Alex asked.

"Of course he is, but not openly. Only a handful of people know. But that's not the problem. I couldn't care less that he's homosexual. I do care that he's a pedophile."

"And your husband works for him."

"Yes, and that complicates the whole thing. Nathaniel's a part of the system. He's a great admirer of Steele. Almost a disciple. If it was ever discovered that I was part of some investigation, my husband would be extraordinarily angry. And he'd probably suffer the most."

"I'm not sure I understand," Alex said.

"Being a judge is Nathaniel's life, more important to him, I'm afraid, than I am. Judge Steele has friends who would never forgive or forget, no matter what he's accused of doing. Those friends would find it far easier to get back at my husband than at me."

"Does Nathaniel share any of your suspicions?" Alex asked.

"I don't know. We don't talk about it."

Alex was incredulous. "You mean you've never asked him about it? Never confronted him? That's hard to believe."

"It's true. He doesn't want to talk about it. We always skirt the subject. I told you, he and Steele are very close."

"So you're telling me things you've never told your husband?"

"Yes."

Alex got up, shaking his head. He walked around the room, hands in his pockets, trying to absorb all he had just heard.

"When we were at the restaurant," he said, "you mentioned something about other important people turning their heads, or their backs, on this thing."

"That may have been a slight exaggeration, but I know other people must be aware . . . must at least suspect . . . what's going on. Every now and then you hear some whispers. Some hints. Even the police must have some idea. But nothing ever happens."

Alex remembered that Barbara's friend Phil had said his lieutenant got nervous when he talked about judges.

"If that's true," Alex asked, "why hasn't anybody done anything?"

"Alex, you just don't understand the enormous power of the judiciary. They talk about three equal branches of government, but that's baloney. A judge, especially a chief judge, has incredible control—over other judges, over attorneys, over prosecutors, even over the public defenders. And, certainly, over the police. Everybody is indebted to a judge for one thing or another. Think about it: when have you ever heard *anybody* talk back to a judge?"

Pat leaned forward, clasping her hands beneath her chin. Her voice was brittle, icy. "And who judges the judges? Other judges, that's who. Just one big happy fraternity. How often do you see a judge defeated for reelection? Usually nobody even dares to run against them. Everybody's afraid. If you want power, and a lifetime job, don't run for governor, run for judge."

"This sounds like a personal vendetta, like a crusade."

"I'm tired of the double standard, Alex. Judges ought to be held accountable just like any of us, especially judges who are molesting young boys."

"It's got to be more than that," Alex argued. "As a public defender, you certainly saw enough injustice and double standards. Why have you settled on this?"

"I suppose part of it is Steele's arrogance, his self-righteous smugness. He thinks he's invulnerable."

"That's part of it," Alex said. "What's the rest?"

She wouldn't look at him, staring at her clasped hands instead. "I've never told you this. I've never told anybody, not even my parents."

"What?" Alex asked.

She took a deep breath. "It's a long story, and it happened a long time ago. When I was in junior high, back in Salina, we went to the Methodist Church. The one over by the skating rink. The pastor took a liking to me. He seemed to single me out for special attention. In confirmation classes, in some of the things the church kids did together. He was like a second father to me."

Alex said nothing and waited for her to continue.

"I was so trusting, so innocent. He was a minister, for God's sake. I worshiped him, almost. He talked to me about my becoming a missionary, doing the Lord's work. He said he wanted to help.

"Then one night, he touched my breast. When we were in the back of a car, coming home from a skating party. He rubbed it, then put his hand between my legs."

"Oh, no," Alex muttered.

"I didn't know what to say. I knew it was wrong; I knew he shouldn't be doing it. But I'd never felt anything like it before. I was only a kid, remember. I pushed his hand away, but I didn't dare cry out. Who would have believed it? I barely did."

She got up and walked to the window, looking down on the leaf-covered lawn.

"It didn't end there. He kept it up, every chance he had. I was like two people. One felt so ashamed, so guilty. The other seemed to come back for more. I didn't want to make him angry, to lose his affection. I kept telling myself: it can't be that bad, he's a minister. I didn't dare tell my parents; I thought they'd blame me . . . that they'd think I had enticed him some way."

"How did it end?" Alex asked.

"When he moved away, when he took over a church in Illinois. It was only after he'd left that I realized what he'd done to me. I felt so dirty, Alex, I can't tell you. That's what made our own breakup in college so hard."

"What do you mean?"

"You were the first guy I really fell for after the whole experience with the minister. The first one I really trusted."

Alex was silent.

"Now every time I see Judge Steele's face, I see that minister. I think Steele is doing the same things to these young guys that the minister did to me. Only Steele uses money and power to screw them over."

Alex considered everything he had heard. *Could such crimes be committed by a man who was so visibly a symbol of justice?* "This seems incredible, Pat," he said, finally. "What should happen next?"

"That's up to you. That's why I came to you. Judges like Steele can't control the media. You're as powerful as they are, and they know it. They fear you as much as we fear them."

"You said you'd be willing to keep helping," he reminded her.

"I will, but I have to be careful. If Steele or his friends get a hint of what we're doing, there could be terrible trouble. I'm sorry to sound paranoid, but I'm scared."

"You realize I can't do this all by myself, don't you?" Alex said. "I'm going to need to keep my boss informed and get some help from other people."

Those intense eyes were on him again. "But you'll keep me out of it, right? That's a promise? These other people don't need to know about me?"

"No, but they'll realize *somebody* has put me on to the story and is feeding me information. They won't need to know it's you."

He briefly debated whether he should tell her about Barbara and decided that he should. No sense in keeping secrets from the beginning. "One person already does know about you. By name."

"You promised," she said, anger back in her voice.

He explained how Barbara had come to know about her, how she had put the pieces together, but that she knew nothing about Judge Steele. How could she? He'd just found out himself.

"Don't tell her anything else," Pat insisted.

"Hold on. She may be one of those I ask to help out, since she already knows as much as she does. She's young, but she seems smart. She's attractive and looks innocent enough that she may be able to get information that I couldn't get. I'll have to think about it."

"I have to be at a deposition in a half hour," Pat said as she got up and started for the door. "We'll have to pick this up later."

"You've yet to tell me how you know all of this," he said, unable to conceal his doubts.

"It's complicated, Alex, but I'll tell you everything I know next time I see you. You can take it from there."

He stepped up to her and held her arms loosely, feeling the warm texture of the wool. She pulled away, but gently.

"Don't, Alex."

He stepped back. "You're right. I'm sorry."

"I'm not looking for an apology," she said. "I'm not a very strong woman around you. I found that out twenty years ago and proved it again last night."

"You're also a married woman," he said.

"That, too. Everything's changed. Maybe I should have just left things alone." She touched his cheek, running her finger slowly along the length of the scar. "Poor Alex," she said.

Then she reached for the door and was gone again.

Ten

The room was dark and seemed the size of a small theater. Each wall was draped or painted in black. The carpet was black, matching the two pieces of furniture: high-backed chairs facing the front of the room, separated by ten feet of blackness.

The only light penetrating the room came from a cone lamp in the ceiling in front, as intense as a spotlight, illuminating only a round area of what appeared to be a small stage squeezed between two large, darkened screens.

The light revealed little else in the room, but Rick could see that one of the chairs was occupied. He saw the outline of a man's arm resting on the arm of the chair, the fingers tapping, trying to match the beat of the blues band Rick had heard in the hallway.

"Good luck." The words were whispered in his ear before Roger backed out of the room, closing the door behind him. The last thing Rick saw of his young escort was the flash of a round earring in the bluish light of the hall.

"Sit down, please." The hand rose from the arm of the high-backed chair and pointed to the other chair in the room. Rick stepped forward, careful not to trip over his long robe, his eyes fixed on the extended hand.

"Please don't look in this direction," the husky voice said. "Just keep your eyes on the lighted area in front of you."

Rick did as he was told, stepping in front of the chair, then settling back into it, his eyes now never leaving the light.

"Listen carefully." The voice seemed to be coming from all corners of the room, with a slight reverberation. Rick realized the words were being amplified, perhaps electronically altered. "We are alone here. You have nothing to fear. But be aware there's an alarm button at my fingertips, and assistance nearby."

The room was warm, the robe heavy, but Rick felt a slight shiver. The walls seemed to close in on him, like a cell.

"I hope you've enjoyed your stay so far. We've tried to make you feel comfortable. I hope you'll relax."

Rick moved his head slightly to the left, pushing his eyes to their very limits, hoping his peripheral vision would give him a glimpse of his host. He saw nothing but a shadowy shape etched in black, wearing . . . what? A hood?

"I'll need to ask you some questions. I hope you'll respond truthfully."

Rick abandoned trying to see more of the man, and his eyes hurt from staring at the brightly lit stage.

"Do you have any idea where you are?"

Rick shook his head. "No, no idea."

"Do you have any idea who I am?"

Again Rick said no.

"How old are you?"

"I just turned sixteen."

"Have you ever been in trouble with the law?"

"A few times. Two car thefts. One burglary."

"Aren't you forgetting something? The truth, remember."

Rick said nothing, closing his eyes against the glare.

"Wasn't there a charge of loitering for purposes of prostitution?"

"Yes, I just forgot." *How would he know that?*

"Do you know what will be required of you here?"

"Not exactly," Rick responded. *That was the truth.*

"I'll explain. But I must have your word that you will tell no one of what happens here. No one. Do I have that assurance?"

"Yes." *What else could he say?*

"Do you know what could happen to you if you ignore that promise?"

"No."

"Then let me tell you. You'll be hunted down and dealt with most harshly, I'm afraid. Russell is quite experienced in that regard. Do I have to say more?"

"No," Rick said, feeling the shiver return.

"Good. Then let's get on with our evening's activities."

Eleven

The sailboat moorings still bobbed in the water of Lake Calhoun, but most of the boats were out of the lake by now. Pulled up on land and hauled away to await the passage of another long Minnesota winter. A few hearty souls kept their boats in the lake until the last possible moment, until the crust of thin ice started to surround the hulls, threatening to lock them in for good.

Alex walked along the lakeshore, feeling empty-handed without his fishing rod and bucket of lures, but enjoying the absolutely clear skies and the warmth of the sun. He was wearing a bulky down jacket he'd found in one of the closets, but wished now he had left it there.

The cold snap had broken, and the early winter sun seemed to be aiming its rays on his back and on the ice along the shoreline. Alex felt a trickle of sweat roll down his neck and wondered if his friends out west would ever believe he was perspiring in Minnesota in November. Probably not.

It was the kind of day which rewarded the patience of a few hearty sailors, and the small, bright sails of their boats dotted the lake. A warming weather system from the Gulf had replaced the cold Canadian high, providing a gentle breeze and moderate temperatures. Everyone knew it would not last long, but in Minnesota people gratefully grasped whatever favors Mother Nature happened to pass along.

Alex knelt by the lake and watched as the sun worked its magic on silvery crystals of ice, transforming them into tiny rivulets. It was a wondrous preview of spring, six months early.

His mind kept returning to his conversation with Pat Hodges, to the enormity of what she had told him. And to how ill equipped he felt to deal with it. *Where to begin? What to do next? Who to talk to?* Pat, it seemed, had far more faith in him than he had in himself.

The specter of the libel suit years before haunted Alex.

It had been his first and only crack at real investigative reporting. A state senator in Illinois had diverted campaign funds for his personal use, which included the support of a mistress and frequent gambling junkets to Las Vegas. Alex had uncovered the story while working for a small newspaper, and had reported it in a sensational exposé. His key source was the mistress.

It was the break he'd been looking for, but in the end it nearly broke him. Nearly killed him.

The night after the story ran, Alex had been cornered in an alley behind the newspaper office by two men wearing ski masks. They'd said nothing, but while one held him, the other had slashed him with a long-bladed knife, aiming for his throat but laying open his jawbone. They'd left him there to bleed to death, but somehow Alex had stanched the blood, and a talented plastic surgeon had done the rest.

The slashers were never caught, and Alex knew he'd been lucky to survive, but he was still plagued by the nightmares.

His story was accurate, but the senator had sued Alex and the paper, claiming they'd been duped, that the mistress had been paid by his political opponents to lie about the affair. The woman mysteriously disappeared before the libel trial could begin—leaving Alex without an important witness in his defense.

The frightened newspaper had agreed to settle out of court. The firing of Alex Collier was part of the settlement.

As he looked back on it now, Alex knew he'd been too eager to get the story to see the dangers. He'd been caught in the middle of power politics and had been too naive, too trusting, to realize it. He'd failed to get sworn affidavits from the woman, and he had lived with his mistake ever since.

The scar on his jaw was a constant reminder.

Since then, through a succession of newspaper and television jobs, Alex had stayed away from investigative reporting . . . and, eventually, from reporting itself.

If Pat was right, he would be back walking that tightrope again.

A judge fucking kids? How was it possible? Shit, he was going to blow this guy off the bench.

The thought terrified him—even as it excited him.

When Alex walked into the newsroom, he found Barbara waiting by his cubicle.

"Well?" she asked.

"Well what?"

"C'mon, don't be cute. Did you talk to her?"

"Yes," he said. "This morning."

"Well? Has she got something?"

Alex looked around, uncomfortable with the idea of talking about it in the middle of a crowded newsroom.

"She thinks she does," he said sotto voce. "She's convinced of it, and she can be pretty convincing herself. But I don't think I should be talking about it here."

"Does it involve judges?" she persisted, quietly.

"Maybe."

"I knew it!" she said, her face brightening.

"How's that?" he asked.

"Just a feeling. Instinct, I guess."

Alex suddenly realized there might be a real reporter living beneath the television mask. That made him slightly uneasy.

"I have a suggestion for you," she whispered conspiratorially. "Our investigative unit, the I-Team, did a story a couple of years ago on the work habits of local judges. Turns out quite a few of them were loafing in the summer. The story caused quite a stink. It could give you some good background. John Knowles, who produced the piece, is still on staff."

If what Pat says is true, Alex thought, this judge could be taking a permanent vacation.

As Barbara watched Alex walk away, she was again struck by his aloofness, his solitary nature. She still knew almost nothing about him, despite her efforts to get closer. He'd made it clear he was a loner and wanted to stay that way.

But he was good, no doubt about that. Maybe the best she'd ever seen. She was learning from him every night. His cadence, the twist or turn of a phrase, the extra beat or extra breath, the studied expression mirroring the mood of a story—all techniques which he had polished to a high gloss.

And which Barbara was now quietly studying with the intensity of a protégé at the feet of the master.

Alex found John Knowles in his tiny office, hunched over a stack of official-looking documents. Alex introduced himself, apologizing that they had not met sooner. "I'm sorry we've missed one another. I've heard a lot about you over the years."

Knowles had a reputation. He had once worked for the network in the Washington bureau, but too many diplomatic parties and too many hotel bars had taken their toll. He'd become a hopeless alcoholic, disappearing for days at a time, sometimes in the midst of crucial news assignments. The network had finally ordered him to get treatment or find another job.

With no other choice, Knowles had agreed on treatment, and was dispatched to the Hazelden Center outside of Minneapolis. When he finished treatment, he'd asked to join the I-Team, where he could work on long-term projects and avoid the daily pressures which had led him to the bottle in the first place.

Knowles stared at Alex over his half glasses, his face looking considerably older than the forty-some years Alex knew him to be. *Makes you wonder if the network rat race is worth it,* Alex thought, contemplating his own future.

Knowles didn't waste any time with get-acquainted small talk.

"I don't have much respect for anchormen," he said, "but I've been watching you on the air, and you strike me as more than just another pretty face. Which is more than I can say for the rest of the blow-dries around this town."

Alex thought that sounded like high praise coming from the station's resident wise man.

"I'd like to ask a favor," Alex said.

"What's that?"

"I'd like to check out your I-Team report on the judges."

"Why the interest?" Knowles asked.

"Barclay thinks he may want me to spend some time around the courts between shows," Alex lied, "and I need some quick background. Your story sounds like a good place to start."

Knowles may have doubted Alex, but he didn't show it. He simply reached behind him and retrieved a videocassette from a crowded shelf on the wall. "They don't like us much over at the courthouse," he said. "Not since this series aired. You may have a tough time of it."

Alex took the tape and caught himself before he offhandedly offered to buy Knowles a drink sometime.

"If I can be of any help later on, let me know," Knowles said. "I don't have much going on right now, and I'd be happy to give you a hand, if you need it."

There was still an hour or so before the early newscast, so Alex stopped by George Barclay's office. He found him on the phone again. This time, Alex stayed outside the office until the conversation was over.

"What's up?" Barclay asked.

Alex shut the office door and proceeded to relate what Pat had told him, without mentioning her name. He expected Barclay to be surprised at the allegations. He was disappointed. Barclay laughed.

"Is that what this mystery story is all about?" he asked. "Shit, those rumors about Steele have been circulating for years."

"Who told you that?" Alex asked quickly, aware Barclay had not been at the station much longer than he had.

"The old man upstairs," Barclay replied. "He told me about it at our first lunch after I took the job. Warned me against going off on any wild-goose chases, said this Steele is a political lightning rod, always in the middle of rumor mills."

The "old man" was Nicholas Hawke, the vice president and general manager of the station. Alex had only met him a few times, but on each occasion left with the impression that Hawke had Teflon skin. It was tough to scratch the surface; you saw only the perpetual smile.

"Why would he take the trouble to tell you that at your first lunch?" Alex mused aloud. "Doesn't that strike you as strange?"

"Not especially," Barclay said. "I didn't really think about it much. I just figured he didn't want me to waste time or money chasing after shadows."

Alex was stunned. The big story was evaporating before his eyes. Was it possible that Pat Hodges was simply using him as a stalking-horse for her own personal or political purposes?

But that didn't make sense, either. She'd have to know he'd find out it was just a worthless rumor. Why go through the motions? Why put on an act?

His confusion showed on his face.

"How much do you trust this source of yours, Alex? It sounds as though somebody may be leading you down a twisted path."

"How much do you trust Hawke?" Alex countered.

"I'm not sure. Not much, now that you mention it. He is slippery, and when I think about it, it *is* strange that he made such a point of steering me away from Steele right off the bat."

"I'd still like to pursue it," Alex said, deliberately masking his own doubts. "On my own time, if need be."

Barclay was studying him, judging, weighing. "I don't know, Alex," he said, still hesitant. "If Hawke finds out we're poking around . . ."

"I'll be careful, believe me," Alex said, certain Barclay was worrying about the old libel suit. Will I ever get that monkey off my back? he wondered.

"Okay, Alex," Barclay said finally, reluctantly. "Stay on it for a while, see what pops up out of the mud. But I want you working on our time, not yours. Don't wear yourself out. We still need you fresh for those newscasts."

"Thanks, George. I appreciate the confidence."

He *does* have balls, Alex thought.

Pat answered the phone on the first ring. She seemed surprised to hear Alex's voice.

"Something's come up, Pat. We need to talk."

"What's the matter?"

"The things you told me. Your story. I found out those rumors have been around for a long time. I'm feeling a little foolish."

There was silence at the other end of the line.

"I'm not sure what you're talking about, Alex," she said, finally. "But I don't think we ought to be discussing it on the phone."

"Can we meet soon then?" he asked.

"How about tonight, after your early newscast? Nathaniel's out of town."

"That's fine," he said. "Where?"

"Do you know where the Lake Harriet bandstand is? It's not far from your house."

"Sure. I caught a concert there at the end of the summer."

"Let's meet in the parking lot at seven," she said. "I'll be driving the BMW."

Pat's car was alone in the big parking lot as Alex pulled in next to her.

"Let's walk," she said, getting out of her car to greet him.

The unusual warmth of the day had lingered into the evening. It hardly felt like a November night, although the wind had picked up slightly and the temperature had dropped with the setting of the sun. But it still seemed more like early spring than early winter, and Alex breathed the air in.

They strolled past the darkened outline of the bandstand and toward the lake, saying nothing. A pair of joggers in sweatshirts and tights passed them from one direction, another couple on a walk from the other, all caught up in their own conversations, paying no heed to them.

After walking for what seemed a long time, they stopped at a bench by the lake; a family of ducks swam contentedly in the open water by shore, squawking quietly, still resisting the call of the south.

"Now please tell me what's going on," Pat said.

"Just what I said on the phone. The rumors about Steele have been around for a long time."

"Who told you that?"

"Barclay, the news director. He says Hawke, the general manager of the station, warned him about the rumors when he first got here."

"I suppose I shouldn't be surprised," she said. "I told you about the occasional whispers I'd hear. I thought other people might suspect the same thing I did."

"Hawke apparently thinks it's just politics—people out to get Steele by planting rumors like this. And Barclay wonders if I'm being played for a patsy."

"And do you think so?" she asked.

"I don't know. I don't want to believe it."

"There's no question that Judge Steele has political enemies,"

Pat said, "but I'm not one of them. I don't like him, but I hardly know the man."

"Then how do *you* explain the rumors."

"Maybe some of Steele's enemies did get wind of what he's doing and found it easier to pass along the rumors than to try to prove them. I don't know. Maybe they hoped the rumors would catch on, that someday somebody *would* prove them."

She caught her breath. "The fact that they're unproven doesn't make them untrue. The fact that the rumors persist only adds to the possibility that they could be true."

She certainly isn't ready to retreat, Alex thought.

"Okay, let's assume you're right," he said. "That brings us back to the basic question. Why are you so *certain* you're right? What have you got besides your suspicions?"

She brushed her hair back, and looked out over the lake.

"When I was with the public defender's office for all those years, I got to see some of the same faces coming back through the system, time after time. A lot of them nothing but kids, caught in the same kinds of crimes. Burglary, car theft, shoplifting. These are the nonviolent kids I'm talking about, not the rapists or the muggers."

"Kids?" Alex asked. "Does the defender's office represent kids, too?"

"*Both* juveniles and adults. The office was organized into teams, and each lawyer on each team spent a couple of weeks every month representing kids in juvenile court. That's how I got to know the ones I saw later as young adults."

"Go on," he said.

"Anyway, I started to notice a disparity in the sentences some of them were getting as adults when they appeared before Judge Steele. It seemed strange. He'd give some the maximum, but a few others only a slap on the wrist and a little probation. It didn't seem to matter what they'd done or how often they'd done it."

"You must have sentencing guidelines in this state," Alex said.

"Sure, but the judges still have lots of latitude."

She got up from the bench, and Alex followed her as she started back down the path.

"At first I thought it was a racial thing," she continued, "since all of the guys getting the light sentences were white. Then I noticed *other* young whites were getting even tougher time than many of the blacks. It just didn't make sense."

"And you never talked to your husband about it?"

"No, not directly. I didn't want to stir anything up. He seemed reluctant to discuss it. Brushed it off with some comment about the prerogative of judges. Then changed the subject."

"So what happened then?"

"You've got to understand that this was happening over a period of many months. But I was curious, so I started doing a little checking. The file of every offender, both juvenile and adult, has to be initialed if it's passed around. Privacy laws and all, you know.

"So I picked a few files at random, files of kids who had been through the juvenile system before facing Judge Steele in district court."

"And?" Alex's question floated in the soft night air.

"And lo and behold, I discovered the judge's initials on the files of the ones who were getting the light sentences."

"I don't get it," Alex admitted. "He has to see those files if he's going to be sentencing the guy."

"Of course. But I forgot to tell you. You not only have to initial the file, you have to date it, too. Steele does not handle juvenile trials, but the dates by his initials went back to the time the kids were still juveniles—*before* he had any official connection to them."

Alex persisted. "I'm still not sure I understand."

"I'm saying that for years Judge Steele has been perusing juvenile court records, picking out kids in trouble, vulnerable, homeless kids, at least the ones that suited him, and *using* them, paying them, frightening them, but promising them a break if they got into trouble later. All in return for sexual favors."

"I'm finally starting to get it," Alex said.

"I kept checking," she said, "and the pattern continued. As chief judge, Steele can handle any adult cases he wants to, and he invariably took those in which he had a 'personal' interest."

"How could he keep it hidden?" Alex wondered aloud. "The kids could talk."

"Ahhhh, now we get into speculation. I don't know the answer to that, but I can guess. I can see how he could protect his identity and still make it clear to the kids that they were doing a favor for a judge. And why should any of the kids talk? They must think they've got a good thing going.

"I also know the judge keeps a few tough guys around him. He's accumulated a lot of wealth over the years, and he can afford the protection—says he needs it because of his job and his visibility. I have no doubt that he would use their muscle now and then."

"Are you serious?" Alex asked. "A judge with bodyguards?"

"Quite serious. I've seen one of them. A big guy who doubles as his driver. A mean-looking man."

They were walking back toward their cars, Alex sorting through everything he had just heard. Almost unconsciously, she reached for his hand and held it. "You still have doubts, don't you?"

"A few, I suppose. It's too much, too soon to absorb all at once. I've got to have time to think it through."

Despite his doubts, Alex marveled at how right it felt to be next to her again.

Careful, he told himself, this is a grown, married woman who's on a crusade, and you just happen to be a handy white knight with a lance.

"What are you thinking right now?" she asked.

"That I ought to be careful," he said.

"Of me?"

"Of the situation."

"Are you afraid?" she asked.

"No, cautious maybe. Let's just say cautious."

Pat stopped. She turned and pulled Alex to her, unzipped his light jacket and put her arms around his body. She brought his face down to hers, their lips not quite touching.

"What are you doing?" he asked softly.

She whispered something he couldn't hear, brushing his lips with hers.

He pulled her against him, feeling again the body he had last touched so long ago. Her breath was warm and moist against his neck, her breasts tight against his chest, her hips pushing against his with a familiar urgency. He could feel the beating of her heart and the beat of his own.

My God, he thought, *how wonderfully sweet this is. Forget the doubts, forget the suspicions. For now, anyway.*

His hands moved over the smoothness of her buttocks, feeling the curves through the fabric, squeezing gently, kneading them, separating them, his hands moving between them.

Their lips had not yet parted, their tongues now exploring, probing, moving gently in and out, their breath coming more quickly, almost in unison.

He felt himself rising, felt her pull her hips back from his, replaced by a hand softly tracing the shape of him. A caress, a loving touch explored as surely as did their tongues, pulling now, tugging, but gently, encouragingly, exquisitely.

Their lips separated, and he smiled at her.

"You still have a wonderful touch," he whispered.

"And so do you," she said, placing his hand on the soft meeting of her thighs. He could feel the wetness, even through the cloth.

"See what I mean," she said. "No one has done that to me for years. I wasn't sure it could ever happen again."

He kissed the nape of her neck, her ears, her hair, all the time gently massaging the soft spot and feeling her move beneath his fingers.

He slowly unbuttoned her jacket, turning her in his arms so her back was to him. His hands cupped her breasts, moving over them slowly, barely touching, but feeling her nipples enlarge, becoming as erect in their own way as he was in his.

"My God." A breathless whisper.

The flimsy brassiere inside her blouse was no barrier, and suddenly, his hands were feeling real flesh, warm, a touch of perspiration between her breasts. Her nipples firm, her head thrown back, her eyes closed, the back of her body pushing against the front of his. His erection was hard against her, straining to be free, eager to be inside her.

They were standing, clinging, at the edge of the parking lot, alone, disguised but not hidden by the darkness and the foliage.

Suddenly, they were bathed in the glare of a spotlight, a police car making its routine rounds. The spotlight passed by them as they turned their heads and allowed their bodies to part.

But the moment was over, and they knew it.

Twelve

Seuss was none too happy when Alex arrived home after the late newscast. The cat was not accustomed to delayed dinners, and he had showed his displeasure. Shredded toilet paper from the bathroom was spread throughout the house, and scraps of magazines were scattered everywhere. The kitchen counter was littered with spilled salt and pepper, the coffee can left teetering on the edge.

His empty food dish had been pushed to the middle of the kitchen floor.

"Christ, cat," Alex muttered when he saw the mess. "Can't you be a little patient?"

He filled the dish and began cleaning up.

He'd left Pat at the parking lot a few hours before and was still trying to sort out his feelings. He knew he had never felt that kind of physical attraction for any other woman, including his ex-wife, and he wondered again if his body and his emotions were overriding his common sense.

Alex couldn't rid himself of his unease. It all seemed so unlikely: he arrives in the Twin Cities, Pat suddenly emerges from his past, swallows her long-simmering anger, and allows their passions to reignite. *Too strange to believe?*

77

In the middle of it all, an explosive story that could lead any-where. Or nowhere.

Time will tell, he told himself. *But be careful.*

After putting the house back in order, Alex put Knowles's vid-eotape into his cassette machine and flipped the switch.

It turned out to be a four-part I-Team series done two years before, a critical report concentrating on the inclination of some judges to spend more time away from the bench than on it.

It was a devastating piece of reporting. The errant judges had been taped with hidden cameras on the golf course, the tennis courts, and in and out of bars, all during time they were supposed to be working. Then it cut to them complaining about a backlog of cases and about the need for additional judges.

Now I can understand why they don't like us too much over there, Alex thought.

He watched the reports once, then rewound the tape to see them again.

Judge Nathaniel Hodges was not among those criticized by the I-Team; in fact, he was one of several singled out for praise for doing his job. Pat had said being a judge was his whole life, Alex remembered. He probably never leaves the goddamned office.

But Chief Judge Emmett Steele was not so lucky. The cameras captured him out sailing one day, swimming the next, playing golf the third, each on a day when he should have been working.

And each time, Alex noted, in the company of young men.

Most of the sinning judges had refused comment on the em-barrassing disclosures, running from the reporter's ambush inter-views or attacking the tactics of the I-Team from the safety of their chambers.

Judge Steele was not so shy. He faced the camera head-on and boldly told the reporter, in effect, to mind his own business. The judges could do what they wanted to do once they had disposed of their pending cases.

But what about the backlog? the reporter asked, the logjam that was tying up the judicial system?

"That's strictly an administrative matter," Steele said, resolutely staring into the camera. "It has nothing to do with the judges' work schedule, believe me. This is a hardworking group of dedicated jurists doing their best to serve the public."

It was hogwash, Alex knew, but it was said with such fervor and confidence that it sounded convincing.

Alex was amazed by the arrogance of the man, by his willingness to slug it out in front of the television camera.

Pat was right: Judge Steele did exude power. He had an almost imperial bearing: straight back, piercing eyes, prominent chin. Unapproachable, almost untouchable. But still, if cornered, he took on the look of a street fighter. He'd tear your eyes out if he had to, Alex thought, or crush your balls in the palm of his hand.

The next morning, Alex stuck his head into John Knowles's office, finding him again nose-deep in a stack of papers. He was surrounded by a clutter of old newspapers, magazine clippings, and overflowing ashtrays. Knowles had licked his booze problem, but had given up trying to conquer cigarettes.

Alex cleared his throat and walked into the office, Knowles's videotape in his hand. "Thanks for the use of the tape."

"What'd you think?" Knowles asked, pushing the half glasses farther up his nose, and leaning back in his chair.

"It's a hell of a series," Alex said. "Didn't it win an Emmy?"

"That's true, but more important, we won a little respect around town. Those guys thought they were untouchable, and suddenly they found people laughing at them . . . asking how their golf game was and all the rest. Taught them a little humility and a little about the impact of television."

"How did you get onto the story?" Alex asked.

"The same way we get onto most of our stories. Somebody called in with a tip, out of the blue. In this case, I think it was a clerk-typist pissed off about working a full eight hours while some of the judges were skipping out early."

"How'd you go about it?" Alex asked.

"Go about what?"

"Proving it."

"We began by quietly checking the court records. Sent young interns in, claiming they were working on a class project on the careers of judges. We wanted to see who was on vacation, who had days off, who was supposed to be working. Then we started doing some random surveillance, hidden-camera stuff, watching the judges come and go from the courthouse. Kind of keeping our own time clocks on them."

"That sounds like a lot of time," Alex said.

"It didn't take that long to discover which ones were fucking off. They were pretty blatant about it. Then it was just a matter of following them and taping them doing their thing. From a distance, of course, with a long lens."

"Flak?"

"Unbelievable. Like we'd used a hidden camera to tape them going in and out of a whorehouse. The legal community . . . lawyers and other judges . . . went bonkers. Bitched, screamed, threatened our license. A bad scene. They're pretty protective of their own."

"So I've heard," Alex said. "How did management here react?"

Knowles lit a cigarette and inhaled deeply, allowing the smoke to escape from his nose like exhaust from twin tailpipes.

"Hawke was up in arms, but there wasn't much he could do about it. It was already on the air. He has a lot of attorney and judge friends, and I'm sure he got an angry earful at the club."

"What did he say?" Alex asked.

"To me, nothing, but he had the old news director on the carpet. I think that's why he eventually got rid of him. And he issued a new edict: no more investigative pieces could air without his personal knowledge and approval. It's a crock of shit, but what do you do? Quit? No, thanks, I need this job."

Alex sat quietly, pondering Knowles's story.

"Watching the tape," Alex said, "I was struck by the arrogance of the chief judge, Steele. You know much about him?"

"I know he's a creep. Brilliant judge, they say, but a tough son of a bitch."

"Anything else?"

"You mean that he's gay? I'm sure he's not the only one."

Alex hesitated, not sure whether to continue. "What if I told you he may be a pedophile? Would you believe that?"

"Are you serious, Collier?"

"Yes."

"I'd have no reason to *disbelieve* it," Knowles admitted. "He certainly seems capable of it. He's a nasty man. Real nasty. But even if it were true, proving it would be something else."

Knowles took off his glasses, rubbed his eyes, and stared across his desk at Alex. Knowles not only looked older than his years, but tired and withered. Alex could not escape his gaze.

"What if I told you I might have a start in that direction?" Alex said, challenging Knowles with his own intense scrutiny.

"In the direction of proving it?"

Alex nodded.

"I'd say who the hell are you? I'd say you sound like the stranger who rides into town at high noon and foolishly pulls your gun on the biggest hombre around. I'd also say you're probably crazy."

Alex got up to leave.

"But I might say I'd like to take the time to hear more, to see just how crazy you are." Knowles was smiling now, a broad grin spread across his wizened face. "What is the world coming to? An anchorman who actually gives a shit about a story. Pinch me."

Alex found himself smiling, too, and settled back to tell Knowles what he knew, but not how he had come to know it.

"Does your source have copies of those files?" Knowles asked. "The ones with Steele's initials and dates?"

"I don't know," Alex admitted. "I didn't ask. But I doubt it, considering their strict procedures and the privacy laws."

"Well," Knowles said, "you're going to need some place to start. What you've told me so far sounds plausible, but it's not proof. I'm not even sure it can get you anywhere."

Alex nodded, aware again of the enormousness of the challenge.

"Tell me something," he said. "Has anyone ever done a major story on Steele? If, as Barclay says, these rumors have been around for so long, why hasn't anybody pursued them before now?"

"They may have," Knowles replied. "I heard a free-lance reporter for the local *City Magazine* was in the midst of preparing a profile on Steele a couple of years ago, but for some reason it fizzled and the reporter disappeared. Left town, I guess."

"Anybody ever hear what he'd found?"

"The magazine's editors and their lawyers must have, but that's only a guess. Certainly nothing ever appeared in print. No one at the magazine was talking about it, even in private."

"The reporter's name?"

"Let me think," Knowles said. "It's been a long time. Dennis Gaboski, or Grabroski, something Polish, anyway. I could find out without much trouble."

"I'd appreciate that. You know anybody at the magazine, anybody who was there when all this was going on?"

"One of the editors. We're on the Press Club board together."

"At some point, you could set up a lunch, maybe. I'd like to poke around a bit, discreetly of course."

"No problem. As I told you, I've got some time now. Anything else?"

"One more thing," Alex said. "Do you still have copies of the time cards for the judges? I'd like to get a closer look at Steele's comings and goings."

"I suspect we do, but the filing system around here stinks. I'll look around and try to get them to you later today."

"Thanks for your help," Alex said. "I may ask for more when the time comes. But I hope you'll keep all of this to yourself. I could end up looking like a jerk, and the fewer people who know about it, the better."

The message light on Alex's phone was blinking when he returned to the newsroom. The message was from George Barclay, telling him they had been summoned to a meeting in Nicholas Hawke's office in a half hour.

Now what the hell is going on? Alex wondered.

His mind skipped over the possibilities: Ratings? No, they'd been getting better; Alex's performance? Not likely. The judge? Could word have spread so goddamned soon?

Slow down, Alex told himself, you're getting paranoid.

Just wait and see.

When he arrived at Hawke's office, he found not only Barclay waiting, but also Cody Strothers.

Before Alex could ask them what was happening, the whole group was ushered into the office. Hawke was seated at the far end, behind an oblong piece of solid ebony which looked more like a huge conference table than a desk.

Hawke wasn't a big man to begin with, but his diminutive size was overshadowed by the nattiness of his dress. He was wearing a carefully pressed dark-blue three-piece suit, with a gold chain draped across the front of his vest. His blue-striped shirt was heavily starched, a gold pin tying the tips of the collars beneath a red silk tie. His Italian shoes looked every bit as soft as the fabric of his suit.

On one wall of the office were three large television monitors, each tuned to a different network. On another wall, a collection of American Indian artifacts, elaborately displayed and lighted.

Hawke's passion for his collection was well known, although some skeptics wondered whether he had ever actually met a real, live Indian.

Hawke came around the length of the desk, shaking hands with everyone and greeting them warmly. He told them to have a seat, asking his secretary to bring them coffee.

With this kind of reception, Alex decided, the news can't be too bad.

Still, Cody seemed scared to death. His face was flushed, his hands tightly clenched in his lap. It was probably the first time he'd ever met Hawke, and it looked like he hoped it would be the last.

The men exchanged small talk until the secretary left, and then Hawke got to the point.

"We've got a problem, boys," he said, fingering a sheet of paper. "I've got a union grievance here from the International Association of Stagehands."

Alex, Barclay, and Cody exchanged glances.

"One of their members, our old friend Derek, claims he was mistreated in the studio the other night. Says he was shouted at, insulted, demeaned in front of his coworkers. The union wants 'appropriate disciplinary action' taken."

Cody sank into his chair, and probably would have disappeared beneath Hawke's desk if that had been possible.

"Bullshit!" It was George Barclay, heaving himself forward in his chair. "Derek is a Class A jerk who shouldn't be anywhere near a television station. He's a menace, and deserves to be fired."

"Hold on a minute, George, calm down," Hawke said sharply. "Just tell me what happened."

"From what I hear," Barclay said, "he was being the same insolent slob he always is. Alex was there."

"I don't like being in the middle of this," Alex said, "but in my opinion, Derek was being an insubordinate smartass, and deserved what he got from Cody. What's more, when he got back to the studio, he said some ugly things to me about a little joke we had played on Barbara. I'd tell the union to take a hike."

"And I'd tell *Derek* to take a hike!" It was Barclay again, still incensed at the whole idea. "It's a disgrace that we employ somebody like that. He's worthless."

"That's another question," Hawke said. "You know about union seniority and proving a just-cause discharge and all the rest. The question is: What do I tell the union?"

"I'd tell 'em to stick it up their ass," Barclay said.

"The last thing I need now is union trouble," Hawke said. "I'll try to fog it out with them, but if they push me, we may have to take some action."

Alex thought Cody might faint dead away when he heard this.

"If you're talking about disciplinary action against one of my people," Barclay said, glancing at Cody, "then we better have another chat first."

Hawke didn't hide his annoyance at Barclay's truculence, but he soon regained his smile and ushered them out, promising to keep them informed.

"Fucking weasel," Barclay muttered as they walked down the hall.

It wasn't clear whether he was talking about Derek or Hawke. Alex was only glad it wasn't him.

Alex had slipped on his sports coat and was tightening his tie, ready to go on the air with the early show, when the newsroom secretary told him he had a phone call.

"It's a Judge Hodges," she told him. "Do you have time to take it?

Alex glanced at his watch. "I've got a minute or two."

His first reaction was a mixture of concern and curiosity. Had someone spotted Pat and him in the park or seen her leaving his house? Not likely, he told himself as he picked up the phone and hit the blinking button.

"Judge Hodges?"

"Alex! Thanks for taking the call. The lady said you're about ready to go on the air."

"No problem," Alex said. "It's good to hear from you."

"I'll make it quick," the judge said. "Pat's birthday is next week, and I'm planning a little party at the house Saturday night. No surprise or anything, just a small get-together with some of our friends and colleagues. I know Pat would love to see you there."

Alex hesitated.

"I realize it's short notice," Hodges said, "but I hope you can make it."

Alex was torn. Part of him wanted to get a glimpse of where and how Pat and her husband lived, to get to know more about her.

But there were problems.

First of all, the pretense could be treacherous. An offhand comment, a stray glance—who knows what could trigger suspicions? Besides, they were getting too close too fast.

Shit, he thought, it's just a party.

"Sure, I think I can make it," Alex said, "but I may be coming by myself, if that's not awkward."

"Heavens no," the judge replied. "You should feel right at home. I know Pat will enjoy seeing you."

After he'd hung up, all Alex could think of was who else might be on this guest list.

When the newscast was over, Alex found John Knowles standing by his cubicle, a bulky envelope under his arm.

"Here's the stuff you asked for," Knowles said. "It's probably more than you wanted."

Alex had never seen Knowles out of his chair and was surprised to find he was a half foot shorter than himself. He stood hunched over, as though he'd been bearing the burden of the world.

This man's been through hell, Alex thought, but the son of a bitch has survived.

"Thanks, John. What's the extra stuff you've got in here, anyway?"

"All of our surveillance data on your friend. I don't know how useful it will be, but I thought you'd want it all."

"Have you had a chance to look at it again?" Alex asked, hoping for some help.

"I glanced at it, but nothing jumped out at me. He likes to fuck off and spend a lot of time away from the courthouse. But so do a bunch of others."

"On the tape," Alex said, "it looked as if he was always with one or more young guys."

"Surprise, surprise," Knowles replied with a smirk.

"Did the same ones keep showing up?" Alex asked.

"I don't remember now. It's been a couple of years, you know. But we could look at the outtakes sometime, see what they show."

Alex knew that on most stories, the outtakes, or unused sections of the videotape, were erased or discarded soon after the story was broadcast. In important or controversial stories, however, where there could be complaints or future lawsuits, the outtakes often were kept for years. They were evidence.

"Will you have a chance to look at them sometime?" Alex asked.

"If I notice anything, I'll give you a call."

"Anything ever shot at night?"

"Not that I know of. We were only interested in what the judges did during the day, when they were supposed to be working."

Knowles pulled out a pack of Winstons, shook one free, got it between his lips, and was about to light it when George Barclay walked up.

"John, you know better than that."

A lot of newspeople snuck into the toilet or out the door for a few quick puffs when George Barclay was around. They never dared light up in front of him.

Knowles sheepishly returned the cigarette to its pack and smiled at Barclay. "Thought you'd gone home by now, George."

"Better luck next time," Barclay said, glancing from Knowles to Alex. "What are you guys up to?"

"John's giving me a hand in my project," Alex said.

"Really? Not enough work of your own, John?" Barclay asked.

"Not at the moment, no," Knowles replied. "That a problem for you?"

"Not unless we end up chasing our own tail," Barclay said, turning away, "which seems more and more likely to me."

"Wait a minute," Alex protested. "What are you talking . . ."

By then, Barclay was walking away, his big body squeezing between the desks. Alex suspected he was sneaking as many Butterfingers and Mars Bars as others were sneaking smokes.

Knowles immediately returned the cigarette to his mouth and lit up, grimacing as he inhaled. "What the hell was that about?" he asked.

"Beats the shit out of me," Alex said. "I thought he was on our side. I wonder if Hawke has gotten to him?"

"Before I forget," Knowles said. "That free-lance magazine writer's name is Daniel Grabowski—the one who was doing the story on Steele. But no one seems to know where he is. Just up and left, disappeared, right after his story got squashed."

"Nobody's heard from him?"

"Not that I can discover. But I guess it's not that unusual. He blew in with the wind, and blew out again. I'm told he was a little strange."

"In what way?"

"Obsessed with the story. Got a little crazy, they say. Ranted and raved about kids getting hurt and nobody doing anything about it. Some of the magazine people thought they had a looney on their hands."

"How do you spell it?" Alex asked.

"Spell what?"

"His name. The writer's name."

"G-R-A-B-O-W-S-K-I. Daniel Grabowski."

"Any relatives around?"

"None that I know of," Knowles said, "but then again, I wouldn't have any reason to know."

Alex picked up the package of surveillance reports. He'd read them over dinner.

Thirteen

John Knowles was right; the surveillance reports provided little of immediate importance to Alex. But they were mildly interesting in a perverse, voyeuristic sort of way, and gave some insight into the habits of Judge Emmett Steele.

The I-Team crew had followed the judge for the better part of four days, timing his arrivals and departures from the courthouse and tracking his movements from the moment he left his home in the morning until he returned in the evening.

The I-Team had used a nondescript converted Chevy van, its windows draped except for small camera openings. Everywhere the judge went, it followed, always at a safe distance, staying out of his view.

Meticulous records had been kept, detailing precisely where and when the judge went anywhere outside the courthouse.

July 3, 10:12 A.M. Steele departs courthouse. 10:23 A.M. Departs ramp, heading south on 35 W. 10:47 A.M. picks up man, identity unknown, at 4612 Laredo South. 11:16 A.M. arrives Minikahda Golf Course. Taping now.

The charts covered ten pages and showed the judge working two to three hours a day and playing the rest of the time. Golfing at Minikahda, swimming at a mansion near Lake of the Isles, and sailing a thirty-two-foot schooner on Lake Minnetonka.

Alex studied some of the still photographs included in the file. He had to give the investigative crew credit: they had even rented their own boat to get clandestine pictures of the judge at the rudder of the schooner, chest bare and tanned, gray hair whipped by the wind, a smile on his face as broad as the beam of the boat.

Alex read the reports three times and was struck by a couple of things. First, Judge Steele never traveled alone; his car was always driven by a chauffeur, a large man dressed in a business suit, whom the I-Team described as looking like a bodyguard.

Secondly, the reports never mentioned the judge in the company of a woman, reaffirming the impression Alex had gotten from the tapes. Steele was always with men, usually young and athletic.

Alex knew those things didn't mean much by themselves, but they did confirm what he already suspected about the man. Maybe the I-Team's outtakes would tell him a little more.

When he returned to the station for the late news, Alex again found Barbara hovering by his cubicle.

"Anything new?" she asked, leaning close, wide-eyed with curiosity.

"Nothing really new. But I am learning a little bit more."

"Did you talk to John Knowles?"

"I did. He's been very helpful."

"I thought he would be. He's a terrific reporter."

"I've seen the series on the judges, and I've read some of their surveillance reports—"

"Can you fill me in on any of it?" she asked. "Is there anything I can do to help?"

Alex looked at her for a moment, trying to decide. Why is she so damned interested? he wondered. *Is she really just intrigued by the story? Is she testing me in some way? Could she be feeding her boyfriend, Phil, information? But why?* Alex decided to take a chance.

"Actually, there is something you can do."

"What's that?"

"I'd like to find a free-lance magazine writer who used to live here, who did an article for *City Magazine* a couple of years ago. He apparently just picked up and left."

"What kind of article?" she asked.

"I'll tell you about that later. It's tied to what I'm trying to follow."

"Can't we just call the magazine?" Barbara asked.

"No. I'm told they don't know where he is, or won't say. And I don't want them to know we're nosing around."

"So what do I do?"

"That's for you to figure out," Alex said, "but I can give you a couple of suggestions. The guy's name is Daniel Grabowski, and he may have some relatives around here. Check all of the Grabowskis in the telephone book, see if anybody knows anything. And if that doesn't work, check the police records . . . driver's license bureau . . . welfare office, that kind of thing. Maybe we'll find a trace of him."

"Okay," she said, "I'll start tomorrow. But you've got to fill in the blanks soon. Promise?"

"Of course," Alex said, hoping his wariness didn't show.

Pat spotted her husband where he said he'd be, at the Sixth Street entrance to the Government Center, standing tall and erect, a head above the other pedestrians waiting for a ride or the bus. He tucked a newspaper under one arm, and he waved to her with the other.

He slipped quickly inside the car as she slowed to a near stop. They said little as she navigated their new BMW through the downtown traffic and onto the freeway—bound for their home in Edina, one of the older suburbs in the Twin Cities, and perhaps the most prestigious.

"I invited a surprise guest to your birthday party," he said after a long silence.

"Who's that?" Pat asked, suddenly wary.

"Not much of a surprise if I tell you, but I will anyway. Your friend from Kansas, Alex Collier."

"Really? Why would you do that?"

"I got the idea as I was watching the news last night. I thought you'd enjoy seeing him, and I did talk to him about having dinner sometime."

"When was that?"

"When he stopped by the courtroom the other day."

Pat lit a cigarette. Nathaniel detested her smoking in the car, but she needed a chance to think.

"It'll be interesting to have a celebrity at the party," he said. "The others will enjoy meeting him."

"So he said yes?"

"He seemed a little hesitant at first, but then he agreed."

"Is he bringing someone?" she asked casually.

"I don't think so. He said he'd probably come alone."

The traffic was backed up, as usual, where the freeway intersected with the Crosstown Highway, and Pat had a moment more to consider what she'd just been told.

"That's thoughtful of you, Nathaniel," she finally said. "It will be nice to see him again, to talk over old times."

"So the guest list is now complete," he said as the traffic began to move again. "Twenty in all."

"You've invited Judge Steele?"

"Of course, Pat. You know how much he adores you. Why would you even ask?"

She slammed on the brakes just in time to avoid driving into the car ahead of them.

"Mrs. Grabowski? Eunice Grabowski? May I have a moment of your time, please?" *Pause.* "No, I'm not selling anything. Believe me. I just need a minute."

Barbara was sitting at her desk, the white pages open in front of her, telephone tucked between her shoulder and ear.

"Mrs. Grabowski. My name is Barbara, and I'm trying to locate a Daniel Grabowski." *Pause.* "No, not Dennis, Daniel. I thought he might possibly be a relative of yours."

It was ten in the morning, and no one in the newsroom could remember the last time they'd seen Barbara Miller at her desk before noon. She had made it clear to everyone that her mornings belonged to her, except in the most extraordinary of emergencies.

"You've never heard of a Daniel Grabowski? Are you sure? He was a writer, a magazine writer, who lived in the Twin Cities a couple of years ago." *Pause.* "Okay. Well, I appreciate your time." *Pause.* "Yes, I'm sure you're up to date on all of your bills. Yes, well, thanks again."

Eunice was the fourth Grabowski Barbara had talked to so far that morning. Three from the Minneapolis phone book, and one from St. Paul. There had been no answer at two others, and she still had twenty-six more to go in the two cities.

This kind of investigative reporting was not quite as glamorous as she had imagined; in fact, it was pretty boring. She wondered if she'd made a mistake volunteering, but knew it was too late to back out now. And she had to admit, it was satisfying to get out from behind the anchor desk and to do some actual reporting, frustrating as it might be at the moment.

"Mr. Grabowski? Ernest Grabowski? I wonder if I may have a moment of your time? My name is Barbara . . . and I'm looking for a Daniel Grabowski. . . ."

Alex was also on the telephone, but at home, talking to Jan in Philadelphia. The kids were already off to school, and Jan told him she was relaxing with her feet up, having her first cup of coffee.

"I don't think I'm going to be able to make it there for Thanksgiving," Alex said. "That's why I called."

"Really? Not again, Alex." She could not hide the anger in her voice. "The kids are going to be very upset. What is it this time?"

"Everything. I just can't ask for the time off yet; it's too early. We're still in the rating period, and I've gotten involved in a story that could lead anywhere."

"A story?"

"It's too complicated to explain on the phone, but it could be important and I don't want to leave it."

"Things never really change, do they, Alex? It's always something else that comes first."

He said nothing; there was nothing to say.

"You have to tell the kids, Alex. I won't. Not this time. I've been apologizing for you for too many years."

"I'll call them in a couple of days," he said. "Maybe we can figure something out for Christmas. Maybe you can come out here."

"Sure," she said, with a short, harsh laugh. "Maybe we can ride out in Santa's sleigh." Then she hung up.

He had no sooner put down the telephone, still hearing the rancor in Jan's voice, when it rang again. It was Barbara.

"I think you'd better get down here," she said.

"Where?"

"The station, Alex, the station."

"You're at the station now? It's not even noon yet."

"Alex, no sarcasm. I'm serious. I think I may have a lead to your Daniel Grabowski."

"No shit. I'll be down as soon as I can get dressed."

Alex could not remember ever seeing Barbara out of her dressy anchor clothes or looking more pleased with herself.

She was wearing jeans and a Southwest State sweatshirt; her hair was tied in a ponytail and she was without makeup. For the first time, Alex got a glimpse of the real woman who lived beneath the media mask. And he was pleased with what he saw.

In front of her, the telephone books were still spread open. And next to them, a yellow legal pad filled with scribbled notes.

"What do you have?" Alex asked, pulling up a chair.

"I took your suggestion and started calling all of the Grabowskis in the phone books. I talked to ten of them before I found something."

"And?"

"I located his uncle, a Frank Grabowski, who lives on Tyler Street in northeast Minneapolis."

"So what'd he say?"

"He wasn't exactly a fountain of information, but he did say Daniel had lived in town until about eighteen months ago. Then he just kind of vanished. The family was puzzled, but not worried. Apparently it's happened before."

"Where did he live?" Alex asked. "Anything else about him? Friends, contacts?"

"Give me a chance," Barbara said. "That's the best part." She looked at her notes. "It turns out Daniel lived with his sister, a Linda Grabowski, who has an apartment on University Avenue. I tried to call her, but there's no answer. The uncle didn't know where she works, but he says she's a nurse."

"Good work. Anything else?"

"No, not really. The uncle didn't know much more. But I got the feeling that Daniel is kind of a black sheep in the family."

"Why?"

"Well, the uncle kept asking if Daniel was in any trouble. He wanted to know if I was with the police or the I.R.S."

Alex asked if there were any other relatives around town.

"Not that the uncle knew of. Most of the family apparently lives out east."

"You're terrific," he said, startled by his own candor. "All of this helps. It may be a wild-goose chase, but I'd sure like to find Daniel Grabowski."

"Isn't it time you tell me what's going on?" she asked.

"I'm still not sure, Barbara."

"Come off it, Alex. You still don't trust me, do you?"

"It's not a matter of trust. I just don't know what I've stumbled into here. I need a little time."

Her eyes locked on his. "Okay," she said, "what's next?"

"You can keep trying to get hold of the sister. If you do, don't pump her on the phone. Just try to set up a meeting, maybe at her place."

"And tell her what? That we're interested in a story that Daniel was working on before he disappeared?"

"That should do it," Alex said.

Then he went to his desk to make a phone call of his own.

"Pat Hodges." The voice was firm, no-nonsense. Like a lawyer.

"Good morning. And happy birthday, in advance."

She laughed self-consciously. "I hear you're coming to my party."

"I'm not sure it's a great idea to be there," Alex said.

"Relax," she replied. "I can't wait to see you."

"I'd like to meet you for a quick lunch," Alex said, changing the subject. "I need to talk to you about a couple of things. Business things."

"I have to be in court at one, so it'll have to be quick."

They arranged to meet an hour later at a nearby Arby's restaurant.

"I hope this isn't one of your husband's favorite spots."

Alex was facing Pat Hodges across the small table. Arby's was jammed with downtown office workers, but they had found a spot off in a corner where he could escape the notice of fans.

"I don't think he'd be caught dead in here," Pat said. "The judges like to take their meals in classier places."

She was wearing a simple but sheer white blouse under a double-breasted blue blazer with brass buttons. Very businesslike, but far less severe than the outfit she'd worn the first time he saw her. However, she looked worried.

"Guess who's going to be at the birthday party," she said.

"Your husband said friends and colleagues."

"Judge Steele," she said.

"Really? I must say it crossed my mind."

"I thought you might be surprised."

Alex grimaced. "In a way I am, I suppose, although I keep expecting to meet him in some dark alley. Since this whole thing started, nothing about Steele would surprise me."

Pat finished her salad, then glanced at her watch. "Sorry I have to rush. What did you need to discuss?"

"Remember telling me about the files you had found? The ones with the judge's initials and dates on them?"

"Of course."

"Did you copy any of them?"

"No, that could have gotten me fired."

"That's what I figured. Still, it's too bad. I need some place to start; I want to talk with some of those kids."

"I may still be able to help. I did jot down the names of several of them, and I've kept the list."

"Any addresses?" he asked.

"Yes, but I don't think they'll do you much good. Most of these cases are a couple of years old, and these kids move around a lot. I wouldn't know where to begin to look."

"I can begin with the names and addresses and see where that takes me."

She told him the information was in her office, and that she'd have it delivered to him the next day.

As he returned from the restaurant, Alex saw Derek Glover waiting on the sidewalk outside the station—watching his approach. Alex started to walk past him, but Derek moved into his path.

"I hear you pissed all over me in front of Hawke," he said, his breath smelling of onions.

"Where'd you hear that?" Alex asked.

"Word gets around."

"Is that right? You heard wrong, Derek. Now get out of my way."

"You took the side of that prick producer, didn't you?"

"I told Hawke what happened. It's that simple. Move."

Derek stood his ground, still blocking the sidewalk. "You really think your shit smells sweet, don't you?"

"My shit smells about the same as your breath," Alex said, pushing past him. "Stay out of my way, Derek. Hear?"

"And you watch your ass!" Derek shouted after him. "We know how to deal with pricks like you."

Alex glanced over his shoulder as he walked through the door. Derek was still standing in the same spot, staring after him.

That evening, at home between newscasts, Alex received two telephone calls.

John Knowles said he had spent much of the day studying the outtakes of the Steele surveillance. Alex's hunch had been right. The same two or three men were with Steele on each of the four days the I-Team followed him.

Sometimes, he said, they were difficult to pick out because the camera was focused on Steele fucking off, but at other times they were quite prominent.

"Recognize any of them?" Alex asked.

"No," Knowles said, "but I took some stills off the videotape so you'll have something to show around. I've also transferred some of the isolated shots to another videotape so you can see the important ones without wading through the rest."

"Thanks, John. One more question: How old did they look?"

"Their late teens or early twenties, I'd guess. Young guys, for sure."

The second call was from Barbara. She'd gotten hold of Linda Grabowski.

"Well?" Alex said.

"First of all, she's a nurse at Methodist Hospital, working the seven-to-three shift in Intensive Care. She *is* Daniel's sister, and she's agreed to see us. Tomorrow morning at ten. It's her day off."

"Did she ask a lot of questions?"

"No, but she does seem quite concerned."

"Then she hasn't heard from him?"

"It didn't sound that way," Barbara said, "but I didn't press her, per your instructions."

"Good. I'll go see her tomorrow morning."

"You mean *we'll* go see her."

Alex paused. "I don't think you need to bother, Barbara. You've done enough. I can handle it from here."

"Wait a minute," she said. "I found the lady for you. She's expecting me to come. Another woman, you know. She might not talk to you alone."

Alex knew she was right, and that he couldn't work with her much longer without telling her what this was all about.

Linda Grabowski lived in a duplex on University Avenue in northeast Minneapolis, the one truly ethnic area remaining in the city. The neighborhood was heavily populated with Russians, Poles, Ukrainians, Latvians, and others from Eastern Europe who preserved the languages and many of the customs of their homelands.

It was the first time Alex had been in that part of town, and as he and Barbara drove toward their destination, he was struck by the neatness of the small homes, the tidiness of their yards, and the old-country feel of the area. You could still see older women in their babushkas, going to morning mass at the large Russian or Ukrainian Orthodox churches.

Alex used the drive to brief Barbara on as much of the Steele story as he knew and on the role Daniel Grabowski had played.

"My God" was all she could manage to say.

"Who knows where it could lead, Barbara. But Grabowski may know more about Steele than anybody right now, and it's important that we find him. He may be willing to work with us since we've got more clout than he did with the magazine, and since we can promise him anonymity."

"Maybe he didn't discover that much," Barbara said.

"We'll never know unless we find him."

"Take a right at the next corner," Barbara said, still trying to get comfortable in the tiny TR4.

"Are you going to drive this all winter?" she asked.

"I guess so. Why?"

"You're going to be sliding around like a sled on a steep hill."

"I've thought of that," Alex said, as they pulled up in front of the duplex. "I think I'll just wait and see."

Linda Grabowski evidently had been watching for them and was waiting by the door as they walked up the sidewalk. The apartment was small and the furnishings were well worn, but everything seemed meticulously maintained. The hardwood floors and the mahogany furniture gleamed with new polish, and not a speck of dust was to be seen anywhere. Yet there was a mustiness in the air, as though the windows were seldom opened to the outside. Nothing was out of place; no picture hung even slightly askew, and the bone china cups on the hutch were posed in perfect symmetry, as if about to perform a close-order drill.

Alex found that the sterility and the uncluttered condition of the apartment, even the faint scent of disinfectant, reminded him of a hospital. Not surprising, he decided, since it's a nurse who lives here.

"I've seen you both on the news lots of times," Linda said with a hint of awe. "You're my favorite station. I almost never miss the ten o'clock news."

Linda Grabowski had a strange kind of attractiveness. Though she was a large and ample woman, there was a delicacy to her features and manner that made her seem like a lovely, overgrown child—helpless in spite of her size. And despite her quick and easy smile, she radiated an anxiety that Alex found unsettling.

Alex and Barbara exchanged a glance.

"Linda, as Barbara told you on the phone, we're interested in locating your brother. We hoped you might be able to help us."

"I don't think I can. I want to find him more than anybody, but he's just gone, and nobody seems to care any more. Can I ask why you want to find him?"

"I'm not sure I can tell you exactly," Alex said. "I've heard he was writing a story for *City Magazine* at the time he left. It's a story we're very interested in pursuing ourselves."

"I know he was working hard on something for the magazine, but I didn't know what. He seemed obsessed by it."

"Did he tell you that he was going to leave, and why?" Barbara asked.

"That's what was so strange. He said almost nothing, and all he took was his briefcase and an overnight bag. He said he had to take a short trip."

"Your Uncle Frank," Barbara said, "told me Daniel had done this kind of thing before."

"He said that? Well, it is true Daniel takes off now and then. But never for this long, and *never* without contacting me at some point. We're pretty close, and besides, he always needs money and usually calls and asks me to send him some."

"Did he take his car?" Alex asked.

"He doesn't even own a car. Do you believe that? He busses everywhere, even on his cross-country trips. Busses or hitchhikes."

They were sitting at the small kitchen table in the apartment, and for a moment the only sound was the ticking of the clock above the stove.

"I keep thinking Daniel will walk in that door any moment," Linda said, her eyes starting to well with her words. "I don't know what I'll do if anything has happened to him."

Alex and Barbara said nothing.

"The last thing Mom asked before she died was that I take care of Daniel . . . keep an eye on him until he could take care of himself. He was never very strong, you know. Now I feel like I've not only failed my brother, but my mother, too."

Barbara cut in. "Did you report him missing to the police?"

"Yes, but not until a few weeks after he left, and not before I'd checked all the hospitals, even the morgues. And not until after the burglary."

"Burglary?" Alex asked.

"Somebody broke into the apartment. They didn't take much, but they sure made a mess of things."

"*After* Daniel left?" Alex asked.

"Yes. A few weeks."

"Do you know what they did take?"

"Almost nothing of mine. Just a few pieces of old costume jewelry and a clock radio from the kitchen. I don't know what they took of Daniel's, because I wasn't sure what he had."

"Did you report the burglary to the police?" Barbara asked.

"Of course," Linda said. "They came out, looked around, and wrote a report, but that's about all."

"Did they ever get back to you about Daniel being missing?"

"Only once, a couple of weeks later, to say they'd gotten nowhere and to ask if I'd heard anything. They apologized, but said they couldn't spend more time looking for someone who was known to take off now and then. They had more important things to do."

"Did you keep pressing them?" Barbara asked.

"No; not really. I didn't see much purpose in it. They didn't seem to care."

"How about the magazine?" Alex asked. "Did you check there?"

"Several times, but they said they hadn't heard anything, either. It didn't seem like they wanted to talk to me."

Alex looked through the kitchen door. "Would you mind if we looked in Daniel's room?"

"There's not much there. Just his computer and some books and magazines. He didn't keep a lot of stuff."

The bedroom was barely big enough for a bed, a dresser, and a small desk. A few photographs hung on the walls, which Linda said Daniel had taken on his travels, and on the closet door, a big Minnesota Twins poster from the '87 World Series.

Alex fingered the Compaq computer on the desk. He switched it on and punched up a directory. He scanned the listings, and saw several files marked "Steele." He retrieved the first and found an empty screen. He hit the second, then the third, and, finally, the fourth. All were blank.

"Did Daniel keep a stack of computer discs around?" Alex asked.

"I used to see them from time to time," Linda said, "but I haven't noticed them since Daniel left."

"Since he left or since the burglary?"

"I can't tell you," she said, with some agitation. "I just didn't notice." Alex could see she was starting to get worked up. "What are you saying?" she demanded, her voice verging on panic. "What do you think's going on here? What's happened to Daniel?"

Alex tried to calm her. "We don't know, Linda, but if you happen to spot the discs, please give me a call. His hard-disc files in the computer have been erased, but maybe he made backup discs. They might help us to locate him."

They agreed to keep in touch, and Linda promised to call if she heard anything from Daniel. But it was clear she had lost most of her hope, and Alex hurried out the door when he saw the first tears roll down her cheeks.

Fourteen

"What is your sexual preference, Richard? May I call you Richard?"

"That's okay," Rick said, although he hated the name. He decided this was not the time to push the issue.

Rick was still seated in the high-backed chair in the darkened room, eyes fixed on the lighted stage, hearing but not seeing the man a few feet away.

"Do you prefer boys or girls?" The voice seemed to deepen.

"Girls, usually. But I've done it with men, too. For money."

"I know, Richard."

The cone light on the stage dimmed, and the two screens on either side brightened.

"To get in the proper mood, we'll be watching some videos. You like videos, don't you, Richard?"

Rick nodded, feeling like a child. But he said nothing.

"On the screen to the right, in front of you, will be a video depicting activities more to your liking. On the screen to the left, in front of me, scenes of the type I prefer. Feel free to watch either or both, but please remember, keep your eyes forward."

The screens came to life.

In front of him, a large-breasted woman was being slowly disrobed by a man who already was nude, erect. On the other screen was Rick, toweling off after his bath in the big tub.

Rick couldn't believe what he was seeing. How in the hell had they gotten those pictures of him? He had seen no camera in that part of the room.

He watched as he toweled dry, fascinated by his own image, but repelled by the obvious effect it was having on the man in the other chair. He could hear the heavier breathing, almost a wheezing.

The images rolled on soundlessly.

Rick felt some relief, but also disbelief, when his nude body was replaced on the left screen. The new tape featured two boys, no older than thirteen or fourteen, wrestling on lush carpeting next to a steaming hot tub. They kept looking toward the camera, embarrassed by their nakedness, but obviously following silent instructions from behind the lens.

On the right screen, in front of him, Rick watched as the man and woman were joined by two other couples, intertwined and constantly moving in a kind of pornographic ballet. Unlike the boys, they took no notice of the camera. Their bodies were covered with the sweat of sex, their faces filled with cinema passion and exertion, their eyes wild, but somehow vacant.

Despite himself, Rick felt a rising sense of excitement in his body. He could not take his eyes off the screen; he heard his own breath quicken, felt his robe lifting.

Next to him, he heard the wheeze turn to a quiet cough as the two boys on the screen splashed in the hot tub, soaping and rinsing one another.

The image made Rick grimace.

The videos ended and the screens went dark. The lights in the front of the room came up.

"Step to the stage, please. Keep your eyes straight ahead, facing the wall."

Rick squinted as he passed beneath the intense overhead light.

"You will find a blindfold on a small table to the right. Please put it over your eyes, and when it is secure, you may turn around."

Rick did as he was told, then turned, feeling the heat of the light, but seeing nothing.

"You may remove your robe."

He hesitated.

"The robe, please."

He found the sash, loosened it, and allowed the robe to fall from his shoulders.

He felt the warm breath on his thighs before he felt the first touch of parched skin.

The sandpaper fingers crept across his body, pausing, probing, exploring, fondling, moving on.

He felt the warm, moist breath, the wheezes like a faint, wet wind in his ears, then on his neck, traveling down his body, following the path of the fingers.

He heard the small moans and muffled cries from the lips pressed against his skin.

Then, suddenly, his body doubled over with an excruciating, penetrating pain from behind, and Rick blacked out, but not before he heard the hoarse, explosive grunt of satisfaction.

Fifteen

Barbara pushed the pillow away, raising her head, leaning on her arm as she watched Phil walk from the bed to the bathroom.

Nice buns, she thought. Not just nice, gorgeous.

It was still dark outside. And cold. She could tell by the frost lines on the inside of the window. But the bedside lamp cast a warm glow inside the room, and the down comforter settled snugly over her body.

She could hear the shower and thought briefly about joining him under the warm spray. Better not, she told herself; he's already late for the early shift.

So she pulled the pillow back beneath her head and pushed herself deeper under the covers, content to close her eyes and wait.

She had met Phil months before at a friend's dinner party, and the relationship had flourished. It was Barbara's first real affair, and she still wasn't sure what it meant or where it would lead. Or what she felt. She was content to let her body do her thinking and her feeling for now.

Her feet felt her nightgown in a ball at the bottom of the bed. She tried to retrieve it with a toe, stretching, still feeling the warmth of his body on the sheets.

She heard the shower stop and quickly jumped out of the bed. The bathroom was steamy, the mirror fogged over, and she was waiting with a big beach towel when he stepped from behind the shower curtain.

"What's this all about?" he laughed.

"At your service," she said, rubbing the towel over his body, pausing now and then to make sure certain parts were dry.

"I'm running late, you know."

"I know, I know," she said, standing behind him, wrapping the towel around both of their bodies. It felt as if they were in an upright sleeping bag, and she laughed as they tried to walk together into the bedroom.

He was a full foot taller than Barbara, lean and strong. *Sinewy.* That was the word. She stroked his stomach and felt his ribs beneath her fingers.

"Barbara! C'mon, give me a break. I'm late." He threw off the towel and grabbed for her tickling fingers.

"I need a favor," she said, pulling him back toward the bed.

"So *that's* what it's about," Phil said, escaping her grasp and reaching for his shorts and pants. "What do you need?"

"Information," she said, back beneath the covers. "I'm trying to find out what happened to a guy named Daniel Grabowski. He turned up missing about eighteen months ago. A missing persons report apparently was filed, but nothing ever came of it."

He finished tying his tie and was putting on his shoulder holster. The sight of the gun always made Barbara nervous.

"Who is this guy?"

"A writer. A journalist. I'm supposed to track him down. I've talked to his sister, but she's as mystified as anybody."

"Why do you want him?"

"For a series I'm doing," she replied vaguely. "Could you check around? Please?"

She pushed the covers off and stretched.

"I think I'm being bribed," he said, as he leaned over to kiss her breast. "You know better than to try and bribe a cop."

"His name is Grabowski," she said, feeling his lips slowly tantalizing her. "And he used to live on University Avenue Northeast. Would you check, please?"

"Okay, okay," he said, reluctantly raising his head. "I'll see what our friendly computer says."

With that, he was gone.

Later that day, Alex met Knowles in an editing room. The tape showing Steele's companions was already cued.

"Let it roll, John. I want to see these guys."

The first image was that of a young blond man, maybe five-eleven, with brushed-back hair and an almost-perfect Nordic face, straight nose, slight cleft in the chin, and piercing blue eyes. He was slouched against the fender of a car, wearing chinos and white deck shoes, his shirt open at the collar.

Knowles had assembled several shots of the man in a variety of poses.

"Looks like an arrogant bastard, doesn't he?"

"Like a fuckin' Nazi to me," Knowles said.

The next series of shots focused on a dark-haired, dark-skinned man who looked Latin, maybe Cuban. He was shorter than the blond, but more muscular. He could have been a professional bodybuilder; in one of the scenes by the pool, he was flexing his biceps and triceps as if he were on stage.

"I bet he's got muscles for brains, too," Knowles mused.

The third young man was blond like the first, but much taller and thinner. Gangly, bordering on delicate. There were only two usable shots of him, both on the golf course, although he was in the background of several of the other scenes. He seemed to stay apart from the others.

"He looks out of place in this group, doesn't he?" Alex noted. "Not the kind of kid you'd think the judge would go for."

"Maybe he's just his clerk or something," Knowles offered.

Also on the tape were several shots of a bulky older man with a protruding nose and a scowl. "That must be Steele's driver and bodyguard," Alex said. "I've been told he has one, and the I-Team reports mention him, too."

Knowles spread out the still photographs, reproductions of some of the scenes on the videotape.

"These may come in handy later," Alex said.

The envelope from Pat was on his desk when Alex returned to the newsroom. It contained three names and addresses. Getting the names was one thing, he realized, finding the individuals was another. But you have to start somewhere, he told himself, tucking the letter away in his desk drawer.

He sat back in his chair and considered everything that had happened in the past few days. It was a singular transformation: from angry frustration to pure exhilaration. He couldn't explain it. His body and mind had reawakened. Life had suddenly taken on a purpose. Remarkably, he found himself thinking less about the pursuit of his career and more about the pursuit of the story.

He knew the exhilaration might not last, that the story might disappear—and with it the surge he felt. And with it too, perhaps, the woman who had walked back into his life after twenty years.

Would that be a bad thing? he wondered. After all, he didn't really know this grown-up Pat that well. He couldn't stop thinking about her, but he still didn't fully trust her or his own feelings; he still didn't know where it might lead.

Worry about that later, he told himself. The story's still alive, and so are you.

His thoughts were interrupted by the newsroom secretary, who stood next to his desk.

"There's a Linda Grabowski in the lobby asking for you," she said. "Want to see her?"

"Who? Oh, sure," Alex said, startled. "I'll go get her."

Linda was standing by the reception desk, an envelope clutched in her hand. She seemed so frail and vulnerable. Yet she showed a determination that Alex found surprising.

"Remember that Twins poster hanging on Daniel's closet door?" she asked.

"Yes, I do," Alex said, leading her to a chair. "A World Series poster."

"I got to thinking about those computer discs yesterday, after you left. So I started looking everywhere. I covered the apartment from top to bottom and finally noticed the poster again."

"Yes," Alex said, feeling his heart beat a little faster.

"I took it down. And behind it, taped to the door, was this envelope with one of those discs in it. And a key."

Her hands trembled as she handed him the envelope. She watched as he pulled the disc and key from inside. Neither bore any markings.

"I . . . I thought you'd want to see them right away," she said anxiously.

"You're right," Alex said as he rushed her toward the elevator. "This looks like a safety-deposit box key," he added, holding up the key as they walked. "Did you rent a box?"

Linda shook her head.

"How about Daniel?"

"I don't know . . . Wait . . . Maybe . . . I do vaguely remember signing something that could have been for a safety-deposit box."

"You don't know where it is? Which bank?" Alex couldn't figure out how someone would forget something as significant as a safety-deposit box.

Linda was starting to break down. "I didn't pay any attention at the time. It didn't seem important," she said as her face grew red.

Alex was too preoccupied with the disc and key to notice her distress as they rode the elevator to John Knowles's office. He knew Knowles also had a Compaq computer and he was anxious to test it out.

Alex quickly introduced Linda and explained the mission to Knowles—who immediately turned to her with a sympathetic nod. "I hope we can help you out, Linda," Knowles said, "we want to find your brother almost as badly as you do."

"Do you really?" Linda said despairingly, but with the slightest hint of hope.

Something imperceptible seemed to pass between the two of them. It was as if Knowles, with his own troubled past and set of frailties, found a kindred spirit in this childlike woman.

Alex took no notice. He handed Knowles the disc and watched as he slipped it into the computer and brought up the directory, including several files labeled "Steele." They looked at one another and grinned. Knowles hit the retrieve key.

PASSWORD? flashed at them from the bottom of the screen.

The grins faded. Password? What the hell?

"He's hidden the files," Knowles said, as he tried the process all over again.

Same thing. PASSWORD? winking at them like a neon light.

"Linda, did Daniel ever say anything to you about a password?" Alex asked.

"No, never," she said. "I certainly would have remembered something like that."

"Did he ever give you a scrap of paper to keep hidden?"

"No."

Alex showed Knowles the key that had been in the envelope.

"Trouble is, all those keys look alike," Knowles said. "No bank name on them. No telling where the box is."

They sat in a semicircle around the computer monitor, staring at the screen, feeling the disappointment seep through them.

"So what have we got?" Alex wondered aloud. "Daniel hides the disc, but not before hiding the files, too. A double dose of protection."

"He certainly didn't want anybody seeing those files," Knowles offered.

"That doesn't make sense, either," Alex responded. "Why wouldn't he just destroy them? He must have hoped somebody would find the disc if something happened to him."

"Why didn't he tell Linda the password then?" Knowles asked.

"If he felt he was in some kind of danger, he probably wanted to protect Linda."

"Oh my God!" Linda cried out. "You think something terrible has happened to Daniel, don't you? Tell me! I have to help him."

Alex recoiled from the outburst. "Calm down, Linda. We don't know what happened. We're just thinking out loud."

Linda sank back in her chair with a small shudder.

Alex watched her uneasily, then continued. "We're back to the same spot, I guess. Hidden files can only be revealed by a password, and that could be anything. And a key that could fit a safety-deposit box anywhere."

"Let's try a couple of passwords," Alex continued. "Just for the hell of it."

"Like what?" Knowles asked.

"Some obvious ones. Like Daniel. Or Steele. Or judge. *City Magazine.* Or pedophile. Who knows?"

Knowles keyed words into the computer, about a dozen in all, but nothing happened.

They both looked at Linda, concerned that all of these speculations were causing her more anguish.

At last they gave up and escorted her to the door.

"Are you okay?" John asked her gently.

Linda nodded slowly, uncertainly.

"What do you think?" Alex said. "Can you remember anything else that might help us find your brother?"

"I don't know . . . I just don't know. I have to find Daniel," she whispered, as if she were only speaking to herself.

"Call Alex or me if you think of anything else," John volunteered as she left the building. "I'll call you if we find something more. And take care of yourself."

Alex knew John's voice didn't carry much assurance.

Cody Strothers collared Alex when he returned to the newsroom.

"Have you heard anything about that union business?" he asked.

"Not a thing," Alex replied. "Have you?"

"Not officially. But Derek claims they're after my ass. Two weeks suspension without pay. He's spreading it all over the station."

"Screw Derek. He doesn't know shit. Have you talked to Barclay?"

"I haven't dared to ask. But I'm telling you, I can't make it without two weeks' pay. I have no savings. I barely scrape by now."

"Don't sweat it, Cody. Not until you know something for sure. I don't think Barclay will let you swing."

"I know Barclay'll do his best," Cody said. "It's Hawke I worry about."

"I'm going to be meeting with both of them tomorrow," Alex said. "I'll see if I can pick up on what's happening."

"Thanks, Alex. Meantime, that prick Derek walks around here like a cocksure asshole."

"Forget him," Alex said, remembering his own angry encounter with Derek on the sidewalk. "He's just trying to piss you off."

It looked like the Knights of the Round Table when Alex and Barbara walked into the conference room the next day.

There was no question who King Arthur was.

Hawke was clearly running the show. He introduced them to Benjamin Farley, a news consultant hired to do research and make recommendations. Farley stood in front of a monitor which would display in graphic detail the results of his audience study. Husky, with a ruddy complexion and darting eyes, he had the quick smile and the self-confidence of a used-car salesman.

Alex couldn't believe he and Barbara had been summoned to sit in on a meeting where their own performance and popularity in the market would be evaluated. But Hawke had insisted—saying they should hear what the public was saying about them, firsthand.

"What a bunch of crap," Alex had muttered to Barbara. "Too much else is happening. I've got better things to do with my time."

George Barclay was also there, seated between Hawke and Justin Scott, the station's promotion director. Barclay winked at Alex and Barbara as they took their places, but turned his back on Scott. Barclay's hatred of promotion people—"double-dipshits," he called them—was well known at the station.

"Isn't it a little unusual to be doing research so soon after I started?" Alex asked Farley. "I imagine half the audience doesn't even know who I am yet."

"That's true," Farley conceded, "but our research measures all the personalities on this station and the other stations. It gives us more complete data on how we're doing.

"Overall, I have good news to report," he continued. "We seem to have stemmed the tide. The audience reaction to Alex has generally been positive, at least among those who know him, and Barbara continues to grow in popularity. The growth curves of the competitive stations seem to have flattened out."

Farley recited the statistics at length, his voice a flat monotone, his words reinforced by a series of elaborate graphs and charts with pies and bell-shaped curves showing audience makeup and personality preferences by age and sex, station strengths and weaknesses, the market's competitive profile.

Alex's eyes were growing heavy, but he suddenly came alert.

"A couple of small negatives did come through about the two of you," Farley said, looking at Alex and Barbara. "Some viewers still perceive you as too young, Barbara, and a few others as too glamorous, too Hollywood."

"Too what?" she demanded.

"Too much of a young starlet, not enough of a seasoned reporter."

"I warned you about that makeup," Alex jokingly whispered.

"Understand, this is only a small number," Farley continued, "but it is something to keep in mind. You can be too good-looking in this business. Other women begin to resent you."

"And what about me?" Alex asked.

"Some viewers describe you as aloof, Alex, arrogant. Not many, mind you, but a few. Viewers expect their anchormen to be down-right homey, like the next-door neighbor."

Alex felt a sharp jab in the ribs from Barbara's elbow.

"So what all of this really means," George Barclay said, finally, "is that we're doing pretty well. Considering that Alex has just joined us."

"That's true," Farley said. "With one major exception."

"What's that?" Barclay asked.

"Your sports guy, Scotty Hansen. He should go."

"What do you mean, go?"

"Replace him. Get rid of him. He's not scoring that well with either the younger men or the younger women."

"But he's been here for years," Barclay protested. "He's prac-tically an institution in this community."

"He's an old man," Farley said. "He's holding you back. He has no appeal to the younger demographics."

Justin Scott, Barclay's nemesis in the promotion department, rose from his chair next to Farley. "I agree," he said. "Hansen's a has-been. A relic. He stumbles around on the air, and still does a sportscast like they did in the fifties."

"What the hell do you know, you ass-kisser?" Barclay roared. "Just promote the fucking news. Don't tell us how to do it!"

"Calm down, George," Hawke ordered.

"I think Scotty does a hell of a sportscast," Alex said, entering the fray for the first time.

"That doesn't matter," Farley said. "His age and lack of younger demographic appeal are the issues. It's your decision, but that's what the research says."

Alex felt as though he were witnessing an execution.

"Wait one minute." King Arthur was speaking from his throne. "You heard the man, George. We're paying him to give us advice based on unbiased, solid research. I don't think we can ignore it. Hansen's a nice guy. I like him. But we can't let our personal feelings get in the way. If he's holding us back, George, he's got to go. Start looking for another sports guy. See what's out there. If we find somebody better, we wave goodbye to Hansen. Let's not sit around talking about it all day."

Barclay pushed himself, with some effort, to the edge of his chair. "I think it *does* deserve more discussion," he said, directing his words at Hawke. "There could be a hell of a backlash if we dump him like this. Think about the public reaction."

"Forget the public," Hawke said. "They don't run this television station, I do. So do what I tell you. This meeting's adjourned."

Barclay got up and walked out, motioning for Alex and Barbara to follow, muttering loudly as he waddled down the hall.

This time, when Alex heard the word *weasel* echo in the hallway, he knew exactly who Barclay was talking about.

Two nights later, in the middle of Scotty Hansen's disparaged sportscast, Alex suddenly snapped to attention. *Why the hell didn't I think of it sooner?* Hansen was describing a trade between the Twins and the Giants, a left-fielder for a second baseman. *That Twins poster that Grabowski hid the disc and key behind. It's a clue. There must be a clue in that goddamned poster.*

After the newscast, he led Barbara to the telephone.

"What's her number?" he asked excitedly.

"Whose number?"

"Linda's. Linda Grabowski."

Barbara searched through her notes and gave it to him.

"She'll probably be sleeping," Barbara said as he dialed.

"She said she always watches the news," Alex reminded her. "Linda? Alex Collier. Sorry to disturb you at this hour, but I have a quick question. Was Daniel a big sports fan? A big Twins fan? No? Never went to a Twins game that you know of. Never watched them on television." *Pause.* "Then why the Twins poster in the bedroom?" he asked, more to himself than to her. "You wondered about that yourself?" *Pause.* "Hold on to the poster, Linda. We'll pick it up as soon as possible. And thanks."

Alex turned to Barbara, a smile lighting his face.

"That has to be it! Why would he have a Twins poster when he doesn't give a shit about the Twins? Why would he pick that particular place to hide the disc? To give somebody a clue, that's why. The computer password has to be on that poster, somewhere. It has to be."

Barbara had never seen Alex so excited.

"Have you got John Knowles's home phone number? Never mind, I'll get it."

His mind was racing as he dialed the number, mumbling to himself, "That has to be it. It has to be."

Sixteen

Since his divorce, Saturday mornings had been tough for Alex.

While almost everybody else he knew looked forward to the weekends, Alex often found them tedious. In most places he had lived, he knew few people, had few friends, and the prospect of two weekend days alone, without the diversions of his job, was not all that pleasing.

Especially when he couldn't go fishing.

So he often slept in late on Saturdays, leaving an extra dish of food for Seuss the night before and closing the cat out of his room. But on this Saturday morning, he was up early, cleaning up the kitchen as the coffee perked.

Alex had been unable to reach John Knowles from the station, but had left a message on his answering machine, telling him he needed to talk to him as soon as possible. So when the phone rang as he was pouring his first cup of coffee, he expected to hear Knowles. Pat's voice was something of a surprise.

"Have you seen the morning paper?" she asked.

"Not yet. I just got up a little while ago."

"Go look. Then call me back—I'm home alone."

Alex walked to the front door, feeling a little foolish as he stepped out onto the stoop in his pajamas. But there was an urgency in Pat's voice that disturbed him.

The headline and picture explained everything.

STEELE TO BE NAMED
TO HEAD STATE SUPREME COURT
Hennepin County Chief Judge to Take Over January 2

The Star-Tribune has learned that Hennepin County Chief Judge Emmett M. Steele, 62, will be named chief justice–designate of the Minnesota Supreme Court by Governor Allen Hamel next Monday. Judge Steele will succeed retiring Chief Justice Lloyd Parker, who has served in the position for the past ten years.

The appointment of Judge Steele could not be officially confirmed, but sources say it will become effective on January 2, one day after Chief Justice Parker reaches the mandatory retirement age of 70.

In Minnesota, no legislative confirmation is necessary, as the appointment of the chief justice is at the sole discretion of the governor.

The selection of Judge Steele had been rumored widely for the past several months, despite some political opposition which has developed over the years. Sources say the governor was persuaded that Judge Steele's "long and distinguished judicial career" in Hennepin County made him deserving of the appointment.

Judge Steele, who is known for his tough stance on law-and-order issues, and for the strict discipline he imposes on other judges, was unavailable for comment.

The article went on to describe Steele's background and accomplishments and to detail the composition of the rest of the Supreme Court.

The picture which stared out from the printed page was of a smug-looking Steele, chin out, with a smile that seemed more of a smirk.

He dialed Pat's number, and she answered on the first ring.

"I can't believe it," he said.

"I knew it could happen, but it's still a shock, knowing what we know. This will make it even tougher. You talk about a position of power; he's really got it now."

"He doesn't have it yet," Alex said. "We've still got six weeks or so. And maybe now he'll let down his guard a bit. This could make him feel even more invulnerable."

"That's certainly an optimistic view," she said.

"There have been a few new developments, which I'll tell you about tonight, if we get the chance."

"Can't you tell me now?"

"I'd rather do it in person."

"All right," she said. "I'll see you tonight."

"Do you think Steele will still show up?"

"Sure. What better chance to puff up and take his bows, all the while denying any official knowledge of the appointment."

"Okay," Alex said, "I'll see you about seven."

There was a moment of silence on the telephone.

"I've missed you, you know," she said.

He was feeling it, too, and wasn't sure he liked it.

The Hodges's home sat high on a hill, brightly lighted, over-looking the twinkling skyline of the distant city. Alex could tell that he was close by the number of parked cars hugging the curbs of the cul-de-sac and by the sight of several smartly dressed people walking up the sidewalk toward the house.

Shit, this may be a big mistake, he thought as he slowly got out of the TR4.

The house was a low ranch-style dwelling, its wings stretching to enfold the curve of the street. He could hear music and muffled conversation through the door as he rang the bell.

Then Pat was there, looking stunning.

Her hair was down, softly settling around her neck and bare shoulders, left exposed by a low-cut dress of deep blue. The color matched her intense eyes.

"Welcome," she said, leading him by the hand into the foyer.

"You're lovely," he murmured as he kissed her on the cheek. "That's a great dress."

"Thank you," she said with a soft smile. "I don't hear compliments like that too often."

She wore little makeup and a scent so elusive it almost wasn't there.

"Let me introduce you," she said.

The house was awash with people, gathered in small groups in various rooms. But the center of activity was a large family room, adjacent to an indoor pool and hot tub. A small combo was playing softly at one end of the room next to a small dance floor and near the bar.

It's like a country club, Alex thought, as Pat led him toward the first group.

"By the way, *he's* not here yet," she said quietly.

"Alex, how good to see you!" Judge Hodges strode across the room, hand outstretched. "I'm *so* glad you could make it. And I know Pat is, too."

They moved from cluster to cluster, introducing their celebrity guest as Pat's old college classmate.

Alex smiled and nodded, trading small talk. Always attentive, always gracious. Still, he couldn't help looking for Pat when she was not by his side.

Later, they were able to walk to the bar together. "You have a beautiful home," he said. "But I remember you asking me what I did with all of the room in my place. I could ask you the same question."

"And I'd have the same answer," she laughed. "We don't use most of it, except on a night like this. It's important to Nathaniel to have a nice home. I'm in no position to complain."

Just as they discreetly touched the rims of their glasses in a silent toast, the people around them started to move toward the front of the house.

"Guess who's here?" she whispered. "I'm not sure I can face him. He makes my skin crawl."

"Go ahead," he urged softly. "Relax, and act natural. Remember, you're the hostess, the guest of honor."

By the time Alex sauntered to the rear of the crowd, Judge Steele had shed his overcoat and was shaking hands all around. His coat was held by a big man with a hawk nose, who stood next to a man Alex recognized immediately as the stringbean from Knowles's tape. The gangly, bony one, Alex thought, the one who looked so out of place. But here he is, all but holding the judge's hand.

Judge Steele reached Pat, shouted a boisterous "Happy birthday!" and gave her a big bear hug. Like an old, dear friend.

Alex could see her shoulders stiffen.

Judge Hodges finally led Steele across the room to Alex, fawn-ingly telling Steele he was not the only celebrity guest.

"From Channel Seven? I watch you all the time. But," he said with a laugh, "I watch all the channels all the time."

Steele's handshake was as firm as Alex knew it would be, his eyes as piercing. But his voice was huskier than Alex remembered from the videotape, as though he had a bad cold.

As Steele spoke, his eyes darted about the room, apparently looking for anyone he might have missed. Alex had seen the searching eyes before, in the face of practically every politician he had ever known.

Judge Steele's arrival was apparently the signal that dinner could begin. Alex was seated next to Pat, across the table from Steele's bony companion.

Alex knew most of the guests were lawyers or judges, and he listened politely to all of the legal talk. His attention was diverted occasionally by the pressure of Pat's leg against his.

"Does Steele always bring his friends along?" Alex asked Pat in a whisper.

"Usually. He seldom goes anywhere alone."

Alex nodded at Steele's companion across the table. "I don't believe we've met. I'm Alex Collier."

"Nice to meet you," he said. "I'm Jerry Caldwell. I work with Judge Steele."

"Really? What do you do for him?"

"Everything really. I'm kind of his aide-de-camp. I make his appointments, keep his schedule, deal with the press."

"It sounds as though you may have some work to do on Mon-day," Alex said. "Have you set up a news conference yet?"

"Good try, Mr. Collier," he replied with a laugh. "But as I'm sure you know, we're not at liberty to say anything about today's story."

"You'll neither confirm nor deny, right?"

"You've got it. Especially when I'm sitting across from a news anchorman."

Alex liked Caldwell. He seemed open and honest, with a sense of humor. There certainly was nothing very sinister about him.

Alex's musings were interrupted by Nathaniel Hodges, who stood up and tapped the edge of his crystal goblet with a spoon.

"May I have your attention, please. We're honored tonight to have Judge Steele with us. Or Chief Justice Steele, if you believe the newspaper."

Steele was beaming, but Alex noticed Caldwell's frown.

"Those of us who work with Judge Steele know the pending appointment is well deserved, and we are delighted that he can be with us tonight."

Has he forgotten Pat's birthday? Alex wondered.

"I know the chief judge is limited in what he can say, but I hope he will favor us with a few words. Judge Steele?"

Pat and Alex exchanged glances, both reluctantly joining the applause as the judge stood up.

"Thank you, Nathaniel. You're a dear friend. But you're right. I am not free to say anything about the speculation in the press. Especially"—with a nod toward Alex—"since a member of the distinguished Fourth Estate is with us tonight. I can forewarn you, however, that I may not be at the courthouse on Monday morning. I may be visiting with the governor."

Caldwell winced and rolled his eyes.

"I thank you for your good wishes, but I don't want this speculation to distract us from the purpose of tonight's party. Happy birthday, dear Patricia."

Finally, Alex thought.

Steele raised his glass, and everyone around the table followed suit, all eyes on Pat.

She smiled sweetly and nodded her thanks.

The catered dinner lasted the better part of two hours and ended when Pat cut the birthday cake, accompanied by the crowd's off-tune choruses of "Happy Birthday." By then, Alex and almost everyone else at the table had had more than their fair share of champagne and wine.

Including Jerry Caldwell. He was wobbling as he rose from the table and began to follow Judge Steele to the door. The judge did not look in much better shape himself as he was helped on with his coat.

"I hope you don't have to drive," Alex said gently.

"Oh, no, we have a driver," Caldwell said. "We couldn't have the chief justice . . . I mean, the chief judge . . . arrested for drunk driving, now could we?"

"That could be embarrassing," Alex admitted, knowing full well that a DWI arrest was nothing in comparison to what he was determined to prove. "I'm sure the judge is avoiding any possible embarrassments at the moment."

Caldwell gave Alex a strange look, but shook his hand. "I hope I'll see you again," he said.

"I'm sure you will," Alex replied.

Some of the guests took their cue from Judge Steele and left shortly after he did. Others stayed on, chatting, drinking, and dancing.

Alex was among them. He found himself on the dance floor, Pat in his arms, moving slowly to "Somewhere Out There." He held her snugly, but not tightly enough to attract attention, her bare back under his hand, her flushed cheek against his.

She moved perfectly on the floor, her body at one with his, her hips lightly against his, undulating to the music.

"You're doing it to me again," he said.

She smiled.

"Can we get away somewhere? I need to talk with you."

She spotted her husband in the midst of a group next to the dance floor.

"Follow me," she said.

She walked to Nathaniel's side. "Alex would like to see the house, dear. Would you like to show him, or should I?"

He didn't even glance at her, apparently irritated at the interruption. "Go ahead, Pat. I'm in the middle of something here."

"I *knew* he'd say that," she told Alex as they walked away.

She led Alex through the wings of the large house, past more bathrooms and bedrooms than he could count. They wound up in the master bedroom.

"I'm not sure we should be here," Alex said, looking around.

"We won't stay long," she said.

They sat on the edge of the bed, and Alex tried to keep his mind on the business at hand. He hurriedly told her of everything that had happened: the pictures from the videotape, including the one of Caldwell, the computer disc and the hidden files, the continuing search for Daniel Grabowski.

"Have you been able to do anything with those names and addresses I sent you?" she asked.

"Not yet," he said, his eyes lingering on her as she got up from the bed. "I hope to start looking next week."

Stick to business, Alex.

But as they walked out of the bedroom, Alex looked down the hallway, and finding it empty, pulled her back into the darkened room. His lips were on hers, his hands touching the fullness of her breasts.

"Happy birthday," he whispered, "and many happy returns."

"I hope there will be," she said softly.

Alex was sitting at the dining room table with the Sunday *Star-Tribune* scattered around him, trying to ignore a dull headache from the wine of the night before, when the door chimes echoed in the empty house.

Barbara Miller was standing on the steps, hugging her coat to her body, her breath turning to steam.

"Barbara. What are you doing here?"

"I was going to call," she said, "but then I thought I'd just drop by. I hope I didn't interrupt anything."

"No, come on in."

"I wasn't doing anything this morning," she explained as she stepped inside, "and I thought you might want to take a walk around the lake. To catch up on things."

"In weather like this?"

"It'll be good for you," she laughed. "Builds the corpuscles for the winter ahead."

Alex hesitated, but then decided the fresh air might help the headache.

They took the plowed path around the lake, buffeted by a stiff wind coming across the ice. Alex's eyes were watering, but Barbara seemed oblivious to the cold.

"Phil checked on Daniel Grabowski in the police computer," she said, "but he didn't find much. The cop who worked on the case barely remembered it, and there have been no computer entries for months."

"Does Phil know what this is all about?" Alex asked.

"No, but he's certainly curious. He wants to help if he can."

"I don't know, Barbara. Too many people know about this already. The whole thing is starting to feel out of control."

"You can't do it alone, Alex, not if you want to get the story on the air anytime soon."

"I'll have to think about it and let you know. I can't wait long, though, not if you believe yesterday's newspaper story on Steele. I want to get him before he gets to the Supreme Court."

Barbara turned her back to the wind, facing him as she spoke. "You're a different person lately, Alex. Did you know that? A lot more likable."

Alex laughed. "Likable? Well, I wouldn't go that far. This thing scares the shit out of me, but I do feel alive again. Like I've got something important to do."

"It's not just your mood," Barbara said. "You seem to care about things. You're not out to hurt people."

"Hurt people?"

"By ignoring them or belittling them—like you did to me in the studio."

"I guess I was just desperate to relieve my boredom."

"I bet Pat Hodges has something to do with it," she teased.

"What gives you that idea?"

"I don't know, just a feeling. A woman's intuition, maybe."

He stopped and tried to wipe the tears from his eyes with a handkerchief. "Let's head back, okay? I'm freezing my ass."

"I think you're changing the subject," she said.

"And I think you're nosy," he replied.

Alex was back inside the house. Barbara was gone, and so was his headache. The phone rang, and he heard John Knowles's voice.

"I didn't get back into town until late last night, and I didn't want to bother you then. What's the urgent message?"

"It may be nothing," Alex said, "but I think I may have a clue to the computer password." He then explained his theory about the Twins poster.

Knowles was skeptical. "You know it's still a long shot, don't you? I haven't seen the poster, but there must be dozens of possible passwords—letters and numbers in various combinations. It could take a long time."

Alex agreed, but said he thought it was worth a try. "He must have hoped the disc eventually would be discovered if something happened to him. He didn't want to make it too easy, but not too tough, either. Otherwise, he would have just thrown the disc away."

"You may be right," Knowles said, "and I don't have any better ideas. Still, it's all hypothesis."

Knowles agreed to pick up the poster from Linda Grabowski the next day, not mentioning to Alex that he was more eager to see Linda again than he was to try cracking the poster password.

The next morning, Alex headed his TR4 across Interstate 94 toward St. Paul.

The Center for Behavioral Therapy was housed in a converted old mansion on Summit Avenue, where the turn-of-the-century rich and famous once made their homes. James J. Hill, the railroad magnate, and many of the millionaire flour millers and grain traders built huge residences along the broad, shaded length of the street. Succeeding generations, however, could ill afford to maintain or heat them, forcing their transformation into offices or multi-unit apartment buildings.

Alex had learned of the Center from another reporter at the station, who had used it as a resource in a story on battered women. Alex had set up an appointment with one of the state's leading experts on pedophilia, Dr. Duane Johnson.

The Center was on the third floor and could only be reached by climbing a wide, carpeted staircase with bannisters of lustrous oak. It occupied what must have once been a labyrinth of bedrooms and bathrooms, converted now to offices and conference rooms. There was a hush about the place, and Alex felt as though he should whisper when he asked to see Dr. Johnson.

"What can I do for you?" Johnson asked once they were settled in his office. "It's not often I'm visited by a television star."

Alex smiled. "I'm hardly that, but I can use your help. The news department is planning to do a series on the sexual abuse of children, an update on what has happened in the area since it grabbed the public's attention a few years ago."

The therapist leaned back in his chair, nodding. Alex guessed they were about the same age, but Johnson looked as though he'd never seen the sun. His skin was sallow, and there were unhealthy dark rings beneath his eyes. His teeth were yellowed, apparently from the pipe which he now held, empty, between his teeth, chewing it like a pacifier. Alex decided he'd probably spent too many hours in dimly lit rooms listening to too many people's problems.

"My assignment," Alex continued, "is to do a piece on pedophiles. Who they are, how to guard against them, that kind of thing. I'd just like to talk today, and maybe arrange for an on-camera interview later."

"I'm not sure where to begin," Johnson said. "As you can guess, it's a big subject."

"How about a general description of a pedophile," Alex suggested. "If there is a typical profile."

"I've dealt with dozens of them, and there *are* some common traits. I'll try to be as concise as possible."

"Mind if I record your comments?" Alex asked as he took out his pocket tape machine.

"Not at all," Johnson said. "First of all, pedophiles are addicts, just like drug users or alcoholics. They're addicted to violating children. They're almost always intelligent, bright people . . . usually in positions of power or authority, like clergymen or teachers. Professional people by and large. Often in jobs where they come in contact with, or have influence over, kids. Or if they don't, they volunteer to work in organizations where they will. Boy Scouts, Big Brothers, YMCA, and so forth."

How convenient, Alex thought.

"And, interestingly," Johnson said, "many hide behind very upright moral values. They can be perceived as very religious, very decent, and often take strong public stands on moral issues. Like, ironically, sexual abuse. Or abortion and premarital sex."

"That is interesting," Alex mumbled, groping for the right questions. "But what would they be like socially? I mean, would they interact normally with everyone else?"

"Well, they tend to be very private people. When they do socialize, they like to travel in classy, visible circles. Again, it tends to deflect suspicion."

"And sexually? What about that?"

Johnson got up and walked to the window overlooking Summit Avenue. He took his time. "That's a more difficult question. Some pedophiles are married, with kids of their own, leading what seem to be very normal family lives. Many are not married, but still maintain lifestyles that seem beyond reproach.

"You've got to remember, these are often very sneaky, clever people, who will do almost anything to protect their fetish. They're great actors who erect elaborate façades around themselves. Most of them have had years of practice; they've learned how to control and manipulate people. They love their secret life.

"And most have had some kind of sexual, physical, or emotional abuse, some trauma, in their own past. Usually as adolescents. That's true just about across the board."

"Are they all homosexual?" Alex asked. "Or is that a foolish question?"

"No, not at all," Johnson said, returning to his chair. "I'm not sure anybody knows for certain. Some pedophiles would be no more interested in an adult male than you or I. Kids are their thing. That's who they dream about."

Alex was struggling to put all of this together, to somehow put Steele's face to it. He just couldn't get his mind around it all. "What is it about kids that's so attractive?" he asked.

"From what my clients tell me, it's their softness, their vulnerability, their naïveté. They can be maneuvered and controlled, and they don't pose a threat. Remember, often the kids the pedophiles target come from dysfunctional families themselves and already are victims of abuse. They're craving attention and love. The pedophiles can prey on that."

The more Alex heard, the more incensed he became. Where is the justice? he wondered. Troubled kids, craving love and help, defiled by the very people specifically entrusted to provide help, not harm. What kind of justice is that? *It's savage.*

"Just another question or two," Alex said.

"No problem," Johnson said. "I spend my life talking to these people, so I don't mind talking about them for a change."

"Are they treatable, the pedophiles I mean?"

"Yes, but with limited success. Pedophiles are quite different from what we call regressed offenders, incest fathers and the like, who often carry on healthy sexual relationships while also engaging in their aberrant behavior. Pedophiles have no healthy relationship to return to, and they know it. So they tend to resist treatment. Some punishment is almost always necessary to get results."

Alex was about to end the interview when he thought of a final question.

"Can they be violent?"

"They can be, but they usually aren't. They tend to be passive. But if they're cornered, if their secret is threatened, who knows what they may do? They do often fantasize about violence, and once they go over the edge, they're likely to continue."

The investigation weighed heavily on Alex. *How in the hell am*

I going to follow the logic of a man like Steele? He is absolutely unscrupulous. Forget all of his self-righteous, high-sounding crap about justice and moral correctness. It's just madness.

Alex checked his watch and saw that the time had sped away. He thanked Dr. Johnson and walked to the office door, but paused. "If they're so bright, so protective of themselves," he asked, "how do they get caught?"

"Usually it's when they get too arrogant, too sure of themselves. And sometimes when their victims, who were once too young or too afraid to talk, grow up. When they begin to understand what happened to them, they sometimes blow the whistle."

We've just got to find a whistle-blower, Alex thought as he walked to his car.

Seventeen

Rick found himself on the bed in the big room, staring at the ceiling. He didn't know how he had come to be there, or who had put the robe back on his body. He didn't care about any of this, though—his mind was filled with extraordinary pain, searing and unrelenting. He tried to shift his lower body, but felt a new stab of agony that made him cry out.

My God, what did he do to me?

His eyes closed against the pain, and when they opened, he saw a blurred figure across the room. A moment later, he heard the sound of running water.

His vision focused as the figure approached him. It was Roger, his face reflecting his concern for the pain he knew Rick was feeling.

"Can you stand?" he asked, softly. "Please try. Lean on me. I'll help you get to the tub. It'll ease the pain."

Rick somehow managed to rise, sliding from the bed with his teeth clenched. He clasped Roger's arm, taking small steps toward the steaming tub.

"What did he do to me?" The words were a hiss through his teeth.

"Don't talk. Don't say anything," Roger whispered. "They can hear and see us."

Finally, the water was lapping at his feet, and he was sliding out of the robe and into the sunken tub, submerging in the soothing and wondrous warmth.

The taste of liquor brought his eyes open. Roger was kneeling by the tub, holding a glass to his lips, urging him to sip. The brandy was as warm and tranquilizing as the steaming water.

Rick tried to speak, but no sound came. He moved his body in the water, lifting, stretching, testing. The pain still there, but more bearable.

"There's medication in the water. Relax, give it time to work."

The glass was at his lips again.

"A little while longer," Roger said, "and you'll be home."

Home? The word echoed in his mind.

He had survived the fear. He had withstood the humiliation and the pain. But that word was more than he could bear.

He started to cry.

Had he ever had a home? A real home? It was so long ago that the memories were splintered, fractured by time and pain. Before his dad left, he'd had a home and a family. *How many years ago?*

There had been cards at Christmas and birthdays, but Rick had seen his father only once since—when his mother died. He'd come back for the funeral, but by then they were strangers. Their only common bond was gone.

The tears eventually stopped. The pain had ebbed. Rick was alone again.

His clothes, freshly cleaned, were spread on the bed.

Rick eased out of the tub, gingerly rubbed his body dry, and wrapped himself in the towel. Walking slowly to the bed, he searched the walls for the hidden camera, then gave up, struggling to put his clothes on without further agony.

He felt something in his pockets and retreated to a corner of the room, hoping he was out of the camera's view.

In one pocket, he found three crisp one hundred dollar bills.

In the other, a key and a note: "*You do have a home, at 3301 Slater South. Courage. Roger.*"

Rick sat cautiously on the edge of the bed, waiting.

A half hour passed. He sipped the drink Roger had left.

The lights dimmed, and the door slowly opened. A hand placed a blindfold on the floor.

"Please put on the blindfold and wait for your escort." It was the voice he had come to hate.

Rick stood unsteadily, blindly. Minutes passed.

Then a hand gripped his elbow, vice-like, and yanked him. "Move!"

Russell was back.

Rick stumbled twice, almost falling, as he was pulled roughly through the house. "Take it easy," he protested.

He got only a grunt for a reply.

He heard the front door open and felt the cold air hit his face. His feet took him down the same five steps and along the gravel path.

"Duck your head," he was told.

The inside of the Continental was as warm now as before, and as quiet. The same muted music, the same hum of the heater, the same deep leather cushions. And he sensed the same man was in the backseat with him, but no words were spoken.

One thing was different. The car was moving faster; there was no feeling of aimless wandering. They were moving toward a definite destination, Rick could tell, and they were wasting little time getting there.

"Watch your speed," said the man beside him.

Another grunt from Russell.

Rick felt the blindfold bite into the side of his scalp. His lower body still ached, and now his temples pounded from the binding of the cloth.

The car slowed, then seemed to creep.

"You can take off the blindfold. We're downtown."

It was his backseat companion, his voice still gentle, his face half-hidden in the shadows.

"Did you receive your money?" he asked.

"Yes," Rick replied.

"Will we see you again?"

"No."

"Do you remember the warnings?"

"Yes."

"Do you take them seriously?"

"Yes."

"Good, Rick. You can get out here."

The Continental stopped opposite the same doorway. Rick

quickly disappeared into the darkness of an adjacent empty lot. He retreated to the deep shadows behind a dumpster—finding refuge and some comfort in the familiar pocket next to the wall, protected from view and from the wind.

How many nights had he spent here, wrapped in newspaper, lying on cardboard, waiting for the first light of day to flee before the giant garbage truck made its early-morning rounds.

He had seen the Continental ease away from the curb, had felt relieved the nightmare was over, but he already missed the warmth of the heater and the softness of the leather cushions.

He slumped against the wall, wrapped his jacket tightly around him, and felt inside his pants pocket. Roger's note and the three crisp bills were there. They were warm in his hand.

Eighteen

"What are you going to do about Scotty Hansen?"

Alex was walking out of the station, taking half steps to allow the ponderous George Barclay to keep up with him.

"I don't know yet," Barclay said, already breathing heavily from the exertion of the walk down the hallway. "I still think it's bullshit, but I've asked Ben Farley to send me a tape of other sports anchors from around the country. I'll look at who's available."

Alex knew that news consultants like Farley kept a computer file of every television personality in the country. Need a black female news anchor? How about an Hispanic meteorologist? Maybe a white sports anchor who's a former jock? The computer would spit out dozens of names, along with their complete background, salary, and contract status.

And for every name in the computer, Alex knew, there was an audition tape somewhere in the consultant's files. Shelf upon shelf of them. Kind of a video supermarket for television talent.

"Have you talked to Scotty yet?" Alex asked.

"Shit no! The last thing I need is him moping around during the rating period. To say nothing of the leaks to the newspapers. They'd crucify us."

"So what will you do?"

"Sit it out for a while. Look at the tapes. Take my time. Maybe

131

find another spot for Scotty on one of the earlier shows, where there's a bigger chunk of older viewers. Who knows?"

Alex walked quietly for a moment.

"I can just picture this happening to *me* someday," Alex said. "Some consultant deciding I'm too old, too demographically unattractive. Bingo! Out to pasture I go. I can hear it now."

"It'll happen to all of us someday," Barclay replied. "So why the fuck worry about it now? Everybody, even anchormen and fat old news directors, get old, retire, and die. I just hope I get to retire before I die."

"You don't worry about it?"

"About getting old? Of course I do," he said, glancing at Alex. "But you, you make a career of worrying about it. Forget it. There'll always be an anchor job for you down in Sun City or Sarasota, with the old farts."

Then he laughed. Alex didn't think it was all that funny.

Seuss was perched atop the bannister, looking lonely and hungry, when Alex walked into the house. He picked the cat up and carried him into the kitchen, stroking his ears along the way.

At least he didn't tear the house apart this time.

He was filling the cat's dish when the telephone rang, again sending Seuss fleeing for cover.

"I hoped I'd catch you," Pat said.

"I'm glad you did," Alex replied. "I tried to get you a couple of times today."

"Thanks for coming on Saturday. You made it a very pleasant birthday. One I'll never forget."

"Nor will I. When can I see you again?"

"That's why I called. Nathaniel's leaving Friday night for a judges' conference in New York. I was hoping I could see you this weekend."

"How about Saturday morning at my place?"

"Isn't that risky?"

"No more so than anywhere else," he said. "It would be nice to be alone."

"I think so, too. About nine?"

"That's fine. We've got a lot to talk about."

As he hung up the phone, Alex remembered he had yet to tell his children that he couldn't be with them at Thanksgiving. No sense in putting it off any longer, he decided, as he dialed their number in Philadelphia. One more disappointment to add to their long list, he thought sadly.

"When will we ever see you?" his daughter, Jennifer, asked after he had broken the news to her.

"I don't know, Jennie. Maybe Christmas if we can work something out."

"Do you really mean it?" Her voice was filled with doubt.

"I can't make any promises, Jennie. You know that. I'll try, but I don't want to disappoint you again."

"You always say that."

Alex had no ready response; she was right. But if his suspicions about Steele were true, he was afraid to have his family too close. He couldn't risk any possible danger to them. He owed them that, at least.

"I'll see you as soon as I can," he said, finally. "Say hi to Chris and your mother, okay? I'm sorry, Jennie, but please don't be sad."

He heard a faint sob, then the dial tone.

The *Star-Tribune* was wrong. But only by a day.

Governor Allen Hamel hated news leaks and loved to tweak the nose of the media. He waited until Tuesday to announce the appointment of the new chief justice.

The news conference was held in the ornate and stately reception room of the governor's office, a room with walls covered by huge oil paintings depicting the state's past and a perimeter dotted with antique mahogany tables and chairs.

Alex had asked to cover the event that morning and was aghast at the raucous scene of the bobbing cameras and lights, the milling reporters, the scurrying minions of the governor's—all in a genteel room steeped in history.

It's like a circus sideshow on the altar of a cathedral, Alex thought. He'd been in similar situations before and was always slightly chagrined by the rowdiness of the news gatherers.

The crowd quieted as the governor strode into the room, flanked by Judge Steele and retiring Chief Justice Parker, and followed by the other justices of the Supreme Court.

"Good morning, ladies and gentlemen. It gives me great pleasure to introduce the new chief justice–designate of the Minnesota Supreme Court, the Honorable Emmett M. Steele."

There was a smattering of applause from the nonmedia people in the room. The justices standing behind their new boss-to-be joined in, politely, although Alex suspected they were disappointed the new chief justice had not been chosen from among their ranks.

"As you all know," the governor continued, "this is one of the most important appointments I am privileged to make, and *the* most important position in the state's judiciary. We are indeed fortunate that a jurist as distinguished as Judge Steele, with his impeccable judicial record, is available and willing to assume these challenging new responsibilities."

You could hear the cameras turn off and see the reporters' attention wander as the governor generously reviewed Judge Steele's record. The yawns were difficult to disguise.

But the cameras went back on, and the reporters snapped to, when Steele stepped to the podium.

"I want to assure Governor Hamel, and the distinguished members of the court, that I accept this appointment with determination to fulfill these new and awesome duties to the very best of my ability, and to use my long experience on the bench to serve the Constitution and the people of Minnesota."

Impressive, Alex thought. Pure bullshit, but impressive.

The first questions from the media were predictable and timid: *What judicial philosophy do you hope to bring to the Supreme Court? Do you see yourself as a liberal or conservative on the issue of abortion? How do you view the controversy over cameras in the courtroom?*

Judge Steele handled the questions with a smiling aplomb, but he stiffened at a question from a St. Paul *Pioneer-Press* reporter in the back of the room.

"Judge Steele, you have a reputation as a tough disciplinarian. I wonder if you plan to oversee the Supreme Court with the same . . . ah . . . zealousness you exhibited in Hennepin County?"

Steele's smile evaporated, and he stared sternly at the offending reporter. "I resent the implications of that question," he said. "I hold myself to a high standard of effort and expect my colleagues to exhibit the same diligence and dedication."

Alex hesitated, then stood up. "In light of that response, Judge Steele, I wonder if you might comment on any change in *your*

work habits since the critical I-Team report of a couple years ago?
I understand you were one of the judges singled out for criticism."

The room became quiet.

"Ahh, Mr. Collier. I might have expected that question from a
representative of your station, but I thought the matter had long
ago been put to rest. The report you mention was yellow journalism at its worst, a tawdry example of a media vendetta. I will not
comment further."

Alex tried to follow up, but the governor abruptly stepped back
to the podium.

"If there is nothing more, I will adjourn the news conference.
Again, my warm congratulations and best wishes to Judge Steele."

A few reporters tried to shout out other questions, but they went
unanswered as the governor's entourage quickly left the room.

It was not until Alex was helping to pack up equipment that he
noticed a couple of familiar faces in the back of the room: Jerry
Caldwell and Nathaniel Hodges. Jerry simply gave him an ugly
look and walked out, but Judge Hodges came over.

"Morning, Judge."

"Alex, I'm surprised to see you here," Hodges said. "I didn't
think anchormen had to do this kind of grunt work." He was smiling, but the smile was strained.

"That's usually true. In fact, the people in the newsroom couldn't
believe what they were seeing. But I have a special interest in this
story, so I volunteered."

"A special interest?"

"Yes. I may be new in town, but I find Judge Steele to be an
intriguing figure, and this an important appointment."

"I think he was offended by your question," Hodges said.

"I don't know why he should be. He didn't answer it."

"Some things are better left in the past," Hodges said as he
walked stiffly away.

Alex had barely taken off his coat in the newsroom before Barclay was by his side.

"What kind of questions did you ask Steele, anyway?"

Alex looked at him. "What are you talking about?"

"Hawke just blistered my ear on the telephone," Barclay said.
"It seems Jerry Caldwell complained to him about your conduct

at the news conference. Said that you asked an impudent question and embarrassed Judge Steele."

"Fuck him. It sure didn't take him long to complain, did it?" Then he explained that since Steele had been extolling his own work ethic, the I-Team question seemed natural and appropriate.

Barclay agreed, but said Hawke didn't want Judge Steele made to look foolish on the air.

"Fuck him, too," Alex said, with increasing anger. "Who's running this newsroom anyway?"

"I sometimes wonder," Barclay said. "I know who signs the checks."

"I don't want to blow my career any more than you do," Alex said, "but I don't want to lie down and play dead, either."

Barclay shook his head and walked away.

"What was *that* all about?" Barbara asked.

"Nothing important, but I'm getting pissed anyway," Alex said as he flipped through the telephone book. He dialed a number.

The answer came on the first ring. "This is Jerry Caldwell."

"Jerry. Alex Collier. I understand you just made a call to Hawke."

There was a long pause. "Word gets back quickly, I see."

"You got it," Alex said. "Next time you've got a complaint about me, why don't you have the balls to tell me directly?"

"Don't get on your high horse, Collier. I thought your question to Judge Steele was inappropriate and that someone in your organization ought to know about it."

"So you just happened to pick Hawke."

"I know Mr. Hawke. He and the judge are friends."

"Well, if you think the judge's lofty position makes him immune to tough questions, you've got your head in the fucking fog."

"You don't have to use that kind of language with me, Collier. It sounds like you can't take a little constructive criticism."

"I don't mind criticism, but it pisses me off when it comes through the back door."

"Well, I think you're being thin-skinned. You're overreacting."

"Thin skin? Me? We'll see who can take criticism, Jerry."

"That sounds like a threat, Collier. We don't react well to threats."

"Call it a prediction then. A prediction for the New Year." And he hung up.

"Bravo! Bravo!" Barbara called, with mock applause.

Alex grinned. "Wait 'til Hawke gets an earful of that," he said. "I'll be on my way to Toledo."

Alex immediately picked up the phone again and placed a call to Dr. Johnson. Alex was still searching for a key to unlock the secrets of Steele's life, to discover what could turn such a man into a sexual monster.

"Dr. Johnson? Alex Collier from Channel Seven. I have a quick follow-up question to our conversation of the other day. Do you have a minute?"

"Sure," Johnson said, "but not much more. A client's waiting."

"It won't take long," Alex assured him. "You told me that pedophiles often have some trauma or abuse in their backgrounds. Usually as adolescents, right?"

"That's usually true," Johnson agreed.

"What kind of trauma?"

"Well, it could be almost anything, from an incest experience to a bad sexual encounter. Maybe even an accident or some other kind of jarring emotional experience. Regardless of what triggers it, the patterns they take on later are often very similar.

"What you'd probably want to look for," Johnson continued, "is some traumatic violation of the child's trust, some kind of abuse. A humiliating experience in school or some relative taking indecent liberties with the child. Even the death of a parent could push some kids over the edge."

Alex sat forward in his chair. "What are they capable of doing as adults? I mean, how far will they go?" Alex could barely get out the questions.

"Depends on what they want and who they are. They want power, for one thing. They always have the edge over the victim. Despite their arrogance, pedophiles really have low self-esteem and see the kids they molest as objects—not as children. Most don't want to change. They get pleasure out of it."

Like the chief justice-to-be, Alex thought bitterly. "Thanks, doctor. I hope I can call again."

"No problem."

But Alex knew he had lots of problems—time being the big one. He immediately started digging through the press release with the biographical information which had been handed out at the news conference. He found what he was looking for.

"Judge Steele was born and raised in New Ulm, Minnesota, the only child of Lester and Martha Steele. His father was a brewery worker and his mother a homemaker until she died in 1939, when her son was twelve years old."

Alex circled the paragraph. Maybe he ought to pay a visit to New Ulm.

Alex asked Barclay to call a meeting for that evening to include Knowles and Barbara. They met in a conference room just off the newsroom.

"We need to move quickly," Alex told the group, "if we're going to get this story on the air in time. We need a plan."

"What's the rush?" Barclay asked.

"We don't want to wait until Steele's on the Supreme Court and becomes totally unassailable," Alex replied. "We've got to get to him before he's sworn in, and that leaves us only six weeks or so."

"So what's the plan?" Knowles asked.

"For one thing, I need to get to New Ulm, Steele's birthplace. It turns out his mother died when he was quite young, and the therapist I've been talking to says a death in the family, or some other trauma, could have had a serious impact on a boy like Steele. Might have set him off even back then.

"In the meantime, I need to find some of Steele's victims. Time is running out, and we don't have anything until we get somebody to blow the whistle on him."

"Maybe Phil could help out," Barbara said.

"Is that your cop friend?" Barclay asked. "I don't want us working with cops, period."

"Wait a minute, George," Alex argued. "All I have is an outdated list of kids Steele may have abused in the past. I'm going to need some help finding them. Phil's badge could get me access to places I can't go, to information I could never get at."

"And he's willing to help," Barbara said.

Barclay was adamant. "No cops. You heard me."

"Okay, I'll try it on my own," Alex said, "but I don't even know the city. I don't know where to begin."

"Try Hennepin Avenue or Loring Park," Barclay suggested. "A lot of those young hustlers hang out around there."

"I'm still working on the computer password," Knowles said. "But there are thousands of possible combinations, and I'm only scratching the surface."

"Keep at it," Alex said. "Hire some expert if you have to. I'm guessing a draft of Grabowski's magazine story . . . or at least some names . . . are on that disc. Maybe a lead to the safety-deposit box."

"What do you want me to do?" Barbara asked.

"I'd like you to continue to try and track down Daniel Grabowski. See if you can contact some of his relatives on the East Coast or friends around here that we may have missed.

"One more thing, Barbara. Work with John to set up lunch or dinner with his friend, the editor of *City Magazine*. Tell him we're planning a feature on the magazine and need some background information. Maybe you can find out something about Grabowski's story, but be careful."

"That leaves me, I suppose," Barclay said. "You seem to be the boss around here now."

Alex laughed. "George, I don't know if you can work any magic with Hawke, but there's no sense in doing this story unless we can get it past him and on the air. Maybe you can soften him up some way."

"Don't count on it," Barclay replied, struggling to raise himself from his chair. "In the meantime, we've got other news to cover. I want to get this Steele business out of the way and on the air so things can get back to normal around here."

Nineteen

Alex felt lost before he began. He drove his TR4 down the ramp and into the darkness—still not sure what he was looking for or what he would find. He'd never tried to pick up a hustler before.

He headed for Hennepin Avenue and was immediately depressed by what he saw. It seemed deserted—like an abandoned, windswept runway. The only sign of life were the few people huddled in the bus shelters.

Hennepin Avenue had once been a vibrant and flashy strip of the city. It had gradually deteriorated, becoming home to the porn shops and a haven for pimps and prostitutes.

The big, glitzy theaters of years past were gone, and so were most of the better bars. Gone, in fact, was one entire block of buildings along the avenue, torn down because it had become such a blight on the city's image.

Alex knew that a restoration of the avenue had begun, anchored by the big new pro basketball arena that had been built nearby, and that within a few years Hennepin Avenue would regain some of its former luster. But for now, he could see, it was a dismal place, an urban combat zone avoided by almost everyone except the lowlife who claimed it as their own.

The avenue was especially foreboding in winter; it was a piece of paved tundra, swept by the swirling winds and home only to the most desperate and pathetic street people, and to the predators.

Alex glanced at the three names on the list Pat had given him. He couldn't believe that anybody trying to sell sex would be out on the street on a night like this.

But he was wrong.

He drove the avenue several times and spotted three promising prospects loitering on the sidewalk or in darkened doorways. What the hell do I say? he asked himself. Just make it clear you're looking for information, not sex, he told himself. And try to make sure they're not police plants.

He silently cursed Barclay for refusing to allow Phil to come along.

All three of the boys were suspicious of him when he stopped, but all seemed willing to listen. Each denied ever hearing of any of the names on Alex's list.

Was he tough enough? Had he pressed them hard enough? Should he offer them money? Shit, he wished he knew what he was doing.

Alex was ready to give up when he passed a figure in an old fatigue jacket, hands deep inside the pockets, stamping his feet to stave off the cold. He leaned over to peer inside each car that slowed as it passed him.

Alex pulled up next to him. "Little chilly standing out there, isn't it?" he said.

The boy looked through the open car window, his face guarded and suspicious like the others. "What do you need?" he asked. "I'm just waiting for a ride from my folks."

"Right, and my father was the pope," Alex said. "I need a little information, that's all."

The boy laughed and started to walk away.

"Hold on!" Alex shouted. "All I want to do is talk."

"All I want to do is make some money," the boy replied, returning to the car.

"Climb in," Alex said. "I can make it worth your while."

The boy stared at him and his eyes widened. "Are you that guy on television?" he asked. "On the news?"

Alex nodded, embarrassed to be recognized.

"What are you doing out here?" the boy asked.

"Just what I said. Looking for information. Now will you get into the car so I can shut the window?"

The boy glanced up and down the street, looked again at Alex, then climbed into the front seat. "I'm no pissant snitch," he said, "but I don't make conversation for free, either."

Alex studied him in the dim light. He couldn't be more than sixteen or seventeen years old. He should be on a basketball court or in a church choir, he thought, not hustling on a street corner.

"I'm trying to find a couple of guys," Alex said. "Let me try these names on you: James Young, Kevin Marcus, and Roger Anderson."

Alex saw no outward sign of recognition.

"They're probably older than you are," he continued, "but hustling, just like you."

"There are a lot of guys out hustling," the boy replied. "They come and go. It's not a fuckin' fraternity, you know."

"Drop the smart talk," Alex said. "Do you know them or not?"

"What's it worth?"

Alex held out five ten-dollar bills. "Fifty bucks if you actually know something. A few minutes in a warm car if you don't."

The boy took the money. "I've heard of two of them," he admitted, "but that was months ago. Kevin Marcus—used to call him 'Sleet'—took off for California, I think. Musta finally got tired of the weather or something."

"Do you know where in California?"

"Shit no, but probably L.A. He might even be back by now, for all I know."

"Who's the second one?"

"Roger Anderson. But I've only heard of him, never met him. He's supposed to work for some big shot in town. Kind of a valet or houseboy or something."

"Some big shot? Who do you mean?"

"I don't know," the boy said. "That's the rumor out there. That he's got some kind of sweet deal. Sure beats workin' the street."

"Who else would know this Roger Anderson? How would I find him?"

"Beats me. I'm just telling you what I heard. I don't even remember who told me, it's been a while."

"Anything else?" Alex asked.

"That's it. Never heard of the third guy."

"How do I find *you* again?" Alex asked.

"Is that part of the deal?"

"That's right, but there'll be another fifty in it for you."

The boy thought for a moment. "Okay, my name's Blake. And you can usually find me around Mr. K's. Just leave a number."

"What's Mr. K's?"

"A bar a couple of blocks over. In the warehouse district."

With that he was out of the car, back on the darkened street.

It was beginning to snow lightly. Alex glanced at his watch. There were still two hours to go before the late news, and he had accounted for two of the three names on the list.

He looked again at the third name: James Young, 3342 Oakley Avenue South.

Alex turned on the dome light inside the car and studied a map of the city. He found Oakley Avenue, and noticed he could get there by driving past Loring Park—another spot that Barclay had mentioned.

George had told him that on summer days the park was a lovely green area surrounding a small and tranquil lake in the midst of a residential apartment area. An oasis in the middle of the city. Ducks and geese populated the pond, living happily on the hand-outs of noontime picnickers and strollers escaping the asphalt and concrete.

But at night, in summer or winter, he'd said, the park's personality changed. With darkness came seclusion, and with seclusion came the cruisers and the hookers, skulking in the shadows of the same great oaks and maples which provided cool shade on a warm day.

"Look closely at those parked cars," Barclay had told him. "Those aren't kids out necking after the prom."

As Alex circled the park, he saw the darkened cars with figures inside. A squad car passed in the opposite direction, its spotlight probing the park.

"It's not only a favorite spot for gays," Barclay had said, "but for gay-bashers, too. We've covered a couple of killings down there."

He drove further south, away from the downtown area and into a quiet, well-kept neighborhood of single-family homes, closed tight against the cold. It was snowing more heavily as he pulled up in front of the house on Oakley Avenue.

The soft glow of a lamp showed through the drawn drapes of the living room, and Alex could hear the faint echo of the door chimes inside when he rang the bell. Then a face peered through the small, square window of the door, eyes squinting to see who stood on the steps under the dim outdoor light.

The face was aged, the skin leathery and deeply lined. It was impossible to tell through the window whether the face belonged to a man or a woman. When the door opened a crack behind the chain lock, however, a woman's voice challenged him.

"Who's there? What do you want?"

"I'm looking for James Young," Alex said, voice raised, face close to the door. "I understand he lives here, or used to live here."

"You don't have to shout. I'm not deaf."

The chain came off, the inside door opened wider, but the glass storm door remained closed. The old woman was no more than five feet tall, her white hair tied in a tight bun, a heavy knit shawl spread over her shoulders.

"Who are you?" she persisted, a gnarled hand holding the shawl tightly around her neck.

"My name is Alex Collier. I work for Channel Seven. I'd just like to talk to Mr. Young."

She opened the storm door. "Well, come in out of the cold, then."

Alex almost tripped over a small stool in the entryway. So that's how she gets up high enough to see through the window, he thought, as he pushed the stool aside with his foot and followed her inside.

The house was very small, but cozy and comfortable. It smelled of the medicated vapors pouring from a humidifier in the middle of the room.

"Aren't you that anchorman?" she asked, looking at Alex. "I don't watch the news much anymore. Too depressing."

She settled into a rocking chair that looked as old as she did. Her legs were barely long enough to reach the floor, but she managed to keep the chair moving slowly.

"Why would you want to talk to James?" she asked.

"Well," Alex began, "I'm following a story for the station, and I believe James could answer some questions that would be very helpful to me."

"I doubt that," she said, looking at him so intently that he had to fight the reflex to look away.

"Why? Isn't he around?" There was no answer, just the stare.

"Are you related to James?" Alex asked.

"I was his great-grandmother," she said, her eyes unwavering.

"You *were* his great-grandmother?"

"Yes. James is dead. He committed suicide two years ago."

The only sounds were the hiss of the vaporizer and a small squeak in the old woman's rocking chair. The squeak was as steady as a ticking clock, a rhythmic reminder of the quiet in the room.

Alex sat in shocked silence. He hadn't expected this.

"I'm terribly sorry," Alex finally said. "I had no idea."

"I'm still wondering why you wanted to see James."

"How did it happen?" Alex asked, deflecting the question.

"We found him in his car in the garage. The doors were closed, and the engine was running."

She lifted her frail body from the rocker and walked slowly toward the kitchen, shawl still clutched around her shoulders. "I'll pour some tea," she said. "It'll warm you up before you go back out into the cold."

Alex followed her into the kitchen, watching as she filled the cups. Her hand was shaking slightly from the weight of the teapot.

"I still don't know why he did it," she said. "Guess you never do. There was a note, but it didn't really make sense to me. Never really could figure the boy out . . . had a bad past. His folks died in a car crash, and he never seemed the same after. He was in and out of trouble, running around with a bad crowd. Always down at court. After his ma and pa were killed, he moved in with my son and his wife, until they passed on a few years ago, too. That's when he came to live with me." She paused and sipped her tea. "I don't know why the Lord saw fit to let me live so long . . . and see them all die."

Alex watched her eyes and wondered the same thing. "How old are you, if I may ask?"

"Ninety-eight next month. Hard to believe, isn't it? People shouldn't live so long. You see too much."

"Did you keep any of his belongings?" Alex asked. "Papers or anything?"

"No. I gave everything away, or burned it. I didn't have the room, and didn't want the reminders around. But I kept the note."

"Would you mind if I looked at it? It could be important."

"I see no harm in it," she said. "I'll go get it."

Alex sat in silence until she returned a moment later, a Bible in her hands. She took a slip of paper from beneath its cover, and handed it to him. "I'll wait in the living room."

The writing was smudged, and barely legible.

Dear Great Gram. Sorry I have to do this to you, to leave you all alone like this. It seems like I'm always causing you trouble. I'm scared. I don't want to die, but I don't want to live either. I met a man I thought would help me, but he turned out like all the rest. I just want to go to sleep forever. Thanks for everything you tried to do for me. James.

"Jesus Christ," Alex muttered to himself, "what a sad story."

He walked to the living room, returning the letter to the old lady in the rocker, who replaced it in the Bible in her lap.

"I can only say I'm sorry," Alex said. "You've gone through a lot."

She seemed to huddle inside the shawl.

"May I ask something else?" Alex said, as he walked toward the door. "The man James mentioned in his note. The one who turned out like all the rest. Do you know who he was?"

"No," she said, still rocking. "Not by name. But before he died, James talked a lot about a man he had gotten to know, someone who was being kind to him. I don't know much about him, but I think he was a judge."

Alex walked out the door, and the cold reached deep inside him.

Twenty

"You did *what*?" George Barclay shouted. "You *paid* a source for information? What fucking school did you go to?"

Alex was afraid Barclay would come across his desk after him.

"Hold on, George," Alex said, feeling anger himself. "I know you don't pay for interviews, but who says you can't pay for information? There's a big difference."

"Like what?" Barclay demanded.

"C'mon, we both know we pay for information all the time. To the wire services, to stringers—to the network, for that matter."

"Nice try. But there's a big difference between them and some goddamned whore on Hennepin Avenue. What are we going to say if the kid gets picked up by the morals squad and claims you paid him the fifty bucks for a blow job?"

"That's why I wanted Phil along," Alex protested, "to prevent that kind of thing from happening. Look, George, I may have to bend the rules a bit if I'm going to get this story. I don't want to violate any of your ethical standards, but shit, I don't think this is that clear-cut a case."

"You start bending the rules," Barclay said, "and pretty soon you're breaking them. Floods start with a drop of rain."

"Let me talk to Phil, will you?" Alex pleaded. "I was lucky to find the one kid and the grandmother. But I'm still missing any of the victims. One of them may be in California, for Christ's sake. I need Phil's badge and his contacts."

"I don't know," Barclay sighed. "Cops and news people don't mix. We're supposed to be watching them, making sure they do their job like everyone else, not working with them. This is the hand-in-glove bullshit I was worried about."

"This is a special case," Alex said. "Phil's willing to work on his own time. Barbara says he's a good guy, that we can trust him. And I need him."

"Collier, you exhaust me."

"I don't want to be a prick, George, but this is important."

Barclay stared at him across the desk. "I don't like cops, Alex. Never have. You can't trust most of 'em."

"I think we have to take the chance," Alex replied.

Barclay finally relented. "Okay, but be careful, and promise me one thing: No payments for interviews, okay? If these kids are going to talk, they're going to do it because they want to put the fucking judge away. Not for a quick buck."

Barbara sat in the lobby of the Hyatt Regency, awaiting the arrival of Barry Stensrud, the *City Magazine* editor. John Knowles had arranged for the dinner meeting with Barbara, telling Stensrud the station was preparing a story which involved the magazine.

"What's he like?" Barbara had asked Knowles.

"He's a good guy," Knowles had said. "A solid journalist who's worked his way up at the magazine, and who's now responsible for some of the tougher investigative stuff they do."

Stensrud was hard to miss when he came through the revolving door and walked across the lobby toward her. He was as Knowles had described him: tall, redheaded, with a face full of freckles and a wide smile.

A hale and hearty fellow, Barbara thought, as Stensrud shook her hand. "I recognized you right away," he said. "I always watch your news; I think it's the best in town."

"That's what they *all* say." Barbara flashed her most flirtatious grin. "I like your magazine, too."

"Maybe we should give each other a quiz later, to see who's really telling the truth." He returned her smile.

The restaurant at the Hyatt was a classy place, with prices to match. Elegant and intimate, and quiet enough for private conversations.

"I always feel like I have to whisper in here," Barbara said.

"I don't think we have to worry about that tonight," Stensrud replied, glancing at the empty tables around them.

Their conversation was easy and relaxed, sprinkled with stories of growing up, their jobs, and their families.

Barbara decided he was one of those men who was exactly what he seemed to be; no more, no less. No pretenses, no phoniness, no airs. Just decent and honest, and expecting others to be the same.

She decided she could not deceive him.

"I have a confession to make," she said. "This dinner is something of a sham. I was supposed to wean some information out of you under the guise of doing a story on your magazine. But I can't do it."

If he was surprised, he didn't show it. "I'm glad, but I can't imagine what information I have that you'd be interested in."

"Daniel Grabowski."

The two words hung in the air.

"That's a sensitive area," he finally said. "How do you know Daniel Grabowski?"

"I don't. We're trying to find him because we're interested in the same story he was pursuing for your magazine."

"Who's we?" he asked.

"The station. Alex Collier. I'm working with him."

He studied her, weighing his words. "Be careful. You're playing with fire, you know."

"Please, we need your help. Do you know where Grabowski is?"

"No, I don't. And I don't want to. You're getting into an area I just can't talk about."

"Why?" she asked.

"It's a long story, and you can't press me on it. Those of us at the magazine have been given orders."

"I can't force you to tell me, and I'm not going to beg. But if what we suspect is true, and if you can help us prove it . . ."

"I can't help you *prove* anything."

"You can help us understand what's going on," she replied, "and that's crucial right now."

He looked around the restaurant, then at Barbara.

"Look, I don't even know you. You seem like a nice young person, and I'd like to help. But you've got to realize that this whole thing is something we're not very proud of. It's behind us now, and all of us just want to forget about it."

"But you *did* know Daniel, didn't you?" Barbara persisted. "You *did* work with him on his story?"

"Give it up, Barbara. Please. I told you I can't say anything."

"Listen," she said. "Alex Collier's not going to give up on this, even though you say we're playing with fire. I don't want to see him, or anybody else, get hurt. I'm sure you don't, either."

"Of course not, but . . ."

"Then tell me what we're up against," she pleaded. "Tell me what you know."

"You're sure Collier won't back off?"

"Positive," she said.

"Then he's a fool," Stensrud said, shaking his head slowly in apparent surrender.

Barbara waited patiently.

"All I know," he said finally, "is that Daniel Grabowski was convinced he had the evidence to prove Judge Steele guilty of the sexual abuse of children. According to Dan, Steele would buy sexual favors from kids, and then buy their silence by promises of courtroom leniency. If that failed, he'd use threats."

"Were *you* convinced?" she asked.

"I never saw any hard evidence, none of the affidavits Dan claimed to have. But I believed in Grabowski, and I knew he was on to something by the pressure that came to bear on the magazine. Not only financial threats, like the loss of every major advertiser, but physical threats. The publisher was scared to death. All of us were."

"I'll be damned," she whispered. "Where were the threats coming from? Could you trace them?"

"They came through the mail, over the telephone, and under the door. All of them were anonymous."

"Did they know Grabowski was at the heart of it?"

"Of course, but they couldn't get to him. He was too determined."

"Did he actually write the story?" she asked.

"I don't know. I never saw it. But I think Dan knew more than he let on."

"Like what?"

"Like others besides Steele who may be involved."

"So what happened?" Barbara asked. "Where did Daniel go?"

"I don't know. We told him we weren't going to run the story, that it was too big for us to handle, no matter how solid the evidence. The magazine would suffer. Somebody could get hurt, maybe even killed."

Stensrud stared down at his plate, his voice barely audible even in the quiet of the restaurant.

"It was the saddest day of my life, telling him that. He was crushed. He asked how we could let a child molester go free and live with ourselves. I didn't have a very good answer."

"Is that why you're talking to me now?"

"Maybe. I don't know. It hasn't been easy to live with. Turning my back on Daniel and on that kind of a story once is enough. I can't do it again."

"Daniel didn't tell you where he was going?" she asked.

"No, and I didn't ask. He said he was going to shop the story around, maybe to a national magazine in New York. That's the last I heard. The publisher ordered us to keep quiet or risk our jobs. It was a horrible experience."

"Would you be willing to tell all of this on camera?" she asked. "If we do get the story?"

"It'd cost me my job. Even talking to you now could, if my boss knew. I've got to think of my family. I just don't know."

For the second night, this time after the late news, Alex was in his TR4—impatiently waiting for it to warm up.

The weather had become even more bitter since the day before. The temperature had fallen to near zero, and with strong winds out of the north, the windchill factor made it to about thirty below.

Alex suspected he'd find no one out on a night like this, but still he cruised Hennepin Avenue twice and then circled Loring Park. He was right; nobody was outside. Even the street people seemed to have found refuge somewhere.

Alex tried to sort things out as he drove, feeling the warmth of the heater spill on to his legs. *We know one kid is dead, another is in California, and the third is working who-knows-where.* Not much progress, he had to admit, and the days were slipping by.

There was still no solution to the computer puzzle, and still no

Grabowski. No proof of anything, and here he was, cruising the frozen streets looking for some kind of lead. It seemed hopeless.

Finding the streets empty, Alex debated what to do next. He stopped and took out his map of the city. He traced the route to Judge Steele's home in the Tyrol Hills section of Golden Valley.

Why am I doing this? he asked himself, as he followed the winding, hilly roads that led past large homes set well back from the street—often protected by fences and locked gates.

Steele's home was one of these, on Merriweather Drive. It sat on a hill, hidden behind a forest of Norway pine that towered fifty feet into the air. The gate was open. Alex paused for a moment, then pulled the TR4 into the gravel driveway.

What the hell am I doing? You want to see the house, don't you?

Even with the car windows closed, Alex could hear the gravel and ice crunching beneath the tires.

The house adorned the hill like a crown, sparkling in the beams of a half-dozen spotlights. Lights were on in virtually every window, but there was no sign of life behind them.

A Lincoln Continental was idling outside the five-car garage, its exhaust made visible by the cold, then swept away by the wind. Alex quickly jotted down the license number: NCA 394.

"Get the fuck out of here," he muttered to himself.

His car was about fifty feet from the garage, hidden in the shadows. Only the trees, blown by the wind, moved around him.

Alex used his hand to wipe away the frost from the side window of the car. As the glass cleared, he found himself peering into the face of Steele's driver, his hawk nose pressed against the window.

"Jesus Christ!" Alex whispered, quickly covering the lower half of his face with one gloved hand while he rolled down the window a crack with the other.

"Who are you looking for?" the man asked, his words almost whipped away by the wind.

"For the Petersons," Alex lied. "Everett Peterson on Hillsdale Drive?"

"This is Merriweather Drive. Nobody named Peterson lives here. I don't know where Hillsdale Drive is. Never heard of it."

Alex kept the glove to his face.

"Sorry about that," he said. "Hope I didn't disturb you."

He rolled up the window and turned the car around. As he glided down the driveway, he glanced into the rearview mirror and discovered he wasn't the onlly one taking down license numbers.

Alex drove slowly back toward the station from Steele's house. It was almost midnight, but he wasn't tired and he decided against going home.

He passed the corner where he'd met the boy, Blake, the night before. The streets were still empty, but he knew the bars would be open for another hour. He took a quick left and headed for the warehouse district.

From the outside, Mr. K's looked like a boarded-up, abandoned building, its windows blackened, its exterior unlighted except for a small neon sign above the door.

Not exactly the Silver Slipper, Alex thought.

He found a parking space across the street and tried to decide on his next move.

I better not go in there looking like myself, he decided. It's not exactly the kind of place I ought to be seen. He pulled out a pair of dark glasses, picked up an envelope from the front seat, and walked hesitantly toward the front door.

The interior was no more inviting than the exterior: low lights, a smoky haze from floor to ceiling, and a too-loud jukebox playing in one corner.

The bartender was young and fat, wearing a sweater which hung open over his protruding belly. He had about a three-day growth of beard that was parted on one cheek by a jagged white scar.

Alex ordered a beer. Only a few patrons sat at the bar, and they seemed to take no notice of him.

"I'm looking for Sleet. I hear he's back from California."

"I don't know any Sleet," the bartender said. "Is that supposed to be a nickname or something?"

"Yeah. Kevin Marcus is his real name."

"No, I don't know him."

"How about Roger Anderson? I'm trying to find him, too. He's supposed to be working for somebody. A kind of a houseboy or valet."

"What are you, a cop?"

"No way. This has nothing to do with the cops," Alex said. "I just need to talk to these guys."

The bartender walked to the other end of the bar, then returned. "Are you the same guy who talked to Blake? The TV guy?"

Alex nodded, then took off the dark glasses.

"He told me about you," the bartender said, studying him.

Alex waited.

"A guy named Roger Anderson used to stop by, but I haven't seen him for a while. And I don't know where he works. It may not even be the same guy."

Alex picked up a napkin from the bar and wrote his first name and his home and work phone numbers on it. "I'll leave my name and numbers in case he stops by again," he said, giving the napkin to the bartender. "You can tell him it would be worth his while to give me a call."

"Did I hear you say you were looking for Sleet?" It was one of the customers, a small, balding man who was sitting three stools away from Alex.

"That's right," Alex said. "You know where he is these days?"

"What's in it for me?" the man asked.

"Depends. A drink for starters."

"I think he's still in California. He went out there a year or so ago, all expenses paid."

"Paid by whom?" Alex asked.

"Some friend of his, I guess. Whoever it is, he set him up in an apartment in Burbank. Sleet wants to get into the movies."

"Have you got an address or a phone number in Burbank?"

"Hell, no. I didn't know him that well."

Alex opened the envelope he had brought from the car. "I've got three pictures here," he said, showing them to the customer. "Is one of these Sleet?"

The man studied the pictures John Knowles had taken from the videotape.

"Yeah," he said, "this is Sleet." He pointed to the shot of Steele's blond friend, the one Knowles thought looked like a Nazi.

"Recognize either of the others?" Alex asked.

"Nope. Just Sleet. But that's him, I'm sure."

Alex pushed a twenty-dollar bill across the bar. "Thanks for the information. If you hear anything more, the bartender's got my number. I'd appreciate hearing from you."

The nets are out, Alex thought. Now we have to see if we land anything.

The next day, Alex found John Knowles in his office, hunched over the computer, staring at Daniel Grabowski's Twins' poster, which he had tacked to the wall, still searching for the elusive password.

"No luck yet?" Alex asked.

Knowles shook his head.

The poster was about two feet wide by three feet long; a four-color collection of pictures of eight Twins players in action, the photos surrounding a center block of lettering with the words "Minnesota Twins" superimposed over a baseball, and beneath that, "World Champions, 1987."

"I've tried a hundred different words or combinations of words and numbers," Knowles said. "Players' names, batting averages, you name it, I've tried it."

"Maybe you ought to give it up for a while," Alex said.

Knowles leaned back and switched off the computer. Alex quickly told him of what he had found the previous two nights, including his encounter with Steele's driver outside his house.

"What the hell were you doing there?" Knowles asked.

"I just wanted to see where the guy lives," Alex replied. "I didn't expect to run into anybody."

"You think he got your license number?"

Alex nodded. "I've still got my California plates. It may take longer to trace those."

"You should get Minnesota plates now, Alex. Don't take chances."

"John, I still don't understand how Steele got to be the powerhouse he is. Why is everybody so goddamned afraid of him, so beholden to him?"

"That goes back a long way," Knowles replied. "He's a brilliant judge, but he's also a consummate politician. He can help you or hurt you. He's done a lot of favors for important people."

"Favors?" Alex asked. "What kind?"

"All kinds. He runs his courtroom like a little kingdom. I remember he once kept the daughter of a former lieutenant governor out of jail after she shot and wounded her husband in some kind of domestic dispute. And he gave probation instead of prison to a guy involved in a big commodities fraud. The guy happened to be the brother-in-law of the speaker of the House. He'll routinely seal the records in messy divorce cases involving his friends. Things like that."

Knowles paused for a moment, dragging on his cigarette. "Over the years, he's accumulated a lot of due bills—and he's not shy about collecting them."

As Alex was about to get up to leave, Barbara walked into the office. "I thought I might find you here," she said.

"How was the dinner with Stensrud?" Alex asked.

Barbara recounted her conversation with the editor, including details of the anonymous threats to the magazine and Stensrud's warnings. "He says we're playing with fire, and that we ought to be very careful. It was a little frightening."

"I was afraid of that," Knowles said.

"Barbara, I think it's time I met Phil. Barclay says it's okay, and I'm going to need his help. Can you set it up?"

"Sure. Just let me know when."

When Alex returned to his desk in the newsroom, he found Cody standing there, anger and frustration written on his face.

"Can you believe this shit?" he sputtered. "We each got a week's suspension without pay!"

"What are you talking about?" Alex asked.

"The union hassle. That idiot Derek gets a week for insubordination, and I get a week for conduct unbecoming a management employee. Can you believe it? Hawke and the union make a fucking deal, and I'm the fucking patsy."

"Settle down, Cody, settle down," Alex cautioned. "Lower your voice. Does Barclay know?"

"Yeah, he's all pissed off, but he can't even get in to see Hawke. He's conveniently tied up all afternoon. Chicken-shit bastard."

"Well, if the deal's done," Alex said, "there's probably not much Barclay can do about it anyway. At least Derek didn't get away clean."

"That's not going to help me pay my bills," Cody said. "I feel like telling Hawke to fuck off and then go find something else."

"I wouldn't be too hasty," Alex warned. "It's a hell of a lot easier finding a job when you've already got one."

Alex glanced up and saw Derek striding across the newsroom.

"Heads up, Cody. We're about to have company."

Derek stopped a few feet away. "Are you pricks satisfied?" he demanded. Two reporters nearby looked up from their desks, startled by the voice. "Got what you wanted, did you?"

"Beat it, Derek," Alex said, rising from his chair.

"Don't tell me what to do, asshole."

"You got what you deserved, Derek. Now get the hell away from us."

Derek started to edge closer to them, fists clenched at his sides. Cody began to retreat.

"What's going on here?" Barclay's voice boomed through the newsroom. He was standing just outside his office door, glaring at Derek.

"Nothing, George," Alex said. "Derek here was just saying good-bye before he left on his week's vacation."

"I suggest you break it up," Barclay said.

Derek backed away. "You may be top shit in here, Collier, but you're nothing outside. I'll find you, that's a promise."

"I'll look forward to it, Derek. Have a nice day."

That evening, after the early news, Alex sat across from Phil in the back booth of a bar a few blocks from the station. He'd never met Phil before, but Barbara had described him in detail.

"He's never wanted to be anything but a cop," she'd told Alex, "not since he saw the first 'Dragnet' reruns on his folks' old black-and-white TV."

Phil listened attentively but impassively as Alex told him of his suspicions about Steele and of the progress of the investigation. "My boss hates the idea of working with cops," Alex said, "but I don't think I have much choice now. I need the help."

"Like what?" Phil asked.

"I need to find Daniel Grabowski. I know Barbara asked you to check the missing persons records, but I need to step up the search."

"I don't know what more I can do without attracting attention," Phil said. "I've already talked to the detective who handled the case. Grabowski's gone, period."

"I also need to locate someone named Kevin Marcus, who's supposed to be in California. He goes by the nickname Sleet. I thought you might know somebody out there who could check the police records."

"I do have a buddy on the LAPD. He could do a computer run, I guess."

"I'd appreciate that," Alex said.

"You understand I have to be a little cautious," Phil said. "I'm

not supposed to be doing free-lance work like this. It's only because Barbara asked me."

"I understand," Alex said, "but if what we suspect is true, I
would think you'd want to get involved officially. Steele's committing felonies, for Christ's sake."

"I work homicide. And, besides, I don't really know what the
big deal is. I've seen a lot of these kids you're talking about, and
they don't look like victims to me. They know what they're doing.
We bring them in every day, and in a few hours they're back on
the streets where we found them."

Alex said nothing.

"They're whores, Alex, standing on the corner peddling their
ass. The fact that the judge is using them doesn't seem like that
big a thing to me. Lots of men are."

"I hear you, Phil, but these are kids—at least some of them are.
Fifteen, sixteen years old, maybe younger."

"They don't act like kids to me. Just hustlers."

"I've got a boy of my own, Phil. His name's Chris. He's eight
years old. I don't see much of him, but I know that once upon a
time every one of these kids was like Chris. I can't believe they
were born to be whores. Nobody is. Every time I see or hear about
one of them, I think of Chris."

"C'mon, Alex—"

"Somebody got to them, Phil. Somebody got them into that kind
of life before they were old enough, or mature enough, to make
the choice for themselves. Somebody like Steele, and it pisses me
off. He ought to be helping these kids get off the streets, not paying
them to stay out there."

"I don't know, Alex. You ought to meet some of these kids—"

"I want to, but I'm going to need your help."

"I'll do what I can," Phil said with a small sigh. "Maybe you're
right, maybe cops get so used to seeing the shit float by, day after
day, that we forget it wasn't always shit."

Twenty-one

The light snow cover made tracking the deer easy, but neither Joe Eichorn nor Wayne Friedman was experienced enough to know just how fresh the tracks were. They'd been out since early morning, moving slowly through the brush of the Wisconsin woods, circling the marshes and small lakes as they tried to follow the tracks.

They'd never been to this area before and feared getting lost. They had seen no other hunters and had heard no rifle shots. Eichorn kept checking his compass and watching for landmarks that could help guide them back out of the woods.

At midmorning, they decided to split up. Friedman would circle north for two miles, then push back south—hoping to drive the deer toward Eichorn. Friedman took the compass, leaving Eichorn sitting on a fallen tree to wait.

It was shortly before noon when Eichorn heard a shot from across a small lake, not a half mile away. Just one shout. And then a shout from Friedman. Another shot, another shout. Sounding urgent. *Was he hurt?*

Eichorn moved quickly through the undergrowth, holding his rifle high, forgetting the noise, forgetting the tracks and the deer. It took him about twenty minutes, and he found Friedman standing near the shore of the lake, not hurt, staring down at the ground around him.

"What the hell's happening?" Eichorn gasped.

Then he saw, too.

The bones were scattered over a small section of ground, no more than ten feet by ten feet. The skull was lodged at the top of what looked like a shallow grave, apparently dug open by animals. Other parts of the skeleton were half buried by leaves and the snow.

"Mother of God," Eichorn whispered.

What looked like the remmants of a briefcase and a small suitcase were lying near the grave, open but empty. Both men seemed to know they shouldn't touch anything.

"We've got to find a phone and call the sheriff," Friedman said, his eyes still on the skull.

"How will we find this place again?" Eichorn asked.

"Let's get a big fire going," Friedman said. "I'll take the compass and try to find my way out of here. Get to a house and a phone. You stay here and keep feeding the fire. We'll find you, even if we have to follow the smoke."

Eichorn didn't relish the idea of camping out with a skeleton, but he agreed—and started gathering wood.

Five hours later, Alex was sitting at the anchor desk reviewing the script of the early news, quietly mouthing the words he would be reading aloud to a quarter million people in a few minutes. Barbara was by his side, doing the same thing; each concentrated on the copy which had been assigned to them.

"What the fuck?" Alex muttered.

Barbara looked up, shocked. It was a cardinal rule of anchoring that you never, *ever*, utter a four-letter word near microphones that could be open. More than one promising broadcasting career had been cut short by that particular indiscretion, and Barbara was stunned that Alex had committed it.

"Alex! Do you know what you just said?"

He ignored her, reading from the page of copy in front of him.

"Authorities in northwestern Wisconsin report that two deer hunters today discovered a human skeleton in a heavily wooded area near Riverside. The remains were found scattered near a

shallow grave in a remote section of Burnett County. Authorities say they believe the body has been there for more than a year.

"No identification was found, but the remnants of an empty briefcase and small overnight bag were buried with the remains. Burnett County officials are checking local missing persons records and have alerted state authorities in Madison, and in Minnesota."

"What are you thinking?" Barbara asked, clearly puzzled. Then her eyes widened. "You don't think . . . oh, no . . . not Daniel Grabowski?"

"I don't know," Alex said. "The stuff about the briefcase and overnight bag caught my eye. Let's hope not."

"What should we do?"

"Can you call Phil? See if he can talk to those Wisconsin cops and get more details."

As Barbara ran to her desk, the light blinked on the anchor-desk phone. It was Linda Grabowski. She'd been listening to the radio and seemed on the verge of hysteria.

Alex tried to calm her. "We don't know anything for sure, Linda. We're trying to check. I'll let you know when we get anything more definite."

He promised to call her back an hour later.

The station helicopter shuddered slightly as it rose from the concrete pad, the engine straining to provide power, the rotor blades whining.

Alex held his breath, as if he were under water, struggling to break the surface and breathe again. He felt a touch of panic as the helicopter fought to break free of gravity's hold.

At about three hundred feet the Jet Ranger broke sharply to the left, darting like a dragonfly above the hangers of the St. Paul airport, the ground falling quickly away.

Phil Tinsley sat facing Alex, and next to him was Linda Grabowski. She looked exhausted but determined, drained from her suffering but somehow empowered by her desperation. She clutched the dental records she had retrieved from the family dentist the night before.

Each of them wore a headset that allowed them to communicate with one another over the noise of the engine and to listen to the pilot talk with the tower.

"What does Barclay think of us riding along in your chopper?" Phil asked.

"He doesn't know about it," Alex replied. "I had to persuade him to let me take the helicopter, and somehow I forgot to mention you. How about your boss?"

"He wonders what the hell's going on, but he likes the idea of you paying for the trip. Saves him money."

The sun was barely above the horizon as they skimmed over the suburbs of St. Paul, heading east toward the St. Croix River and then north to the empty grave in the Wisconsin woods.

"Are you okay?" Alex asked Linda. She looked at him abstractedly and nodded, but her eyes quickly returned to the window and the ground flashing by below.

"David?"

The pilot, David Eastman, looked over his shoulder.

"We'll set down in Siren first," Alex said, "then take off for Riverside. A couple of cops are still at the scene."

"Okay," Eastman said. "We're about forty-five minutes away."

Siren was the county seat of Burnett County, a hundred miles or so from the Twin Cities, and the new courthouse was located right next to the airport. The sheriff had promised Phil he'd have a deputy waiting to meet them.

"Once again, Phil," Alex said. "What do we know so far?"

"Not a lot, really. The skeleton was definitely that of a man, about the size of Daniel. And the description of the briefcase and suitcase seem to match Linda's memory of Daniel's stuff, but you know, those things tend to look alike. Only a few shreds of clothing were found, and they had no labels or anything."

Alex glanced at Linda, but she didn't seem to be listening.

"But," Phil continued, "Wisconsin has no reports of any missing person who matches, and no recent homicides where the victim is still unaccounted for. That's not a very good sign."

"How about Minnesota?"

"I checked the state crime wire last night, and there's nothing that seems to match on that, either."

The helicopter was following the river north, staying low, flying at about five hundred feet. High enough to avoid the power lines and water towers, but low enough to cause a few whitetail deer to scamper from the open and into the woods.

The terrain whitened and grew more rugged as they flew farther north, more snow, more woods, fewer towns. The snowmobile trails weaving through the countryside formed elaborate patterns.

"Siren is ten minutes ahead," Eastman said over the intercom. "We're cleared for landing, and the deputy is there waiting."

Alex knew the skeletal remains and the other physical evidence had already been moved to Siren. They would have the task of carrying them back to the Twin Cities, where forensic facilities were better. A final identification and perhaps a cause of death would be determined there.

Linda's hand was clammy where she held the dental records. Her heart hammered at the prospect of seeing her brother's briefcase and suitcase, of *knowing* for sure. But that's what she was here for, why she had insisted on coming along.

Alex noticed Linda's agitation and, for an instant, thought he heard her mutter something to herself.

The helicopter swept in over the Siren airport, hovered above the runway, and settled smoothly to earth not fifty feet from the deputy's squad car. They were all out of the chopper and on the ground before the rotor blades slowed to a stop.

"Fred Jensen's my name," the deputy said, holding his hat on with one hand, opening the car door with the other. "The sheriff is waiting to see you. His office is just a minute or two away."

The sheriff was a big fellow in his fifties, and looked even larger because his tight-fitting uniform hid neither his small potbelly nor his barrel chest. His name was Mike Tolliver, a man Phil said was known around the county with a mixture of affection and respect. A friendly fellow you don't fool with, Alex decided.

"Can I speak candidly?" Tolliver asked Phil while looking at Alex and Linda.

"Sure. Don't worry about these two. We wouldn't be here if it wasn't for them. They'll respect any confidential information."

"Okay. Here's what we know. The grave, as you'll see, is in the middle of nowhere. Not far from a small lake that's really more of a swamp. Nobody fishes it, and the only way you can get in there is on an old logging trail. It's county land, and until this year, had been closed to deer hunting."

"How far off the nearest road?" Alex asked.

"Maybe a half mile, but understand, even the roads up in that area are pretty rough, pretty desolate.

"At any rate, these two deer hunters were tramping around and came across the grave. It looks as if animals had dug it open, and parts of the . . . uh, remains . . . were scattered all around. Pieces of clothing, too."

He looked at Linda, but she was lost inside herself, as if she were preparing herself for a more important moment.

"We spent the better part of yesterday collecting everything we could find. The briefcase and suitcase were still near the grave, and because they're vinyl and not leather, there's quite a bit left of them. Enough to tell what they looked like, anyway. Nothing in either of them, though."

"No tracks or anything?" Phil asked.

"Nothin'. Time and weather took care of that. But you can look for yourselves when you get up there."

"Where are the . . . ?" Linda spoke suddenly, as if rising from a sleep.

"Just down the hall," Tolliver replied. "The coroner and a local dentist are standing by, so you can give them your records and look at what's left of the suitcase and briefcase at the same time. I wouldn't recommend looking at anything else, though."

After Linda left, Phil turned to the sheriff. "Now you can tell Alex what you told me about the skeleton."

"Well, we haven't had a lot of time, and don't claim to be experts in these things, but the coroner says it looks like three fingers of the right hand were all broken. Probably before the guy died, and probably one by one. No indication that a single blow broke 'em all."

"Goddamn them," Alex muttered. 'So they may have tortured the poor son of a bitch before they killed him."

"Looks that way. The killer may have done other things to him, too, but that'll have to wait for the full autopsy."

There was a tap on the door, and the deputy walked in.

"The lady says the briefcase and suitcase look just like her brother's," he said. "She's sure they're his. The state she's in, I'd get someone to take care of her. I don't think she's fit to travel right now. The dental exam's going to take an hour or so, anyway, and she wants to wait."

"Okay," Phil said. "Will you keep an eye on her, Sheriff? We'll pick her up on the way back."

"No problem. I've got a woman deputy who can stay with her."

The helicopter landed about thirty miles north of Siren—in the yard of an abandoned schoolhouse that was surrounded by a dense growth of red and white pine. A gravel road, rutted and potholed, passed by the front of the old school. A rusted swing set and a twisted slide stood off to one side, not far from a wooden outhouse as decrepit as the school.

One of Tolliver's deputies stood by the fender of a four-wheel-drive Blazer, the car's exhaust suspended in the cold November air.

"Quite a rig," he said, pointing to the helicopter.

"It gets us places in a hurry," the pilot agreed as he picked a small video camera from the cockpit and followed the others into the Blazer. David Eastman was a better pilot than photographer, but he had enough camera skills to do the job in a pinch.

"Have you talked to folks around here?" Phil asked the deputy, as they drove down the rutted road. "Anybody remember anything?"

"We've been to every house within five miles," he replied, "and my partner is still out knocking on doors. But nobody can remember nothin'. Who knows how long the body was buried, and there aren't that many houses. You could stand on this road for days and not see anybody."

The logging trail that was carved into the forest was barely passable, even with the four-wheel-drive vehicle. Old rotted logs lay across it, and low-hanging branches scraped the car's roof and blocked the view. The half mile seemed like ten miles, and Alex was glad he'd left Linda behind.

The burial site was as Tolliver had described it. The grave was no more than two feet deep, part of it covered by snow and leaves and dead branches. Two big oaks hovered over it, not more than twenty feet from the edge of the frozen lake.

Alex had known what to expect and had tried to prepare himself, but he was still shaken and saddened by what he saw. While he had never met Daniel Grabowski, in the past few days he felt he had grown to know him. And this is what was left, Alex thought, a half-open hole in the ground that denied Daniel dignity even in death.

"We've searched every inch of this place," the deputy said, "but until the snow melts in spring, we won't really know if we missed anything."

"We can't wait until spring," Phil said. "Can't you scrape everything up, melt the snow, and sift it through a screen?"

"Don't know about that," the deputy conceded. "You'll have to talk to the sheriff. Be a hell of a lot of work, that's for sure."

Alex and Phil divided the area into two rings and walked in ever-widening circles, eyes on the ground, with Eastman recording it all on videotape. They found nothing more.

"I told you we checked it over real good," the deputy said.

"You know," Alex said, looking around, "you don't just happen onto a place like this. It's too remote, too out-of-the-way. Somebody had to know this area, to have some idea this spot was back here."

"What are you getting at?" Phil asked.

"I just think somebody ought to check out whoever owns the land around here. I know this is county property, but how about the adjoining land?"

"The sheriff should be able to do that," Phil said. "All the records ought to be back in the courthouse."

"Does anybody own any big cabins or hunting lodges up here?" Alex asked the deputy. "Or big chunks of property?"

"Not that I know of. But we don't get up to this part of the county often. There's never been any trouble up here, until now."

When the helicopter returned to Siren, they found Linda sitting in one corner of the airport flight office, head in her hands, sobbing uncontrollably.

No questions were necessary.

Sheriff Tolliver was standing by the door, obviously relieved they had arrived.

"The coroner can't be absolutely certain, but the dental X rays seem pretty positive," he said. "Not much question that it was Daniel Grabowski in that grave."

Alex walked over to Linda and knelt beside her, resting his hand on her arm. He didn't know what to say, but he thought he should try. "At least it's over, Linda. no more wondering, no more waiting. You can get on with your life now."

"I just don't understand," she whispered. "Who would do this to him? Just let him lie there until the animals . . ."

"Take it easy, Linda."

"It's unbearable. What am I going to do? They killed Daniel."

As Alex was trying to comfort Linda, leading her back to the helicopter, Phil pulled Tolliver aside. "Since the body was found up here," Phil said, "I know you have the primary jurisdiction. But because he came up missing in Minneapolis, I'd like to keep working with you as closely as possible."

The sheriff agreed, saying he'd check all the property tax records and bring in additional personnel and equipment to search the burial site more thoroughly.

"We haven't had a murder up here in years," he added. "I'll be looking for all of the help I can get."

"You'll have it," Phil said as he closed the helicopter door. "We'll pass on the autopsy results as soon as we hear."

With that, the helicopter lifted off, carying its passengers back to the Twin Cities—along with a cargo of bones.

Twenty-two

The words Alex had written moments before stared back at him from the TelePrompTer. He could barely bring himself to read them.

"Channel Seven News has confirmed the identity of the man whose skeleton was found in a shallow grave in northwestern Wisconsin. He was thirty-four-year-old Daniel Grabowski, a free-lance writer from Minneapolis who disappeared almost a year-and-a-half ago."

Eastman's videotape then appeared on the screen.

"The grave was discovered yesterday by two deer hunters in a remote area of Burnett county, near Riverside. Authorities searched the burial site, but found only remnants of clothing and a briefcase and small suitcase which belonged to Grabowski. The remains of the body have been brought to the Twin Cities, where an autopsy will be conducted to determine the exact cause of death.

"Burnett County sheriff Mike Tolliver says it's not known whether Grabowski was slain in Wisconsin or killed elsewhere and his body buried there. Minneapolis police are cooperat-

168

*ing with Tolliver in the investigation, but so far, he says, there
are no suspects and no apparent motive for the murder."*

Alex noticed Barclay standing in the shadows of the studio, waiting for the newscast to end. His face was grim. "What do you make of this?" he asked as Alex walked off the set. "Puts a whole new light on things, doesn't it?"

"No question about it," Alex replied. "Suddenly, we're in the middle of a murder. I wasn't counting on that."

"What do you want to do?"

"Keep going, I guess, but it isn't going to be easy. We're never going to know everything Daniel knew about Steele, and it means this whole thing could be a lot more dangerous than we had let ourselves believe."

Barbara intercepted them as they walked across the newsroom. "I just got a call from Barry Stensrud. He says he'll do anything we ask; he blames himself for Daniel's death. The poor guy sounded really broken up on the phone."

"He was right about one thing," Alex said.

"What's that?"

"About playing with fire. He knew what he was talking about."

Alex found John Knowles waiting by his desk, looking more morose than ever. "I give up," he said. "I've tried every fucking combination I can think of. I'm seeing baseball players in my sleep. It's impossible."

"Relax, John. It's not the end of the world. Maybe I was wrong about the poster; it seemed like a good idea at the time."

"You may still be right, but I don't know what to try next."

"It's a pity we can't figure it out," Alex said, "because it looks now like the password died with Daniel."

"What have I missed?" Knowles asked, more of himself than Alex. "I've tried names, uniform numbers, batting averages. . . ."

"Maybe we've been taking the poster too literally," Alex said as he led Knowles toward the elevator. "We know Daniel didn't know or care much about baseball. Maybe he used the poster in a more generic sense."

"Keep going," Knowles urged.

"Even if Daniel wasn't an expert, he may have known some of the common terms. Like diamond, or home run, or triple. Some-

thing that had nothing to do specifically with the Twins or the
World Series."

They left the elevator and walked into Knowles's office. John sat
down at the computer.

"Why don't you try a few?" Alex said. "Like umpire. Ballpark.
Stadium. Sacrifice. Stolen base."

Knowles typed the words into the computer as quickly as Alex
said them. PASSWORD? kept blinking back at them.

"What was the last thing you mentioned?" Knowles asked. "Stolen base?"

"Christ!" Alex shouted. "That has to be it."

Knowles was typing in the word: STEAL.

God, why hadn't they seen it before? The computer screen was
suddenly filled. Daniel Grabowski's secret had finally been unlocked.

They stared at the words, which now took on a ghostly quality.
They were the words of a dead man, words buried in a computer
file for longer than their author lay buried in a shallow grave.

If you are reading this, it means two things: my fears about
my own safety were well founded, and you were smart
enough and caring enough to discover the disc and the key,
and to solve my little password puzzle.

I assume you are friends, since I am confident my enemies
would have simply destroyed the disc and made no effort to
discover its contents. I also assume you are aware of the story
I was working on, and are as determined as I am to reveal
the truth about Judge Emmett M. Steele.

I hope you will treat part of what I tell you as confidential.
I would not like Linda, who's very fragile and given to break-
downs, or other members of my family to know the entire
truth, and I trust you will respect my wishes.

I first became interested in Judge Steele because I am gay
. . . yes, I can say that now! . . . and through some of my gay
friends, I heard rumors of a judge who was abusing his power
to entice young boys into a life of degradation and prostitution. Some of his young victims were treated viciously and
made the subject of pornographic videos without their knowledge or consent.

I also heard that Judge Steele enforced their silence

through promises of leniency in court or, failing that, through threats and intimidation.

I believe every person should have the right to pursue his or her own sexual preference and to live a life free of ridicule and harassment. I despise pedophiles and other predators of the young, whether gay or straight, who turn the innocence of childhood into fodder for their own sexual appetites. They ruin young lives before they have a chance to flower and mature.

I especially despise adults who are in a position to help young people get past their problems and who take advantage of them instead.

Judge Steele is such a person. He is a truly evil man. He must be exposed. He must be stopped.

I desperately wish I had declared my own sexual preference years ago, that I had come out of the closet and lived my life in the open, so that Linda and others could know and remember me as I really am. I lived a lie, and I regret that now. I planned to declare my sexuality as part of the article on Steele, to demonstrate to skeptics that we in the gay community are as sickened as the rest of society by the atrocities of pedophiles.

But it's too late now. The story was stillborn. You'll have to carry on where I left off, and I can only wish you Godspeed.

The key you found with the disc is for safety-deposit box #2301 at the Lincoln Bank, on Lake Street. You'll need Linda's signature to get into it. In the box, you'll find signed affidavits from three of Steele's young victims, all of whom have sworn they were paid to have sex with the judge when they were still juveniles. I have promised them confidentiality for purposes of my story, but all three have agreed to testify before any grand jury that might subsequently be called.

I can only hope they're still around, and still willing to cooperate. I found them by weeks of searching and talking, finally persuading them to step forward and tell their stories. I was able to establish a trusting relationship with them. May you have the same luck with them, or with others you may find.

Also in the safety-deposit box, you'll find the first part of my story on Steele, as much as I was able to get done. When

City Magazine told me they wouldn't publish the story because of the pressure they were feeling, I decided to seek another outlet. I am leaving on that mission now, and leave behind this disc and the contents of the safety-deposit box in case something happens to me.

I can't ignore the threats, but I hope these words will be seen by no one but me, and that I can laugh at my paranoia as I erase this disc, holding a printed copy of the Steele story in my hand.

Alex and Knowles said nothing as they stared at the screen. They scrolled back the computer pages and read them again.

"The last will and testament of Daniel Grabowski," Alex finally said. "Poor bastard. The saddest thing is that he had to face this all alone. He didn't have anybody to fall back on, even to talk with. It was just him and the story. Him against the judge, and it sure as hell was no contest."

"I'd like to know what happened on that last day, the day he took off on—what'd he call it?—his mission."

"We'll probably never know," Alex said. "Poor guy had to take the bus, for Christ's sake. Who knows how far he got?"

"We'll have to tell Linda we discovered the password," Knowles said, "because we'll need her signature to get into the safety-deposit box. Do we tell her about him being gay?"

"No. To my mind, by reading this, we've given Daniel our word. We can tell her everything but that part. And we should get to that safety-deposit box tomorrow."

"Not tomorrow," Knowles said. "It's Thanksgiving, remember? Banks aren't open."

"That's right. I forgot. We'll just have to wait till Friday then."

Alex was surprised to learn that he and Barbara had been given Thanksgiving afternoon off. The televised football game would wipe out the normal local news programs during the day, leaving little for Alex and Barbara to do.

Barbara took advantage of the break to invite Alex, Phil, John Knowles and Linda Grabowski to her apartment for Thanksgiving dinner.

"Can you really cook?" Alex had asked her.

"I'm a farm girl, remember? I learned to cook almost before I learned to walk."

At dinner, Linda seemed very withdrawn. She said little, but nodded and laughed quietly to herself from time to time.

Out of deference to Linda, they had discussed everything except the death of Daniel and what it meant to their investigation. But after the dishes were cleared, as they were sitting, sipping coffee, the subject finally came up.

Suddenly Linda began speaking, to no one in particular. "It's funny. I keep seeing him, remembering him as a little boy. That's when we were the closest, after our dad died, and when Mom was so sick. I was kind of a second mother to him, and we spent a lot of time together."

Barbara was pouring more coffee, but Linda didn't notice.

"Later, we kind of grew apart. He still lived with me, but I didn't know many of his friends. He seemed to spend a lot of time alone or traveling by himself. I always felt guilty that he wasn't happier, that I couldn't do something to make him happier. But he seemed to live in his own little world, and he never really let me be part of it. I could have helped him, but I failed him. Someone has killed my baby brother, and now I can never tell him how much I loved him."

John reached out to comfort her, and when she did not respond, they sat quietly around the table. The silence was broken by the beeper on Phil's belt. He went to the phone to collect his message and was back a moment later.

"Two things," he said. "The autopsy's done and the report is ready, and Mike Tolliver is faxing the list of property owners in the Riverside area. The list should be at my office in a half hour."

"What about the autopsy?" Alex asked.

"They wouldn't tell me anything over the phone, said it's all in the report. The medical examiner will be around for a while to explain, so we ought to get over there soon."

They grabbed their coats, said their goodbyes, and hurried out the door, leaving Knowles to help Barbara clean up and to get Linda home safely.

The medical examiner, Dr. George Huffman, was still in his white lab coat when Alex and Phil arrived at the St. Paul-Ramsey Medical Center.

"Do you always work on Thanksgiving?" Alex asked.

"Not usually, but on something like this, yes. We don't see these kinds of things often."

Alex guessed Huffman to be in his early forties, but he knew he could be off by ten years in either direction. Huffman was slight of build and balding, with a few strands of brown hair brushed to one side to cover as much as possible. He wore thick glasses, which kept sliding down on his nose, and which he nervously kept pushing back up.

"So what can you tell us?" Phil asked.

"I'll try to keep it as nontechnical as possible," Huffman said. "The technical stuff is all in the report, if you're interested."

"We appreciate that," Phil said.

"The first thing you have to understand is that dealing with a skeleton is a lot different than dealing with a body. It makes it much more difficult for us. No organs, no skin tissue, not even all of the bones makes the job very tough. Most of our normal tests and techniques are of no use."

"I can understand that," Phil said, "but you found something."

"Something, but not much. Just so you know at the outset."

"Okay. Go ahead."

"First, an inventory. The skull was pretty much intact, although a number of the teeth were missing. They probably just fell out of the sockets when the gum tissue disappeared. Most of the vertebrae were there, about half the ribs, and most of the extremities, although not the right foot or the left hand. Animals must have carried those away."

Alex swallowed hard.

"The local coroner was right about the right hand fingers. They appear to have been crushed, maybe with a pliers or something similar. It doesn't look like the work of an animal."

"The cause of death?" Phil asked.

"Just coming to that. There were no signs of gunshot wounds, of any holes in the skull or notches or metal tracings on any of the bones. Similarly, there'd be no evidence of stab wounds. I can't rule either method out entirely, but I don't believe the victim was shot or stabbed."

"So what does that leave?" Alex asked, trying to hide his impatience.

"On the basis of my examination," Huffman said, "I'd say the man was beaten to death. Beaten about the head, with some kind of blunt instrument. There were several fracture lines on the skull, coming from different directions, as if he'd suffered a series of blows. The nose seemes to have been broken, too, although I'm not certain on that."

"God Almighty," Alex breathed. "They broke his fingers and then beat him to death."

"It wasn't a pretty way to die, that's for sure," Huffman agreed.

"What kind of blunt instrument?" Phil asked.

"It could have been anything. A rock, a hammer, a fence post. Again, if there were a body instead of a skeleton, I could tell you a lot more."

"Any ideas on *where* he died?"

"None. It's impossible to tell from what I have. Blood or some other evidence at the scene may tell you, but I can't. It's too long ago and there's too little left to even venture a guess."

"Anything else?" Alex asked.

"Not really. I'm going to call in a couple of my colleagues from the university for a second opinion, since this is such an unusual case, but I suspect they'll reaffirm my findings.

"As I say, this fellow died a pretty horrible death."

Alex and Phil said little to one another as they moved quickly through light holiday traffic. Each was caught up in his own thoughts, trying to translate the dispassionate dissertation they had just heard into the reality of a violent death.

"I'll bet they killed him there, in the woods," Phil said.

"Why's that?"

"Think about it. You don't torture a guy, then beat him to death, in the middle of the goddamned city. Not when you're trying to get him to talk. I bet they took him out there in the middle of nowhere and let him scream until they ran out of patience."

"You're probably right," Alex muttered. "And when they didn't get anything out of him, they shook down the apartment. Faked a burglary."

"I still don't understand why they didn't try to get to Linda," Phil said, "to find out what she might know."

"That is strange. They must have thought it wasn't worth the trouble. I'll bet they kept an eye on her, though."

They took the Fifth Street exit off the freeway and pulled up in front of City Hall, finding no shortage of parking spots on the holiday. The homicide office, like the street, was nearly empty, too.

Sheriff Tolliver's list of property owners was on Phil's desk. Maybe a hundred names or so, in alphabetical order, complete with legal descriptions of the properties, their tax bills, and the home addresses of the owners.

A note from Tolliver said the list included everybody who owned land within a ten-mile radius of the grave site.

Phil and Alex split the list in half, their eyes moving down the pages, looking for any familiar names, checking off anyone from the Twin Cities.

Alex had the "A through L" half of the list, and was on the next-to-last page when he suddenly stopped and took a sharp breath. A gasp, really.

There, halfway down the page, was a familiar name: HODGES, NATHANIEL F., 2242 PINETREE DRIVE, EDINA, MINNESOTA.

"I'll be a son of a bitch," Alex said.

"Isn't he the judge your friend is married to?" Phil asked. "The one Barbara asked me about?"

"That's right. There's got to be some explanation."

"It could be nothing," Phil said. "Still, it's strange, isn't it?"

They went over the list of names again, more carefully this time, and still found no others that were familiar.

"I'll run all of Twin Cities' names through the computer," Phil said, "and see if anything else turns up."

Alex knew the Thanksgiving dinner didn't account for the funny feeling in his stomach.

Twenty-three

The dog bounded across the park, tail high, neck outstretched, lunging against the leash. A squirrel dashed into its path, defiantly scampering toward a huge elm. The dog broke free and made a headlong but futile attempt to reach the squirrel before it reached the tree.

"Jesus," Rick gasped, trying to catch his breath. "Is this what you call taking him for a walk?"

Roger leaned against the tree, trying to unwrap the leash from around the trunk. "He sleeps all day and all night—until I take him out. Then he goes crazy."

The dog, a black Lab, whined feverishly, waiting to be freed.

"If I don't take him out twice a day, he pisses all over the rugs. I should get rid of him."

The cold was numbing, and the sweat from the run seemed to freeze on their faces almost instantly. They knew they couldn't stand and rest for long.

Rick had arrived at Roger's house several nights before, accepting the scrawled invitation on Roger's note, trading his cold refuge by the dumpster for the warmth of a real bed.

"You're welcome to stay as long as you like," Roger had told him. "I'm not here that much, and I've got plenty of room."

"I don't understand," Rick had said. "Why are you doing this? You don't even know me."

"In a way, I do. I've been there; I think I know what you're feeling. I'd hate to see you make the same mistakes I did."

"How did you wind up in that place? With *him*?"

"I started just like you, only he was gentler with me for some reason. The money was good and I had nowhere else to go."

"What do you do for him?"

"Not what you're thinking. Not anymore. He likes 'em younger than me. I just keep the house clean, do some shopping and cooking, and now and then tend to somebody like you."

"Why do you keep doing it?"

"To stay off the streets, to earn enough money to afford my own place."

"But you've got your own place now, and you're still there."

"Not for long, I hope. Not after seeing what he did to you. He's getting worse all the time."

The leash and the dog were now free of the tree and back in Roger's grasp. They began walking back toward Roger's house, pulled along by the Labrador.

For days, Rick had pressed Roger to tell him about the man who had hurt him: who he was, and what he had done to him. Roger had remained silent, saying only that the time was not yet right.

"When will it be right?" Rick had asked.

"When I figure a way to get out without getting hurt."

Linda stood with Alex and Phil in the small, vaultlike basement of the Lincoln Bank, surrounded by rooms of floor-to-ceiling safety-deposit boxes. The clerk, a woman about fifty, was solicitous as she examined Linda's signature and the key to the box.

"I'm terribly sorry about your brother," she said. "I heard about it on the news."

"Did you know Daniel?" Linda asked.

"Not really, but I do recall him coming in a couple of times. The name stuck in my head for some reason. Funny how you remember some names and not others. He seemed shy, never said much."

"Was he always alone?" Phil asked.

"Yes, I think so," the clerk said as she handed them the box and started to leave. "I don't recall ever seeing him with anyone."

The box was long and narrow and crammed with papers. One small sealed envelope, the size of a greeting card, was addressed to Linda. She retreated to one corner with it while Alex and Phil sorted through the other documents.

The three affidavits varied in length from one to three pages; each told the story of various sexual encounters with Judge Steele, but each differed significantly in language and style, and each bore a different signature. All apparently were typed by the same person.

"It looks like Daniel may have recorded these statements and then transcribed them," Phil said. "But he got each of the kids to sign them."

Alex and Phil read through them quickly, immediately noting that one had been signed by Kevin Marcus.

"Our friend Sleet," Phil said. "No wonder he wanted that one-way ticket to California."

The other two affidavits bore names they did not recognize: John Martin and Rico Sanchez.

"We've got a problem," Phil said, after skimming the documents. "Only one of these guys, Marcus, claims to have actually seen Steele at the time they were having sex. The other two say they were blindfolded and that they recognized his voice during later court appearances."

"Isn't that good enough?" Alex asked.

"Depends on whether we can find Marcus, and whether he's still willing to cooperate. The voice identifications would be useless in court. Steele would tear those guys apart."

"What *about* Marcus?" Alex asked. "Did you ever hear from your cop friend in L.A.? How many days has it been, anyway?"

"We've missed each other on the phone a couple of times, but I hope to connect today. I do have other cases I'm working on."

"Sorry. I get too anxious."

In their statements, all three of the boys claimed they were between fifteen and seventeen years old during their first encounter with the judge. All three described similar experiences: a contact shortly after they got out of juvenile court by a man they'd never seen before, then a medical exam by a doctor whose name they never learned, and finally a blindfolded trip by car to what they said was the judge's house.

"*When this happened the first time,*" Martin's statement said, "*I was only fifteen. I didn't have no money, didn't have no place to go. My folks kicked me out of the house. I'd never done what I did there before. He liked hurting me, but the money was good so I kept going back. I saw movies of myself with a man in a hood. He had a real hoarse voice. I heard it again later when I was back in court. It was Judge Steele.*"

Sleet's statement said he had started out the same way, but that he later had become a houseboy for the judge, and no longer was blindfolded.

"*I finally got sick of it,*" the affidavit said, "*sick of the judge and what he was doing to me and the others. He doesn't just like sex, he likes to control people, to hurt people. I'm getting out, and I've told him so. He said he'll help me get to California if I promise to never come back.*"

Linda joined them, tucking Daniel's note in her purse. Her eyes welled with tears, and her voice wavered. "He just said goodbye. He knew if I ever read the note, something would have happened to him. He thanked me for taking care of him and said he loved me." Her eyes could not contain the tears. "It makes me angry. He got to say goodbye to me, but I didn't have the same chance. Why would he do that to me?"

"Because he wanted to protect you," Alex said.

They gathered up the papers and left, Alex and Phil on either side of Linda, helping her up the stairs and out into the bright sunshine of another cold November day.

Alex met John Knowles when he returned to the station, and showed him what they'd found in the safety-deposit box.

Knowles studied the documents and Grabowski's article. "Did you read his story?" he asked.

"Not yet," Alex said. "We just looked at the affidavits."

"Shit, it's no surprise Steele knew about his story. Daniel confronted him, for Christ's sake. The story's full of Steele's denials and denunciations of Daniel."

"No shit," Alex said.

"The story even quotes Steele threatening Daniel. '*If you print this heap of lies, you'll forever regret it.*'"

"No wonder Steele was so desperate to find the documents and the computer file," Alex said.

Knowles nodded. "Which reminds me, now that we've found the password and the safety-deposit box, what can I do next? I don't want to just sit around."

Alex thought for a moment. "How'd you like to go to New Ulm?"

"What's in New Ulm?"

"Steele's boyhood home, remember? I'd been planning to go myself to see if I could dig up anything out of his past. But even more, to see if there's any clue as to how he's survived this long without being caught. I know he had a human mother and father, so how could they deliver this monster into the world?"

Knowles seemed unconvinced, and perhaps worried that Alex was becoming too obsessed. "I'll give it a try," Knowles said, "but don't blame me if it bombs, and if word gets back to Steele."

"We've got to get all the information we can on this man," Alex insisted.

"Are you worried about a lawsuit later?" Knowles asked.

Alex pulled back. "Maybe," he answered bitterly. "I just don't want to be accused of leaving any of the proverbial stones unturned."

"What do you suggest?" Knowles asked.

"Check old school records, old newspapers. Talk to any old family friends who may still be around. You're the investigative reporter, for God's sake."

"How do I explain this little inquiry of mine?"

"If anybody presses you, tell them we're planning a special tribute to the judge when he ascends to the Supreme Court. Kind of a surprise 'This Is Your Life' special, and that you're responsible for researching his childhood."

Knowles still found it difficult to hide his skepticism. "Ten to one it'll turn out to be a waste of time. But if you're really serious, I'll go down next week—right after the memorial service for Daniel."

Alex woke early on Saturday, about seven. Two hours to go, he told himself—two hours until Pat arrives. He quickly showered and dressed. Then he made coffee, fed the cat, read the paper, and watched the clock.

Still an hour to go.

He nervously wandered the house—tidying up, checking himself in the mirror, fixing the fire, putting a tape into the stereo.

Still a half hour to go.

Think about something else, he told himself. He walked to the kitchen and poured another cup of coffee, trying to sort through his feelings about Pat and the problems he still faced in the investigation.

Like, where is Sleet, and if I find him, will he be willing to talk? Who are John Martin and Rico Sanchez, the other names on Daniel's affidavits? Where should I begin looking for them? Then there was Roger Anderson, the elusive valet. Would he ever contact the bartender at Mr. K's? And what did Pat know about the Hodges's Wisconsin property?

Christ, Alex thought, it's damn near the first of December, and in a lot of ways, I'm no closer to the end of this story than I was two weeks ago. And, in a month, Steele's going to be chief justice of the Supreme Court. *Get going, Alex.*

He walked to the living room as Pat's car pulled into the driveway. He watched her striding up the sidewalk. He didn't wait for the doorbell to ring.

Alex wasn't sure how much time had passed, how long they had slept. He could only marvel at the wonder of what had happened. He could hear Seuss pawing and pushing at the closed door of the bedroom, waking him but causing no stir in the warm body next to his. Alex lay on his back, staring at the speckled, shadowy finish of the ceiling, feeling her warm, steady breath on his neck.

It was day, but the room was dark, the blinds closing out the light of morning. Her head was cradled against his shoulder, her leg lay over his, warm and smooth, her hand resting lightly on his stomach. He matched the rhythm of his breathing to hers, allowing only his eyes to move, fearing anything more would threaten her sleep and his overwhelming sense of peace and satisfaction.

Even Seuss seemed to understand his wishes and finally retreated from the door.

Alex had been determined to remember every moment, every explicit, exquisite detail. But now, in the darkened calm of the bedroom, it was all a maddening blur. Like a videotape in fast-forward: images, yes, but no single frame distinguishable from the one before or the one after. It had all happened too fast. She was at the door, then in his arms, their clothes falling away as they somehow moved through the house and fell onto the bed.

Then a dizzying jumble that made his mind and memory spin— until at last, the sweet silence of exhaustion.

Had they spoken even one word? They must have, but he had no clear memory of words—only the rush of the most intense and urgent physical desire he had ever felt.

How could he explain it? He couldn't, not to himself, and certainly not to others. But he had known since the night in the park that it would come to this. And it was now clear that Pat Hodges had known it as well.

Her breathing did not change, her eyes did not open, but he felt her hand move slowly down his stomach to cover the softness of him. She had the touch of a butterfly, the tips of her fingers landing lightly, never still . . .

"Good morning," she whispered into his ear, snuggling closer. She lifted her leg slightly, guiding him into her. "Ahhh," she breathed, "a perfect fit."

They lay still, content this time to simply absorb the extraordinary sensations their coupled bodies created.

"You're wonderful," he said, kissing her still-closed eyes. "You know that, don't you?"

"I hope so," she answered, shifting slightly to draw him deeper into her. Then her body lifted, and she was above him, her eyes fastened on his, unwavering. Her breasts tickled his chest, her hips moving ever so slowly.

This time there would be no blur. They were in slow motion. Even at the end, a building, blinding surge welded them together for what seemed like minutes, neither of them willing to release their grip until the last flame subsided.

"God, you're lovely," Alex said, standing at the bathroom doorway, watching her towel down after her shower. She was just as he had imagined that first day at the restaurant: hair wet and mussed, skin a steamy, misty pink, her eyes alive, face radiant.

"I've never felt better in my entire life," she said, turning to face him, watching his eyes, showing no shyness, making no effort to cover herself.

Alex walked to her and took the towel. He kissed her neck and her shoulders, feeling the dampness of her hair against his face, touching the towel to the drops of moisture still clinging to her back and between her breasts.

"I don't know what you do to me," she said, "but you always have. It's unbelievable."

Alex wrapped the towel around her and took her hand. They walked slowly to the living room, and she watched as he put more wood on the fire. They could feel the warmth across the room as they snuggled on the couch.

"If Nathaniel knew about this . . . about us . . . he'd be terribly hurt and angry," she said. "His ego would be hurt. He'd think this shouldn't happen to people like us; we're too respectable. But deep down, if he'd ever admit it, I don't think he'd really care. We haven't made love for a long time. He lost interest long ago."

"I have to ask you something," Alex said. "It has to do with Nathaniel, and I don't pretend to understand it."

"What's that?" she asked, suddenly nervous, on guard.

"Do you and Nathaniel own any property in Wisconsin?"

She pulled back, looking puzzled. "Sure. But how'd you know?"

"It just came up," he said, avoiding a direct answer. "Can you tell me about it?"

"Nathaniel bought it a long time ago. Before we were married. As an investment, he says. It's about ten acres or so, on a lake. We haven't been up there for years. I've only seen it once or twice, and then just to walk around a bit."

"No cabin or anything?"

"No, we've never had the time, although we did talk once of building a retirement home up there. Like a lot of plans, that one kind of got lost. I think there's an old boat on the lake, but not much else. What's this all about anyway?"

"We got a list of all the property owners within ten miles or so of Daniel's grave, and Nathaniel's name was on it . . . the only one that popped out."

"What? Our property was that close to Daniel's—"

"Just a few miles north."

"I can't believe it," she said.

Alex wanted to believe her, to give her the benefit of the doubt. "It's probably just a coincidence," he said. "We're running all the local names on the list through the police computer system to check any other possible connections to Daniel or to Steele."

"Who else saw the list?" she asked.

"Phil Tinsley, the Minneapolis cop who's investigating Daniel's death. Barbara's friend."

"What did he think?"

"That it was strange."

"So he knows about me, too?"

"Only that you're married to Nathaniel."

Pat slowly shook her head as Alex continued to probe. "You said you haven't been up there for years. But does Nathaniel ever go up by himself? To fish or hunt?"

"I don't think so," she said. "He's certainly not much of an outdoorsman, and he's never talked about it. I don't keep close track of what he does or where he goes."

Alex saw a slight shiver pass through her body. "Worried?" he asked.

"Yes, but, as you say, it's probably just a crazy coincidence."

He could not keep the old doubts at bay. "Maybe it's time to get dressed, huh?" he said.

"Maybe so," she replied.

Few words were exchanged as they slowly, now shyly, returned to the clothes they had so hurriedly abandoned only hours before.

The talk about the Wisconsin property had given Alex pause, suddenly renewing his mistrust, reminding him again of how deeply he had gotten into all of this. And Pat clearly noticed the change in his mood, the new distance between them.

As Alex led Pat to the door, both tried to act normal, but it was difficult to disguise their confusion. And when they exchanged goodbyes, the memory of their lovemaking was already fading.

"I'll call you," Alex said absently and turned back into the house as she left.

Spending Saturday night alone was nothing new to Alex, but this night he felt more alone than he had in years.

The hours since Pat had left had passed slowly, and he found himself thinking of little else. The more he thought about her, the more confused and angry he became. He knew he was falling in love again, but—hard as he tried—he could not escape the feeling that he was being set up. Where was she leading him?

Calm down, calm down; you're panicking.

But he could not ignore his suspicions. The stronger his feelings, the more anxious he became.

What next? he wondered. Where did he want it to lead?

He thought again about his own marriage, and the wreck he had made of it. Two children he seldom saw and hardly knew anymore, and a former wife growing increasingly bitter by his estrangement from them.

Without answers to any of his questions, he drifted off to sleep, the shadows from the flames in the fireplace still dancing on the walls.

Twenty-four

The interior of the tiny St. Kungunda Polish Catholic Church would have been dim on a sunny day, but under a cloudy day almost no light passed through the row of small stained glass windows.

"We are gathered here to remember our friend and loved one, Daniel Grabowski, a young man, one of God's chosen, who died long before his time . . ."

Only the first two pews of the church were filled with mourners—not more than two dozen in all. Linda and her Uncle Frank and a handful of Grabowski cousins and spouses were huddled together in the first row, eyes still dry and staring straight ahead.

Alex, Barbara, John Knowles, and Barry Stensrud sat behind them, and across the aisle, some of Daniel's friends and a few parishioners who had stayed on after morning mass. Phil Tinsley was at the back of the church, trying not to look like a cop, watching as the guests arrived and noting who did and did not sign the register.

"God does not always provide easy answers to difficult questions, and we must have the faith to believe Daniel's life was not in vain . . ."

The priest's voice sounded distant, although he was no more than twenty feet from them. A small man, his body was almost lost in the folds of his white chasuble and his words echoed in the unpeopled space of the sanctuary.

"We must have the courage to go forward," he said, looking directly at Linda, "to put this tragedy behind us. To remember Daniel with fondness and with love, to reserve a special place for him in our hearts and our memories. But we must live our lives to the fullest, as Daniel would have wanted us to do, trusting in God's wisdom and His ways."

Linda leaned against her uncle's shoulder, and from behind, Alex could see her body heave in silent sobs.

As the mass ended, the soft sounds of the Polish "Dobry Jezus" echoed in the church, three times over. "A nasz Panie, die mu wiechnie spochewanie. Good Jesus, our Lord, give him eternal rest."

The priest walked from the altar and touched Linda's hand, whispering words of comfort to her, before moving slowly toward a door at the side of the church.

The memorial service was simple, as Linda had wanted it to be. No testimonials from friends, no reception afterward. Just a gentle goodbye to Daniel.

Linda was still in her seat, head bowed, as the rest of the small crowd walked quietly to the back of the church; mostly strangers to one another, they were bound together for a moment by the death of a young man many of them had not even known.

"Alex, can you step over here for a minute?" It was Phil, beckoning him toward one of the mourners, a young man who stood near the door looking uncomfortable.

"I'd like you to meet John Martin," Phil said, as Alex extended his hand. The signature on the affidavit in the safety-deposit box flashed in front of Alex's eyes. "I recognized the name on the guest register."

"Hello, John," Alex said. "I'm glad we found you. We didn't know where to start looking. I'm sure Daniel would appreciate you being here."

"How'd you know about me?" Martin asked, glancing at the door.

"We'll be glad to fill you in," Alex replied. "But I don't think this is the right place or time. Can you tell me where you live or work? Someplace to contact you. I know Daniel would have wanted you to help us—especially now."

"I don't know anything," Martin protested. "I just came because I was Daniel's friend."

His nervousness seemed to be edging toward real fear, and Alex tried to calm him.

"Look, we just want to talk. No big deal. If you really were Daniel's friend, I'd think you'd want to help." Martin started to walk away. "Please don't make things difficult, John," Alex said, grabbing his arm, deciding to try a more persuasive tactic. "Mr. Tinsley here is a police officer, but we want to keep this whole thing unofficial for now. Just a conversation between you and us."

Martin looked at Phil, then back at Alex, and saw no escape. "Okay, okay, I don't want any trouble," he said, freeing his arm of Alex's grasp. "I live at the Marymount apartments on Lyndale, and work at the Phillips gas station on Park and Franklin. You can usually find me at one place or the other. But, remember, I don't know anything. I was just his friend."

As Martin walked out the door, Alex realized that only Barbara was still waiting. Linda was inside the church, John Knowles sitting next to her, saying nothing. Everyone else had left, including Barry Stensrud.

"Barry was on deadline at the magazine and had to leave," Barbara said, "and John says we should go on ahead. He'll wait for Linda and take her home when she's ready to go."

"Am I missing something?" Alex asked, as they walked down the sidewalk.

"You mean with John and Linda?"

"Yes. Is something going on between them?"

"I'm not sure," Barbara said. "I first noticed it at dinner on Thanksgiving. They've become very good friends, but I think it may go beyond that."

"No kidding. They seem like an unlikely couple."

"Oh, I don't know," Barbara said. "They're both alone now, and Linda certainly needs the support."

"I thought she seemed better on Thanksgiving," Alex said, "but I'm not sure now. She looks like she's had a relapse."

"I know," Barbara said. "I wish I knew what more to do."

Roger was sprawled on the living room couch, the black Lab's head nuzzled against him. Rick sat across the room. A game show was on television, but neither of them seemed to be watching it.

"Have you ever heard of Judge Emmett Steele?" Roger asked suddenly.

"That's him, isn't it?" Rick said, leaning forward in his chair. "I knew I'd heard that voice before! He was hanging around juvenile court the last time I was there, holding some kind of a meeting with the judges. That son of bitch!"

"Did he see you?" Roger asked.

"Damned if I know. I was just sitting there waiting for my case to come up when he walked around the halls. But I remember his voice."

"What were you up for?"

"For boosting a car with a couple of other guys. I got sent to Red Wing for a few months, and got a year's probation."

"Your first time at reform school?"

"Yeah," Rick said. "It's the last time I want to be in a place like that."

"That's probably how you ended up at his house," Roger said.

"What do you mean?"

"Steele probably spotted you that day in court, liked what he saw, and then kept track of you. That's how he usually does it."

"Why'd you decide to tell me about him now?" Rick asked.

Roger pushed the dog's head aside and stood up, stretching.

"Because I think I know what I'm going to do now."

"What's that?"

"Leave," Roger said. "Quit. As soon as I can figure a way to get out."

"Fuck him. Just walk out," Rick said.

"It's not that simple. Steele won't be happy. I know too much; I've seen too much, too many kids fucked over, too much pain."

"What the hell can he do?" Rick asked.

"That's what worries me. He could make life miserable, if he wants to."

"Like what?"

"Like trying to keep me from getting another job. Bad-mouth me, blackball me. I don't have a lot of references, you know."

"What are you going to do for money?" Rick asked.

"I don't know. I'm sure as hell not going back on the streets, not again. I hope you don't, either. We'll figure something out."

"You still haven't told me what he did to me," Rick said.

"I told you I'm not sure you want to know."

"Yes, I do."

Roger paused, trying to choose his words carefully. "Let's just say a . . . foreign object was thrust into your body with force. That's how he gets his final kick."

"A 'foreign object'? C'mon, what are you talking about?"

Roger stared at him. "A bottle."

"A what?"

"You heard me. A bottle."

Rick felt the pain all over again, the stupefying agony, the double-over shock, and he heard again the piglike grunt of ecstasy.

"Let's get the son of a bitch," he said.

When Alex returned to the station, he went directly to George Barclay's office to fill him in on everything they'd discovered in the past several days. He found Barclay leaning back in his chair, eyes closed, looking asleep.

Alex coughed politely at the doorway, then watched as Barclay's eyes slowly opened. "Sorry to bother you," Alex said. "Should I come back later?"

"No problem," Barclay said, straightening in his chair. "I try to get a few minutes of meditation in every day. Relaxes me."

Alex told him about the affidavits and Grabowski's partial script in the safety-deposit box and of finding John Martin and the leads to the whereabouts of Sleet.

"We've also got a couple of other names that may get us somewhere," Alex added. "I think we're getting closer, but time is getting tight. The rating period's over, and I'd like a few days off the newscasts to work on this thing full time. I may not be around much."

"I don't know, Alex. Hawke is keeping close tabs on us. What'll I tell him if he asks where you are?"

"Tell him I'm sick, that I've got laryngitis. You'll think of something."

Barclay hesitated.

"C'mon, George, just for a few days."

"Okay. We'll try it. But if Hawke gets too goddamned nasty, I may have to put you back on. Agreed?"

"Agreed," Alex said. "And thanks."

"God, it's cold out there." Barbara was just coming into the station, stamping her feet and blowing on her hands, as Alex was on his way out.

"I know,' he said.

"You're supposed to ask me *how* cold it is."

"Okay," Alex said, humoring her. "How cold is it?"

"I just ran into a flasher," she said, "and it was *so* cold he kept his coat buttoned and tried to *describe* himself to me."

Alex grinned. "Very funny. You ought to be in show business."

"Thanks," she said. "Where are you off to?"

"Barclay gave me a few days off the shows to work on the story."

"Good for you," Barbara said. "Is there anything else I can do? I feel as though I haven't been much help lately."

"Not at the moment. But a few things are starting to come together, and I may need your help later. Meantime, just keep those ratings up while I'm gone, will you? I don't want to have to save your ass again."

He gave her a quick flash with his coat, and was out the door.

Barbara's jocular warning had not quite prepared Alex for the extraordinary cold which awaited him outside the door. It bit deeply into his lungs and made his nose feel like a frozen pipe.

Temperatures had plummeted to well below zero in a matter of hours, and they were still falling as Alex scurried toward the skyway system a couple of blocks away.

Abandoned storefronts on the street level were stark evidence that Minneapolis had become a second-story city; downtown life now centered on the skyways, warm pedestrian thoroughfares that linked all of the major buildings. The walkways were lined by stores and shops of all descriptions and jammed by office workers and shoppers untouched by the extremes of Minnesota weather.

It was the center city's answer to the success of the enclosed suburban shopping malls, but it left the downtown streets all but deserted.

Alex had no trouble finding Phil's office again. The homicide division was on the first floor of the old Minneapolis City Hall, which was built before the turn of the century and showing its age.

A receptionist directed him to Phil's office, but not before shyly asking Alex for his autograph. "I didn't watch Channel Seven before you came," she said. "Now I won't watch anything else."

Alex thanked her, signed a small piece of paper, and followed her pointed finger down the hall. He found Phil with his feet on his desk and the phone on his shoulder. Phil pointed to an empty chair next to an overflowing file cabinet, and Alex sat down.

"Okay, Mike. Thanks. We'll keep in touch."

Phil placed the receiver on the hook. "That was Mike Tolliver up in Siren. Something's screwy."

"What are you talking about?" Alex asked.

"Tolliver says he just drove up to the Hodges's property. He was curious because the tax bill seemed so high for a piece of empty land. Turns out it's not empty. There's a new year-round house, more of a lodge, really, sitting on the property."

"*What?*" Alex was on the edge of his chair. "That's crazy. Pat said they'd never done anything with the land. That there's just an old boat sitting there."

"Really? Well, hold on, there's more. Tolliver says the building permits were in Hodges's name, but the contractor who built the place told him he was paid by somebody else."

Alex waited. "C'mon," he said, "don't fuck with me. Who?"

"Jerry Caldwell, Steele's right-hand man."

"I'll be a son of a bitch," Alex said. "That brings Steele one step closer to Grabowski, doesn't it? And Hodges one step closer to Steele. Hodges must know about the place if the goddamned building permits were in his name."

"You'd think so," Phil agreed.

"No wonder he hasn't taken Pat up there for years," Alex said.

"If she was being straight with you."

Alex gave him a sharp look. "She's being straight, believe me. She has no reason to lie."

Phil was taken aback. "Don't get so damned defensive. I was just thinking out loud."

"You don't have to worry about Pat," Alex said. "She's as mystified about all of this as we are."

"Would her husband benefit if Steele gets taken out?" Phil asked. "Would he be in line for Steele's job?"

"Shit, I don't know," Alex said, chagrined he had not thought of that himself. "She says he's damn near a disciple of Steele's."

"Reporters must be more trusting than cops," Phil said.

"Is there anything else?" Alex asked, turning the discussion.

"Yeah. I finally heard from my cop friend in L.A. this morning. Our friend Sleet, or Kevin Marcus, currently resides in the Los Angeles County Jail. He got busted for running some kind of male call-service, but he's due out before Christmas. They try to clean out the jailhouse for the holidays, and Sleet's one of those set for early release."

"It's all coming together, isn't it?" Alex said. "Can we get to him before he gets out?"

"I'm booked on a morning flight two days from now. Do you want to come along as an *observer*? You'll have to pay your own way."

"I wouldn't miss it," Alex said.

Twenty-five

Alex flipped on the television set as he walked into the house. The news was just beginning.

"Good evening everyone, I'm Don Sergeant, sitting in tonight for Alex Collier . . ."

Alex stopped and watched. It felt strange seeing someone else sitting next to Barbara, like his ghost, reading the same words he would have been reading, making the same camera moves, attempting the same inflections.

Sergeant was the weekend anchor and backup for Alex. He was a few years younger, but had obviously been studying Alex's style. We may not be twins, Alex thought, but at first glance you can't see a hell of a lot of difference.

As he walked toward the kitchen, the phone rang.

"Is this Alex Collier?" The voice was muffled.

"Yes, that's me."

"I'm told you've been looking for me."

"Who is this? And who told you that?"

"The bartender at Mr. K's gave me your name and number, said you'd been asking about me. He said you're that TV newscaster."

"Right. Are you Roger Anderson?"

"You got it. Why are you trying to track me down?"

"I need to talk to you about a story I'm doing," Alex said. "It's important that I see you."

"What kind of story? Why me?"

"I don't want to talk about it on the phone," Alex said. "Can I meet you somewhere? Buy you a drink or a cup of coffee?"

"Maybe. Is there anything in it for me? Time is money, you know."

"There could be. We'll talk about it, but I can't promise anything over the phone."

"Okay," Roger said. "When and where?"

"How about tomorrow?" Alex asked.

"No. Not tomorrow. I'm tied up."

"Well, I've got to be out of town for a day or two after that. How about Monday morning at ten at the Perkins restaurant near Southdale? Know where it is?"

"Sure. I'll be there."

"How will I know you?" Alex asked.

"Don't worry. I'll find you. You're a TV star, right?"

In his apartment, Roger put down the phone and looked at Rick.

"Do you know what you're doing?" Rick asked.

"I think so," Roger said.

"Calling a television guy?"

"The bartender at Mr. K's said this Collier was looking for me. Said he was also asking about Sleet and a couple of other guys."

"Who's Sleet?" Rick asked.

"The guy that I replaced at Steele's house. He took off for California or someplace."

"What do you think this Collier wants?"

"He didn't say, but it figures to have something to do with Steele."

"Why get mixed up in that?"

"I'm not mixed up in it yet. I haven't even talked to him."

"But you said you would."

"I'll listen to what he has to say. It may be an answer."

"What do you mean?"

"It may help me get out of there. If Steele's face is all over some TV screen, he sure as hell isn't going to worry about me."

Rick said nothing.

"Besides, this shit's got to end sometime, Rick. Otherwise,

there'll be more kids like you, and like I was a few years ago. The parade will never stop, not unless he's stopped."

Rick remembered the bottle, and the pain.

"Can I come along?" he asked.

"Why not," Roger replied.

After the call, Alex changed to his robe, and with a cup of decaf coffee by his side he finally got around to opening the day's mail. There wasn't much: a White Sale circular from Dayton's, a pre-Christmas electronics sale catalog from Best Buy, and two other letters.

The first was from Jan.

> *I'm disappointed we haven't heard from you, but I'm as-suming you may still want us to come for Christmas. The kids are out of school on the 22nd, and we'd plan to be on the plane the next day. I'm going to get the tickets while they're still available, but if there's a problem, or if you've changed your mind, let me know. The kids have learned not to count on anything, and so have I. I'll just wait to hear from you. Jan.*

God, how could I have forgotten to call? he asked himself. Too goddamned much going on, that's the problem.

His name and address were scrawled on the envelope of the second letter, the writing almost unreadable, and certainly not recognizable. He tore open the envelope, and found a single sheet of paper with a simple message printed in block letters in the middle of the page.

WE KNOW WHAT YOU'RE UP TO
BACK OFF BEFORE IT'S
TOO LATE
YOU'VE BEEN WARNED

Alex almost laughed. What is this shit? C'mon, you can't be serious—a threatening note? To me? *You've been warned.* Give me a break.

But as he thought about it, it didn't seem so funny. It had caught him so off guard that he had momentarily forgotten the kind of people he was dealing with, the same ones who'd broken Daniel's fingers one by one and then beaten him to death.

No, he decided, there was nothing funny here. For the first time since he began all of this, he felt a touch of fear. He had the urge to go to and check the locks on the doors.

C'mon tough guy, he told himself, unpucker your ass; it was only a note.

Alex picked up the phone and called Barbara at the station.

"Enjoying your night off?" she asked.

"I was until a few minutes ago. Can you do me a favor?"

"Sure. What do you need?"

"Call Barry Stensrud at *City Magazine* tomorrow and see if he still has copies of the threatening notes sent to the magazine. If he does, maybe I can pick them up before Phil and I go to L.A."

"No problem," she said. "Why the sudden interest?"

"Because I just got one."

Alex read the message to her and described the envelope and the printing inside.

"My God," she said. "Barry said something like this could happen, but now that it has, I can't believe it."

"I thought it was a joke at first," he said, "but now I don't think so."

"Alex, be careful. Okay?"

"Don't worry."

The flight to Los Angeles was uneventful. Alex and Phil had spent the first half-hour of the flight comparing Alex's note to the copies of the notes Stensrud had provided. They decided at least a couple of the messages were probably written by the same hand.

Phil slept for the rest of the trip while Alex went over the story in his mind, dividing it into columns: what they suspected, what they knew, and what they had to prove. The third column was by far the longest, but at least now they had a shot. *If* Sleet, John Martin and Roger Anderson would cooperate, and *if* they could get the story past Hawke and on the air. Big ifs.

Phil's eyes opened the moment the wheels of the 747 touched down on the runway. The flight attendant announced that it was seventy-six degrees outside.

"Jesus," Phil said, watching the airport workers scurry about the tarmac in shirtsleeves, "do you realize we'll be almost seventy degrees warmer than we were just a couple of hours ago? It's amazing."

They found the Los Angeles County Jail on the northeast edge of downtown, a gray, windowless structure made of cement slabs. Once inside the complex, neither Phil nor Alex had any real notion of where they were; they'd been led through the maze of hallways by a sheriff's deputy, and left alone in a small room to await Sleet's appearance.

The meeting had been set up by Phil's friend, who also arranged for a police stenographer to be present during the interview. Phil had a copy of Sleet's affidavit in his pocket, the document they had found in Daniel's safety-deposit box.

Alex and Phil had struck a deal: Phil would handle the interrogation as part of his investigation of Grabowski's death. But, depending upon Sleet's reaction, Alex would get a chance to ask some questions of his own and to try and arrange for an on-camera interview with Sleet. One of the station's I-Team cameramen was waiting back in the Twin Cities, aware only that he might have to board a plane for California.

When Sleet was led into the room, Alex was shocked, and for a moment he thought they had brought the wrong man. He bore little likeness to the arrogant young blond Alex remembered from the Knowles videotape. He walked with a slouch, eyes averted, staring at the floor, wearing a full beard as shaggy and unkempt as the stringy hair that hung below his shoulders. Alex decided that life in California had not been so good to Kevin Marcus.

The police stenographer followed Sleet into the room, and set up her recorder on a small table.

"Hello, Kevin, I'm Phil Tinsley of the Minneapolis Police Department. This is Alex Collier. He works for a Twin Cities television station and is also interested in talking to you."

Sleet still had not looked directly at either of them. His eyes moved from the floor to the ceiling, then to the walls, then back to the floor again. His hands were clasped together in his lap, as though bound by nonexistent handcuffs, and there was a slight tremor in his voice when he finally spoke.

"I haven't been in Minnesota for a couple of years. What do you need me for? I got enough problems."

"We don't want to add to your problems, Kevin, believe me," Phil said. "But we do need your help. Nothing you will say here today will ever be used against you in any way. That's why we've got the stenographer here . . . so it's on the record that you're talking to us voluntarily. There's no danger of incriminating yourself. Understand?"

"What do mean, voluntarily? I'm not here voluntarily. I'm in a fucking jail, and I was brought here."

"You can leave right now if you want to," Phil said, deciding to bluff. "But I won't guarantee I won't be back here next week, or the week after, with an extradition petition to get you back to Minnesota. Then it *will* be official police business, and then what you say *could* be used against you. Take your choice."

"Extradition petition? For what?"

"As a witness," Phil replied, still bluffing.

"What's this all about, anyway?" Sleet asked.

"Do you remember Daniel Grabowski?"

"The magazine writer?"

"That's him," Phil said. "How well did you know him?"

"What's the difference?"

"C'mon, Sleet, answer the question."

"Not that well. We were friends, I guess, and I gave him some information. But then I took off, and I haven't heard anything from him. Why are you asking this stuff?"

"Because he's dead," Phil said. "Murdered. They found his body a couple of weeks ago, buried up in Wisconsin. It looks like he was killed a few months after you came out here."

Marcus shook his head. "Poor bastard. I knew he was asking for trouble. I told him so. That's why I got the fuck out of the state."

"But you signed this affidavit before you left," Phil said, pulling the document out of his pocket and showing it to Marcus. "You did tell Grabowski these things, didn't you? You did sign this?"

Sleet looked at the paper, reading it slowly, studying his signature. Then reading it again.

"Should I have a lawyer here?" Sleet asked, turning to the stenographer for advice. She stared back at him blankly.

"I told you, you don't have to say anything," Phil replied. "But, remember, you can't get yourself in trouble by talking now. I've given you that guarantee."

"Guarantees from cops don't mean shit," he said. "But what the fuck. Yeah, I told Grabowski this stuff," he said, pointing to the paper, "and yeah, I signed it. It's true."

"Would you be willing to update it, and re-sign it? So there'd be no question that it's genuine? That you still swear to it?"

"You're asking me that after just telling me that Grabowski got killed? You got to be kidding."

"No, I'm not kidding," Phil said. "We need your help. You told Grabowski you'd be willing to come back and testify before a grand jury if need be. That may not be necessary, but we need to know if you're still willing to cooperate."

"Lookit. When I signed that thing, I knew Steele could be dangerous. That's why I split. But I didn't know he'd kill anybody. That puts a whole new light on this thing."

"We don't *know* that Steele had anything to do with Grabowski's death," Phil said.

"C'mon," Sleet said, "don't shit me, okay? Who else would've wanted Daniel dead? He was a harmless little guy."

Alex had been standing against a wall of the room, fidgeting with impatience, and now he moved directly in front of Sleet. "You're right. We won't shit you. We know Steele or some of his cronies probably killed Grabowski. But proving it is almost impossible because of the condition of the body and the lack of any other real evidence. It happened too long ago.

"So we're stuck with trying to do the next best thing. To prove that Steele is a goddamned pedophile, a trusted public servant who has been violating kids for most of his adult life, turning a lot of them into whores or worse. You worked for him, for Christ's sake, you know what he did. That's why you talked to Daniel, that's why you signed the affidavit. Nothing has changed, except that it's probably gotten worse. Steele is about to become chief justice of the Minnesota Supreme Court in less than a month. We can't let that happen. We don't have much time."

Sleet started to say something, but Alex waved him quiet.

"Maybe, just maybe, if we can get him on this thing, something will break on Daniel's murder. That's what we're hoping for. But it's not going to happen unless you and some others give us a hand. You said Daniel was your friend, didn't you?"

"What's this got to do with you?" Sleet asked. "He says you're a reporter, not a cop."

"So was Grabowski," Alex replied. "I want to expose Steele just like Daniel wanted to expose him. I want the public to see him for what he really is. A goddamned criminal in the robes of a judge who preys on kids."

Alex glanced at Phil, who was watching him closely.

"I wouldn't make a very good witness, you know," Sleet said, his resistance crumbling. "I'm not exactly a model citizen."

"Let *us* worry about that," Phil said. "The important thing is you knew and worked for Steele, and he paid you to have sex with him when you were still a juvenile."

"Christ Almighty," Sleet said. "I just want to get out of jail and take off for somewhere new, like New Mexico."

"We'll try to help you do that," Phil said. "But we need your help now."

"Okay," Sleet sighed, "I'll sign the fucking thing. But I don't want to go back to Minnesota. Steele scares the hell out of me. And you got to help me if I get in trouble later."

"We'll do what we can," Phil promised.

"I need one more thing," Alex said. "I'd like you to tell your story on camera. We'll disguise you and your voice, and won't use your name. Would you be willing to do that?"

"I guess so. Why not? But forget the disguise, they'll know who I am anyway."

As Phil was taking a new statement from Sleet, Alex searched the jail's hallways, frantically trying to find a phone for an urgent call to a cameraman waiting in Minneapolis.

Twenty-six

John Knowles stood on the doorstep, his arms hugging his coat to his body, his breath turning to instant frost.

Thank God Alex is back from L.A., Knowles thought as he heard the chimes ring inside.

"C'mon in, John," Alex said, holding the door open.

Knowles had called Alex three hours before, telling him he was returning from New Ulm and asking if he could talk to him right away.

"What have you got?" Alex had asked.

"I'll tell you when I see you," Knowles had said, "but you won't believe it."

Now he stood in the entryway, rubbing the cold from his hands as Alex hung his coat in the closet.

"How about a cup of coffee?" Alex asked, leading him into the living room.

"With a little cream and sugar, thanks."

Knowles was sitting on his knees by the fire, absorbing the heat, when Alex returned from the kitchen.

"So what's the deal down there?" Alex asked.

"I ought to win a duPont award or a Peabody or something," Knowles said.

"Don't be so modest, John. Just tell me what you found."

"I didn't find much going through old newspapers and school records, but then I started talking to some of Steele's old neighbors and classmates."

"And?"

"I finally ran into an old guy, must be ninety now," Knowles said. "He talked about young Emmett having a tough time of it after his mother died. Something about a baby-sitter and some kind of a scandal that was hushed up."

"A scandal?" Alex asked.

"After Steele's mother died, his father went back to work at the brewery. From what I could learn, the kid was in pretty bad shape. He and his mother were real close. He was an only child, you know, and she was what you'd call a doting mother. Anyway, he took her death pretty hard, wouldn't talk to anybody, not even his dad, or teachers, nobody. Just went into a deep funk.

"His dad worked long hours at the brewery, and was back and forth between the day and night shift. Somebody had to watch the boy, so they hired a high school kid to keep an eye on him when the father was at work. Turns out the baby-sitter was a creep, and they found out later that he'd been molesting Emmett."

"Son of a bitch," Alex whispered. "How'd they find out?"

"Emmett went a little bonkers. They had to put him away for a while. Therapy wasn't the best in those days, you know. At any rate, Emmett spilled the beans, told everything. Nobody believed him at first; they passed it off as a kid's crazy accusations. Then they discovered the baby-sitter butt-fucking another kid, so they put him away.

"But that's not the end of the story," Knowles continued. "It gets worse. By the time he got back home, after this whole god-damned ordeal, his father was drinking more beer than he was brewing. Can't really blame him, I guess. His wife was dead, his son stuck away in some cuckoo's nest."

"You said the story gets worse?" Alex asked.

"It got better for a few years. Emmett went back to school and his dad apparently went on the wagon. But the kid was never the same. He didn't have many friends, stuck to himself. But he was a hell of a student. Valedictorian of his class, according to the yearbook. Things seemed to be going okay until they found the body."

"*Body?*" Alex came up out of his chair. "What body?"

"The body of the old baby-sitter. He'd gotten out of jail, or wherever he was, and had come back to town. He acted as if nothing had ever happened. He even tried to see Emmett again, according to one of Steele's old classmates. Well, they found his body in the local dump, roped-up like a rodeo calf. A banana was stuffed in his mouth, a clamp on his nose, and a catchup bottle up his ass. He'd suffocated. Pretty brutal stuff."

"No shit. So what happened? Who did it?"

"The case was never solved," Knowles said, "although I'm not sure they ever really tried. Steele was never connected to it. He was a senior in high school at the time and left town shortly after to go to college. He hasn't been back since, except for his dad's funeral."

"How'd you dig all of this up?" Alex asked.

"By a lot of hard work, thank you. Combing through old records, talking to people, bullshitting. Whatever it took. It happened a lot of years ago, and it's not the kind of thing people like to talk about in the first place. But I think it's a pretty accurate account."

"It's an incredible tale," Alex said, knowing it was also much more than he had bargained for. "If this is Steele's doing, we've got more than a pedophile on our hands. We've got a killer."

"Don't forget about Daniel, either," Knowles reminded him.

"This man's an absolute animal," Alex said, beginning to feel real terror.

Yet the bastard was a victim himself. Abuse begets abuse. Is that what it all comes down to? Does that make it less evil?

"Now that you know," Knowles said, "what the hell are you going to do with it? It's ancient history."

"I'm not sure." Alex was feeling desperate. "But we'd better start getting some evidence. And soon."

Twenty-seven

Pat sat across the breakfast table from her husband. The sun poured in through the kitchen window, sliced by the slats of the venetian blinds, warming her back. Nathaniel sat across from her, and one of the lines of light was directly in his eyes.

"Would you please close the blinds further," he asked, squinting to see her.

They were still in their robes, the breakfast dishes scattered on the table, the Saturday morning paper divided between them.

What a difference a week can make, Pat thought, remembering the wonderful erotic delirium at Alex's house. Seven days had passed, but it seemed like only yesterday. The memory was that fresh.

She adjusted the blinds and started to clear the dishes.

"What are we doing this weekend?" she asked.

"Pardon me?" Nathaniel said, not taking his eyes off the newspaper. "What did you say?"

"I asked what we're going to do. I don't want to sit around the house all weekend, do you?"

"I hadn't thought about it," he said, finally looking up at her. "I have a lot of work to do, you know that."

"Can't that wait? Why don't we drive up to Wisconsin and spend some time at the lake? Just wander around. Maybe rent some cross-country skis. We haven't been up there for years."

Pat asked the question casually, but carefully watched for his reaction. She couldn't see his eyes, they were back on the paper, but she noticed him shift in his chair.

"Oh, I don't think so," he said, slowly turning a page. "It's too far and it's too cold." He still did not look at her. "Why don't we wait until spring, when it warms up a bit and the lake thaws?"

"We could drive up and back in a day," Pat persisted. "We wouldn't need to stay overnight."

"I can't spare a full day; I have too much work to do." Now he was studying her. "Why the sudden interest in Wisconsin? I can't remember the last time you even mentioned it."

"I don't know," she said. "I just feel like going outside and doing something. I thought it would be fun to see the place again. Remember talking about a retirement home up there?"

She was facing the sink, her back to him, but she could feel his stare. The seconds of silence seemed like minutes.

"Well, it'll have to be another time," he said, closing the discussion.

It was unusual to find George Barclay at the television station on a Saturday morning, but he was there now, standing in front of a television monitor—watching the raw videotape of Alex's interview with Sleet in Los Angeles.

"Damn, this is great stuff," he said.

Alex and Phil stood with Barclay in the viewing room.

"He may be a slimeball," Barclay continued, "but he sure as hell is believable."

"He's willing to take a lie detector test," Alex said. "Just to back up the affidavit and the interview. He's locked in."

The tape rolled on, Sleet looking directly into the camera, revealing in explicit detail the sordid sexual practices of Judge Emmett M. Steele.

"How'd you get this stuff?" Barclay asked, not able to hide a hint of admiration. "What in the hell did you say to him?"

"You should have heard Alex," Phil said. "He damn near had me in tears. Sleet must have a decent streak in him somewhere, and Alex found it. Maybe he really does want to start life over again."

"Let's make a transcript and a couple of dubs of these tapes," Barclay said, "and tuck them away until we're ready to edit. I don't want them circulating around the station, to take the chance of their falling into Hawke's hands."

"What *about* Hawke?" Alex asked.

"He'll find out eventually, but I don't want him seeing anything until we've got it all together. It's not going to make him happy, that's for sure."

Alex had planned to spend the rest of the weekend at home. He was still exhausted from the hurried trip to L.A. and wanted time to digest what he had learned from Sleet and from John Knowles.

Instead, the next day he found himself in Pat's BMW, sitting by her side, traveling north on Wisconsin highway 35.

Toward Steele's lodge.

The highway followed what used to be the railroad tracks north to Superior. The rail line was now abandoned, the tracks torn up, the right-of-way turned over to snowmobiles and three-wheelers. The giant loads of pulpwood once carried by the trains now traveled on huge flatbed trucks, but even they were missing from the road on this Sunday.

Endless stretches of forest flashed by. They hadn't seen another car for miles, and they began to wonder if anybody really lived in the area. Alex decided it looked as desolate from the ground as it had from the helicopter weeks before.

"Does your husband know where you are?" he asked.

"Of course not," Pat replied. "He's at home with his nose in the lawbooks. I told him I was going to the Walker Art Center, and then shopping. He won't miss me."

Alex had called Pat the night before, urging her to get up to see the Wisconsin property, but not explaining why. Not then. He wanted to see her face. She told Alex that Nathaniel had refused to go, and asked if he'd like to come with her instead.

"You're in for a surprise, you know," Alex told her now in the car.

"What do you mean?"

He explained what Tolliver had found when he explored the property and the confusion and contradiction over the building permits and the payments to the contractor. He watched for her reaction.

She seemed genuinely shocked. "What can it mean?" she asked.

"I don't know, Pat. I'm at a loss. It's amazing that Nathaniel hasn't said anything to you about it."

"It's downright scary, Alex. I thought I knew my husband pretty well. Maybe I don't after all."

Alex then told her about his conversation with Sleet in Los Angeles, and about the anonymous note in the mail. "It's pretty obvious they know what I'm up to," he said. "I just wonder how much they know. They sent the same kind of notes to the magazine people and succeeded in scaring them off."

"What about Daniel? They didn't scare him off, and look what happened to him. I wouldn't take this lightly, Alex."

"I'm not, believe me. But I'm not going to run away, either."

The miles slipped by, and so did the time. After two hours, Alex knew they were getting close. They weren't that far from Daniel's grave site.

Pat slowed the car, downshifting as they approached a gravel road which branched off the highway to the left.

"It's about a half mile from here," she said.

The driveway was plowed, and there were signs of recent tire tracks in the snow. "We ought to be a little cautious," Alex warned. "No telling what we'll find."

"Don't tell me that," Pat said, "I'm uncomfortable enough as it is."

You're uncomfortable, Alex thought. He still couldn't swallow his suspicions. The tension in the car was as thick as the trees surrounding them.

The driveway dropped away toward the lake, the house hidden by the dense stand of birch and poplar, blocking the view even without summer folliage. Pat kept the BMW in first gear as they crept down the incline, inching their way.

"What *do* we say if someone's here?" Pat asked. "How do we explain what we're doing?"

"We're taking a look at your property, I guess."

"What about you?"

Alex shrugged. "I'm just a friend keeping you company. Let's hope nobody will be here to ask."

Tolliver was right. The house *did* look more like a lodge. It was situated halfway down the hill, with a clear view of the lake below, its exterior made of rough-hewn logs, its roof of natural cedar shingles. A massive stone fireplace dominated one end of the building, a three-car garage the other end.

No cars were in sight, but a thin trail of white smoke rose from the chimney, and the smell of burning birch was in the air as they got out of the car.

"I can't believe it," Pat said, clearly puzzled. "How could all this happen without me knowing? This was all woods the last time I was here. The driveway stopped at the top of the hill, and we had a hard time walking down, the trees and brush were so thick."

Alex would never forget the moment. Looking at her, seeing the confusion and fear in her face, he knew for the first time with absolute certainty that she was as much in the dark as he was. It was as though a giant weight had been lifted from his back, and he felt a surge of relief.

He looked around, watching the wisps of smoke vanish in the air. "Certainly looks as though somebody's living here. Might as well act like we belong."

"Maybe we should leave," she said. "We've seen the house."

"You didn't come all this way just for that, did you?"

They walked to the door, greeted by a door knocker carved in the shape of a woodpecker. Alex hesitated, then rapped the bird's beak against the side of the door. There was no answer. He rapped again, and then pounded on the door with his fist. Still no response.

"Let's take a look," he said, trying to shake off his sense of unease.

A window just off the back door gave them a glimpse of the kitchen, but when they walked around to the front, a big picture window provided a panoramic view of the interior. Alex and Pat cupped their eyes against the glass and examined the expanse of space inside. The fireplace wall ran across the length of the living room to the attached dining area, and next to that was a circular staircase to a loft which overlooked the living area below.

The interior had the same rustic look as the exterior, the furniture carved out of the same kind of logs used to build the house.

"Pretty impressive," Pat whispered.

They had just stepped back from the window when they heard a car door slam behind the house. The sound seemed to echo in the trees.

"Shit, somebody's here," Alex said.

Pat grabbed his arm, then released it.

They walked back around the house as calmly and casually as their jittery nerves would permit. Alex didn't know what to expect, but he stopped short when he saw the Lincoln Continental parked next to Pat's BMW. Standing between the two cars were Judge Steele, his hawk-nosed driver, and a young boy.

No one said anything for a moment. It was hard to tell who was the more surprised.

"Patricia? Mr. Collier? What in the world are you doing here?"

"Looking at our property, I thought," Pat replied quickly. "It's changed a lot since I was here last."

"Nathaniel hasn't told you?" Steele asked, feigning total surprise. "He hasn't mentioned that we're partners in this little project, that he provided the land, and I provided the house? I'm amazed. Perhaps he meant to surprise you with the news."

"Perhaps so," Pat said. "And perhaps we ought to keep it that way. A surprise, I mean."

"If that's what you'd like, certainly. And, Mr. Collier, how about you? Just along for the ride?"

Alex had to give him credit. After the first moment of shock, Steele had recovered completely. He seemed in absolute control of the situation now. But Alex could not look at him now without thinking of the roped-up baby-sitter in the New Ulm dump.

"I'm on the lookout for some lakeshore property of my own," Alex lied, "and Pat offered to give me a tour of the area. Nice day for a drive."

"Too bad Nathaniel couldn't have made it, too," Steele said, with the slightest hint of innuendo.

"I asked, but he wasn't interested in coming," Pat said. "He said he had too much work to do. I decided to come anyway."

They stood uncomfortably in the cold, the driver and the boy shifting their feet uncertainly in the snow. "I'm terribly sorry," Steele said, "I've neglected to make introductions. This is my driver, Russell, and my nephew, Steven."

"Really?" Alex said. "Your nephew? I didn't know you had brothers or sisters. I thought you were an only child."

"That's true," Steele said, unperturbed. "Steven is actually my godchild, the son of some very good friends. But I think of him as my nephew."

"What's your last name, son?" Alex asked.

The boy didn't answer, and started to walk toward the house.

"He's shy, I'm afraid," Steele said, "but he'll be fine. He's going to stay with us for a couple of days."

Pat and Alex glanced at one another, excused themselves, and started to walk toward her car.

"Won't you come in and warm up?" the judge offered. "Have a cup of coffee?"

"No thanks," Pat said, climbing into the car. "We've got to get going. Besides, I want to leave something for Nathaniel's surprise."

The BMW went up the hill faster than it had come down, leaving Steele and the others in a spray of snow and gravel.

"Nephew. Godchild. What a bunch of crap."

"He can't be more than thirteen or fourteen," Pat said, visibly shaken.

"We shouldn't have left him there," Alex said. "Who knows what Steele will do with him."

"What were we supposed to do, kidnap him? Maybe he really is his godchild."

"Not likely," Alex said.

"Steele certainly can lie with a straight face, can't he?" Pat said. " 'Perhaps he meant to surprise you with the news.' Ugh."

"He'll tell Nathaniel, you know."

"I know," she said. "But I also know Nathaniel won't say anything to me. He'll be too embarrassed, so he'll pretend he doesn't know and wait for me to say something. It'll be a standoff, a mutual silence."

They were back on the highway, heading for the Twin Cities.

"What do you think's going on?" Alex asked.

"I wish I knew. It seems clear there's a part of Nathaniel's life I know nothing about."

The sky was beginning to darken on the short winter day. Alex touched her cheek, feeling the softness and warmth. She took his hand to her lips and kissed his fingers gently, lovingly.

Then she drove on, lost in her own thoughts.

Leaving him with his.

The next morning Alex sat at a small table in the Perkins restaurant, pretending to study the menu, but glancing up now and then to see if anyone was approaching.

He was on his second cup of coffee and had long since put the menu aside when two young men walked up to his table. They were about the same height, both good-looking, one younger, the other slimmer, with a gold earring hanging from his left ear.

"Alex Collier?"

Alex stood at the table and shook their hands.

"I'm Roger Anderson," the slimmer one said as they sat down, "and this is Rick. You look a little older in person than you do on TV."

"Thanks a lot," Alex laughed, "that's just what an aging anchorman likes to hear."

Roger apologized for being late, explaining his car battery had died and they had needed a jump-start.

"I appreciate your coming," Alex said, "especially in this weather. I won't waste your time or mine. I'm guessing you work for someone I'm quite interested in, someone I'm trying to do a story about. If I'm right, I'd like to ask for your help."

Roger and Rick studied him across the table, and then looked at each other. "Assuming we could help, why should we?" Roger asked. "We don't even know you."

"I don't know," Alex said. "Maybe for the same reason you agreed to meet me here this morning, why you decided to call me in the first place. Maybe we're interested in the same thing."

"I'm interested in money, for one thing," Roger said. "Are you paying?"

"For breakfast, yes. For your help? No, I'm not. The ethics of the news business don't allow for that."

"The bartender at Mr. K's said you paid some kid on the street and some guy in the bar," Roger said.

Alex wished now he had listened to Barclay. "That was different. A few bucks for a little information. I'm looking for more than information now, and I can't pay for it."

They didn't seem satisfied, but each went ahead and ordered steak and eggs with side orders of pancakes.

"So you want to know about Judge Steele, right?" Roger asked, waiting for the breakfast to be delivered. Alex nodded. "That wasn't hard to figure out, especially since the bartender also said you asked about Sleet."

"I found him," Alex said. "He's willing to help."

"No kidding? That's amazing. I know he was scared shitless

when he left Steele's house. I didn't know why at the tme, but he sure as hell wanted out."

"Do you know now?" Alex asked.

"I guess that's why we're here," Roger replied.

The breakfasts came and Alex settled back to watch them eat, knowing conversation would be impossible until the food was gone.

"So what do you need from us?" Roger asked, wiping his mouth with the napkin.

"You know what Steele is and what he's been doing for years. I want to expose him, to flush him out. I know I'm taking a chance by even telling you this, since you still work for him, but I don't have much time, and I'm going to need your help."

"So? What do you need?"

"I need everything you know about Steele. What you've seen, what you've heard. I need to know the names and how to find more of his victims. I need a statement, a signed affidavit, swearing what you're saying is true. I need an on-camera interview, in disguise, if you prefer. I need his videotapes. I may even need to get a camera inside his house."

"Do you know what you're asking? Do you understand what he could do to me?"

"I can guess," Alex said. "But I need your help. I know I can't force you. I can only ask."

"And what do *I* get out of this?" Roger asked.

Alex smiled wanly. "Nothing. Not a goddamned thing, except for the same satisfaction I'm going to get out of it. That's all I can promise. It'll have to be enough."

"We'll let you know," Roger said, pushing back from the table. "Thanks for breakfast."

It was only after they'd left that Alex realized Roger's friend Rick had not said a word. He wondered what he had to do with Emmett Steele.

Twenty-eight

When Alex returned to the station, he was immediately summoned to George Barclay's office. "Into my confessional," Barclay said, shutting the door behind them. "Tell me what the hell is going on."

"What are you talking about?" Alex asked.

"I understand from Hawke that we're doing a special on Judge Steele. Kind of a 'This Is Your Life' program to coincide with his Supreme Court ordination. Interesting, huh? Hawke was very pleased. In fact, he congratulated me on my foresight. I accepted all of his praise, of course. Now can you tell me what the fuck is happening?"

"How did Hawke find out?" Alex asked.

"He got a call from Jerry Caldwell, who apparently found out from the judge's friends down in New Ulm. Jerry said he understands you're responsible for the idea, and he told Hawke how pleased he is to see a change in your attitude since the governor's news conference."

"Shit, Knowles warned me word would get back. Sorry."

"*What* word, for Christ's sake?"

Alex explained how he had sent Knowles to check on Steele's childhood, and how he had invented the story of the special as a cover—to deflect any suspicion about the purpose of the inquiry.

"I'll be dipped in shit," Barclay muttered. "And why didn't you tell me about any of this? I do still run this place."

"I didn't want to bother you with it," Alex said, "and I wasn't sure you'd go along with it. I had to bend the truth a little."

They looked at one another across the desk, Alex at a loss for anything more to say. But Barclay wasn't. "So what do we do now?" he asked. "Hawke's expecting a special on Steele."

"He'll get one," Alex said, grinning, "only it won't be exactly what he was looking for."

"This isn't a fucking joke, Alex. It could cost us our jobs."

"What do you want to do, George, back away?"

"No, but I don't want to be sticking my chin out, either. Hawke's no one to screw around with."

"Neither are we," Alex said with more confidence than he felt.

Barbara did not hear the door open behind her. She didn't know how long he had been standing there.

She'd been in the editing room for about a half-hour, watching the videotape of Alex's interview with Sleet in the Los Angeles jail.

"I worked for Judge Steele for almost two years, and I must have seen thirty young kids come through the house. Many of them came back several times. He'd average about one a week, I'd guess." Sleet stared directly and calmly into the camera. *"The routine would always be the same: The limo would bring 'em there, blindfolded, and they'd be tucked away in this room until Steele was ready for them. He'd watch dirty flicks while the kids got ready to go."*

Alex's voice was heard off-camera. *"How many of these 'young kids,' as you call them, were juveniles? Do you know?"*

"Most of them, I'd say. They sure looked young. And I know a few were. I looked through their billfolds when they were in the room with the judge."

Alex again. *"You'd swear to that?"*

"Sure," Sleet replied on the tape. *"I saw it with my own eyes."*

"Did the judge pay them for sex?" Alex asked.

"Sure, I gave his money to a bunch of them myself."

It was at that moment in the tape that Barbara heard the rustling behind her. Startled, she turned quickly in her chair. Derek stood by the door, grinning at her.

"What are you doing in here?" she cried. "How long have you been standing there? What's wrong with you, anyway?"

"Pretty hot stuff on that tape," Derek said, pointing to the monitor. "Is that *the* Judge Steele he's talking about?"

"Derek, what do you want? Why are you here?"

"They need you down in the studio," he said. "They sent me to get you. They're shooting a promo."

"I don't know how long you've been watching this," Barbara said, taking the tape from the machine, "but forget what you saw. It's confidential. Do you hear me?"

"Sure," he said. "But, man, that's hot shit."

That night, Alex arranged for another meeting with everyone working with him on the Steele story. "This thing is moving so fast," he told them, "it's hard to keep track of."

He spoke for a half hour, trying not to skip over any of the important details.

When he'd finished, John Knowles pushed himself forward in his chair. "I think the key is this Roger guy," he said. "If he agrees to help, if he doesn't run to Steele, he could be of immense value. He's got more credibility than Sleet, he has more recent information, and he has access to the house—an inside source."

"You're right," Alex said, "but he's still a question mark. We certainly can't plan on him at this point."

"What if he does get us those sex tapes?" Knowles asked. "Can we use them? After all, they'd be stolen property."

"I'm not sure. You know more about this than I do," Alex said. "But if we don't steal them, if Roger *gives* them to us, I don't think it's our problem. How he gets them is none of our business."

"That's a pretty fine line," Knowles argued. "It's one thing if he steals them on his own and brings them to us. It's another if we ask him to."

"How about a camera inside the house?" Alex asked.

"No way," Knowles said. "That's a clear invasion of privacy."

"What worries me," Barclay said, "is how we're going to keep our investigation separate from the cops'. I may sound like an echo, but I don't want us to be an arm of the goddamned police department."

Phil spoke up. "I'm going ahead whether you do your story or not. It's true you've provided me with a lot of information, like the stuff in the safety-deposit box, but I'm trying to keep my collection of evidence separate from yours. Hopefully, I'll have enough to take to the grand jury without any help from you."

"Does anybody else at the department know what you're doing?" Barbara asked.

"Everybody thinks I'm just pursuing the death of Daniel Grabowski. There are so many leaks over there, I don't want to tell anyone else until I have everything together."

"Isn't it time we bring an attorney into this thing for our own protection?" Knowles asked.

"Not yet," Barclay replied. "Too many people know what we're doing already. Let's keep the circle as small as possible."

"A couple of final points," Alex said. "I've still got to meet with John Martin, the guy at the memorial service, although I don't know how much help he'll be. And John, I think we ought to get set to do some nighttime surveillance of Steele's house. I'd like to see where that Continental goes at night, and get it on tape. And, Phil, can you find out anything about Steele's driver? His first name's Russell, that's all I know. Maybe he's got a record."

"You should know one thing," Barbara said. "Derek walked into the viewing room this afternoon while I was watching the tape of Sleet's interview."

"How much did he see?" Alex asked.

"I don't know. I'm not sure how long he was there."

"Shit," Alex said.

As Alex walked into the house that night he noticed Seuss was not waiting on his usual perch atop the bannister.

Strange, he thought, and wondered for a moment if he had left the cat outside that morning. But no, Alex remembered seeing him sitting inside on the windowsill as he got into the car and drove off to the studio.

Alex walked through the house and into the kitchen, calling out, stooping to look underneath pieces of furniture where Seuss liked to hide. He returned to the stairway and shouted into the darkness above.

The house was still.

What the hell, he thought. Where can he be? How could he get out? He's a smart cat, but he can't open the goddamned doors.

It was when he returned to the kitchen that Alex heard the first plaintive cry. He stood stock-still, listening. Another soft meow, with an edge of pain. It had to be coming from the basement, through the closed door. Alex felt a touch of fear.

He opened the basement door. "Seuss? *Seuss?* Hey, cat."

Nothing for a moment, then another soft cry. Alex was down the steps, three at a time. Fuck, he thought, forgot the light switch. But the glow from the kitchen was enough to reflect the two luminous eyes peering at him from a corner of the basement. Alex went up the stairs and hit the lights.

There was a terrifying screech from the basement.

The lights went out immediately. *A blown circuit breaker?*

Alex felt his way down the stairs and across the basement floor. He found Seuss in a heap, legs bound with a rope, a bare electric wire running from his body to a socket in the ceiling.

Alex ripped the wire away, picked up the cat, and carried him through the darkness and up the stairs. By the time he reached the top, he knew Seuss was dead. He had killed Seuss by flipping the light switch.

Jesus Christ, what is going on?

A piece of paper was tied to the cat's collar. Alex tore it off—knowing what it would say before he opened it.

THIS IS YOUR
LAST WARNING
DON'T BE A FOOL

As Alex looked at the still form of Seuss, his first thought was of his kids: Whoever did this might be capable of hurting them, too. No way, he thought. He couldn't let that happen, not ever.

He realized there was a more immediate and troubling issue. Whoever had gotten into the house had captured and tormented Seuss and had departed without leaving a trace. There were no broken windows, no smashed locks.

Alex suddenly felt very alone. He was standing in the middle of a silent, empty house—the only living tie to his past life now lying dead at his feet.

The next morning, there were two messages waiting on Alex's desk at the station. The first was from Phil Tinsley, and Alex phoned him at his office.

"Remember Rico Sanchez?"

"Yeah," Alex said, "the name on the third affidavit."

"Well, I found him."

"How?" Alex asked.

"I located his mother. She says Rico died of AIDS two months ago down in Rochester."

"God Almighty."

"I don't know if the disease had anything to do with Steele, or the kid's hustling, but it makes you wonder. He was twenty years old, Alex. *Twenty years old.*"

"It never seems to end, does it?"

"One other thing," Phil said. "I checked on Steele's driver. His full name is Russell Tosier. He's got a record as long as your arm: armed robbery and assault. He was a real mean bastard in his younger years."

"And now?" Alex asked.

"Nothing for the last four or five years, not since he's been working for Steele."

"How did he end up with Steele?"

"No one's quite sure, but apparently Steele was active in some kind of prisoner rehabilitation program and befriended Russell in prison. He got him out on a work-release program and has kept him out of trouble since."

"A humanitarian gesture?" Alex asked sarcastically.

"The word is that Russell's like a puppy dog to Steele, devoted and dedicated. He's a combination driver and bodyguard."

"From the looks of him, I believe it," Alex said.

Alex then told Phil about Seuss's death and the second note.

"How'd they get into the house?" Phil asked.

"Who knows, Phil, but I don't mind telling you, this is getting scary."

Phil said he'd ask for more police patrols around Alex's house. "I'll tell them you've been getting a bunch of crank calls. Loonies on the loose or something like that."

The second message surprised Alex. It was from Jerry Caldwell, who answered on the first ring.

"I think it's time we talked," Caldwell said. "In private."

"Really?" Alex replied. "About what?"

"About some rumors I've been hearing."

Alex paused. What's this about? he wondered. Another warning, delivered personally? His mind quickly weighed the possible risks of a meeting against the potential gains. "Can you tell me any more?" he asked.

"Not on the phone," Caldwell said.

"Okay," Alex said finally. "Where would you like to meet?"

"Do you know the Como Park Conservatory in St. Paul?"

"I'm sure I can find it. When?"

"How about tomorrow morning at ten?" Caldwell said. "And no cameras or microphones, right?"

"Right," Alex said. "I'll be alone."

Alex found John Knowles sitting behind his desk in his cluttered office, hands clasped behind his head, staring into space. A cigarette sat smoldering in an ashtray, untouched and unnoticed by Knowles.

Alex quietly sat down across the desk, snuffing out the cigarette but saying nothing, afraid of breaking whatever spell Knowles was under. Finally, he cleared his throat, and said gently: "John, are you okay?"

Knowles blinked his eyes, and slowly turned his head.

"Oh, Alex. Sorry. I was just thinking. When did you come in?"

"A minute ago. You got a problem? Anything I can help with?"

"No, not really. Some personal matters, that's all."

"Can I guess? None of my business, but do they have anything to do with Linda Grabowski?"

Knowles looked surprised. "Has it been that obvious? I thought I was being pretty circumspect."

"No, it hasn't been obvious."

"I'm worried, Alex. Linda's still so upset over Daniel's death that I worry about her mental health."

"It's only been a few weeks since she found out about Daniel," Alex said. "I'm sure she'll come out of it. You'll just have to be patient."

"I'm not so sure," Knowles said, slowly shaking his head. "She seems consumed by Daniel. He's become something of a martyr to her, and she seems determined to devote her life to his memory. It's a little strange, really."

The Como Park Conservatory was an island of summer in the middle of an ocean of winter, a domed glass edifice rising from the snowdrifts that was filled with the warmth, color, and smells of a tropical paradise.

Hundreds of different flowers and plants extended in every direction, protected by the glass wings of the Conservatory. Red and pink azalias, hibiscus, poinsettias of every shade, amaryllis and cyclamen. Winding stone walkways led beneath giant palms and through lush growths of grapefruit and coconut trees.

Alex spotted Jerry Caldwell across the way, his tall frame throwing a shadow against the sunlit glass. Alex navigated his way through the pathways, stopping now and then to smell the fragrant buds. He was in no hurry for this meeting.

He again wondered if he'd made a mistake in coming. Although Alex liked Caldwell, he had no real reason to trust him. He was, after all, part of the enemy camp—the right hand of the man Alex was determined to expose. But Alex had come to rely on his instincts, and they all seemed to be pushing him down the path.

Caldwell saw him and walked to meet him. "Collier, nice to see you. Thanks for coming. Let's just stroll, shall we?"

They walked without speaking until they reached a stone bench next to a fountain and pool, hidden away from everyone but the goldfish gliding through the water.

"I'll get right to the point," Caldwell said. "We are receiving disquieting reports that you and your station may be preparing another critical report about Judge Steele."

"Where did you hear that?" Alex asked.

"It's not important," Caldwell said. "But because of our previous conversations, I wanted to speak to you in person before taking my concerns to Mr. Hawke. We're approaching a very important point in Judge Steele's career, and we'd be *extremely* disappointed if anything were to be broadcast or published which would tarnish the judge's image at this most critical juncture."

"Jerry, let me ask you something," Alex interjected. "Just how well do you know your boss? I know you've worked for him for a long time, but how well do you *know* him? What he does with his time away from the bench?"

"I don't know what that has to do with this," Caldwell said. "I do know Judge Steele is a real scholar, a distinguished jurist. Tough and controversial, perhaps, but a great thinker."

"I don't think anybody questions that, but that's not what I asked you. What do you know about his *character*, about the kind of *person* he is? I'm sure you'd agree the life of any public official should be beyond reproach . . . but especially a judge, and most especially, a chief judge who is about to become chief justice."

"I don't like the direction this conversation is taking," Caldwell said. "Judge Steele's private life should be his own. I don't know much about the judge outside his chambers, and I've never felt it was any of my business."

"You ought to make it your business."

"What are you saying?" Caldwell asked, his tone less certain.

"Try to figure it out," Alex replied. "You seem like a decent guy. I think if you knew what I know, you wouldn't be sitting here now, telling me to lay off Judge Steele. You should open your eyes, take Steele off your little pedestal."

"If you pursue this, you must know word is going to get back to Hawke," Caldwell said.

"I know that," Alex replied, getting up to leave. "I only hope that after what I've just said, Hawke doesn't hear it from *you.*"

Alex left him there, considering his words, staring into the fountain waters.

Twenty-nine

"Are you okay, Alex? I just heard about your cat."

Barbara was standing by his cubicle, her coat in her arms, a bright red scarf still wrapped around her neck.

"I'm fine," he said.

"I can't believe this," Barbara said. "Why would they pick on your poor cat?"

"It was just Steele's way of getting his message across. Seuss happened to be handy. He wanted me to know they could get to me, and hurt the things close to me. That could include all of you."

"Is Steele capable of this?" Barbara asked.

"Personally? Maybe not, but he's certainly capable of ordering it. Look what they did to Daniel Grabowski, for Christ's sake. Look at the threats the magazine got. Look at his history. Judge Steele is crazy, crazy like a fox."

"So what happens now?" she asked.

"I don't know. I've had some supposedly pickproof locks installed on the doors, and Phil has beefed up the police patrols in the neighborhood, but I'm not naive enough to think that's going to provide real protection. I'll have to be more cautious, and so will you, but I'm not going to run away from this thing. I'm sure that's what they'd like to see. My biggest fear is telling Jan and the kids about the cat. I don't know if they'll ever forgive me."

"What's this about your cat?" George Barclay had walked up behind them.

Alex repeated the story and showed both Barbara and Barclay a copy of the note attached to Seuss's collar.

"Y'know, in all my years in this business, I've never seen anything quite like this," Barclay said. "It's like a fucking movie. I've also never had a reporter of mine get hurt, and I don't want you spoiling that spotless record, Alex."

The statement was made casually, but he was clearly concerned.

"By the way," Alex said, "I talked to Jerry Caldwell. He knows something is up, and predicts Hawke will hear soon. So you may want to get your howitzer out and loaded."

"Thanks," Barclay said gravely. "I hope I don't end up like your cat."

John Martin pumped gas at a Phillips 66 station on Franklin Avenue. When Alex pulled in, he was bending under the hood of a Grand Am, testing the battery. He was hard to recognize at first, covered head-to-toe in a snowmobile suit and hood and wearing big leather mittens.

Alex waited inside the station, and when Martin came in, his eyebrows and small mustache were covered with ice. "I've been out jump-starting cars all morning," he said, "freezing my ass. That's where the other guy is now. We take turns running the truck."

"Do you want to do this another time?" Alex asked.

"No, that's okay. I'll just take the phone off the hook. We're booked for the next two hours anyway."

He stripped off his mittens and brushed the ice crystals from his face. His cheeks were splotched with white, the first sign of frostbite. "I don't remember a cold snap lasting this long," he complained, rubbing his cheeks, trying to restore circulation.

"John, I think you know what I want," Alex said, showing him the affidavit. "You signed this before Daniel disappeared, and I'd like your word that you're going to live up to it. For Daniel's sake, if nothing else."

Martin looked at the paper, holding it up to the light. "Listen, I've been thinking about this since the service for Daniel, and I don't know what to tell you. All this stuff is behind me, okay? I've been trying to start over again. That's why I'm working at a place like this. I feel sorry for Daniel, but I don't want any more trouble, understand?"

"Did you know Rico Sanchez?" Alex asked.

"Yeah, he was another friend of Daniel's. I'd see him on the street. He did the same shit with Steele as I did."

"Well, he's dead. Of AIDS, a couple of months ago."

Martin said nothing.

"Did you ever know James Young?"

Martin shook his head no.

"I think he was another of Steele's young studs. He committed suicide a couple of years ago, leaving his great-grandmother to fend for herself. Then there's Daniel, and maybe others. What about yourself? How many others are there like you? Lives fucked up, trying to start over. Don't let this guy keep doing it, John. Help us."

A car drove in next to the gas pumps. Martin pulled on his mittens and lifted the snowmobile hood over his head.

"I hear what you're saying," he said, "but I also know what happened to Daniel. Find somebody else. I want to stay out of it."

Then he walked back out into the cold.

"Has Nathaniel said anything?" Alex was sitting across from Pat in a small bar atop the IDS Building, the tallest structure in the Twin Cities.

"Nothing, as I predicted. But it's decidedly cool around our house right now. I *know* he knows, and he *knows* I know. It's very strange."

Alex had called Pat at her office to arrange for the drink after work. He thought she'd want to know about the episode with Seuss and the second warning note. Her face paled.

"Alex, I don't know what to say. What did I get you into?" She leaned toward him, her expression a mixture of pain and concern. "I feel so badly."

A light snow was falling outside, big, fluffy flakes, obscuring the view of the downtown streets far below.

"What now?" she asked. "I won't blame you if you want to give it up. Not after all of this."

"The thought has crossed my mind, but only for a second—I know I'd never forgive myself."

"What are you doing to protect yourself?" she asked.

Alex told her about the extra police patrols and the new locks on the house. "One thing to remember is that I'm not quite as vulnerable as Daniel Grabowski was. He was pretty much alone. Steele must know others are working with me on this story and that if anything happens to me, all hell would break loose. They'd like to scare me away, and hope I'd tell the others to drop it, too."

"You could be right," Pat said, "but what if you're not? What if there's a vendetta against you?"

"All I can do is to keep my eyes open and wait to see what they try next. I want to keep the pressure on, see what happens."

She touched his foot with hers beneath the table. "Promise me something, Alex. That you'll give it up if it gets too scary. Please? The thought of Steele getting away with it is horrible, but the thought of something happening to you is much worse. Promise?"

"I don't think I can, Pat. What's 'too scary'? I'm scared right now, but I'm also more convinced than ever that Steele has to be stopped. Besides, it's a hell of a story."

The snowfall covered the big windows like a lace curtain. For a moment, Alex and Pat felt the world had been closed out. For a moment, at least.

If anything, the snow was even thicker when Alex left Pat and began walking back to the station. He had decided against the skyways, choosing to feel the snow against his face, to suck the fresh air into his lungs. He thought he was alone on the sidewalk until he felt the two bodies next to him, one on either side.

"Mind if we walk along?" It was Roger Anderson, collar up around his neck, but bareheaded. Rick McDaniel was on the other side, in a coat and cap.

"Not at all," Alex said. "Have you been keeping tabs on me, or is this just an accidental meeting?"

"We were watching for you when you left the TV station," Roger replied, "but there was no chance to talk in the skyways, so we waited. Who's the lady in the bar?"

"Nobody you'd care about," Alex said. "Just a friend."

They walked three abreast down the Nicollet Mall, surrounded by the brightly lighted Christmas decorations and sparkling store windows. Feeling conspicuous, Alex finally ducked inside a bus shelter, and his companions followed.

"We've thought about what you told us," Roger said, "and we

want to help, if we can. But we're scared of what Steele may try to do to us if he finds out. And we don't know what I'm going to do for work if you do get him."

"So what can I do?" Alex asked.

"You can help us both get a job once this thing is over. Maybe at the station—you must have lots of connections. We're going to need some bread and a fresh start."

Alex looked at the two of them, weighing the request. "I don't want to see you go back on the street, either, but I can't make any promises. *I* may not even have a job when this is over, but I will try to help you find something. That's all I can do."

Roger glanced at Rick, who shrugged his shoulders. "Okay," Roger said, "if that's the best you can offer. What should we do?"

"I want you to walk back to the station with me and meet a man named John Knowles. He'll take statements from both of you, and arrange for on-camera interviews. If you're willing, a lie detector test will come sometime later. Still interested?"

They both nodded.

"Another thing, Roger. Can you get any of Steele's private tapes? You know the ones I'm talking about."

"I'll try, but I don't know. I've never looked for them. He locks them away, I know that. But I'll give it a shot."

"Good. Now, let's go meet Mr. Knowles."

The next morning, Alex was back on Summit Avenue, back in the office of Dr. Duane Johnson, who looked no healthier today than the last time Alex had seen him. He needs a vacation, Alex thought. Me, too.

"I appreciate your seeing me again on such short notice," Alex said, "and I want to apologize."

"For what?" Johnson asked.

"For misleading you in our earlier conversations. We are doing a story on pedophiles, but not in a general way. We're focusing on one particular pedophile."

"Really?"

"When I talked to you the first time," Alex said, looking at his notes, "you told me pedophiles are rarely violent, that they tend to be passive people who might turn violent only when they're cornered . . . when facing discovery. Did I get that right?"

"Pretty much. But you do understand that there are no hard and fast rules. Each case can differ dramatically."

"Understood," Alex said. "But let me give you a hypothetical case. Say someone was sexually brutalized as a boy . . . over and over again . . . and that his tormentor was himself later murdered in an especially brutal way . . ."

"By the boy?" Johnson asked.

"We're not sure. In any event, is it possible that this kind of experience could lead the boy to an adult life of torturing other kids in the same way?"

"That's tough to answer," the therapist said. "Even in a hypothetical sense."

"Please try," Alex urged.

"It sounds as though you may be describing more of a psychopath than a pedophile, a man more interested in hurting kids than he is in fondling them. He may get his pleasure from their pain. I don't deal with that type often."

"Are you telling me this man's insane?"

"It sounds that way to me. Hypothetically, of course."

Alex paused, then continued. "You also told me that once a pedophile turns violent, he's likely to continue to be violent. Right?"

"That's true. But, again, we're talking about a relatively small sample. We've all heard about men who abduct small boys and end up killing them. But it's just not that common."

As Alex was walking to the door, Johnson stopped him. "I realize everything we've discussed is only *hypothetical*," he said, not disguising his concern. "But if I were you, I'd be careful."

Alex smiled at him ruefully. "You're not the first to say that, Dr. Johnson. I'll try."

When Alex returned to the station, he found Barclay waiting with a man Alex only vaguely recognized.

"Alex, I'm sure you remember Joel Petersen of the *Star Tribune*. He'd like to chat with the two of us, in private."

Alex had met the television columnist for the newspaper only once, when Alex arrived at the station and Hawke had held an informal press briefing to introduce the new anchorman to the local media. It had not been a memorable event, and Alex had not seen Petersen since.

They shook hands and Alex was impressed by the strength of his grip and by the bulk of the man. He and Barclay could both be sumo wrestlers, Alex thought as he followed them to Barclay's office.

Petersen wrote little about the local news programs in his column, concentrating instead on the network scene. Alex was surprised to see him making a personal visit to the newsroom.

"What can we do for you, Joel?" Barclay asked. "You probably want to do a feature on the best station in the country, right?"

Petersen was not in a joking mood. "No. In fact, I feel a little strange being here. I just thought I ought to give you a warning."

"A warning? What are you talking about?" Barclay asked, his mood darkening.

"Our city desk got an anonymous telephone call late last night, from somebody who sounded legit. He said he was going to give the paper an exclusive story . . . that a major TV anchorman in town had been convicted of libel many times and was found to have falsified evidence in a number of cases. He said this anchor skipped out of every city after each of these revelations and is here under an assumed name, Alex Collier."

"Jesus Christ," Alex muttered. "We wondered what would be next."

"What'd you say?" Petersen asked.

"Nothing," Alex replied. "Just talking to myself. But I can guess the rest: they called shortly before your deadline, after it was too late to check with anybody, and threatened to give the story to the St. Paul papers if they didn't see it in your next edition. Right?"

"Even better," Petersen said. "They gave the desk a number to call in California for confirmation. Of course, it's two hours earlier out there, so the desk guy tried it. Sure enough, somebody answered, identifying himself as an assistant district attorney."

"What the fuck is going on around here?" Barclay shouted.

"Of course we didn't bite," Petersen continued, "but the young guy on the desk called me at home. When we did more checking today, we confirmed that it was a lot of bullshit. I thought you ought to know that somebody's out to get you."

"Shit, we better call the St. Paul papers, and the AP and UPI," Barclay said, reaching for the phone.

"Don't bother," Petersen said. "I've already done it. I thought you deserved that favor."

"How about that California phone number?" Alex asked.

"I tried it as soon as I got in this morning," Petersen said. "It's already been disconnected."

Alex and Barclay looked at one another, both realizing how narrow the escape had been.

"I've got a nagging feeling that this call wasn't just out of the blue," Petersen said. "Anything you'd like to tell me, on or off the record?"

"Not yet," Alex said. "But, believe me, after what you've just done for us, you'll be the first to know."

At about the time Alex and Barclay were talking with the columnist, Judge Steele was stepping out of his car and onto the sidewalk in front of the Government Center. Russell, his driver, was behind the wheel, pulling away from the curb.

"Are you Judge Steele?"

"Yes," he said, and turned to face a tall young man with long, black hair, drooping eyelids and insolent smile.

"What can I do for you?" Steele asked.

"It's not what you can do for me," the young man said, with a smirk. "It's what I can do for you."

Steele clearly did not recognize him. "Who are you?" he asked, a tone of annoyance in his voice.

"Don't get so uptight, Judge. My name is Derek Glover. I think you and I have some business we need to discuss."

"What kind of business? Make it quick."

"I work for Channel Seven. With Alex Collier. Do you know what he's up to these days, Judge?"

Steele stared at him, saying nothing.

"From what I can tell," Derek continued, "you may need a little inside help. Call it consultation. I'm in a position to provide it. For a price, of course."

"I don't know what you're talking about," Steele said.

"If you don't, you should," Derek said.

"What do you do at Channel Seven?"

"I'm one of the little people who work behind the cameras. But I get around the station, I know what's going on."

Steele glanced up the street, apparently watching for the return of Russell. He appeared undecided.

"Why don't we continue this conversation in my chambers," he finally said.

"You won't regret it," Derek said.

Thirty

Roger walked through Steele's house, alone. It was late afternoon and the winter sun had retreated beneath the horizon, leaving the house in a twilight gloom.

Roger moved from room to room, straining to see in the half-light, knowing he was where he shouldn't be. These areas were forbidden to anyone but the judge.

He paused, listening, ready to bolt for safety at the slightest sound. But there was nothing, just the wind through the big pines and the soft rattle of the windows. He leaned against a wall, breathing deeply, his shoulders sagging.

The door to Steele's study was locked, as Roger knew it would be. Would his master key work? He didn't know; he had never dared to try it.

The key slipped in, the knob turned, and the door swung open, squeaking slightly on its hinges. Holy shit, he thought, what am I doing here? A single drop of sweat rolled down the back of his neck.

He resisted the urge to turn on a light, knowing the windows of the study could be seen from the driveway. He felt his way around the perimeter of the room, tracing the outline of the books on the wall shelves, finally reaching the rolltop desk by the window. Its cover and drawers were locked, and he had no key.

Across the room was another desk. The drawers were unlocked, but there were only papers there.

He went back to the book shelves. Eyes pressed close, his fingers moved across the rows of books. There! Near the bottom. Mixed in with the volumes were new shapes. Not books but cassette cartons!

Roger quickly pulled two of the tapes from the shelves. It was too dark to see any markings. Take a chance, he told himself, tucking the tapes into his pants, beneath his sweater.

The glare of headlights through the window temporarily blinded him, paralyzed him. The Continental was in the driveway, its doors slamming shut before Roger could move. He heaved himself toward the study door and sprinted down the hallway, holding the tapes tight against his stomach.

He reached the kitchen before he heard the key turn in the lock of the front door.

"Roger?" The hoarse shout echoed in the house. "Are you here? Why is everything so dark?"

"In here," Roger replied, hoping the quaver in his voice did not betray him. "In the kitchen. Getting ready to start dinner."

The judge came in, faced him, with a puzzled expression. "What's going on?" he asked. "Why no lights?"

Where was Russell? Must still be with the car.

"Sorry," Roger said, trying to busy himself at the sink. "I was taking a nap and didn't wake up until I heard the car pull in. I didn't expect you so soon. Dinner may be a little late."

"Take your naps on your own time, okay?" Steele snapped. "I don't like to be kept waiting. I'll be in my study. Call me when it's ready."

Roger leaned against the kitchen counter. His chest felt tight, his stomach knotted. He took a deep breath, feeling relief and a small sense of triumph. Then he heard the voice from down the hall.

"Roger!"

My God, he thought, did I shut the study door?

Alex never dreaded making a phone call more.

He had purposely waited until late in the evening, long after the kids would be in bed. It would be hard enough to talk to Jan, but the notion of facing the children—even on the telephone— was more than he could bear.

The phone rang four times before Jan answered, her voice filled with the huskiness of sleep. Alex apologized for the lateness of the hour.

"What's going on, Alex?"

"It's a long story, Jan, but things have changed since you wrote. I don't think you and the kids ought to be coming out here for Christmas. It may be too dangerous."

"*Dangerous?*" she said, now fully awake. "What in the world are you talking about? This isn't some joke, is it Alex?"

"It's no joke, Jan. Seuss is dead, killed by somebody who was trying to give me a warning."

"Seuss is *dead?* My God, what's happening, Alex? What kind of warning? Are you all right?"

"I'm okay, Jan. I can't explain it all on the phone, but I keep wondering what might have happened if you or the kids had been here. It's too frightening to even think about."

There was silence at the other end of the line.

"Are you there? Jan?"

"I'm here. What should I tell the kids about Seuss?"

"I wouldn't tell them anything for a while," Alex said.

He listened to her slow breathing. "The kids will be heartbroken if they don't see you. They've been counting the days on the calendar, Alex, crossing them off one by one. Maybe all this will be over by Christmas."

"I doubt it," Alex said. "It could be at its worst."

"We've still got a couple of weeks," she said. "I'll keep the airline tickets until we decide definitely not to come. Okay?"

Alex again voiced his reservations.

"Well, in the end, it's going to be up to you," she said.

"I know. And I'll end up being the bad guy again."

"Sometimes the shoe hurts," she said, and hung up.

"So what the hell happened then?" Rick asked, leaning forward in his chair. They were sitting at the kitchen table in Roger's house, reliving Roger's experience with the judge the night before.

"I thought I'd shit my pants," Roger replied. "I stood there like a goddamned statue, didn't know what to do. I still had those tapes stuck inside my belt. So I just stood there, like I was nailed to the fucking floor. I've never been so goddamned scared."

Roger felt the same fear again, remembering the hoarse shout echo down the hallway. *"Roger!"*

"I couldn't for the fucking life of me remember if I'd shut that door. I remembered going *through* the door, running down the hall, and sliding into the kitchen. But that was it."

"So what *did* you do," Rick asked, with obvious impatience.

"I didn't do anything. I'm telling you, I couldn't move. I just stood there until he yelled again. Figured I'd had it. Then I got my legs moving, poked my head around the corner and saw him down the hall, standing by the study door. 'Are you deaf?' he says, 'What's wrong with you?' And then he says 'I forgot my study keys at the office. Do your keys work in this door?' I say something like 'Don't know, never tried.' And he says 'Well, bring it here, and let's see.' So I do, and he opens up the fucking door."

"Jeez," Rick breathed. "Talk about a close call."

"Tell me about it. I thought I'd had it. That's the last time I'll ever try something like that. I don't give a shit what that Collier wants. It's too goddamned risky."

"So you got the tapes?" Rick asked.

"Damned right," Roger said, sticking a tape into the VCR.

The lighted stage in Steele's house was the first image on the screen. A figure in a long robe walked into the picture and on to the stage. He put on a blindfold and turned to face the front.

"Son of a bitch," Rick whispered.

The muted blues music he had heard in the hallway of Steele's house was now at full volume on the tape. Rick saw the robe drop around his ankles.

"I can't watch any more," he said as he picked up his coat and walked out the door.

Roger finished viewing both tapes, then dialed the phone.

"Collier?"

"Right. Who's this?"

"Roger Anderson. Can you talk?"

"Yes. For a minute. Where are you?"

"Home. I have the tapes. Two of them, at least."

"Good. Any problems?"

"It was a bitch getting them, and I'm afraid he'll miss them if I don't get them back soon."

"Have you seen them?"

"Yeah, I just watched them," he said. "They're what you're looking for."

"We'll need to make copies. Can you get them down here, or
can I pick them up?"

"Maybe you should come out. I don't want to be seen around
the TV station."

"Give me your address, and I'll be right there."

"Make it quick, okay? I don't like this shit."

Alex called John Knowles, then hurried to the engineering sup-
ply area to sign out a portable videotape recorder. Knowles met
him at the back door of the station.

"What's up?" Knowles asked, as they walked to his car.

"We've got to make dubs of a couple of Steele's tapes," Alex
said, recounting his conversation with Roger Anderson. "The kid
sounds scared, and I want to get copies of those tapes before he
can change his mind."

Traffic was light as they moved from downtown toward Anderson's Slater Avenue address. Despite the recent fresh snow, the
accumulated vehicle exhaust, factory emissions, and other pollu-
tants had already turned the streets a dirty, dingy gray.

"What's the latest on the lie detector tests?" Alex asked.

"I think I've found the right guy. He's in St. Paul, former FBI
polygraph tester. Great credentials, and very discreet, I'm told.
When do you want to start?"

"As soon as we can, I guess," Alex said. "But what about Sleet
in Los Angeles? He sure as hell doesn't want to come back here
for any tests."

"The guy in St. Paul says he can go with us, if we give him a
little notice. One of us will have to be there, too, with the photographer."

"Why don't you do that," Alex said. "I'm just not going to have
the time. Besides, I don't know a goddamned thing about lie de-
tectors."

It took them about twenty minutes to get to the house and to
find a parking place on the street about a half block away. Roger
was waiting inside the door, nervously watching the traffic pass by
outside. The black Lab was by his side, but Rick was nowhere to
be seen.

While Knowles set up the equipment in the house, Roger told

them about sneaking into Steele's study and of his close encounter with the judge. "I didn't know what I was getting into when I agreed to this," he said. "I was scared shitless."

"Sounds as though you handled it well," Alex said. "Now you've just got to get the tapes back where you found them."

"No shit," Roger muttered.

As Knowles was dubbing the tapes, Alex caught a glimpse of Rick shedding a robe on a lighted stage.

"Is that who I think it is?" he asked, looking around.

"You got it," Roger replied. "That's why he's not here. He didn't know he was on this tape, and when he saw it, he got pretty upset. Like he was in shock or something. He just got up, put his coat on, and walked out."

"Well, you took a big risk," Alex said to Roger, "and we appreciate it. I know it must have been scary—it is for all of us, believe me—but we're finally getting somewhere. These tapes should clinch it."

"There's got to be more," Roger said, "but I don't know how to get at all of them. I know he tapes every one of his sessions, and there's still one room I haven't been in. It's next to his study. At the far end, by the garage."

"What do you think's in there?"

"I have no idea. But it may have something to do with these tapes. Where he makes them, or stores them, or something. I don't know."

"Don't take any more chances," Alex said. "You've done enough already."

As they were packing up the equipment, Rick walked in the front door. His face was flushed from the cold, and he wore a pea jacket and stocking cap. The dog leaped to greet him.

"Are you going to show those tapes on TV?" Rick asked, barely inside the door. It was the first time Alex had ever heard him speak.

"Parts of them, maybe," Alex replied. "But not enough to permit recognition of anybody. You don't have to worry."

"I'm not worried," Rick said. "Not if they'll help stick it to Steele. He's one sick son of a bitch."

Rick stood with Roger by the door and watched as Alex and Knowles walked down the sidewalk toward Knowles's car.

Knowles stowed the videotape recorder in the trunk and then slid into the car.

"How's Linda doing?" Alex asked as he buckled the seat harness around himself.

"About the same," Knowles said. "I see her two or three times a week, but I can't notice much change. She still seems to be in mourning for Daniel. She says she wakes up hearing his screams and finds herself crying all the time."

"Is she getting professional help?"

"I've been pushing her," Knowles said, "but she thinks she can deal with it herself."

"How about the two of you?" Alex asked.

"I wish I knew. She seems to want to keep seeing me, but it's almost like she's using me to fill in for Daniel."

"Patience," Alex said. "Patience."

"Easy for you to say. You don't feel like somebody's ghost."

"Got time for a cup of coffee?"

Scotty Hansen was standing next to Alex's cubicle, holding two paper cups of coffee, looking as though he hadn't slept for a week. His collar was open and wrinkled, tie askew and stained, pants drooping around his waist.

Alex was startled; Hansen was normally a fastidious dresser. "Scotty, you look like shit," he said. "Are you sick or something?"

The sportscaster shook his head, and pulled up a chair close to Alex. "No, I just haven't gotten a lot of sleep lately. I need to talk, if you've got the time."

Alex guessed Hansen was in his mid-to-upper fifties, but he had the physique of someone much younger. As a running back at the University of Minnesota, he had set a number of Big Ten yardage records. He'd played two years with the Green Bay Packers before a knee injury ended his professional career. As a local sports hero, he had had no problem getting a job in broadcasting when he returned to Minnesota.

But that was thirty years ago. His running records had long since been surpassed, and the memories of his athletic exploits had faded further with each generation. Now he was simply an aging ex-jock who was fast becoming an old sports anchor.

"Have you heard the rumors?" Hansen asked.

"What rumors?" Alex replied, his expression unchanged.

"That they're looking to replace me. The guys in the mailroom tell me Barclay is getting in dozens of tapes from sportscasters all around the country."

"Have you talked to Barclay?" Alex asked.

"No, not yet. My contract's up in a few months, and I thought I'd wait to see what happens with that."

"I don't think you should wait," Alex said. "Talk with Barclay. He'll be straight with you."

"Have *you* heard anything?" Hansen pressed. "You seem to be in tight with those people."

Alex tried to skirt the question. "Me? Tight with who? Shit, I've bounced around more in the past five years than most people have in their careers. I don't have time to get tight with anybody. You know, a moving target is hard to hit."

"I can't believe it," Hansen said, more to himself than to Alex. "If they're not happy with me, why doesn't somebody say something? Why do I have to hear things from guys in the mailroom? It just doesn't seem fair after all these years."

"Look, Scotty, I'm not the one who should be telling you anything. Talk to Barclay. The business has changed, with the consultants and all, and fairness isn't as important today as it once was."

"I don't know what I'll do," Hansen said, slumping in the chair. "I haven't done anything else since I quit playing ball. I don't *know* anything else. I've still got two kids in college, and a mortgage to meet. And the union pension plan isn't worth a damn."

"The first thing you should do," Alex said, "is to try to get yourself back together. Get some sleep, some fresh clothes. Then forget all of this shit for a while. Maybe we can turn this thing around."

"What do you mean?" Hansen asked.

"I'm not sure, but I've got an idea."

Alex waited until Hansen walked away. Then he picked up the telephone.

Thirty-one

The bedroom was pitch-black and absolutely still when the phone rang for the first time. The sound brought Barbara straight up in bed, out of a deep sleep, disoriented and sightless in the dark.

She pushed the covers back with one hand and reached for the bedside lamp with the other. The light blinded her momentarily, but quickly restored her sense of her surroundings. The phone was across the room, on the dresser, and she stared at it without moving—until it rang again.

"Yes?" she said. There was silence at the other end. "Hello? Who is this?"

"Get wise, cunt. Back off!"

Barbara recoiled at the words. They were like a sharp slap in the face, and she felt the sting. She was now fully awake.

"Who is this?" she stammered again.

The line was dead.

Barbara unplugged the phone from the wall. But she could not forget the words or the voice—filled with a cold hatred and calculated contempt.

She couldn't sleep after that. She prowled the apartment, drawing the drapes more tightly, double-checking the dead-bolt lock. She thought about calling Phil or Alex, but decided against it. What could they do? She slipped back into bed, pulling the covers tight around her neck, keeping the lamp lit, her eyes fixed on the ceiling.

How had they found my phone number? she wondered. The number was unlisted, known only to her close friends and family and to a few people at the station. It was protection against crank calls, and the number was to be revealed to no one without Barbara's personal permission.

Yet somehow someone had gotten hold of the number. She was still staring at the ceiling when she thought of Alex's notes.

Were they more than empty threats?

Her eyes opened as they had closed, staring straight up. She didn't feel as if she'd slept, but she knew she must have: hours had passed, and the suffused light of morning was now trying to push its way past the drawn drapes. The lamp was still on, and soft music was coming from the clock radio. Nine A.M.

She tiptoed to the window, pushed aside one edge of the drape, and looked down on the empty street below. She didn't know what she had expected to see, but was relieved it looked as it always did.

She was in her robe, pouring her first cup of the coffee when the buzzer of the intercom sounded. "Barbara?" It was Phil. "Are you okay? I've been trying to call for an hour."

"Hold on, Phil. Let's talk up here, okay?" She pressed the button opening the security lock on the front door, and he was there in a few moments.

"I'm fine, Phil. C'mon in, and I'll tell you why I unplugged my phone." She led him into the kitchen, holding his hand tightly, recounting details of the phone call. "It was silly, I suppose, but I haven't been that frightened in years. I felt that if someone like that could get my phone number, they could also get inside my place," she said, looking around. "I keep thinking of Alex's cat."

"Who would know you're involved in this story?"

"I don't know," Barbara said. "I haven't exactly broadcast it around. It's a pretty small group that knows . . . just Alex, Barclay . . ." She stopped.

"What's the matter?"

The picture of Derek standing silently behind her in the editing room flashed through her mind. And his words: *"Is that the Judge Steele he's talking about? Pretty hot stuff!"*

"Nothing," she said. "I just can't forget Derek standing over my shoulder, watching the tape, sneering. But it's probably nothing."

Pat was riding the escalator up to the main floor of the Government Center when she spotted Judge Steele opposite her, going down on the other escalator. She tried to avert her eyes, but he saw her at the same time.

"Patricia! Do you have a minute?" he asked as they passed.

She reached the top as he arrived at the bottom, and they stood for a moment, a floor apart, looking at one another. Steele finally stepped on the escalator and rode up toward her.

"I was hoping we'd run into one another sometime soon," he said, as he reached her and took her arm—leading her to a small bench on one side of the atrium.

"I'm due at a pretrial hearing in a minute," she said. "I have to run." Her tone was firm, and she declined his invitation to sit next to him on the stone bench.

"Who's holding the hearing?" he asked.

"Judge Siransky."

"If there's any problem, I'll speak to him," Steele said. "I want a word with you. Please sit."

Pat was torn. She wanted to escape, but she didn't think she could rudely walk away from him. So she reluctantly sat down, careful to keep a distance between them.

"I don't need to tell you I was very surprised to see you and Collier show up at the lake place in Wisconsin. Surprised and perplexed, Patricia. I still don't understand what you were doing there."

"*You* were surprised?" Pat said. "What about me? The last time I saw the place, it was all trees and bushes."

"It is a pity Nathaniel decided not to mention our arrangement to you. He must have his reasons. What troubles me more, however, is your relationship with Collier—"

"Really, I don't think—"

"Allow me to finish, Patricia. I don't believe Collier is a person deserving of your friendship. I am told he is pursuing an almost *maniacal* mission to discredit the bench and those of us who serve it. That certainly could include your husband."

Pat studied the judge closely. Seated, he had lost some of his imposing strength and stature. But his eyes had lost none of their penetrating power. They were fixed on her like a laser.

"Judge, I don't believe this is an appropriate discussion," she said. "What Alex Collier does on the job is none of my business."

"Patricia, let's be candid, shall we?" Steele moved closer, his voice a hoarse whisper. "To a great extent, Nathaniel's future in the judiciary is tied to my own. Some would call him a protégé. He's still quite young, and very ambitious, someone who could, with enough time and a right word here and there, follow in my footsteps to the Supreme Court.

"On the other hand," he continued, "his judicial career could hit an unexpected snag. A *wrong* word here or there could do great damage, politics being what they are. He could wind up back where he began, or worse."

Pat stood up, abruptly. "I don't like what you're implying, Judge." She started to walk away, but Steele rose quickly and grabbed her by the arm.

"Come now, Patricia. Let's not play games. I know there is more between you and Collier than old college memories. I'm imploring you for Nathaniel's sake, if not your own, to use your influence to persuade Collier to retreat."

Pat jerked her arm free, her words a hiss. "Don't touch me like that again. *Ever.* You may be Nathaniel's mentor, and he may be your protégé, but you're nothing to me."

He was still standing there by the stone bench when Pat got into the elevator. She could feel his eyes through the steel doors.

Alex found a hand-scrawled note from George Barclay on his desk. "Come see me, pronto!"

Barclay was in his office, sitting at his desk, half-hidden behind an open *Star-Tribune.*

"You wanted to see me?" Alex asked, trying to look over the paper. "George?"

The page slowly lowered, and Barclay's bearded face appeared. He was not smiling.

"You wouldn't know anything about this, would you?" he asked, pointing to the top of the television section. It was Joel Petersen's column, with a bold headline:

LET'S SAVE SCOTTY!

"What the hell's that?" Alex asked, innocently. "Something about Scotty Hansen?" He bent over the paper, reading the words, avoiding Barclay's probing eyes.

"Informed sources at Channel Seven report that veteran sports-caster and former Gopher football great Scotty Hansen may be on his way out. The sources say that Vice President/General Manager Nicholas Hawke has ordered News Director George Barclay to begin a nationwide search for Hansen's replacement. Barclay is said to oppose the decision, but is now in the process of reviewing audition tapes of potential sportscasters from around the country."

Alex glanced up at Barclay, who was watching him in stony silence. Alex returned to the column.

"The action reportedly is the result of the latest research con-ducted by the station's news consultant, who is said to believe Hansen's age and long tenure at the station are hurting Channel Seven's efforts to attract younger viewers to its newscasts.

"Hawke was unavailable for comment, but if true, this would be only the latest example of the high-handed and insensitive treat-ment dished out to some of our television favorites by know-it-all consultants and weak-kneed station managers. I think Scotty Han-sen deserves better, and I would urge all Channel Seven viewers, and all Minnesota football fans, to begin a 'Save Scotty' campaign. Just address your cards and letters to Nicholas Hawke at Channel Seven. If enough of you do, I'm sure he'll get the message."

"Hell of a piece," Alex said. "Has Hawke seen this yet?"

"He's at a network affiliates meeting in L.A." Barclay replied, "and, no, I don't think he knows about it yet. I'm not looking forward to what he'll say when he finds out."

An excited Barbara poked her head in the door. "Have you read it?" she asked. Their looks told her they had. "Well, you ain't heard nothing yet! Two of the morning-drive deejays on radio have joined the 'Save Scotty' campaign, and are telling all of their listeners to call Hawke with their vote for Scotty. Our switchboards are jammed, and Hawke's secretary is about ready to jump out the window."

"Jeeesus Christ!" Barclay exploded. "He'll have my ass for breakfast."

"Why should he be pissed at you?" Alex asked. "You didn't tell Petersen any of this stuff. It's not your fault it leaked. You know you can't keep secrets in a newsroom. Besides, you warned him this could happen, remember?"

"He'll sure as hell know *somebody* who was in that research meeting leaked it," Barclay shouted. "And he knows it wasn't him or the consultant. That leaves you, me, Barbara, and that prick from promotion."

"Not necessarily," Alex said. "The rumors are flying all around the station. Even the guys in the mailroom know about the audition tapes. And a lot of people know we had a research meeting. Put two and two together and you've got a rumor. *Anyone* could have leaked it."

"In this kind of detail?" Barclay asked, looking unconvinced. "Maybe he'll buy it, maybe he won't. But he's going to be madder than hell, no matter what he believes."

"It ought to buy Scotty a little time, anyway," Alex offered, "and maybe the public response to this 'Save Scotty' campaign will prove to Hawke that the research was wrong."

"You sound as if you've thought this all out, Collier. As if you maybe even planned it this way."

"You have a very suspicious mind," Alex deadpanned. "But I must admit, it does occur to me that with all of this commotion going on, Hawke may have less time to worry about any reports or rumors he might hear about an investigation of his friend Steele."

"Collier, you are one devious son of a bitch," Barclay said, a hint of admiration in his voice.

Nicholas Hawke did not like surprises. Nor did he like trouble.

He was expecting neither as he stood by the reflecting pools at the Century Plaza Hotel in Los Angeles, quietly sipping his dry vodka martini and listening to a small group of network executives complain about the soaring costs of prime-time programming.

"Why do you think there are so damn many public affairs shows on in prime time?" one of them asked. "Because we're public

spirited? Bullshit! Because they're a hell of a lot cheaper to pro-
duce, that's why. You don't have to pay the news people what
you've got to pay these fucking Hollywood stars."

Hawke had to laugh. He knew these same network executives
who dumped on the Hollywood stars in private would kiss their
asses in public. He was moving in closer to the group, ready to
enter the discussion, when a bellboy walked up and handed him
a note with a terse message:

> Mr. Hawke. Please call your
> office. Urgent! Marie.

"Marie" was Marie Stickney, Hawke's secretary, whom he knew
would never bother him at an affair like this unless there was a
genuine crisis at the station.

Hawke excused himself from the group, which hardly noticed
his departure ("Most of them are a bunch of fucking fairies, you
know, and we're paying them millions!") and walked to a pay phone
in the lobby. Marie's line was busy. He waited two minutes and
tried again. Still busy. He dialed his private number and let it ring
eight times before finally hearing the harried voice of his secretary.

"Oh, Mr. Hawke! I'm so glad you got my message. It's going
crazy around here. I've never seen anything like it!"

"Settle down, Marie. What's happening?"

She read him Petersen's television column and told him how
everybody was climbing on the "Save Scotty" bandwagon: the radio disc jockeys, viewers by the hundreds, even reporters from
the other television stations. "The phones lines are all plugged
up," she said. "You can't even get a line out."

Hawke couldn't believe what he was hearing, but before he
could say anything, Marie pressed on: "The newspapers and the
radio and TV stations are calling for a statement from you, and I
don't know what to tell them. They want to know if Scotty's going
to be fired or if you're going to reconsider because of the public
outcry. It's just *terrible*, Mr. Hawke!"

"Don't say anything to anybody, Marie. Just tell people I'm out
of town and unavailable for comment. Got that? I'll be on my way
back first thing in the morning. Now, get me George Barclay."

"I'm afraid I can't, Mr. Hawke. The phone lines won't handle
any internal transfers. The whole system's gone wacky."

"Okay, Marie. Then walk down to his office and have him call me in my room here at the hotel. I'll be there in a minute."

Nicholas Hawke didn't like surprises, and he didn't like trouble. Now he had both.

Somebody was going to pay.

Alex was seething. Phil had brought Barbara to the station and told Alex of her early-morning phone calls. He had also learned of Pat's courthouse encounter with Judge Steele.

"Those chicken-shit bastards! Why don't they confront *me?*"

"Because they know this will probably be more effective," Phil said. "Looks like they're right."

They were sitting in George Barclay's office, awaiting his return. Marie Stickney had summoned him moments before, and he had quickly waddled away. They guessed Hawke must have gotten the word about Scotty Hansen. Poor George.

"So what do I do about Steele?" Alex asked. "We can't just sit around and take this shit."

"We don't have a lot of options," Phil said. "You say you're not ready to go with your story yet, and we're sure as hell not ready to go for an indictment. Steele must know his only chance is to scare you off the story. He probably doesn't even know I'm involved yet."

"So? What do we do?"

"Barbara's had her number changed, and the only ones who will know it are George Barclay and you. She's promised to watch her step, and either I'll be at her place, or she'll be at mine, every night."

"Tough duty," Alex said with a smile.

Phil ignored the jibe. "So that should take care of Barbara. From what you say, Pat Hodges can probably take care of herself. If I were her, I'd be more worried about her husband."

"What do you mean?" Alex asked.

"Think about it. If Steele and his boys are as alarmed as we think they are, and if this little ploy with Pat didn't work, don't you think he'd go after her husband? Start putting pressure on *him* to put pressure on *her* to put pressure on *you?* Makes sense to me. Hodges and Steele must already be tight, with that cabin deal and all, and I can just hear Steele telling Hodges his fucking career is over unless he plays along."

"Maybe Steele already did that," Alex said, "and when that didn't work, he went to Pat himself. Besides, why would Nathaniel think Pat could pressure me?"

"You'll have to answer that," Phil replied. "But Steele obviously thought she could. Why wouldn't Hodges? At the very least, he must know you two were at the cabin together. Why wouldn't he suspect more?"

"I still don't think we can just do nothing," Alex said. "I've got to send some kind of message to get them to back off. Otherwise, anything could happen."

"I'd be careful," Phil cautioned. "You start playing those kind of games, and anything *could* happen. You should just keep your cool and get that story on the air as fast as you can."

Barclay hung up the phone, his ears still stinging from Hawke's tirade. Barclay had been right; Hawke *did* blame the Hansen leak on somebody in the research meeting, and he was determined to ferret out the culprit. Hawke ordered a meeting on his return the next morning—to figure out a public response to the rumors, and to *fix* the leak.

Hawke's reaction had been no surprise to Barclay. Like every bureaucrat or executive ever born, television general managers hate news leaks, especially those which come from their own news-rooms. They consider the leakers to be traitors and are always determine to plug the leaks, although they usually don't have much success.

Barclay had tired of telling his bosses they were pissing into the wind. News people love to gossip, to pass on the latest rumors from their station to friends at other stations or to the newspaper columnists. So he'd simply listened patiently to Hawke's hysterics, denying any knowledge of how the rumors got started, and promising to do all he could to track down the source.

"Have you talked to Alex and Barbara yet?" Hawke demanded.

"Of course," Barclay replied. "But we have to be careful with that. They're the franchise right now, and I'd hate to get them all hacked off. They're too important to us."

"How about Hansen? Have you talked to him?"

"No," Barclay said, with some relish. "I thought I'd leave that to you."

Late that afternoon, Scotty Hansen showed up at the station, looking fit but a bit sheepish. He ignored the catcalls and wolf whistles from the newsroom crew, giving them all a grin and a sweep of his middle finger as he walked directly toward Alex's desk.

Before he got there, someone hoisted a three-by-twelve-foot "Save Scotty" banner over the assignment desk, and someone else started a tape with a deafening rendition of "The Minnesota Rouser," the university's fight song.

Alex grinned, half expecting to see cheerleaders and pom-pom girls running into the newsroom. But they weren't needed: everyone was on his feet, cheering and clapping to the beat of the Rouser. "Rah, rah, rah for Ski-U-Mah, Rah for the U of M. . . ."

Hansen was obviously touched, but embarrassed. "Look what you've done," he said, as he reached Alex.

"Who, me?" Alex said, spreading his hands apart in mock innocence. "I'd say you're seeing a genuine outpouring of support and affection."

"I can't believe it," Hansen said, looking around. "I've been hiding all day, trying to avoid the newspaper and radio people. There's even a camera crew from the competition out in front of the station. I had to sneak in the back."

"You're the center of attention, no question about that."

"What the hell should I say?" Hansen asked. "What can I say?"

"Don't say anything if you don't have to," Alex offered. "Just carry on as you always do. But if you're pressed, just say you don't know where the rumors got started, that you're overwhelmed by the public response, and that you hope to be here for many years to come."

"Does Hawke know about this?"

"He does now," Alex said. "He's in L.A., but he'll be on his way home soon."

"Christ, what do I say to *him*? What do I do?"

"Shit, if I were you, I'd ask for a raise," Alex said.

Thirty-two

Roger carried the two tape cassettes under his jacket until he was inside Steele's house, until he was sure no one else was there. Then he walked calmly down the hallway, opened Steele's study door, and replaced the cassettes where he had found them on the library shelf.

He glanced around the room, feeling no fear now, but still recalling the terror of the headlights in the window, of his flight down the hall. In the light of day, he could see what he had only felt in the darkness: the desks, the chair, the lamps, the row upon row of books.

What he didn't see as he came or left the study was a small piece of toothpick that fell silently to the carpet when he opened the door.

After making sure the door was locked, Roger returned to the kitchen and began preparing dinner for the judge and Russell. He knew they'd be there in a couple of hours, and he was determined this time to be ready when they arrived.

An hour after dinner, as Roger was preparing to leave the house, Judge Steele invited him into the living room for a drink. It was a rare invitation, and Roger accepted with some hesitancy.

He sat on the couch as Steele busied himself at the private bar,

talking over his shoulder, excitedly explaining plans for his swearing-in as chief justice. As he moved about, his pet parakeets rustled
in their cage, chirping and flitting from side to side.

Roger had seldom seen Steele so relaxed, so animated. Strange,
Roger thought, knowing what he knew, but he shrugged off his
qualms and joined the judge in a toast to the future.

It was after his second sip of the drink that Roger felt his first
touch of drowsiness, and after his third sip that he felt his eyelids
droop.

Steele's image was blurred, but Roger could see him holding
something tiny between his thumb and forefinger.

"Know what this is, Roger? Can you see it, Roger?"

The voice grew more distant with each word.

"It's a toothpick, Roger. See it? Guess where I found it, Roger?"

Roger's consciousness slipped away before he could guess.

At about the same time, Rick stood at the edge of the circle of
light thrown by the streetlamp, half in, half out of the shadows.
He was five steps back from the curb, where he knew he'd be
picked up—but just barely—by the headlights of passing cars. It
was a fine art, hustling was, a game of hide-and-seek; visible to
some, invisible to others.

Rick had done this a few times before. After his first arrest for
soliciting, he had quickly learned the small tricks of the trade.
What to say, where to stand, how to act, and most important, how
to tell the real johns from the vice-squad plants.

Rick was alone on the street tonight, as he suspected he might
be. He knew business always fell off during the Christmas season,
when many of the regular customers were preoccupied with family
holiday activities. He knew that when the johns weren't out, most
of the hustlers wouldn't be, either.

But he was on a mission that couldn't wait until after Christmas.

Rick pulled his cap down over his ears, not to warm them, but
to cover the small earpiece and cord running from his right ear
down the back of his neck. He could feel the weight of the wireless
transmitter on the back of his belt, under his coat, and could touch
the small microphone which had replaced one of the buttons on
his coat.

The unmarked I-Team van was parked half a block away, at an

angle against the curb, to provide a clear shooting lane for the camera behind the curtained window.

His earpiece crackled: "Remember, Rick, if a car pulls up, step out into the light, and get as close as you can to the guy inside, so we can pick up as much of your conversation as possible." The voice was Alex's, from inside the heated van.

Rick stepped into the light of the streetlamp and nodded, hoping he could be seen through the long lens of the camera.

"We see you fine, Rick. That's good. Can we get another voice check?"

Rick could think of nothing to say. "Anything at all, Rick," Alex said. "We just need a voice level." Rick's mind was blank. "C'mon, count, sing, do anything." Rick finally said the first words that came into his mind, straight out of his childhood. "Now I lay me down to sleep, I pray the Lord my soul to keep . . ." Then he stopped, embarrassed.

"That's fine," Alex said, exchanging glances with the cameraman. "Just remember not to touch the mike or to rub it against anything. It'll cause static."

Earlier in the day, when they'd decided to begin the nighttime surveillance, it had been John Knowles who suggested trying a decoy in hopes of getting some general footage of johns on the prowl, cruising in their cars. There was also the remote hope that one of those cars might be a Lincoln Continental.

"It's going to be a hell of a lot easier than trying to follow Steele's car around," Knowles had told Alex. "Maybe we'll luck out, and they'll come to us. Can't hurt to try for a night or two."

"Where in hell do we find a decoy?" Alex had asked. "What do we tell him to do? We sure as hell wouldn't want him to actually get picked up. Or busted, for that matter."

"The cops do it all the time," Knowles had argued. "Nothing illegal or unethical about it if the decoy just stands there and listens to the offers."

It was then that Alex had thought of Rick, and when he'd called, he had found him anxious to help out. So after a hurried briefing he'd been carefully wired and taken to his decoy position on "the hill" near Loring Park, perhaps the most popular roost in the city for young chickens.

That had been two hours ago, and so far only two cars had even slowed as they passed him. Neither had stopped. Rick was getting cold and frustrated. "I don't know if this is going to work," he whispered into the button-mike. "Nobody seems to be out looking."

"Just take it easy," Alex replied, through the earpiece. "Let's give it a while longer. I know it must be cold out there, but try to make the best of it. We'll take a break if something doesn't happen soon."

Another half hour passed, and two more cars slowed as they drove by. Fifteen minutes later, one of the cars returned, almost crawling. It was a Pontiac Grand Prix. It stopped fifty feet away. Rick stood still. Another of the rules: don't make the approach, let them come to you.

Rick could see the outline of a head behind the wheel, staring back at him, studying him. Finally, the car moved away, as slowly as it had arrived. Five minutes went by before it was back, this time stopping directly in front of Rick, inside the circle of light. The passenger window rolled down with a hum, and Rick stepped up, leaning inside, remembering to push the microphone as far forward as possible.

"Need a ride?" the driver asked.

"I don't know," Rick replied. "Where you heading?"

"Where do you want to go? In the mood for a little party?"

"Depends," Rick said. "Who'll be there?"

"Just you and me so far."

The man was heavy-set, dressed in a cashmere coat, his body squeezed between the seat and steering wheel. He wore a hat pulled down over his eyes, but Rick could see his flaccid cheeks and a double chin in the glow of the dashboard lights.

Rick waited, knowing he could not make the first monetary suggestion. "I don't know . . . A friend is supposed to pick me up."

"You're not working for the cops, are you?" the man asked, suddenly. The question always arose, sooner or later.

"Do I look old enough to be a goddamned plant?" Rick responded. "Shit, I'm not even out of high school."

"Okay, okay," the john said. "How about the party? I can make it worth your while."

"How worth my while?" Rick asked, glancing toward the truck, hoping they were getting all of this on the tape.

"Thirty for a nice simple little favor. Won't take more than fifteen minutes."

"What kind of 'little favor?' " Rick asked.

"Don't be cute. What are you, a pricktease? Do we play or not?"

"I'll need at least fifty," Rick said, hoping to end the conversation.

"For a blow-job? C'mon, you got to be kidding."

"Fifty. That's it. Take it or leave it," Rick said.

"Fuck off," the man growled, as the car window closed and he drove off.

"And Merry Christmas to you, too," Rick muttered.

Three more cars, a Toyota, a Cadillac, and another Pontiac, were drawn to Rick's post in the next three hours, and each time the scenario was the same: guarded overtures, a wary proposition from the john, quibbling over price, and a rebuff.

Each car's license plate was dutifully recorded, and between each approach the I-Team van changed locations slightly, to vary the angles of the camera shots, and to deflect suspicion. Alex noted that not one of the prospective johns had bothered to ask Rick's age. They'd probably prefer him even younger, he thought.

"Let's call it a night," Alex finally said, talking into the microphone in the van. "We got some good stuff, Rick. Just relax until we can get you unwired."

"Good," Rick replied, "my ass is freezing."

As Alex was pulling back the van door, another set of headlights swung around the corner, moving slowly down the street. "Hold it!" the cameraman whispered. "We got another customer."

Alex leaped to the mike button. "Hold on, Rick. Be alert. We've got more company."

A small black BMW crept along the curb and stopped, still in the dark. Rick didn't move. Neither did the car.

"C'mon, asshole, pull up," the cameraman murmured from behind his camera. "Get into the light."

But the standoff continued. After several minutes, Rick finally sauntered to the car, ignoring the no-approach rule.

"Looking for somebody?" he asked, leaning into the open window. The words were hardly spoken when the engine roared and the car sped away, leaving Rick openmouthed on the curb.

"What the hell was *that* all about?" Alex asked.

"Did you get the license number?" Rick responded.

"No, he never got far enough into the light. Why?"

Rick walked down the sidewalk to the van and opened the door.

"Because," he said, "the guy in that car was the same guy who was in the back of the Continental with me, that's why. One of Steele's delivery boys."

"Did he recognize you?" Alex asked.

"I guess so, the way he took off. Wonder who the hell he is?"

There must be lots of black BMWs around, Alex thought, but he knew of only one: it belonged to Pat and Nathaniel Hodges.

The next morning, Nicholas Hawke was back from Los Angeles. He stood in front of his desk, arms folded across his chest, looking down on his seated audience: Alex, Barbara, Barclay, and Justin Scott, the promotion director.

The power posture, Alex thought, studying Hawke. No-nonsense Nick. He looks like he was born in a business suit, Alex mused, as though he emerged from the womb with his pants pressed and tie straight.

The research meeting had been reconvened, but for a different purpose. Hawke wasn't smiling.

"I was shocked to hear about the Scotty Hansen rumor," he said. "And I'm disturbed by the adverse impact the rumors, and the resulting public outcry, will have on this television station."

"Did you see the ratings from last night?" Barclay asked, quickly. "Best ever. Forty-three fucking share of audience."

"Come off it, George. What do you take me for? Who the hell wouldn't be curious enough to watch after the uproar we've had? But that's beside the point. There's been a betrayal of trust here; somebody leaked that information—very private information—to the newspaper columnist, and I want to know who it was."

"Are you accusing one of us?" Alex asked, righteous anger in his voice.

"You're damned right I am!" Hawke said. "You're the only ones who had access to that information."

"I don't like what I'm hearing," Barbara said.

"That's too bad, Barbara, but I'm going to get to the bottom of this," Hawke said. "I plan to talk to the columnist and to his editors."

"They won't tell you squat," Barclay said.

"Maybe not, but I'm putting you on notice that I won't tolerate this bullshit. These rumors have got to stop."

"But Mr. Hawke," Barbara said, "it wasn't really a rumor, was it? As I understand it, you are planning to get rid of Scotty. I remember George warning you that this kind of thing could happen if the news ever got out."

Alex gave her an admiring glance, but Hawke glared at her—his face reddening.

"I agree with you, Mr. Hawke." It was Justin Scott, speaking for the first time. "I think the rumors have been destructive. And there's no doubt they originated in the newsroom."

"Fuck you, Scott," Barclay said. "You're just a frustrated newsman yourself, bitter because you never made the fucking grade."

Scott was out of his seat. "I resent that, Barclay . . ."

"Settle down, both of you," Hawke shouted angrily. "We're getting nowhere this way."

"What are you going to do about Scotty?" Alex asked, hoping to break the tension. "He's the one hanging out to dry."

Hawke eyed Alex suspiciously. "Can't forget him, can we, Collier? For now, I've decided to call off the search for his replacement. I will tell the public that no such search was ever planned or conducted, that the rumors are false."

Chalk one up for the good guys, Alex thought.

"The search for the leak will continue, however," Hawke said, "and I won't rest until I've plugged it. Is that clear?"

Clear as ice, Alex thought, as they got up to leave.

"One more thing. Collier, it sounds like you've recovered from your laryngitis. I want you back on the air tonight. Understood?"

"No problem," Alex muttered, pushing his way through the door.

When they were back in the newsroom, Barbara stopped at Alex's desk.

"Have you still got those tapes?" she asked.

"Which tapes?"

"The sex tapes from Steele's house," she replied.

"Yeah, they're in my desk. But I don't think you want to see them. They're pretty graphic."

"Look in your desk."

He opened the desk drawer. The tapes were gone. "What the fuck?" he said. "Where the hell are they? Knowles must have them."

"Don't count on it," Barbara said. "Do you have other copies?"

"Not unless John made another set. What's happening, any-way?"

"Derek."

"What do you mean, 'Derek?' "

"Somebody from graphics saw him rummaging around my desk last night," she said. "I knew he'd seen me viewing the tape of Sleet's interview, but thank God I'd already taken those tapes back to John. Then I thought of the tapes you had."

"Fuck me," Alex muttered, opening drawer after drawer of his desk. "We *need* those goddamned tapes." He slammed the last drawer shut and sat back in his chair. "I should have locked the drawers, for Christ's sake. I'm not thinking straight."

Barbara knelt next to him. "Maybe John did make more copies."

"I doubt it," Alex replied.

"I'll give him a call," Barbara said, starting to move away.

"I don't get it," Alex said. "How would Derek know about those tapes? And what would he want with them?"

"Maybe he just gets a thrill out of looking at that kind of stuff."

Alex shook his head. "I don't think so. He's looking for any chance he can get to fuck things up for me."

As Barbara left to make her call, Alex's phone rang. It was Rick. "Have you seen or heard from Roger?" he asked Alex. "He wasn't here when I got home last night, and he hasn't come in this morn-ing."

"No, I haven't heard from him, Rick. You should try Steele's house," Alex suggested. "Maybe he stayed there last night."

"I did," Rick replied. "Several times. No answer. I'm worried. This isn't like Roger."

"Relax, Rick. He'll show up. But let me know when he does, will you? I need to talk to him."

Alex's voice was calm and reassuring, but that was not how he felt.

Thirty-three

Roger awoke to the sound of the birds. Not Steele's parakeets in the cage, but wild birds, chickadees, and pine siskins, thumping against the outside of the window in their greedy haste to get to the feeder.

No, not the parakeets. This time, he was in the cage and the birds were free.

Roger had no notion of where he was. The room was small, maybe ten by ten, finished in a shiny knotty pine. Even the ceiling was pine. He was lying on a single bed, more of a cot, really, and a small dresser stood across the way. A single window allowed a shaft of sunlight to hit one wall, and he could see the minuscule particles of dust dancing in the light.

He sat up slowly, feeling a dull ache at the base of his skull, and a slight unsteadiness when he stood. He slowly walked to the window and saw the birds fluttering around the long glass feeder suspended from the overhang of the roof. Beyond it was nothing but trees, as solid as a wooden wall, allowing the sun to penetrate only through their upper reaches.

The window would not open from the inside, and the door, when he tried it, was locked. Some of his clothes hung from a rod in the closet, others filled three of the dresser drawers. They were clothes he had kept at the judge's house.

Roger listened for any noises in the house, no matter how faint. Creaking floors, the ring of a telephone, the sound of a radio or television. There was nothing. He was sure he was alone.

He tried the door again. There was no give to it. He went to the window, rapping on the glass with his knuckles, then scratching the surface with his ring. It wasn't glass, but some kind of hard plastic. He felt the window frame. Not wood, but painted metal.

He stood quietly, then cupped his hands around his mouth.

"Help! Hello, Anyone. Can you hear? Help!"

A minute passed. Then he heard the first footstep.

He was not alone.

Roger sat back on the bed, his eyes fastened on the door, his ears cocked at the sound of the approaching footsteps. They moved across the floor above, then down the steps, one by one.

The footsteps stopped outside the door. He heard the key in the lock, he saw the doorknob turn, watched as the door opened a crack. The first thing he saw through the crack was his visitor's hawk nose.

The door opened all the way. Russell's body filled the doorway.

"Pipe down, Roger. Nobody can hear you anyway."

His first name was Russell, but that's all Roger knew.

"Where am I, Russell? Why are you keeping me locked up? Where's the judge?" He tried to keep his voice calm, to hide the tremors of fear.

"I can't say nothing. But I'm supposed to bring you food and something to drink, if you want."

"C'mon, Russell. What's the deal? What's this all about?"

Russell didn't budge. "You want something or not?"

It was like talking to the door. "Sure. Whatever you've got."

The door closed, leaving Roger alone again.

For the second night, Alex knelt inside the I-Team van, his legs cramped after two hours of stooping, his eyes weary from peering into the darkness. He almost envied Rick's post on the street; he needed to stretch his legs, to breathe in the fresh air.

Tonight, John Knowles was with him in the van. "How much longer, John?" Alex asked. "Hawke wants me back for the news."

"Let's give it another fifteen minutes," Knowles replied. "Never can tell what might turn up."

Tonight was even slower than the night before; only two cars had stopped, and neither was the one they were looking for. Rick patiently stood his ground, never complaining, despite temperatures in the teens and a biting north wind that swept down the empty street.

He didn't look like the same person; the decoy was now in disguise. They had given him a new coat and hat, elevated shoes, and a small mustache, in hopes of again attracting the mystery BMW.

The trap remained baited, but unsprung.

The fifteen minutes passed, but there were no more cars.

"Here, Rick, let me help you get unwired," Knowles said, once Rick was back inside the van.

Rick said nothing, allowing the equipment to be stripped from his body. Alex watched him, knowing where his thoughts were.

"No word yet from Roger?" he asked.

"Nothing," Rick replied. "It's been almost two days now. I know something's wrong. It has to be. He wouldn't just up and disappear. Not with me and the dog at the house. He'd leave some kind of word."

Alex was not able to escape the thought of Daniel Grabowski. "I've alerted a cop friend of mine, and he's spreading the word to the precincts around town. A lot of cops are keeping their eyes open for Roger."

"If anything happens to him, I'll kill that fucking Steele myself," Rick exclaimed.

"Cool it, Rick," Alex warned. "Talk like that can only get you in trouble, and we've got enough of that already."

"I'm not shitting you," Rick persisted. "Roger's the only real friend I've ever had. He put his ass on the line for me."

"Let's give it a little more time," Alex cautioned. "He may be sitting at your place right now."

Alex slept fitfully that night and was barely awake when Pat showed up at his door the next morning.

"Good morning," she said, slipping past him into the house. "Don't look so sleepy; this was your idea, remember?"

Before he could respond, she was out of her coat and in his arms, her cheek against his chest, hands clasped behind his back.

"And good morning to you," Alex whispered into her ear.

"I've missed you, you know." Her voice was muffled, concerned. "I've been worried about you. Are you okay?"

"I'm fine," he said, "and I've missed you." He held her against him, feeling the beat of her heart and the tightness of her hug. "I'm glad you could come."

They had arranged this meeting the night before, before Alex had begun his vigil with Rick on the hill.

"I have to ask you something," he said, once he had poured them each a cup of coffee. "But you have to promise not to ask me why I want to know, okay? Not now anyway."

She looked puzzled, as he knew she would. "I'm not sure I understand," she said, "but go ahead, ask."

"Do you happen to know where Nathaniel was the night before last? Was he home? At the office?"

She stared at him across the table. "There's something else, isn't there? Tell me."

"You promised not to ask, remember?"

"The night before last?" She was thinking. "No, he wasn't home. He left after dinner, said he was going back to work. He had to finish writing an opinion."

"When did he come home, do you know?"

"Not until after I was asleep, that's for sure. Otherwise, I would have heard him. I only saw him for a minute the next morning."

"Was he driving the BMW that night?"

"I guess so. He always does when I'm not using it. What's this all about, Alex?"

He couldn't tell her. Not until he knew for sure.

When Alex walked into the newsroom later that morning, he found an apoplectic George Barclay nose to nose with a young overnight dispatcher who was responsible for monitoring the police radios.

"We broadcast *news* around here, not *excuses*," Barclay thundered, his bulky body puffed up and quivering. Alex thought he might explode, and ducked into his cubicle to escape.

"We pay you to listen to those goddamned police radios," Barclay shouted, "not to sit around here and play with yourself."

The dispatcher was near tears, cowering at his desk.

"What the hell's going on?" Alex whispered to a passing reporter.

"The kid missed a double homicide last night," the reporter replied. "The first we knew about it was from watching the competition this morning. As you can tell, Barclay's pissed. He doesn't like to miss a story."

"One more fuckup like that," Barclay fumed, "and you're out on your ass. There are plenty of kids around who want to *work* and who give a shit about the news."

Barclay stomped back to his office, still muttering to himself, leaving his young prey standing alone, in a mild state of shock. No one offered him any solace; he had caught an instant case of newsroom leprosy.

After giving Barclay time to cool down, Alex knocked on his open office door.

"What do *you* want?" Barclay snarled.

Alex decided he should have waited a few minutes longer.

"I've got a problem," he said, quietly.

"I don't need any more problems," Barclay said. "Now now." He hoisted himself out of the chair. "Fucking kids. What do they teach them over at that goddamned J-School anyway?"

"I think he got the message," Alex said. "If he's worth a damn, he'll remember it."

"I hope so." Barclay was standing, staring out the window. He turned and faced Alex. "Enough of that. What's *your* problem?"

"Derek. Somebody saw him going through Barbara's desk, and now those tapes from Steele's house are missing from my desk. I think he may have taken them."

"Why Derek?" Barclay asked. "What's he got to do with this?"

"I don't know. I just wanted you to know that I'm going to use a little gentle persuasion to try and find out."

"Shit, you can hang 'em by his balls from a telephone pole for all I care," Barclay said. "Just don't get another union grievance. I don't need that."

"Thanks," Alex said. "That's all I wanted to hear."

When Alex left Barclay's office, he found Barbara at her desk.

"Can you get the crew out for a drink after the late show?" he asked her. "And invite me along?"

"I can try," Barbara said. "Why?"

"I want to get Derek alone for a minute, and I'd rather not do it here at the station."

Barbara gave him a long look. "You want to ask him about the tapes?"

Alex nodded.

"Okay," she said, "but I suggest you talk to him before he gets too many beers in him."

Rick waited patiently in a phone booth just outside the Tom Thumb store. Waited and watched.

He had learned long ago that Minnesota drivers like to keep their cars warm in the winter, often leaving them unattended and idling when they made a quick stop at the store.

Three drivers had done just that in the past twenty minutes, but all of them were men. Rick preferred to wait for a woman, guessing she might spend more time in the store and hoping she would be slower to call the police.

Rick didn't like the idea of stealing a car, but there was no other easy way to get to where he wanted to go. He knew Steele's house was in the boonies, not close to any bus line, and he sure as hell didn't want to ask a cab to drop him off at the front door.

Besides, he might need to get away in a hurry.

So he waited until he knew the cops were changing shifts, figuring it would take at least an hour to get the stolen car report through police channels and out into the squad cars. That was all the time he would need.

He felt sorry for the lady whose car he took, but he consoled himself that she would learn a relatively painless and inexpensive lesson: a cold car is better than no car.

Alex found the crew crowded around a small table in the corner of the otherwise empty bar. The table already was littered with empty beer bottles, peanut shells, and crushed potato chip bags, and Derek was calling for another round from the bartender.

"Alex! Glad you could make it," Barbara shouted as he walked toward the group. "We were wondering if you'd forgotten about us."

There were eight of them in all, including Barbara, Scotty Hansen, Charley Nichols the weatherman, Derek, and four other studio technicians.

"We were just talking about Barclay's temper tantrum," Barbara said as Alex sat down. "Was it as bad as everybody says?"

"He got his point across, that's for sure," Alex said.

"Did the kid *really* piss his pants?" Derek asked, too loudly.

"No, but he looked like he was ready to. He sure as hell had his ears glued to the police radios tonight when I left."

As the bartender was delivering the beers, Scotty Hansen walked around the table and pulled Alex aside. "I've never really had the chance to say thanks for what you did," he whispered. "I know you saved my job, and I just want you to know I'll never forget it."

"I hope you *do* forget it," Alex said. "Hawke still isn't certain who the leak is, and I'd just as soon he never finds out."

"Hawke's talking to me about a new contract," Hansen said, "with a raise, just like you said."

At that moment Derek got up, gave a booming burp, and headed toward the restroom. Alex waited a minute, then followed.

Derek was standing at the urinal when Alex walked into the small men's room and leaned back against the door.

"Get in line," Derek said, over his shoulder.

"I want to talk."

"When we get back to the table," Derek said, tucking himself in and zipping his pants.

"No," Alex said. "Here. Now."

It dawned on Derek that something was wrong. "What's going on?" he asked, uneasily. "You got a problem?"

"*We've* got a problem. I need the tapes back. Now."

"What the fuck are you talking about? What tapes?"

He started to push past Alex, squeezing between the sink and a toilet stall. Alex put his arm against the wall, on a level with Derek's neck, blocking his way. "Don't fuck with me, Derek. I want the tapes. And I want to know why you took them."

"Are you crazy?" Derek sputtered.

"How do you know Steele?" Alex demanded, taking a chance. "How'd he get hold of you? Or did you go find him?"

Derek hesitated, but only for a split second. "Move aside or I'll fucking deck you," he shouted.

"Settle down, asshole," Alex said. "You don't know what you're into here. Somebody saw you pawing through Barbara's desk, and that's enough to get you canned right there. A couple of tapes are now missing out of *my* desk. I think you've got them."

"You're full of shit," Derek said, but he had lost some of his bravado. "You got no proof. Now get out of my way."

Alex's arm stayed against the wall.

"Derek, wise up. I'm not playing games here. Your ass is going to be out on the streets. The union won't do you any good now."

Derek stared at him, mouth open, his beer breath almost overpowering Alex. Then he tried to lunge past him, but Alex wrapped his arm around his neck and squeezed. He heard the choking sounds in his throat and increased the pressure.

"Think about it, Derek," he hissed into his ear. "You've got until tomorrow afternoon to get those tapes back."

Alex loosened his hold, expecting Derek to turn on him. Instead, Derek reached for the door and hurried out, rubbing his throat. He wasn't at the table when Alex returned.

Thirty-four

The last time Rick was there he'd been wearing a blindfold, but thanks to Roger he had no trouble finding Steele's house again. Even in the dark. He parked the stolen car a block away, tucked between two other cars on a small side road with no streetlight.

If some cop finds it here, Rick thought, he deserves a medal.

He walked casually down Merriweather Drive, ignoring the headlights of passing cars, acting as if he belonged there. He strode past two other driveways before reaching the closed gate with the name STEELE emblazoned in brass above it.

He walked on, waited for another car to pass, then quickly returned to the gate. It was locked and the fence was spiked. Was there an alarm system or guard dogs? Roger had never mentioned either, but he'd find out soon enough.

Rick grasped the top bar of the fence on his fourth leap. *Pull!* he told himself. Every muscle in his arms was stretched under the strain, and his legs flailed in the air, trying to get traction on the steel posts. His gloved-hands began to slip from the bar.

PULL!

He got one leg on the crossbar, wedged between the spikes. As he rested, he saw no dogs, heard no alarms. Rick pulled the rest of his body to the top of the fence, straddling it, then eased himself down the other side, falling the final three feet. *Jesus!* The frozen

267

ground sent sharp pangs shooting up his legs, like little bolts of lightning.

He made his way along the edge of the driveway, using the tall pines to cover his movement, the fresh snow to deaden any sound. The front of the house was ablaze with lights, so Rick moved around the back, staying in the rim of shadows.

The ground sloped sharply away from the house on every side. He had to fight to keep his footing in the snow, crawling part of the way as he circled the house, creeping closer as the front lights faded to darkness.

Every window was draped but one: the kitchen. He could see the top of the refrigerator and the cupboards. He moved closer, hugging the house, stretching his legs and neck to peer inside. Steele was there, talking on the phone. He was wearing an overcoat and hat, so he was either coming or going. Which one?

Rick moved to the other side of the window, but he could see no one else. *Where was Russell?* Steele was hanging up the phone.

Rick scurried away, low to the ground, around to the other end of the house. He flattened himself against the wall next to the garage and waited. Five minutes passed. Then he heard the hum of the garage-door opener and the growl of the Continental's engine.

Be ready! he told himself, edging closer to the corner.

The tail of the Continental backed out. Steele was alone, looking back over his shoulder, watching the driveway.

Go! Rick was around the corner and inside the garage, squeezed against the wall, before the door could close.

Alex was in his robe watching the last of the Letterman show when the phone rang.

"Mr. Collier?"

"Rick? Is that you?"

"Right. Hope I didn't wake you up."

"No problem. Where are you?"

"At Steele's house."

"*What?*"

"I'm inside," Rick said. "Standing in the kitchen."

"What are you doing there? Where's Steele?"

"He left, and I snuck in. Roger's not here. I've looked everywhere. His car's not here, either."

"You broke in?" Alex was incredulous.

"Kind of. Just after Steele left. I stole a car, too."

"Christ, Rick, You could be in deep shit."

"I've got a bunch more tapes from one of the rooms in the house. It looks like your TV station, there's so much equipment."

Alex remembered Roger talking about a room he'd never been in.

"How did you get into the room?"

"Picked the lock," Rick replied.

"Rick, listen to me. Put the tapes back. Leave everything as you found it, okay? Then get the hell out of there."

"I thought you wanted more tapes," Rick said.

"I do. But I didn't plan on any burglaries."

"Roger stole the ones *he* got," Rick countered. "What's the difference?"

Alex paused. He had a point. "I'm not sure, Rick. But at least Roger worked there. He didn't break in, for Christ's sake."

"I'll just take a couple, then," Rick said. "But what about Roger? If he's not here, where do you think he is?"

"I don't know, Rick. We're looking all over. For now, just get the hell out of the house, will you? Before Steele comes back."

"I don't care if he does," Rick said. "I'd like to coldcock the sucker."

The next morning, Alex found Rick waiting for him at the station. He took him immediately to John Knowles's office.

"What's going on?" Knowles asked.

Alex told him what Rick had done the night before, and what he'd discovered.

"You broke into his house?" Knowles asked, astonished. "You didn't run into Steele?"

"I saw him, but he took off. All by himself."

"What about the car you stole?" Alex asked.

"I dropped it off where I got it. Even put some gas in it."

"Judas Priest!" Knowles murmured.

"What's done is done," Alex said. "Let's not worry about it. At least now we know Roger's not at Steele's house."

"What about his place in Wisconsin?" Knowles asked.

"I've thought of it," Alex said, "but I think Steele's smarter than

that. He knows *we* know about the place, and that we'd be bound
to look there sooner or later."

"Maybe he's figuring on later rather than sooner," Knowles said.
"He may not even realize we know Roger's missing." He turned
to Rick. "Does Steele know anyone's living with Roger?"

Rick shook his head. "I don't think so."

"I still think we should check out the Wisconsin place," Knowles
persisted. "It won't hurt to have somebody take a look."

"What's this about Wisconsin?" Rick asked. "What place?"

"Forget it, Rick. You've done enough exploring for a while,"
Alex said. "Remember what I told you. What you did last night
was dumb, and you were lucky to have gotten away with it."

"What about it?" Knowles persisted.

"Okay," Alex said. "You're right. I'll call Mike Tolliver and ask
him to take a drive up there to check. Then, Rick, you, and I are
going to take a short trip ourselves."

"Where the hell's Derek, anyway?" Alex asked Cody when he
returned to the newsroom. "I told him I wanted those tapes by
this afternoon."

"Didn't I tell you?" Cody replied. "Derek called in sick this
morning, said he was going to take some vacation days he has
coming. It pisses me off because I have to bring in somebody on
overtime to fill in for him."

"Has anybody seen him?"

"I don't think so," Cody said.

The idea of Derek on the loose, unaccounted for, was not exactly
reassuring to Alex.

The elevator ride seemed to take forever.

Rick stood silently by Alex's side, watching the lighted floor
numbers above the door change as the elevator glided upward.

6, 7, 8.

There were two other passengers, attorneys apparently, talking
in hushed tones about some kind of writ. They got off on nine.

The last time Alex had been on this elevator was the day he had
paid his visit to the courtroom of Judge Nathaniel Hodges.

Today, a return trip.

10, 11, 12.

On the fourteenth floor, the elevator again slowed to a stop and the door opened. Alex took Rick aside in the empty hallway and pointed to Judge Hodges's courtroom.

"Remember, I want you to just walk into that courtroom and stand at the back until the judge sees you. I want to know if he's the man you recognized the other night in the BMW."

"What do I do then?" Rick asked.

"If he's not the man, just walk out as if you made a mistake. If he *is* the man, play reporter. Watch his face, note his reactions when he sees you. Remember them so you can describe them to me later."

"Why don't you come in, too?"

"I told you. I don't want Hodges to know I have any connection to you. It's important."

"Okay," Rick said.

"I'm going back down to the main floor. I'll meet you there when you're done."

The ride down seemed even longer to Alex.

He had to wait only a few minutes before he saw Rick get out of the same elevator and amble toward him—hands in his pockets, gazing up into the empty expanse of the atrium.

"Well?" Alex asked, when he finally arrived.

"It's not him," Rick said.

"It's not? Are you sure?"

"I'm sure. I've never seen that guy before."

Thirty-five

The leg shackles forced him to take small steps. Russell was by his side, helping him up the stairs. He held Roger's arm, but loosely, knowing he wouldn't be going anywhere.

Roger didn't know how much time had passed, having finally fallen asleep on the narrow bed. The sun was high in the sky, flooding the house with light as they reached the top of the stairs. Roger had to squint to see, and he paused for a moment to allow his eyes to adjust to the glare.

"This way," Russell said, tugging slightly on his arm.

The shackle chain jangled between his legs as Roger was led across the kitchen and into a large open living room. Two big birch logs were ablaze in the grate of a towering stone fireplace that reached two stories high.

A wall of windows brought the outside in, and Roger felt the urge to reach out and touch the bark of the trees, to scoop the snow from the deck.

"Where are we?" Roger asked absently, still staring out the windows.

"Never mind," Russell replied, moving him to a chair by the fireplace. He left him there, the heat from the fire warming his legs. Roger tried to spread his feet, but stopped when the shackles cut painfully into his ankles.

"Sorry about the manacles, Roger," said Steele's voice from behind him. Roger turned his head as the judge walked across the room. "Neither Russell nor I was foolish enough to believe we could catch you if you decided to run, although I don't know how far you'd get in this weather."

Roger waited until Steele sat down across from him. He tried to keep his voice level, steady. "What's this all about, Judge? Why am I a prisoner?"

"Ohhh, Roger. Poor Roger. Such innocence. I think you know why you're here."

"*No! I don't!* All I know is we were sitting having a drink and I passed out. Next thing I know, I'm here, wherever *here* is."

"Roger, come off it! Let's be honest, shall we? I placed great trust, great confidence in you. Provided a home for you, an income, and many favors over the past couple of years. Then you turned your back on me. You violated that trust and confidence—betraying me to people who are intent on doing me great harm."

"I don't know what you mean," Roger protested. "What people?"

Steele simply stared at him, an amused expression on his face. "You invaded the privacy of my study, you stole two tapes and gave them to Alex Collier. I am about to retrieve them, however."

Roger was astonished. *How could he know all of that? Where did I fuck up?* "Why do you think it was me?" he demanded. "If your tapes were stolen, it could've been anyone."

"Once I discovered the tapes were missing," the judge said, "I recalled using your key to open the study door. After that, it was simple. I left a toothpick wedged in the door, and came home to find the tapes back in place and the toothpick on the floor. You were the only one who'd been in the house."

That's what he was holding when I passed out, Roger remembered vaguely. *A fucking toothpick.*

"But that's history," Steele continued. "What I'm interested in now is what else you've told Collier. How much of my private, personal life you have revealed to him."

The heat from the fire seemed more intense, and Roger felt it spreading from his legs through the rest of his body. Even his face seemed to be burning.

"I don't even know Collier!" Roger lied, looking directly at the judge. "I've only seem him on television. And even if I did know him, why would I tell him anything?"

He wasn't sure which came first: the stinging slap across the face or Steele's hoarse shout: "Russell!"

Steele's hand had moved as fast as a whip, and with no warning. Even more frightening was his face: eyes tight and narrow, lips pulled back over his teeth, a grimace that also showed the hint of a satisfied smile.

Before Roger could react, Russell had bounded into the room, moving as fast as an outside linebacker, pinning Roger's arms to his sides. "Easy does it," he breathed into Roger's ear.

As if he had a choice.

Steele settled back in his chair, anger gone, looking as calm and comfortable as he would be in his club chatting with another judge.

"You should understand, Roger, that we are not dealing with a trivial matter here. My reputation, my career, everything I've ever worked for, hangs in the balance. Do you understand that?"

Steele got out of his chair and walked to the window, looking down the snowy slope to the frozen lake below. Roger could see only his silhouette against the glass.

"I can't expect you to understand, Roger, but I've struggled all of these years to achieve the position which is now within my grasp. *Struggled*, Roger. *Studied. Fought.* Overcoming obstacles and enemies which would have stopped a lesser man dead in his tracks."

Roger was spellbound. Steele slowly turned around, arms folded across his chest.

"I will not be denied, Roger. I will stop Collier in this crusade of his. I will marshal whatever resources it takes to thwart him. Believe that, for your own good."

Steele stood over Roger, looming above him. His hands were clenched, and spittle showed at the edge of his mouth.

"We can proceed in one of two ways," Steele said, sitting back in his chair. "Cooperatively or antagonistically. It is entirely your choice, Roger. I'm in no hurry, and neither is Russell. But you should know there's a limit to our patience."

Roger felt helpless, but was determined to disguise his fear. "You can't hold me forever," he said softly. "I'll be missed."

"By whom?" Steele scoffed. "All of your friends at Mr. K's?

Come now, Roger. We both know you have no real friends, no one besides me. That's why I kept you. You're a loner."

"You don't know *everything* about me," Roger said, angrily. He was immediately sorry he'd said it.

"That's what I'm discovering," Steele admitted. "Perhaps you do have a friend in Alex Collier. But I doubt—"

Steele was interrupted by a rap at the front door.

"We've got company," Russell said, grabbing Roger by the arm.

Russell had not only the speed but the strength of a linebacker. He picked Roger out of his chair and slung him over his shoulder, shackles and all, before Roger could understand what was happening.

"Don't make a fucking sound," Russell warned, as he raced toward the stairs. "Not one fucking sound!"

Roger was awed. It happened so fast—there was no time to think, let alone to shout. He felt like a baby, the way he was handled. Across the kitchen, down the steps and then thrown back into the knotty-pine room.

"Afternoon. I'm Sheriff Mike Tolliver. And this is Deputy Jensen."

Steele held the door halfway open. "Sorry for the delay," he said. "I was at the other end of the house."

"No problem," Tolliver said. "And what's your name?"

"Steele. Judge Emmett Steele. From Minnesota."

"Nice to meet you, Judge," the sheriff said. "I thought I knew most of the folks living in Burnett County. Sorry we've never met."

"I'm sorry, too, but we just recently built this place," Steele explained, "and I don't get up here that often. You know how busy the courts are."

Tolliver wasn't sure exactly what they were looking for. Alex had told him only that one of Steele's young victims, his houseboy, was missing, and that it was possible Steele was holding him at the Wisconsin lodge.

Standing on the step in the cold was becoming awkward, which is what Tolliver was counting on. He wanted to be invited inside, but Steele seemed just as determined to keep him out.

"What can I do for you, Sheriff?" Steele asked. "I don't mean to be discourteous, but I'm up to my neck in paperwork."

"You don't happen to have the coffee pot on, do you?" Tolliver persisted, in his best good neighbor voice. "I don't often have the chance to talk to a big city judge."

"I'm truly sorry, I don't. Never drink the stuff myself. Now, if you don't mind, what is it you wanted?"

"Well," Tolliver said, "we've had some reports of random vandalism around here, mainly to vacation places like yours. I'm just checking to see if you folks have had any problems."

"No problems here," Steele said. "We have a pretty elaborate alarm system. But I do appreciate your concern."

He started to shut the door, but Tolliver held it open.

"Haven't seen any strangers around, have you? *Young guys?*" He paused, watching Steele.

"I haven't seen anyone," Steele said. "I'm just here by myself. Good luck, Sheriff."

Steele pulled the door shut, slowly but firmly, and Tolliver and his deputy walked back to their squad car, studying the black Continental standing outside the garage.

"I may be just a small country sheriff," Tolliver told Jensen, "but I think the honorable Judge Steele is lying through his teeth."

"What are we going to do?" the deputy asked.

"I want you to get your car and sit up on the highway," Tolliver said. "If that Continental leaves with anybody but the judge inside, or if any other car leaves, I want you to stop them. For anything. Just see who's inside the car. Got it?"

"Got it. But for how long?"

"Until I tell you to quit," Tolliver said.

Roger sat on the edge of the bed, a handkerchief stuffed in his mouth. Russell leaned against the locked door of the bedroom, breathing hard but poised to leap if Roger's hands moved toward his mouth. Roger strained but could hear no movement upstairs, no voices. Finally, there was a soft rap on the door, and Steele's words. "May I see you upstairs, Russell?"

Russell found the judge back by the windows overlooking the lake. Steele quickly explained the visitor. "I don't like the feel of this, Russell. That sheriff was not looking for vandals. He was here for another reason, I'm almost sure."

Russell listened intently, although Steele seemed to be talking more to himself than to him. And while Russell was never one to question his boss, he made an exception now. "What makes you think that, Judge? They didn't stay long."

"I think the sheriff wanted to get into the house, to get a look around. He almost forced his way in. And he said something like 'I don't often get a chance to talk with a big city judge.' I didn't tell him I was from the Cities . . . just Minnesota. He knew who I was before he ever asked."

"I hear what you're saying, Judge, but how would a sheriff way up here ever know about Roger?"

"I can't answer that, Russell. Maybe he doesn't. But when he asked if I had seen any *young guys* around, he had a funny look on his face. It's worrisome."

Steele walked the length of the living room twice. "At the moment, the sheriff thinks I'm here alone, working. He has no reason to believe otherwise. Certainly no reason to investigate further." It was as though Steele was talking to himself. "But if my suspicions are justified, he may be keeping an eye on the house. That would argue against doing anything rash with Roger . . . with taking him anywhere for the time being."

"So what *do* we do with him?" Russell asked.

"We talk to him once more, a little more persuasively, I trust, and then I will return home tonight. You will stay here with him, keeping him company. Keeping him out of sight. You don't mind a little baby-sitting do you, Russell?"

After their trip to the courthouse, Alex dropped Rick off at Roger's place on Slater Avenue with orders to stay put. No more wandering around in stolen cars or breaking into people's houses, he told him.

Alex was just getting into his own house when the phone rang.

"Can I buy you a drink after the news?" Pat asked. "Nathaniel's out of town again, and it would be nice to spend some time with you."

"Sure," Alex said. "Where do you want to—wait a minute. *What did you say?* Nathaniel's out of town? When did he go?"

"This morning," Pat said. "To Atlanta. Why?"

"Wasn't he in court this afternoon?" Alex demanded, almost harshly. "I thought he had a trial."

"They settled it just after jury selection yesterday, so he took off for some seminar in Atlanta this morning. What's wrong with you, anyway?"

"So who was using his courtroom this afternoon?"

"It could have been anybody," she replied, sounding puzzled. "A couple of the courtrooms are being repainted so they use any one that's vacant. What's this all about, Alex?"

Rick's words, *I've never seen that guy before,*' spun around in Alex's head.

"I thought I'd answered one puzzle, but it turns out I haven't. It seems like every corner I turn, I run into another surprise."

"I don't get it. Do you still want to have that drink?" she asked.

"Sure. How about the Monte Carlo at eleven?"

"I'll meet you there," she said, "with more questions."

"We've had a change in plans, Roger," Steele said. "I have to leave in a few hours, but I don't want to go without talking to you again."

They were in another room in the basement, this one with no windows and no furniture, except for three straight-backed chairs. The judge was seated properly on one of them, Russell straddling the other, his arms folded loosely across its back.

Roger was bound to the third chair, his legs still shackled, his arms now tied securely behind him. "Why won't you believe me?" Roger pleaded. "I told you! I don't know Collier. I've never seen him except on television."

"That's bullshit, and we both know it," Steele said. "I want the truth. I want to know what you've told Collier about my private life."

"Nothing, I swear—"

Steele's hand shot out again, the impact snapping Roger's head, almost tipping him over in the chair.

"*The truth!*" Steele shouted, then swung again with the back of his hand. His knuckles cracked across Roger's nose.

Roger could taste the blood running into his mouth, mixed with the salt from his tears. "My God, why are you doing this?" he sobbed.

"For all of the reasons I described upstairs," Steele said, impatiently. "I told you I have nothing to lose. You are simply another obstacle in my path. I have dedicated my life to the truth, and I shall have it from you now."

"But I *am* telling you the truth. Why would I do anything to hurt you? I know what you've done for me."

Steele nodded to Russell, who nonchalantly rose and walked to the back of Roger's chair.

They must believe me, Roger thought, relieved.

That's when he felt the first finger crack.

The Monte Carlo was jammed with fans who had come from the Timberwolves basketball game. Alex knew he could have picked a quieter place, but he wanted to be in the middle of a crowd with Pat. Alone, but surrounded. He knew it was risky, but so far they had gone unnoticed in the crush.

He leaned close to her. "I love being with you, you know that? It feels right."

Pat smiled and touched her fingers to his. "To me, too," she said. "It feels right, but still not real. I keep thinking you'll suddenly disappear again."

Alex thought he saw a flicker of sadness in her eyes.

"I wish we could just walk away," she said wistfully. "Have a little time to figure out what's going on between us. I know we probably never will . . . but that doesn't keep me from wishing.

"It's all so complicated, Alex. Not knowing about Nathaniel. Not knowing what my own feelings are, or what yours are. Maybe they'll change when all of this is over."

"I don't expect my feelings will change," he said. "I think—"

Alex saw her eyes leave his at the same time he felt the hand on his shoulder. "Hello, Collier. Hello, Mrs. Hodges. Nice to see you both."

Alex recognized the voice before he turned. It was Jerry Caldwell, a half glass of white wine in his hand, and a short, slender woman on his arm. "Alex Collier, Patricia Hodges, meet Janet Dawson."

They exchanged greetings, Caldwell displaying no surprise at finding Alex and Pat together. Alex offered no explanation, but did offer to pull up a couple of chairs. "No thanks," Caldwell said. "We're just ready to leave. But I would like to have a quick word with you if I could."

"Sure, if Pat doesn't mind."

"Of course not," Pat said, inviting Janet to join her.

Alex and Caldwell walked to one end of the bar, away from the crowd. "I just wanted to tell you that I've said nothing to Hawke or anyone else," Caldwell said. "But I don't think things will remain quiet much longer. Judge Steele's going to deal with the matter personally. So I'd be ready for the assault, if I were you."

"I appreciate the warning," Alex replied, "but why are you telling me this?"

"Because I've thought about what you said to me at the Conservatory. I realized I've been kidding myself, not seeing things I should've seen, mostly because I didn't want to see them."

"Like what?"

"Suspicious behavior, I suppose. His strange friends and his secretive, solitary lifestyle. Lots of little things which I tended to ignore because of my admiration for Judge Steele's intellect and his work on the bench."

"So what are you going to do now?" Alex asked.

Caldwell hesitated, draining the final sip of wine from his glass. "I plan to leave the judge's staff and begin another career after he's sworn in as chief justice."

"*If* he's sworn in," Alex said.

"Don't sell him short," Caldwell warned. "He's got great power and influence. Everybody in this town owes him a favor, and he's as determined as I've ever seen him."

"I believe you," Alex said, as they returned to the table. "I've seen enough evidence of his determination to scare the shit out of me."

Caldwell gave him a quizzical look. "I don't think I want to know any more," he said, taking Janet by the hand and saying their goodbyes.

"What was that all about?" Pat asked after they'd left.

"Another warning of sorts," Alex said. "God knows I've had enough of those."

Thirty-six

Deputy Fred Jensen never would have admitted it, but he was damn near dozing when the glare of the headlights popped his eyelids open. They were coming straight at him, on the road across the highway. The car was moving fast, the headlights on bright.

The deputy's unmarked squad car was backed into the brush, well out of sight. The Continental braked to a quick stop at the corner, then powered onto the highway, heading south toward the Twin Cities.

Jensen didn't have a chance to see who was in the car.

The deputy put the supercharged Plymouth into gear and bolted onto the road, already a half mile behind the speeding Continental. He waited until the other car was over a hill before turning on his own lights, and then pushing the pedal to the floor.

"Just see who's in the car," Tolliver had said. *"Got it?"*

Jensen quickly closed the gap between the cars and drew up tight behind the Continental. He saw the outline of only one head inside the car, but to be sure he quickly changed lanes and roared past, leaning on his horn to make the driver look his way.

He must think I'm quite a prick, Jensen thought.

But the deputy had accomplished his mission: the angry face he saw inside the Continental was definitely Judge Steele's.

Jensen had to make a quick decision: to stop the car to make sure Steele was alone or to quietly return to the house—to make sure it was empty.

What would Tolliver do? Use your own judgment, Jensen! he told himself. That's what they pay you for.

Deputy Jensen made his decision. He pulled to the side of the road and allowed the Continental to speed by.

Then he turned around.

The throbbing pain in his finger brought Roger awake.

The room was dark. He held his hand close to his eyes, but could see nothing. He touched the finger lightly, but recoiled in agony. He felt his face. Was his nose broken, too? The caked blood chipped away and fell onto his lips.

Roger didn't know how long he'd been passed out. He didn't care. He could think only of the pain.

He'd been thrown back into the first small room. He pushed himself up from the bed, one arm hanging limply by his side. He stumbled to the wall in the dark, found the light switch, and flipped it on with his other hand. He made himself look, and saw that the ring finger of his right hand was badly swollen and had a purplish tinge.

It hurt like hell.

A small basin of warm water and a washcloth had been left on the dresser. Roger used his good hand to wet the cloth and wipe the blood from his nose and mouth. Then he put his crippled hand into the water, knowing it would provide little relief, but not knowing what else to do.

Fred Jensen had never been a particularly brave fellow.

Even as a kid growing up on a dairy farm near Luck, Wisconsin, he'd been terrified of rounding up the cows for fear of confronting the big bull who roamed the south pasture, the one who fiercely pawed the ground and snorted menacingly every time young Freddie appeared. He'd always been the last of the kids to volunteer to scale the silo chute or to climb high in the loft to stack the bales of hay.

He certainly didn't think of himself as a coward, but he knew he'd never win a medal for bravery, either. Conservative, he called it. Cautious. He had learned to sidestep danger whenever possible.

The only real danger he'd ever faced as a deputy was a crazed farmer who came after him, pitchfork in hand, during a farm foreclosure. Fred had jolted the man to his senses with a shotgun blast into the air, and barely kept from pissing his pants in the process.

For some reason, Fred was thinking of the farmer and the pitchfork now, as he got out of his Plymouth on the hill above the lodge. Maybe it was because he had the same shotgun in his hands. Or maybe because he had to piss. He wasn't sure which.

Maybe it was because he was afraid.

He had tried to contact Tolliver by radio to get instructions, but was told by a snickering dispatcher that the sheriff was unavailable for the next hour. Fred knew that meant Mike was getting laid at Mary Jane Bigelow's house at the other end of the county, and he sure as hell wasn't about to bother him there.

Fred told the dispatcher he was going to look around and then started to walk down the hill, cautiously, looking for lights, pausing every few steps to listen. He gripped the shotgun, chiding himself on his fear.

It began to snow again as he crept down the driveway and circled the dark house, satisfying himself it was deserted. He was ready to retreat to the safety of his squad car when he saw the window light come on.

Fred hadn't figured on this. He couldn't knock on the door. *What the hell would he say? What would Tolliver do?* He'd look in the goddamned window.

True to his nature, Fred decided to play it safe. He'd look, but from a distance. He crouched down, duck-walking through the snow to within about ten feet of the lighted window. He slowly straightened up, and through the falling snow saw somebody inside. It was a young guy holding something to his face. A cloth?

Fred felt a blow against the back of his head and, before he blacked out, the cold of the snow against his face.

He came to inside his Plymouth, the radio squawking. "Jensen? Please respond. This is Tolliver. Fred, where are you?"

It took the deputy a moment to regain his senses. He tried to raise his head, but his hair stuck to the headrest. Blood, he knew instantly. He was frozen to the leather.

"Jensen. Car Two. This is Tolliver at base. Come in, Two!"

The pain in the back of his skull pounded like a piston. Still dazed, he moved his head from side to side to pry it free, but it was stuck fast.

Fear was high in his throat, choking him.

Hands! Use your hands, asshole, to pull your head free. Then he realized his hands were cuffed to the steering wheel.

"Fred, if you're out goofing off, I'll have your badge! Respond, Car Two. This is Tolliver. Respond. *Now.*"

C'mon, he told himself, Tolliver can't help you now. Give your head a jerk. Be brave for once. Ready, set, go! His face flew forward, his forehead slammed into the steering wheel. He felt the hair pulled from the back of his head, felt the agony of a thousand needles jabbing him at once.

The radio was quiet. He slumped forward, his head resting on the steering wheel, chest heaving against the pain.

That's when he heard the sound of the chain saw. He raised his eyes. It was dark, except for the glow from the half moon. His head swiveled and he saw it, there behind the car, a figure, dark against the snow, holding a chain saw.

"This is Sheriff Mike Tolliver making a priority call to Deputy Fred Jensen. Please answer, Fred. This is urgent. All other cars, stay off this frequency. Car Two?"

Jensen was helpless. He wanted to kick at the radio in frustration, but his feet were bound, too. His eyes were riveted on the figure behind him, and he watched as it bent over, pointing the chain saw to the ground. He heard the engine rev, then roar, and saw the chain dig into the snow. Snow? No, not snow.

Ice.

Jensen suddenly understood. His car was not in the middle of some snow-covered field. It was in the middle of an ice-covered lake, in the middle of nowhere. The chain saw was cutting through the ice in a circle, tight around the car.

He could not hold back a scream. He pulled at the cuffs, then smashed them back against the wheel. The steel rings tore into his wrists. He pushed his feet against the floorboard, pulling with all his strength.

"Let me out of here! For God's sake, let me out!"

He pounded his head against the horn, again and again, but there was no sound.

The chain saw roared on.

He searched frantically in every direction for cabin lights, for any sign of life.

Nothing. Just the moonlight on the ice, and the man with the chain saw.

"Car Two? Jensen? Come in, please. This is Tolliver. Don't make me come up there looking for you. Please respond, Two!"

Come! Come! Jensen silently pleaded.

But he knew it would be too late.

The chain saw was halfway around the car, cutting through the ice relentlessly. Jensen was cold and exhausted. His wrists were raw and bleeding, his head ached, and his voice was hoarse from shouting to no one but himself.

He knew it would not be much longer before the ice gave way. Then the car would slowly sink, and the freezing water would rise to engulf him. The open hole would freeze over by daylight, and with the new snow, leave no trace of the car or its panicked captive.

The chain saw finally stopped, and even inside the car, Fred could hear the sharp cracking of the ice. The car started to sink. The frigid water hit his ankles first, then his knees.

The last thing Fred saw was the figure throwing the chain saw into the water.

The last thing Fred heard was the radio. "I'm on my way, Fred. Hang in there, wherever you are."

Too late, Tolliver, Jensen thought, as the water rose to his neck and he took his final breath.

Roger heard feet pounding across the floor above him, then down the steps. The door was flung open, and Russell stood there, breathing deeply. He smelled of gasoline and his snowmobile suit was covered with slush and ice.

"C'mon," he shouted. "We're leaving. Now!"

"What's going on, Russell?" Roger asked. "Where's Steele?"

"Shut up," Russell said. He pulled Roger out of the room, half dragging him up the stairs, then through the house and into the garage. Roger tried to protect his broken finger, but it seemed to throb more with every jarring step.

"Jesus, Russell, take it easy, will you?" he pleaded.

The Continental was not in the garage, but Roger's car was. Russell shed his snowmobile suit and left it in a heap on the garage floor. He spun Roger around and pulled a blindfold over his eyes,

then threw him into the car with a grunted warning: "Make a move
and you'll be out that fucking door at seventy miles an hour."

"Where are we going, Russell? What the hell did you do?"

"Never mind," Russell said as he backed the car out of the garage
and roared up the slope of the driveway.

Somewhere along Highway 35, heading south, they passed Mike
Tolliver, heading north. Their headlights met in the night.

When Alex got to the station the next morning, he found an
urgent message from Phil on his desk.

"We've got problems," Phil said. "Mike Tolliver's missing a deputy. He said he left him near Steele's place late yesterday and he
hasn't seen him or his car since."

"Who was at the house?" Alex asked.

"Steele was there when they checked, and he told Tolliver he
was alone. But he's not there today. Nobody's there."

"Son of a bitch," Alex muttered.

"Tolliver's pulling out all stops in the search. He had the dogs
out early this morning, and found what he thinks is a trace of blood
near the house. He's got cars all over that part of the county and
will have planes going up when the weather clears."

"Anything we can do?" Alex asked.

"Tolliver wants me to talk to Steele, find out what time he left
the place and whether he saw the deputy. I'm heading over to see
him now. Then I'm going to Wisconsin to see if I can give Tolliver
any help with the search."

As Alex hung up the phone, he found Barclay by his desk. He
had no jovial smile or smart wisecracks, just a somber stare.

"The day of judgment has arrived," Barclay said. "In Hawke's
office. At three. Seems the head of the state bar association, the
chief of the judicial conference, and the governor's top aide would
like an audience."

Alex's mind was still on the missing deputy. It took a moment
for Barclay's words to register. When they did, he once again felt
overwhelmed. "We knew it would come eventually," he said,
trying to disguise his distress. "Shit, what's the worst he can do?
Fire me?"

"After carving you a new asshole," Barclay replied.

Phil was ushered into Judge Steele's chambers by Jerry Caldwell, who paused before quietly shutting the door.

"What's this urgent meeting all about, Detective?" Steele asked brusquely. "I have a busy court calendar. I can't afford these kinds of interruptions."

Phil remained standing, as did the judge. "Sorry to bother you, Judge, but I'm here at the request of Sheriff Mike Tolliver of Burnett County, Wisconsin, as part of a current investigation."

Phil watched him closely, but there was no hint of surprise.

"More trouble with vandals?" Steele snorted, sitting down, but not offering Phil a seat. "The sheriff was at my lake place yesterday about a rash of vandalism."

"This is more serious than that, I'm afraid," Phil said. "Sometime after visiting with you, Tolliver's deputy disappeared. He's still missing, along with his car, and he was last heard from in your area. The sheriff was wondering when you left your place, and whether you may have seen anything of the deputy."

Steele sat back in his chair, his fingers together, steepled beneath his chin. "I'm sorry to hear that," he said, "but, no, I saw no one when I left. I pulled out after dark and got back to the Cities about midnight. I didn't notice anyone on the way."

"Were you alone at the house?" Phil asked. "Was anyone else there who might have seen or heard something?"

The judge gazed at him with a strange intensity. "No," Steele finally said. "As I told the sheriff yesterday, I was alone, trying to get some work done. He must have told you that."

"No, he didn't mention it," Phil lied. "Do you have any neighbors on the lake?"

"No, we're all alone. We own practically all of the lakeshore, and the remainder is county land. I like my privacy."

Phil could think of no more questions, and felt awkward and off balance standing while the judge sat. "Well, if you think of anything further which might be of help, I'd appreciate a call."

"Of course, Detective. I hope the deputy turns up."

The three men waiting for Alex and Barclay in Hawke's office appeared fully as dapper and corporate as Hawke himself. Cut out of the same Brooks Brothers cloth.

"We need to set the record straight," Hawke said. "These gentlemen believe we're preparing an exposé on Judge Steele. I have assured them that, to the contrary, we're planning a special tribute to the judge. Right, George?"

Barclay said nothing, glancing at Alex instead.

"We're planning a special series on the judge, that's true," Alex said evasively. "The exact nature of the program is not fully decided. It's still being researched."

"What kind of double-talk is that?" said the chief of the state judicial conference. "It's another hatchet job, and you goddamned well know it."

"What's the source of your information, if I may ask?" Alex said, trying to take the offensive. "I won't respond to rumors."

"These aren't rumors," said the governor's aide. "We understand that the broadcast is imminent, deliberately aimed at embarrassing the chief justice–designate and the governor immediately prior to Judge Steele's swearing-in."

"What are they talking about?" Hawke said, his eyes moving from Barclay to Alex and back again. "Is there any truth to this?"

"This is something we should discuss in private," Barclay said. "It's an internal news matter that is no business of outsiders."

"You didn't answer my question!" Hawke roared, rising out of his chair. "Judge Steele is a respected member of this community, one of its finest citizens. He's also a friend of mine. I will not have him slandered by this television station."

"Then you'd better talk to your boys here," said the governor's aide, "because you're obviously being deceived by them."

"Wait a minute!" Alex said, rising out of his own chair. "I may be new to this town, but I'm not new to the news business. I've never heard this kind of discussion before. Where I come from, if it's news, you broadcast it."

Hawke tried to interrupt, but Alex rushed ahead.

"Here you sit, the four of you, not knowing a goddamned thing about what we are or aren't going to report. *We're* not even sure yet, for Christ's sake. But I will tell you, if we don't report our story, somebody else will."

Barclay started to get up to leave. "We're supposed to be operating in the public interest," he said, standing, "and I won't be told what we should or shouldn't report. I don't think we should have to sit here and listen to this bullshit."

"Sit down, George," Hawke ordered. "We're not done yet."

"Let me ask *you* something," Alex said to the governor's aide. "How thoroughly did your office investigate Judge Steele before the governor announced his appointment?"

The aide hesitated. "Routine," he said. "We disregarded the

slander of his political enemies. His reputation is beyond reproach."

"If you had done your homework," Alex said, "you wouldn't be sitting here now, because the governor wouldn't have made the appointment."

Hawke interrupted him. "You know what happened the last time you got mixed up in this kind of business, Collier," he taunted. "I won't tolerate it."

Alex started to protest, but was cut off by the representative of the bar association. "How long do we have to put up with this nonsense, Hawke? Who runs this television station, you or a bunch of renegades from the news department?"

"Make no mistake," Hawke said sharply. "I run it. These people will do as I say or they'll be working for someone else. And I say there will be no critical report on Judge Steele on this station. No trial by television here, no character assassination. If someone else wants to do it, Collier, so be it. Then it's their problem, not mine. Good day, gentlemen."

This time, "fucking weasel" rang out in unison as Alex and Barclay walked back to the newsroom.

"What do we do now?" Alex asked as he and Barclay slumped in their chairs.

Barclay stared out his window, his big body sagging, as if all his energy had seeped out of him. "You know, when I came here, I hoped this would be my last stop. I thought it was a great town, a great television station. I wanted to buy a house, settle down."

Alex said nothing, feeling only regret that he had gotten his boss, now his friend, into this mess.

"But if we back down on this, we might as well get out of the business. I'd never be able to look a young reporter in the eye again. When it comes right down to it, all we've got is our reputations and whatever principles we've been able to hang on to."

"So what are you saying?" Alex asked.

"Haven't you guessed, Mr. Anchorman? I'm not going to buy a fucking house. We're going to get that goddamned story on the air. Don't ask me how, but we'll do it."

Thirty-seven

By the time Phil arrived at the Wisconsin search area, almost eighteen hours had passed since Fred Jensen's disappearance. Sheriff Tolliver had set up a command post at a rest stop along the highway, about a mile from Steele's lodge.

The northwest winds that had brought clouds during the night had pushed them out by early afternoon, leaving the skies clear and a few inches of fresh snow on the ground. Four Civil Air Patrol planes were in the air to assist more than a hundred volunteers on the ground.

Phil found Tolliver ready to get aboard a highway patrol helicopter. He had not slept or shaved, his eyes were bleary, and the stubble of his beard made his face look gray. "Come on along," he told Phil, handing him a headset and a pair of binoculars.

"I can understand how a *man* can get lost in this country," Tolliver said after they were aloft, "but I don't know how a fucking *car* can up and disappear."

From above, the sight was awesome: patrol cars poked down virtually every backwoods road, snowmobiles by the dozens scooted along the trails cutting through the forests and swamps, and people on skis and snowshoes explored thickets the cars and snowmobiles couldn't reach.

"The new snow has wiped out damn near every track," Tolliver said, "and makes it a hell of a lot tougher to spot a parked car."

"At least you don't have all of the foliage to contend with," Phil said. "If this were summer, you'd probably never spot a hidden car from the air."

"We'd better find it soon. Jensen could be freezing to death. A man can't survive in this weather for that long, and Fred isn't what you'd call a survival expert. He gets cold if his damned car heater isn't going full blast."

Tolliver had decided that with the deep snow cover, the car would almost have to be near a road. But he also knew it could be hundreds of miles away by now.

"Did he have any family?" Phil asked.

"His folks are in a nursing home in Luck."

"No wife and kids?"

"Nah. I'm not sure he ever had a date," Tolliver replied. "Kind of a meek little guy. Shy, kept to himself. That's what I don't understand about this. I just can't see Fred gettin' himself in trouble."

They had been in the air about a half-hour when the chopper passed over a familiar spot: the old grave site of Daniel Grabowski, still cleared and roped off, waiting for spring. Tolliver pointed to it.

That's where all of this began, Phil thought, as the shadow of the helicopter passed over the site.

He wondered where it would end.

Roger still wore the leg shackles, but his blindfold was off. He had no idea why he'd been brought back here to his old room at the judge's house on Merriweather Drive, but he knew something had happened to frighten Russell and force the change of plans. Russell had given no clue; he'd said little in the car, grunting only an occasional threat when Roger shifted in his seat or tried to talk.

Hours had passed and Roger was sitting on the bed when he heard the first muffled sounds of an argument down the hall. He shuffled to the door and pressed his ear to it. The voices seemed closer, but were still indistinguishable.

He slid to the floor and tried to listen through the crack at the bottom of the door. One of the voices was Steele's—raised, almost shouting. Roger could hear his anger, but only fragments of the conversation.

". . . no other choice? You imbecile, the place will be swarming with . . ."

Roger knew the other voice had to be Russell's, but it was softer, more controlled.

". . . never find him. . . . The snow will cover the . . ."

What the hell are they talking about? The voices quieted for a moment, then Roger heard Steele again.

". . . the chain saw. . . . What did you do with it?"

Chain saw? Roger remembered the smell of gasoline on Russell's snowmobile suit.

". . . in the lake?" It was Steele again. ". . . be able to trace it, you fool!"

". . . had no time . . . never find it." Russell's voice seemed to be on the verge of breaking. ". . . didn't have time to think . . . had to get away . . ."

The argument seemed to end as suddenly as it began. The house fell silent again. Until Roger heard the heavy footsteps of Russell coming down the hall, stopping outside his door. Roger pushed himself across the floor, dragging his legs behind him, hoisting himself onto the bed just as the key turned in the lock and the door opened.

Russell stood in the doorway, a food tray in his hands. The hands were trembling.

Darkness was closing in on the Wisconsin woods. Many of the searchers had gone home, and the CAP planes were returning to the Siren airport one by one as they ran low on fuel.

Sheriff Tolliver slumped in his squad car at the roadside command post and watched as the search effort wound down. Phil was sitting next to him, but ready to get into his own car for the return trip to the Twin Cities.

"What are the chances of finding him alive?" Phil asked.

"Not good," Tolliver said. "Somebody would have spotted his car by now."

"I hope you're wrong," Phil said, "but if he is dead, I hope there's something that ties it to Steele."

"So do I, but the odds aren't great. We've got to find him first."

"What about the blood in the snow by Steele's lodge?"

"Type O," Tolliver said. "Same as Fred's, and a billion other people."

One of Tolliver's deputies approached the car as Phil was walking away. "What about tomorrow?" the deputy asked.

"Same time, same place," Tolliver said. "Get as many of these people back as you can, okay? We'll need the planes again. Find the pilots a place to stay, will you?"

"Sure. Anything else?"

"Yeah. Stick with me awhile. I want to check every house around here, see if anybody remembers hearing or seeing anything last night."

"Already done that. Two or three times," the deputy argued. "Nobody remembers anything."

"Sure," Tolliver said. "But somebody who was home last night may have been working today."

"Whatever you say," the deputy replied.

The yard light came on as they pulled into the driveway. A Doberman pinscher, fangs bared, was straining at a chain next to the back step of the old, ramshackle house. A '65 Buick with two of its wheels and hood missing was sitting up on blocks, half covered with snow, just a few steps away from a decrepit Dodge pickup and a pile of rotting tires.

Tolliver and his deputy got out of the squad car, shading their eyes against the floodlights, stepping over debris littering the yard. This was their fourth stop, and both were growing irritable.

"Who lives here?" Tolliver asked, keeping his distance from the lunging dog.

"Clarence Janklow, an old guy who lives alone. Traps for a living, I guess. If you call this a living."

As Tolliver was about to cup his mouth and shout, the back door opened and a small, withered figure emerged, a shotgun held loosely in one hand. "Who's there? What do you want?" he yelled.

"We're the law, Clarence. Call off your dog. We need to talk to you."

The old man pulled the Doberman inside the door and walked down the steps, still holding the shotgun.

"Why don't you put that thing down," Tolliver said. "It makes me nervous."

Clarence leaned the gun against the house and stood waiting.

His beard was long and matted, stained brown from dribbling tobacco juice.

"Were you home today, Clarence? Did anybody stop to talk to you about a missing deputy?"

"I've been out trappin' since daybreak," the old man said. "Up in the Trego country. Didn't get home but a little while back."

"Well, one of our men disappeared around here last night. We've been searching all day. Can't find him or his car. Did you happen to see or hear anything during the night? Anything unusual?"

"Nuthin' unusual that I can think of," he said. "Unless you call a chain saw unusual."

"A chain saw?" Tolliver said. "Last night?"

"Yeah. Somewhere off in that direction," he said, pointing south. "Barely heard it. Thought it was a might weird that somebody was cuttin' trees or a fishin' hole that time a-night."

Tolliver and his deputy looked at one another.

"Wouldn't a-heard it if the dog hadn't got up to take a leak," he continued. "Didn't think much more about it after that."

"What time you hear it?"

"Don't have a clock. Just know it was late."

"Okay, Clarence. Thanks. I don't know if it means anything, but we appreciate the help."

Back in the squad car, Tolliver turned to the deputy. "What did he say? It's weird to be cutting trees or a fishing hole at that time of night?"

"That's what he said."

"You know," Tolliver said, "I think he's right."

Alex was preparing for the early newscast when he saw John Knowles approaching him from across the newsroom.

"Welcome back," Alex said. "How was L.A.?"

"Fine. Sleet sends his warmest greetings," Knowles said. "He's off to New Mexico or someplace, but he passed the polygraph test without a problem. All of them did, except for Roger, of course. Any sign of him?"

"No sign. But a lot of other things have happened," Alex said, telling him of the deputy's disappearance and of the confrontation with Hawke and his friends.

"So as it stands now," Alex said, "we've got the lie detector tests done, we're getting the people we need on tape, and we still have all of the writing and editing left to do."

"You're going to go ahead?" Knowles asked.

"I think we should, and Barclay agrees. But it could get real ticklish. You may want to back out while you can. If Hawke finds out what we're doing, he may fire our asses before we can get the piece on the air. He won't tolerate anybody directly defying his orders."

"Shit, he can't fire the whole staff," Knowles said, dousing his cigarette in a half-filled coffee cup.

"Don't count on it. He was pretty adamant in that meeting, and after the Scotty Hansen business, I don't think he's in the mood for any more foolishness."

"Maybe we can talk to him again," Knowles offered. "He's got to understand what's at stake here."

"I don't think it'll do any good."

"Aren't you and Barclay worried?" Knowles asked.

"About being fired? Hell, yes. But I've traveled around so much that one more station won't make much difference. Besides, I think if we can get the piece on the air, he'll be hard pressed to dump us. The danger is between now and then. We don't want to get caught."

"I'm not sure what I'd do if I wasn't working here," Knowles said. "I'd make a piss-poor PR man, and I sure as hell can't get back into the network rat race."

"John, believe me, we'll understand if you want out. As much as I'd like to have your help, I can't ask you to risk your job."

"Let me think about it," Knowles said. "But in the meantime, I'll get all of the stuff together on the lie detector tests."

Alex asked him about Linda. "I don't know," Knowles replied, "I haven't seen her for a while. She's seeing a shrink, and she's taken a medical leave from her nurse's job. She seems to be regressing . . . getting more bitter, more angry all the time."

"Is there anything we can do?" Alex asked.

"Not that I can think of," Knowles said. "She sits and stares at Daniel's picture all day or rummages through old photo albums from when they were kids. It's bizarre, and I only hope the therapy helps."

Barbara overheard part of Alex's conversation with Knowles from her cubicle. "Why haven't you told me anything about the meeting with Hawke?" she asked after Knowles left. "Don't I deserve to know, too?"

"Sorry," Alex said. "I didn't want to drag you in."

"I've got a stake in this, too, Alex. I know I haven't done as much as you or John, but I'm not exactly uninterested, either."

"I know, Barbara. But I think you should keep out of it from now on. Hawke wasn't fooling around."

"Don't you think *I* should decide that?" she asked, anger in her voice. "You still want to treat me like a kid, don't you?"

"Knock it off, Barbara. It's nothing like that. But you do have a whole career ahead of you. Barclay and I have bounced around and we'd survive getting canned a whole lot better than you would."

"What a bunch of male chauvinist crap! Don't patronize me. You're not my father."

"You've got a great thing going here. Why the hell risk blowing it?"

"I want to see the Steele story air. I don't want to see Hawke kill it. And I don't want to work here if he does."

Alex studied her, embarrassed to remember that just a few weeks before he'd told her she'd have to earn his respect.

"Okay, Barbara," he said, "it's your choice."

The lake in front of Steele's lodge was about two miles long and about three wide, with a half dozen big bays indenting the shoreline. It had taken Tolliver much of the day to recruit and assemble the volunteer snowmobilers. He'd divided them into four groups, each with a team leader, and each assigned to a certain section of the lake. If they found nothing after the first sweep, the teams would trade sections and try again. After two unsuccessful sorties, they'd move on to the next lake.

"What are we looking for, Mike?" one of the volunteers asked.

"I know this sounds crazy, but I think some fucker *sank* Fred," Tolliver told him. "I don't think we're going to find him in the woods or under some snowbank. He's under the ice somewhere . . . him and his car . . . and we have to find some sign of them."

"What are you talking about?" another had the courage to ask, but they all looked doubtful.

Tolliver told them about the old man who'd heard the chain saw.

"I know people do strange things around here," Tolliver said, "but I've never heard of anybody chain-sawin' in the middle of the night. Not for the hell of it. And the more I think about it, the more I'm sure somebody sank the car with Fred in it. Otherwise, we would have found him by now."

"You mean somebody drowned him? On purpose? Why the hell would they do that?" The man's skepticism had not disappeared.

"So we wouldn't find him, I suppose. At least not for a long time. Maybe never. They had to get rid of him and the car, quick."

"There's a hell of a lot of ice out there," one of his deputies muttered.

"And there are a hell of a lot of lakes to cover," Tolliver said, "so let's get going."

Later, sitting on the shore astraddle his snowmobile, Tolliver watched the searchers come in through the twilight, one after another, the headlights of their snowmobiles bouncing crazily across the lake.

He had counted fifteen of them when he saw the bright burst of a flare across the bay. Somebody had found something.

"Look!" Tolliver shouted, gunning his Skidoo, leading the pack toward the flare. They raced across the ice, the freezing wind in their faces, a deafening roar in their wake.

"What'd you find?" he yelled, as he leaped off the snowmobile.

"I'm not sure, but I thought you should see it," the deputy said, pointing toward the ice. "I damn near flipped the snowmobile when I hit it."

"Get more flares going!" Tolliver shouted, "so we can see something here." He walked to where the deputy stood and found a ridge of ice about eighteen inches high and about eight feet wide. It was as if the slab had been raised up, then slammed back down on the surface of the lake, forming a ramp of sorts. Tolliver walked the length of it, pushing the snow away with his boots, trying to picture the imprint a sinking car would leave in the ice.

"Would the weight of a car going under push the ice away as it sank?" he asked the deputy.

"Got me," he replied. "Only cars I've seen go under went through thin ice when the lake never had the chance to freeze over like this. But it makes sense, I guess."

"Anybody got any ideas?" Tolliver asked the group.

"I don't know what else would make a ridge like that," one of the searchers said. "Not all by itself in the middle of the lake."

"Okay. Let's get the chainsaws and the divers out here first thing in the morning, cut us a hole and go down to see what's under there. Anybody have any idea how deep it is?"

"I've heard this lake is a hundred feet deep or so in spots," another searcher said. "But it could be a lot less here."

"I guess we'll find out in the morning," Tolliver said.

The next day broke cloudy and gray, and Tolliver could almost feel the snow poised somewhere above him, ready to drop. He knew the weather was due to worsen within a few hours, and he waited anxiously for the sky to lighten enough to proceed.

It took them only a few minutes to cut a hole in the ice big enough for the scuba diver to slip through. The diver was tethered to an ice spud drilled into the surface while another diver, the tender, stood watch over the rope. A third, fully outfitted in a dry suit and tank, stood by in case the first diver got into trouble beneath the ice.

"How long do you think it'll be?" Tolliver asked the rope tender.

"Hard to tell," the man replied. "Depends on how deep it is, and whether the mud's still stirred up at the bottom. Fifteen or twenty minutes, I'd guess."

It was actually sixteen minutes when the diver broke the surface and was hoisted up on the ice. He pulled off his hood and took his mouthpiece out.

"It's there," he said, breathing deeply. "About fifty feet down, up to the wheels in mud. And your guy's there, too. Not a pretty site. Looks like he's handcuffed to the steering wheel."

"Sweet Jesus," Tolliver muttered, feeling his stomach heave.

"Car was all closed up, doors locked. He'll have to come up with the car. The chain saw's down there, too. I saw one end sticking up out of the mud. Whoever did it must have thrown it in after the car went down."

"Get the tow truck out here," Tolliver told Slater. "Get the car up, and don't forget the chain saw. Don't touch anything in the car until I get back. I've got to go see Fred's folks."

Thirty-eight

Alex and Judge Steele heard the news at about the same time, but in different ways.

The judge was driving to work, listening to the local news on the radio, when the newscaster reported the discovery of Fred Jensen's body entombed in his car at the bottom of a Wisconsin lake.

"Authorities believe Jensen's killer cut a hole in the ice of Lake Jordan with a chain saw and allowed his squad car to sink with the deputy handcuffed to the steering wheel. So far, there are no leads to the identity of the killer."

Steele quickly pulled to the side of the road, and turned off the radio. He sat in his car, trying to think, as the traffic roared past.

Alex got the news at home, in a phone call from Phil.

"They found him in Steele's lake?" Alex asked, amazed.

"Not that far from the lodge. Whoever dumped him obviously did it in a hurry and thought he'd stay put for a while."

Phil described the condition of the body and said they'd also found the chain saw that apparently was used to cut the hole in the ice. "They're trying to trace the ownership of it now," he added.

"What does Tolliver say?" Alex asked.

"He'd like to search Steele's house," Phil replied, "but he doubts he can get a warrant."

Minutes after he said goodbye to Alex, Phil's phone rang.

"Detective Tinsley?"

Phil thought the voice sounded as though it were coming from a car phone. "Yes, this is Tinsley," he said. "Who's this?"

"This is Judge Emmett Steele. I just heard the news about the deputy on the car radio. I'm terribly disturbed about it, happening as close as it did to my place. It must have happened the evening I left, and I hope you'll tell Sheriff Tolliver that I'll be happy to cooperate in any way I can."

"I'm sure he'll be pleased to hear that," Phil said, careful to keep his tone neutral. "They'll be looking for all the help they can get."

"It's a pity I left the house," Steele said. "Perhaps I could have done something to help the officer. It seems such a horrible way to die."

"You're right about that, Judge. I'll pass on your message to the sheriff."

Alex met Pat in a small coffee shop just off the skyway in the Pillsbury Building. She had not yet heard about Fred Jensen.

"That's why I wanted to see you, Pat. The deputy was supposed to be watching Steele's place when he disappeared. Nobody knows what happened to him, but it must be more than a coincidence."

"I can't believe all of this, Alex," she said. "It's unreal. Is there anything I can do?"

"Two things, maybe. One, if you could find a key to the lake house, I think Tolliver would like a chance to look around inside without having to get a warrant and without Steele knowing. Since you and Nathaniel seem to own part of it, you should be able to give him permission."

"I have no idea where the key would be or whether we even have one," Pat said. "I suppose I could look at Nathaniel's key chain, but that would be tricky. I'd never know which key is which, anyway."

"Which brings me to the second point," Alex said. "Maybe it's time you and Nathaniel finally talked about this lake property."

He could almost see the color drain from her face.

"Do you know what you're asking? It'd open everything up, and who knows where it would end? I don't know if I can do it, Alex."

"His connection to the place is bound to come out at some point," Alex countered. "It's just a matter of time, the way things are going."

"The truth is, I'm afraid to find out what he knows about it," she said, as she took a final sip of her coffee.

"Is Nathaniel in court today?" Alex asked.

"He's at the courthouse, but I don't know if he's hearing a trial. You're not going to talk to him, are you?"

"No, not if I can help it. I was just wondering."

When Alex returned to the station, he found Derek slouched on a chair in the studio, alone and reading a tattered magazine. It was the first time Alex had seen him since their confrontation in the toilet.

"Have a nice vacation?" Alex asked, walking up to him.

"Buzz off, Collier," Derek replied, hardly looking up. "I got nothing to say to you."

"How about the tapes, Derek? They're still missing. I still want them back."

Derek pulled himself up off the chair, looked around, and bellied Alex backward into the wall. "Listen, you prick," he hissed, "stay away from me, *understand*? You're getting on my nerves. I don't know nothing about your fucking tapes."

Alex was pressed against the wall, the foul breath from Derek's mouth almost making him gag. Without thinking, his knee came up like a piston, doubling Derek over. He made no sound, except for a sharp grunt.

"Wise up, Derek. This isn't some fucking game. *Understand?*"

Then Alex walked out of the studio and toward the newsroom, leaving Derek grimacing and holding his balls with both hands.

"You've become a major inconvenience, Roger, and I'm facing a serious dilemma as to your future."

They were sitting in Steele's living room, where the nightmare had begun with the drugged drink days before. Steele was lounging comfortably in an easy chair, one leg draped over the knee of the other. Roger was on the sofa, legs still chained together. Russell was not in sight.

"We cannot immediately return to our former location," Steele said, "nor can we keep you here indefinitely. And we certainly can't release you."

"What about my hand?" Roger asked, holding up his swollen, misshaped finger. "You can't leave it this way."

"Your finger is the least of your problems, Roger," the judge said.

Roger sat quietly. There was nothing to say.

"Since I'm still not certain exactly what you have told Collier, it is difficult for me to assess the danger you pose to me in the future."

"I'm no danger to you," Roger pleaded. "Even if I wanted to talk, who'd believe *me*, anyway?"

"Alex Collier would believe you. He'd believe anyone with disparaging things to say about me."

Roger slumped in his chair.

"I may have blunted Collier's plans temporarily," Steele said. "However, that still leaves the question of your future unanswered."

Steele looked at his watch.

"It is now eleven o'clock on Thursday. You will have precisely seventy-two hours—until eleven o'clock on Sunday—to tell me what I want to know. If you refuse, you and Russell will take a little trip. It will not be a pleasant trip, Roger, and you are unlikely to return from it. Need I say more? Think about it."

Alex and Rick stood to one side of the Government center atrium, well away from the crush of the noon-hour rush, but well within view of the bank of elevators. They'd been there for fifteen minutes, and Rick was beginning to fidget.

"Calm down, Rick, it shouldn't be much longer."

"I don't like crowds," he said, scrunching up his shoulders.

"Keep your eyes open," Alex urged. "He could be —"

The middle set of elevator doors opened, and Judge Nathaniel Hodges and three other men emerged, engrossed in conversation, paying no heed to anything else.

"There!" Alex said softly, resisting the urge to point. "That group of guys walking over there. Recognize any of them?"

Rick's eyes followed his, and he edged forward to improve his angle of vision. "Yeah," he said excitedly. "The one in the gray coat with the Russian hat. That's him. The guy in the back of the Continental with me, and in the black BMW."

For a fraction of a second there was a void in the babel of the atrium crowd. And in that silence, as though a conductor had brought down his baton, Rick's last words rang out.

Hodges stopped mid-step, and his head snapped around, as if searching the air for Rick's words. Instead, he found Alex, then Rick. His companions stopped and looked at Hodges, but he stood rooted to the floor, his eyes moving back and forth between Alex and Rick—the confusion on his face changing first to disbelief and then to understanding.

Alex returned the gaze unblinking. He watched, transfixed, as Hodges seemed to shrink before his eyes, the upright judicial bearing melting like snow in the spring.

Finally, Hodges turned away and walked haltingly to join the others.

"Man, is he freaked out," Rick whispered. "For a minute I thought he might keel over."

Alex said nothing, but took a deep breath. He felt a little faint himself.

Now what would he tell Pat?

That evening, after the early news, Alex called an informal meeting at his house. Faced with Hawke's threats, Alex had decided it would be wise to hold the meeting outside the station. Barclay was there, filling one of the easy chairs, along with Barbara, Phil, and John Knowles.

"Okay," Alex said, once everyone was settled. "We all know the situation. The question is: How do we put the story together and get it on the air without Hawke finding out what we're up to?"

Knowles was the first to speak. "I'm not sure it's possible, but I can take the interview tapes home and start logging and transcribing them there. I'll pick out the best segments so you'll know what you have when you start writing."

"We've got to limit the number of people who know what we're doing," Barclay said. "We can trust Cody, and he was a tape editor before he became a producer. I'll free him up to edit your piece."

"Good," Alex said. "Barbara, can you try to get the magazine guy, Stensrud, to tell his story on tape? You said he'd be willing."

"I'll try," Barbara said. "I just hope he hasn't changed his mind."

"How about Judge Hodges?" Barclay asked. "Are we going to try and tie him into this? We don't have much besides Rick's I.D."

"I don't know," Alex admitted. "I just wonder how deep it goes. Remember that Grabowski thought it went beyond Steele, and Hodges seems to be the first link to that. But maybe he's just Steele's errand boy, doing a few favors in return for a few."

"How about the murders?" Phil asked. "Daniel and the deputy. What can you say about those?"

"John, what do you think?" Alex asked. "We can report that Daniel was investigating Steele when he disappeared, can't we?"

"Yeah, but I wouldn't mention the proximity of Daniel's grave to Steele's lodge," Knowles replied, "or anything about the dead deputy. I don't think we want to be accusing Steele of murder, even by implication."

"Speaking of the murders, Phil, how are you guys doing?" Barclay asked.

"The murders are in Tolliver's jurisdiction," Phil said, "but I'm giving him all of the help and support I can."

"How about your own investigation of Steele?" Alex asked.

"For abusing the kids? We're finally starting to get our shit together, thanks to you guys. I've got my lieutenant working with me now, and we're trying to find a prosecutor we can trust— somebody who's not in Steele's pocket. I'm sure we can get an indictment against him for soliciting juveniles for prostitution. And maybe for child abuse. But, face it, nothing's going to happen until your story breaks. Then the sky's going to fall in."

"How so?" Alex asked.

"Watch and see. Everybody's going to be demanding a grand jury investigation the next day. We've got to have everything ready to go for the county attorney when the time comes."

"Okay," Alex said, glancing at his watch. "I'll start writing a rough draft tonight. George, John, I'm counting on some writing help from you. The last time I did this kind of story, I got my ass sued."

"Glad to help, Mr. Anchorman," Barclay replied. "Even if we have to do it standing in the unemployment line together."

After the group had left, Alex placed a call to his family in Philadelphia. Jan answered the phone.

"I think you'd better cancel those plane tickets," Alex said.

"Why? What's happened?"

"Things are getting worse," Alex said.

"Worse?"

"I can't explain it, Jan, and I don't want to worry you. You'll have to trust me until I can see you and fill you in."

"When will that be?" she asked. "The kids are very anxious."

"Soon after the first of the year, when this is all over. Tell the kids I'll bring their Christmas gifts with me."

"What about Seuss? What should I tell them?"

"Don't say anything, Jan. I'll tell them when I come."

Pat sat in her living room, watching the flames slowly die in the fireplace. The newspaper lay open but unread on her lap.

She heard the garage door open and close and listened as her husband's footsteps crossed the kitchen and continued, without pause, to his study. She could not hear the door close, but she knew it had.

She did not stir, studying the pulsating glow of the embers in the grate. She was content to wait until the coals turned from red to black, if necessary. Until he emerged and faced her.

It was almost midnight when Pat heard his footsteps again.

"Nathaniel?"

The steps paused, then resumed, the creaking of the floor her clue that he was walking in her direction.

"You're still up?" he asked, standing in the archway.

"I've been waiting. I thought we should talk."

"It's late and I'm tired. Maybe tomorrow."

"I think we should talk *now*," she said. "We've already waited too long. We can't just keep avoiding each other, can we?"

The embers had turned to ashes, still smoldering, but providing neither light nor warmth. Only the Christmas tree lights burned in the living room, leaving both Pat and Nathaniel shrouded in shadows.

"I'm not up to it," he said, his body sagging against the wall. "It's been a tough day."

Pat stood and walked to him. She took his hand and led him to the couch. "What's happening, Nathaniel? What's going on? I'm not sure I know you anymore. I'm not sure I ever did. Please."

He stared at the lights on the tree, blinking red and blue and green, seemingly hypnotized by them.

"Nathaniel?"

"It's too complicated, Pat. Too impossible to explain. I wouldn't know where to begin."

His words were a whisper, and Pat could not see his lips move.

"Try," she said.

He leaned his head back against the rim of the couch, eyes closed, breathing deeply. His face revealed nothing but weariness.

"It's funny, you know. I just wanted to be a good judge, Pat. Just a good judge. And I was—I am. But something happened along the way. Suddenly, and I don't know when exactly, just being a good, *ordinary* judge wasn't good enough anymore."

Pat waited for him to continue. His eyes were still closed.

"I saw others around me . . . You know who they are, Richter and Sampson, Guyter, and the rest of the lightweights . . . They were starting to get the better cases. I couldn't figure it out. At first, I thought it was just the luck of the draw, but when it kept up, month after month, I knew it was more than that."

"Steele."

"Of course," he said, looking at her for the first time. "It became clear I was on a slow track to nowhere, because I wasn't on Steele's list. It wasn't only the assignments. He'd pick me apart in the meetings, as only he can do it. Piddling stuff, almost laughable. But nobody was laughing, least of all Emmett Steele."

"Why didn't you tell me all of this at the time?" Pat asked.

"Because it was my problem, not yours," he said, bristling. "I had to solve it. And the solution was obvious: to make peace with Steele. To cozy up. Being a good judge clearly wasn't enough. You didn't even have to be *good*, for God's sake."

"And?"

"And I did what I needed to do. A little ass-kissing at first. A few favors. No more than a lot of others were doing. But then more and more. I started to get a few of the bigger cases. You know the ones I'm talking about."

"But I didn't know how you got them," she murmured.

"Now you know. It wasn't because of my brilliance on the bench, believe me. I had become one of the favored few."

"At what price?"

"Aha! Now to the heart of it, right? Just like a lawyer, Pat. Well, remember, I'm not on the witness stand, and you're not cross-examining."

"Nathaniel," she pleaded, "I'm just trying to understand."

"Well, you'll *never* understand. No one who hasn't been there can grasp the power of that man, his charisma, the euphoria of sitting at his right hand and getting his approval. Talk about having it made: reputation, respect, an unlimited future. I had it all."

"What did Steele demand in return?" she asked.

"Don't give up, do you?" His eyes closed again. "Too much, I know that now. I gave up my self-respect, my independence, maybe even my manhood. Willingly, too, for a long time. Until I realized what I'd given up. By then it was too late."

He stood up, looking down at her. "Now I'm going to bed."

"What about the land in Wisconsin?" she blurted.

He paused. "Couldn't forget that, could we? Part of the price, Pat. Steele wanted an out-of-the-way place. A hideaway, but not in his name. A retreat, he called it. He knew about our land and the lake. I did plan to tell you about it, but there never seemed to be an appropriate moment."

"There's more, isn't there, Nathaniel?"

"Nothing you'll ever hear from my lips," he said, starting to walk away.

"The kids, Nathaniel. *What about the kids?*" The words rushed out of her. Followed by tears that clung to her cheeks.

His expression didn't change.

"Why don't you ask your friend Collier? He seems to know all about it, Pat."

Then he left, the same creaks in the floor tracing his path to the bedroom, and out of her life.

Nathaniel was not in the house when Pat awoke.

She had slept little, feeling his restless stirrings in the bed across the room, knowing his eyes, like hers, were staring into the same dark space.

Before dawn, sleep finally came to her. She did not hear him leave his bed or the house.

Pat walked from room to room, pausing to look at the familiar pictures and mementos of their marriage, noticing how the morning sun made the same latticed patterns on the rugs.

Nothing looked different, but her life had changed.

Now I know how a widow must feel on the day after the funeral, Pat thought.

As she stopped at the door of Nathaniel's study, she suddenly recalled Alex's words: *"If you could just find a key to the lake house . . ."*

Thirty-nine

Rick knew he must look odd, waiting at the bus stop with the little Christmas tree tucked under his arm, but he didn't care. And the driver didn't blink when he boarded the bus.

Rick realized he should be at Roger's, staying put as Alex had asked him to. But he just couldn't, not without Roger there. So he packed up the little tree he had bought at a corner lot and headed for the bus, hoping Alex would understand.

The bus dropped him off a block from the cemetery. From the gate, it seemed to stretch for miles. Winter made it all the same, the snowdrifts erasing the small rises and gullies, hiding the grave markers which used to guide his way in summer.

Rick saw row upon row of pine wreaths and plastic crosses stuck in the snow, but he didn't see a decorated Christmas tree anywhere, and that made him feel good. His mom always loved the holidays, especially when his dad was home, and he knew she'd like having her own tree this Christmas.

Rick finally found the small maple and dug through the snow to uncover the flat gravestone. He piled the snow carefully on each side of the marker, hoping it wouldn't slide back. Then he buried the tiny trunk of the Christmas tree in the snow at the head of the grave, and opened his knapsack. There were only a few decorations: four glass bulbs, two silver bells, a tiny wooden manger, and a silken white angel with golden hair, which he hung at the top of the tree.

Then he talked to his mother, and thought he heard her laugh.

Maybe it was just the wind whispering through the bare branches of the maple.

It didn't take Pat long to find the keys in Nathaniel's study. They were stuck away in a small cuff-link box in the bottom drawer of his desk. She had never seen these keys before, and tried them in every door of their house and garage. They opened nothing.

In twenty minutes, she had driven to the hardware store and back, copies of the keys in her purse, the originals tucked away again in the desk drawer.

She felt no guilt, no regret, as she dialed Alex's number.

"Alex? I'm sorry to bother you."

"No problem, Pat. What's up?"

"I found some keys. They may be for the lake place, I don't know. At least they're not for here. I don't know what to do with them."

"Where are you?"

"Home. Nathaniel could be back at any time. I don't know where he is."

"Is something wrong? You don't sound like yourself."

"It's a long story," she sighed. "But we had our talk last night. It kind of drained me, and I didn't sleep very well."

"I'm sorry." He didn't know what else to say.

"So am I."

"About the keys," Alex said. "Can I pick them up from you somewhere. You should also sign something that gives Tolliver the right to use them."

"Okay. Can we meet in the Southdale parking lot right away? I don't want to be away from the house for long."

"Fifteen minutes," Alex said. "And thanks."

Alex spotted Pat's black BMW on his second swing around the parking lot. She gave him the keys and the note authorizing their use. "I don't know how legal this is," she said. "I don't even know if they're the right keys. But it's the best I could do."

"Let's hope they work, Pat. The county records say you and Nathaniel own the place—and that'll be enough for Sheriff Tolliver. He doesn't have much to go on, and I think he's getting desperate. I'm taking the keys up to him myself."

"Good luck," she said, as she put the BMW into gear. She seemed in a hurry to get away.

"Can you tell me any more about your conversation with Nathaniel?" Alex asked.

"Not now, Alex. I just want this to end. Soon."

Then she drove away.

As soon as Rick returned from the cemetery, he dialed the number of Steele's house. The voice he heard on the other end was familiar; Rick remembered Russell's words from his very first visit to the house (*"His name is Rick. He's clean. All checked out."*) and knew it was him.

"May I speak to Roger Anderson, please?" Rick asked Russell. He covered the mouth of the phone with a handkerchief, like they did on TV.

"No Roger Anderson lives here" was the gruff reply.

"But doesn't he work there?" Rick persisted.

"Not anymore. Who is this?"

"A friend."

"Well, friend, you'd better check somewhere else."

Russell slammed the phone down and walked quickly to Roger's room. He unlocked the door and pushed it open. Roger was lying on the bed.

"You had a phone call," Russell said.

"I did? Who?" Roger sat up on the edge of the bed, the shackles still on his legs.

"That's what the judge will want to know," Russell replied. "The guy said he's your friend."

Roger immediately thought of Rick, the only real friend he had. "The judge doesn't think I have any friends," he said.

"Don't get smart, kid. The judge isn't going to like you getting phone calls. It's going to make him nervous. He may not want to wait until Sunday to settle up."

Roger glanced at the clock on the shelf. More than thirty hours had passed since Steele's warning, almost half the allotted time. Roger was now counting the minutes, not the hours.

"Why are you doing this, Russell? You know there's going to be big trouble for you."

"I do what I'm told," Russell said. "You should do the same."

He left and locked the door.

Rick waited until the dark of late afternoon, then stood again in a phone booth outside another convenience store. He waited, hoping he would see an older woman with a common-looking car, nothing fancy or flashy.

He knew he had to be more cautious now; he couldn't wait for the police shifts to change, and he wasn't sure how long he'd need the car.

This time, it took forty-five minutes for the right lady to come along. She left her '86 Buick Century at the edge of the lot, unlocked and idling, and walked slowly to the store.

Rick was behind the wheel and on his way before the woman was through the door of the store. He needed only five minutes to get to the parking lot of a theater ten blocks away. He cruised the aisles of parked cars, guessing the lot would remain safe until the theater emptied out.

He pulled into a space between two cars, took a screwdriver from his pocket, and quickly exchanged the license plates of his stolen car with those of the car next to him. With luck, no one would notice the trade until morning, maybe longer.

It took less than two minutes, and Rick was again on his way to Merriweather Drive.

He stopped at a SuperAmerica gas station and a Target discount store to pick up the items he needed. Then he drove past Steele's house—checking the gate and looking for an outdoor phone nearby. He found one three blocks away.

The chain on the gate was old and rusted, and proved no match for the boltcutters he had just bought. Rick allowed the gate to swing open, crouching low against the fence, watching for car lights in either direction. His car was a few feet away, parked on the side of the road, hood up, as though it had engine trouble. He hurried to it, grabbed his supplies from the trunk, and raced up the driveway before the first car passed by.

Nathaniel Hodges had spent the full day in his chambers, passing the hours pacing the floor, staring out of his window, watching the annual Christmas parade wind through the streets below. There was office work to be done, opinions to be written, but he appeared to have little appetite for any of it.

His court clerk stopped by, but found Hodges deep in thought and in no mood to talk. So he backed out of the chambers quietly, to work by himself in the outer office. When he finally left, hours later, after day had turned to evening, the door to Hodges's chambers was still closed.

The clerk met Emmett Steele in the hall.

"Is Judge Hodges in?" Steele asked.

"He's there," the clerk replied, "but he seems depressed. Hasn't moved out of his office all day."

"Thanks," Steele replied, smiling. "I'll try to cheer him up."

Steele rapped on Nathaniel's door, then pushed it open. He found Hodges curled up on his couch.

"Nathaniel?"

Hodges's eyes opened slowly, as if he were emerging from a deep sleep.

"Nathaniel? Are you all right?"

Hodges closed his eyes again. Steele reached down and shook his shoulder.

"Come on, Nathaniel. Get up. What's the matter?"

Hodges's eyes opened again. "It's all over, Emmett. I know that now," he whispered. "All I ever wanted was to be a good judge."

"What are you talking about?" Steele demanded. "Pull yourself together, Nathaniel. Show some backbone."

He pulled Hodges up by the arm.

"Are you blind?" Hodges asked. "Can't you see them closing in? Even Pat knows about it, and Collier knows Rick. They were together downstairs yesterday, waiting for me."

Steele studied him. "It shouldn't surprise me that your wife knows," he mused, sitting down next to Nathaniel on the couch. "I should have realized it sooner. She must be at the bottom of all this."

"What are you talking about?" Hodges demanded.

"Why else would Collier, new in town, and knowing nobody, really, except Patricia, develop this sudden interest in me? Someone had to plant the seed, Nathaniel, and I'm sure it was your wife."

"You can't be serious, Emmett. Why would she do that? She

knew nothing. Collier must have told her about Wisconsin. About the kids. He's learned everything, and now Pat knows, too."

"And I suppose you still think they're just friends, eh? Don't be naive, Nathaniel. Collier's fucking her, don't you know that?"

Hodges looked stricken. "I won't believe that!" he said. "How can you say it? There's no proof—"

"You just don't want to believe it," Steele said.

There was a sharp knock on the door.

"Go away!" Steele yelled. "We don't want to be disturbed."

There was another knock, and the door opened.

"Didn't you hear me?" Steele demanded of the young woman in the doorway. "No interruptions."

"Judge Steele, please," she said, her voice trembling. "I have an urgent message for you."

"What?" he asked, his nose almost in her face.

"Somone just called. Your house is on fire!"

Steele was disbelieving.

"My house is on fire? Who called?"

"He said his name was Russell," the woman said, still standing outside the door. "He said I should find you right away."

Steele bolted past her, leaving Nathaniel alone again.

Roger smelled the smoke before he heard the sirens. *Had the fireplace backed up?*

He hobbled to the door and pounded on it. Wisps of smoke seeped under it.

He heard heavy footsteps running down the hall. He shouted and pounded again.

That's when he heard the sirens.

The lock in the door turned, and the door swung open.

"Stay put!" Russell shouted. "It's just the garage. Don't say a fucking word!"

The door closed again, and the key turned.

Rick stood back among the pine trees as an interested neighbor would, his face half lighted by the leaping flames. He watched as the firemen played their hoses on the south wall and roof of the garage, waiting for them to bring Russell out of the house.

He knew one thing already: Roger's car *was* in the garage. Not much was left of it now, but he was sure Roger would understand.

It had worked as Rick had hoped it would: he'd splashed gasoline on the side of the garage, carefully lit a long, gasoline-soaked rope, and run for his car. He'd made it to the phone booth and dialed 911 in less than three minutes. The firemen were arriving as he walked back to the scene.

In the excitement and confusion, no one noticed the young man saunter through the gate and up the driveway before it could be cordoned off. None of the firemen missed the single fire axe taken from one of the trucks.

Russell came out the front door, his upper body wrapped in an old mackinaw.

"Anybody else in there?" a fireman shouted, pulling him away from the house.

"No, nobody," Russell coughed. "Just get the goddamned fire out, okay?" He sat on the ground, breathing deeply.

Rick moved quickly around to the back of the house, away from the fire. One swing of the axe splintered the back door. And in a minute he covered the now-familiar house and found the locked door. Quickly, he cracked through it.

Roger was huddled by the bed, his face buried in a pillowcase. He looked at Rick with surprise and disbelief. "Rick! How the hell did you get here . . ."

"Never mind," Rick said. "Just follow me, quick!"

He led Roger through the splintered back door. Roger moved as fast as the shackles allowed, holding on to Rick for support. Together they slipped and slid down the hill behind the house, the glow of the burning garage lighting the night sky.

Steele was into the Continental and down the courthouse ramp in minutes. But the crowds along the Nicollet Mall, gawking at the Christmas store windows, filled the intersections and blocked him through two changes of stoplights. On the third green, Steele's car lunged ahead, scattering the lingering pedestrians still in the crosswalk.

Fifteen minutes later, he sped through his gate and up the driveway—as far as the parked fire engines would allow. Only smoke now poured from the charred garage. The firemen were beginning to wrap up some of the hoses, which were stiff with cold.

Large icicles hung from the eves of the unburned section of roof, and the ground around the front of the house was as slick as a skating pond. Steele struggled to stay on his feet as he rushed to the first fireman he saw.

"I'm Emmett Steele. I own this house. What happened here?"

"We're not sure," the fireman replied, "but it looks as if somebody tried to torch your place. It smells like a gas station over by the garage, and we found some pieces of charred rope that may have been used as a fuse."

Steele's eyes searched for Russell.

"You're lucky," the fireman continued. "We got a 911 call, and got here quick, in time to keep it from spreading to the house."

"A 911 call? From whom?"

"Anonymous. The guy just gave us the address and said there was a fire."

Steele pushed past the fireman and strode to the front door.

The house was still filled with smoke, and Steele found Russell in the kitchen, staring into the haze.

"Where's Roger?" Steele demanded, rushing down the hall.

"Gone," Russell replied, his voice flat. "Somebody broke down the door and took him."

Steele stared at the shattered door, the words of Nathaniel Hodges echoing in his mind:*"Are you blind? Can't you see them closing in?"*

Alex was home between newscasts when the phone rang.

"Mr. Collier?"

"Rick? How are you?"

"I found Roger. I have him with me now."

"You found him? Where?" Alex was astonished. "Is he okay?"

"At Steele's house. He's not too bad. Got a broken finger and some bruises. But he'll be all right."

"How'd you find him?"

"I'll tell you about that later, but for now, we're taking off. I don't know where, yet, but somewhere Steele can't find us. We'll call you when this thing is all over."

"Rick, wait a minute! Don't hang up. Can I talk to Roger?"

"He's in the car. He doesn't want to talk. Just wants out of here."

"How can I find you?" Alex asked. "You said you'd help."

"We have helped, Mr. Collier. It's only gotten us trouble."

"We may need you again, Rick."

"We'll be watching. We'll know when you need us. Bye, Mr. Collier."

Then the phone line went dead.

Forty

Mike Tolliver was waiting for Alex the next morning in the driveway of Steele's lake lodge. The sheriff was alone.

"Hell of a way to spend Christmas Eve, isn't it?" Tolliver muttered after shaking Alex's hand. "I appreciate your coming up."

"No problem," Alex said. "I just hope they're the right keys."

They were.

Moving through the house, they opened drawers and closets, checked beneath beds, even took pictures off the wall. They were careful to restore everything to its original position.

"Anything more on your deputy?" Alex asked.

"Not really." Tolliver turned away. "Autopsy showed he drowned, which was no big surprise. He also got hit on the back of the head. Hard to tell the time of death."

"Phil told me you recovered the chain saw from the lake. Have you been able to trace it?"

"We're still trying," Tulliver said. "It's a Homelite brand and they sell lots of them around here. But we're still looking."

They continued to search the house, but found nothing unusual except for a towel and a basin full of pinkish water in one bedroom, and what could have been a trace of blood on the floor of another basement room. Then they reached the garage.

Tolliver pushed a pile of clothes on the floor with his foot. It didn't move. It was frozen to the floor, a small slick of ice still surrounding it. He knelt beside the clothes and leaned over.

"Smells like gas," he said.

Then they noticed the boxes stacked in one corner. There were about ten in all, ordinary brown cardboard boxes sealed with masking tape with no labels or other identification.

"What do you think?" Tolliver asked.

"Don't you need a warrant?" Alex asked.

"Fuck it," Tolliver said, slitting the top of a box with a pocketknife and folding back the flaps. It was filled with tapes and magazines and a few newsletters.

"What the hell's this?" Alex asked as he picked up one of the newsletters. It was from a man-boy love association whose slogan read: "Sex After Eight Is Too Late."

"God Almighty," he muttered, thumbing through its pages.

"This is a goddamned pornographic stockpile," Tolliver said, as he picked out one magazine after another, all of them with young boys on their covers and in their pages. "I got a good idea what's on those tapes."

"We shouldn't be touching this stuff, should we, Sheriff?" Alex said. "Walking through the house is one thing, tearing open somebody's private boxes is another, right?"

"I don't see any names on them," Tolliver countered.

"C'mon, Mike. You're the law, but I think we should get the hell out of here."

"Okay," Tolliver agreed. "But I'm gonna' borrow these clothes. They'll never miss them. We'll see what the lab says about the gas smell."

Judge Steele surveyed the fire damage by the morning light. Russell was by his side, having said virtually nothing since the night before.

The portions of the garage not burned had been ruined by the water and smoke. Roger's car was an icy, blackened hulk, the tires melted into the garage floor. The adjoining wall of the house was scorched, but otherwise intact.

"I want someone out here to repair this damage," Steele said.

"I've already called," Russell said. "They won't work on Christmas, but they'll be here later in the week."

They picked their way through the debris, stepping carefully to avoid the ice and the ashes. Steele stooped to pick up the remains of a burned rake.

"How did the firebug know Roger was here, Russell?" he asked suddenly. "No one knew but us."

"It could have been the guy on the phone," Russell replied. "Somebody called and asked for Roger, said he was a friend."

Steele straightened up and stared at him. "Why didn't you tell me?"

"I was going to as soon as you got home, but the fire started first."

"Russell, you're an imbecile! You should have notified me immediately." Steele moved closer. "You've made two big mistakes, Russell. First the deputy, now this. Your incompetence has become a threat to me. Do you want to go back where I found you?"

Russell stood mute. He felt shame and, for the first time, anger with his boss. He tried to respond, but Steele cut him off. "No backtalk, no excuses, Russell. You've been warned."

Steele turned abruptly and again surveyed the damage. He walked around the perimeter of the charred garage, muttering to himself. Russell followed a few steps behind, keeping his distance.

"I'll be damned if I'm going to let this spoil my Christmas," Steele finally said. "I want everything boarded up and cleaned up, Russell. You've got two hours to get it done."

"Yes, sir, I'll try."

"Don't try. Do it!"

"Yes, sir."

"When's the insurance adjuster coming?" Steele demanded.

"He said within the hour, Judge."

"Okay. When he's done, and when you're done, we're going to get away from this stinking mess. I can't stand to be around it."

"Get away, Judge?"

"We'll spend Christmas at the lodge," Steele said.

"You really want to leave it like this?" Russell asked.

Steele glared at him. "I'm not paying you to question me, Russell. Now get to it!"

On Christmas morning, Pat sat alone by the tree, still in her robe in the utter silence of the house. She had no heart for opening the gifts beneath the tree, knowing the packages would seem empty—no matter what they contained.

She had stayed awake most of the night and still felt groggy and listless when the doorbell rang. She could barely find the energy to walk to the door.

"Merry Christmas," said the man outside, handing her a telegram in a brightly colored holiday envelope. "Hope it's good news," he added with a smile.

Pat carried the envelope to the kitchen, knowing who it was from, dreading to read it. She put it on the table and stared at it, finally slitting it open with a paring knife.

> PAT. CAN'T FIND IT IN MYSELF TO RETURN HOME.
> NOT YET. TOO MUCH TO SORT OUT. SORRY.
> I NEVER INTENDED TO HURT YOU. NATHANIEL.

Pat read the words over and over.

"Merry Christmas," she said quietly to herself, not bothering to try to stop the tears.

In his downtown hotel room Nathaniel sat on the edge of his bed and listened to the Christmas chimes ring out from the steeple of the nearby St. Olaf's Catholic Church. He'd been awake since before dawn, sitting where he now sat, undressed and unshaven. The world seemed to have closed in on him.

Nathaniel had checked into the hotel after Steele rushed out of his office almost thirty-six hours before. He had told no one where he was—ordering his meals through room service, and watching from the hotel window as last-minute shoppers scurried through the streets on Christmas Eve.

He had ventured out of his room only once, to send the telegram to Pat. Now, on Christmas morning, the streets were quiet, except for the chimes.

Alex had never spent a Christmas alone, not in all of his travels and in all of the years of separation from his family. He had always managed to find a way to be with them on the holiday, enduring crowded airports and winter storms and complaining bosses to do it. Now he was not only without his family, but also without whatever meager company Seuss might have offered.

He had already talked to Jan and the children in Philadelphia, wishing them a long-distance Merry Christmas and promising again that he would fly out to see them once the investigation was over. The children had seemed pleased to talk to him, but their voices were subdued and they sounded unconvinced by his promise.

Who could blame them?

Alex stood by the large front window, watching the first flakes of a new snow settle featherlike on the drifts covering the lawn. Despite the snow and the holiday music playing softly on the radio, there was no feeling of Christmas. He had had no time to think about a tree or decorations, and the house felt barren and joyless to him.

He had tried to phone Pat the night before, after his return from Wisconsin, but his calls had gone unanswered. He decided he would try again, and was relieved to hear her voice.

"Are you okay?" he asked.

"Nathaniel's not coming home, Alex. I just got a telegram."

"Where is he, Pat?"

"I don't know. Hiding out somewhere, I guess."

"Why?"

She read the telegram to him. "That's all I know, Alex."

"Pat, what the hell did you say to each other?"

"Please, Alex. I can't talk about it now."

"Why not?"

"Because it's too painful, because I don't know what's going to happen to Nathaniel. I don't want to think about it."

Alex told her about his trip to Wisconsin, and described what he and Tolliver had found in the garage. He also told her that Rick had found Roger in Steele's house and had freed him.

"What does it all mean, Alex?"

"I think it means we're getting close, Pat."

"I'm afraid, Alex. I wish I'd never started this."

Alex wanted to reassure her, to calm her, but he couldn't. Not knowing what he knew.

John Knowles took Linda Grabowski to church on this Christmas morning. Linda hadn't left the house for weeks except to go to therapy and mass, seeking comfort in the services, still unable to heed the priest's urgings to put Daniel's death behind her.

As they knelt in the pew, heads bowed, John could hear Linda's plaintive murmurs. She seemed to have retreated to some primitive part of herself and was unable to find her way back. Even her physical appearance was beginning to show the weight of her rage and suffering; she looked almost haggard.

Now, on this morning of joy, John felt chilled by this solitary stranger kneeling next to him.

Forty-one

Alex faced his computer terminal with a mind as blank as the monitor screen.

It was not the first time. He'd made several unsuccessful attempts to begin the Steele story, but on each occasion had given up in frustration. He knew time was running out.

Where do I begin? he wondered. How in the hell do I tell this story concisely and objectively?

The empty screen provided no answers, so he began to write.

"Channel Seven News has learned that Hennepin County Chief Judge Emmett Steele, who is about to be sworn in as the new chief justice of the Minnesota Supreme Court, has been sexually abusing children for years. He has recruited juvenile males and paid them for sexual favors with money and special treatment in his courtroom. And without their knowledge or consent, he has made videos of his sexual encounters with them.

"These allegations are the result of a six-week investigation by Channel Seven News, and will be substantiated by the words of several of Judge Steele's victims . . ."

Alex was interrupted by George Barclay, whose hulk cast a shadow over the computer screen.

"A word to the wise," Barclay said. "My spies tell me Hawke's not exactly brimming over with trust in us. He's got some of his own gremlins nosing around the newsroom, trying to make sure we're sticking to the straight and narrow."

"Not surprising, I guess," Alex said with a wan smile. "What should I be doing differently?"

"Just keep that computer file hidden," Barclay replied, "and do as much of the writing as possible at home. I'll try to cover for you here. We're too close now to lose it."

Alex thought for a moment. "You know, we're going to have to confront Steele soon. We can't run this story without some kind of reaction from him. . . . We have to give him the opportunity for a denial. And when we do that, Hawke will be the first to hear."

"You're not telling me anything I don't know," Barclay said.

"Is there any way we can get Hawke out of town?" Alex asked. "Is he planning a vacation?"

Barclay looked at him. "Not that I know of, but you may have just given me an idea. Come with me for a minute."

He led Alex into his office and closed the door behind them. Then he picked up the phone and dialed.

"Who—"

"Just listen," Barclay said.

"Affiliate Relations," a voice on the other end answered.

"Anthony Logan, please."

Alex looked at him quizzically. Barclay covered the mouthpiece and said: "An old friend. Works for the network."

They'd worked together ten years before at a small Florida station, Logan in sales, Barclay in news. Tony was one of the few TV salesmen George had ever liked, and they'd kept in infrequent touch as they each moved to different stations.

"Anthony Logan here," said the deep voice at the other end.

"It's George Barclay, Tony."

"George, you fat son of a bitch. How are you?"

"Okay. But I need a favor."

"What's that?" Logan asked.

"It's going to sound a little weird, but I need to get our general manager out of town for a few days."

"Jesus Christ, George. What are you up to now?"

"Don't press me," Barclay replied. "I just wondered if you knew of any conferences or panel discussions going on in the next few days which might be short a speaker? Last-minute fill-in kind of thing. Hawke loves to perform in public."

"Not offhand," Logan said, "but I can check around. It's always pretty quiet between Christmas and New Year's, you know."

"I know. That's a problem. But I've got to get him gone in the next few days. It's important, Tony."

"Okay, okay. Let me look. But I've got to cover my own ass, you know. The invitation will have to come from somewhere besides here."

"That's fine," Barclay said. "I appreciate the help."

After he hung up, Barclay turned to Alex. "It's a long shot, but it's the only way I can think of to keep Steele and Hawke apart."

"I don't have any better ideas," Alex admitted.

Alex returned to his computer, forcing himself to write page after page of the story. It was a rough draft, which he knew would have to be honed down later in the editing process. But he wanted to tell the whole story as he had come to know it, fact by degrading fact.

Knowles had provided him with transcripts of the taped interviews with Sleet in California and with Rick and Roger before they disappeared. Alex used excerpts of those interviews in his narration, along with scenes from the tapes Rick had stolen from Steele's house.

"*The pictures you see on your screen are not pretty,*" he wrote, "*although they've been carefully edited to conform with television standards. They were taken inside Judge Steele's home in Golden Valley, and were given to Channel Seven News by one of his victims. The boy on the lighted stage is a juvenile, brought to Judge Steele's home to perform sexual acts with the judge. . . .*"

He wrote of Daniel Grabowski's futile efforts to report on the activities of Judge Steele, and of Daniel's death in the woods of northern Wisconsin.

"*Before his death, Grabowski had obtained signed affidavits from three of Steele's alleged victims. He had confronted the judge with the allegations of his aberrent behavior. Grabowski disappeared a short time later. . . .*"

Alex was hunched over the computer, still writing, when he found Barbara standing over him.

"Stenrud's going to do the interview," she said, "but he's scared out of his wits. He thinks it will cost him his job."

"Tell him that if the piece gets on the air, he'll probably be a hero."

Barbara grinned. "I hope you're right," she said.

"Russell!"

Steele's shout came from the garage of the Wisconsin lake lodge and caught Russell by surprise. He'd hardly spoken to the judge since they'd arrived at the lodge late on Christmas Eve, two days before. Steele had been closeted in his study since then, working on what he said was his chief justice acceptance speech.

Russell rushed to the garage, and found the judge standing next to a stack of boxes.

"Have you been fooling around with these boxes?" Steele asked.

Russell shook his head.

"Well, somebody has," Steele said, pointing to the open top of one box. "Are you sure?"

"Yeah, I'm sure," he said. "You know I'd never do that."

"Did you lock up when you left?"

"Yes, sir. I always do. Even when I'm in a hurry."

"Who else has a key, Russell?"

"Judge Hodges. But he hasn't been here in a long time."

As Steele stared at him, Russell glanced down at the floor where he'd dropped his soaked clothes the night he'd fled. Only a spot of ice remained. He couldn't take his eyes away.

"What's the matter with you, Russell?"

"Nothing, Judge," he lied. "I was just thinking."

"Somebody's been inside here, Russell. I want all these boxes moved into the basement. Lock them up."

Russell nodded and started to pick up the first box.

"I'm going back to the Cities," Steele said, "to make sure the repairs begin on the house. I want you to stay here and keep an eye on the place."

"I won't have a car," Russell said.

"You won't need one. I want you here."

Pat never liked retrieving her car in the parking ramp. There had been a number of crimes committed there, and while security had improved, Pat vowed never to go in search of her car without the small cannister of Mace in her hand. She was clutching the Mace now as she approached the BMW, watching the

shadowed corners and dark spaces between cars. Looking everywhere but inside her car, she inserted the key and opened the
door.

"Hello, Pat."

She jumped back and brought the Mace up in one motion, her
arm outstretched, pointing inside the BMW.

"It's me, Pat. Relax."

"Nathaniel! What are you doing here? You scared me!"

"Sorry, Pat. Get in, please. We need to talk."

She slid behind the wheel, her body still trembling as she
slipped the Mace into her purse. "Where have you been, Nathaniel? I've been worried."

"That doesn't matter," he said. "I have to ask you some questions. I need the truth."

"I need the truth, too, Nathaniel. I don't think I got it all the
other night."

They stared silently at one another in the darkness of the car,
two feet apart, and a world between them.

"Are you having an affair with Collier?" The question was mat-
ter-of-fact, asked without emotion.

"Who told you that?" she asked. "Never mind, I can guess."

"Is it true?"

She paused only a moment, deciding she could not demand the
truth from him without revealing it herself. "It's true," she said.

"Did you lead him to the sordid business about Steele?"

"Yes. At least I got him interested."

"Will he broadcast the story?"

"I don't know. He wants to. I want him to."

"Do you realize it will ruin me? Ruin us?"

"Why *us*?" she asked. "Now it's time for the full truth from you."

"I'm involved. More deeply than you can imagine, more deeply
than I can explain. If Steele is destroyed, I will be destroyed."

"How did this happen, Nathaniel? How could you do it? Make
me understand, *please.*"

"For all the reasons I talked about, Pat. Ambition, frustration.
It was the only way to move ahead, and I thought Steele was
untouchable. It looks like I may have been wrong."

"Did you . . . participate . . . in what Steele—"

"I'm leaving, Pat." He slipped out the car door and was lost in the shadows of the ramp.

Barclay was on the phone with Tony Logan the next morning.

"You may be in luck," Logan said. "There's a small conference going on out in Vail—'Local Television in the 1990's' or some such shit—and a buddy of mine from the Affiliate Board is running it."

"Perfect," Barclay said. "Hawke loves to ski, too."

"Hold your horses. They don't really need another panelist, but this guy is willing to invite Hawke as a favor to me. He'll cook up some reason and see if Hawke bites. But you're going to owe me one because I'm going to owe him one."

"You got it," Barclay said. "I'll give you my secret diet."

"Terrific," Logan laughed. "I'll let you know what happens."

The message was brought to Alex by someone from a personal delivery service.

Alex: Could you please see me late this afternoon, say around four o'clock, in my chambers? If you can't make it, please call my clerk. I would appreciate your visit. Nathaniel Hodges.

What the hell's this about, Alex wondered as he picked up the phone and dialed Pat's number. She answered on the first ring, and he told her about the message.

"Why would he want to see me?" Alex asked.

"He knows you've found out everything," Pat replied, finally telling him of her two conversations with Nathaniel, leaving out her husband's admission of his own involvement with Steele.

"He knows about us, Alex. I told him."

"He does?"

"He asked me point-blank. I couldn't lie to him. He also knows you're trying to run the story."

"You told him that, too?"

"I had to. I also told him I was your original source."

Alex couldn't believe what he was hearing. "My God, Pat, why would you do all of that?"

"Because I wanted to tell the truth for once," she said. "I'm tired of the lies."

"And was he truthful to you?" Alex asked.

"Yes. But only to a point."

"What did he say?"

"I can't tell you more, Alex. Not right now."

"I won't press you, Pat. I don't want this to come between us, either."

"You'll have to be patient, Alex. That's all I can say."

By four o'clock the Government Center was beginning to empty out. Alex was one of the few people taking the elevator up.

He paused outside the chambers of Nathaniel Hodges.

What the hell am I doing here, he asked himself. It's crazy. Pat has told Hodges everything. He's probably waiting inside with a gun, ready to blow me away. No, not Nathaniel.

"Screw it," he muttered and walked through the door.

Alex was greeted by Hodges's clerk, an officious little man wearing oversized horn-rimmed glasses, who ushered him into the judge's office.

"You may leave now, Gerald," Hodges told the clerk. "I won't be needing you any more today."

Hodges closed the door and led Alex to a chair across the room. "Have you talked to Pat?" he asked.

Alex acknowledged that he had. "I was curious about the purpose of this meeting," he said. "She wasn't much help."

"I assume she told you about our talks," Hodges said.

"Some."

"Well, in light of those discussions, it seems appropriate that you and I should talk. We appear to be rivals of sorts, since you seem intent on pursuing both my wife and this vendetta of yours."

"It's not a vendetta, Judge."

"Semantics," Hodges said. "Is there any way you could be persuaded to abandon this crusade?"

"No. As I told Steele's bar association friends, if I don't do it, someone else will."

"Do you know what Judge Steele and I mean to this community? Do you know the contributions we've made to the judicial system, to civic organizations and charities?"

"That's kind of superfluous now, isn't it?"

Hodges stood and walked to the window, staring down. Alex thought he looked exhausted.

"Since I assume you won't consider some kind of monetary enticement," Hodges said, "I wonder if my willingness to step aside quietly for you and Patricia would help persuade you? It could be quite messy, otherwise. You and I are both in the public eye."

Alex was stunned and angry. He got up to leave.

"I've heard enough, Hodges. Pat wouldn't appreciate being used as a pawn in your game."

"So you'd ruin Judge Steele and me?" His eyes were pleading, his voice almost breaking. Alex had never seen anyone on the edge of a nervous collapse, but he guessed this was what it was like.

"He should've thought of the consequences before he started abusing those kids," Alex said, slamming the door behind him.

The elevator doors were closing when Alex heard the glass shatter. By the time he reached the first floor, a small crowd had begun to gather outside.

He looked up. There was a gaping hole in one of the windows on an upper floor. The edge of a drape was flapping in the wind outside.

Alex elbowed his way through the circle of people, and felt pieces of glass grind beneath his feet.

He looked down. At his feet was the broken form of Nathaniel Hodges, his body as grotesque in death as it had been imposing in life. He had landed on the red patio tiles of the courtyard, his arms and legs bent at unnatural angles like a child's doll with movable appendages. A pool of blood was spreading across the tiles.

People looked, then turned away, sickened by what they saw. Alex started to do the same, but before he could, he saw the impassive face of Emmett Steele staring at him from the fringes of the crowd.

Alex's first thought was of Pat. *Who would tell her? Should he? What could he say?* He wasn't sure he could bear to see her face, to hear her grief.

His dilemma was solved by Judge Steele. He quickly took charge of the situation, summoning the police and an ambulance, enlisting courthouse acquaintances to help disperse the crowd, and dispatching another judge to bring Pat to the hospital.

"Don't tell her anything," Steele ordered, "except that there's been an accident. Understand?"

Alex moved back, well away from the body, but he could not escape Steele's vengeance for long. Steele sought him out, pushing him farther away from the crowd. "Satisfied, Collier? How does it feel to drive a man to his death? I wonder if Patricia will think your story worthwhile now?"

His face was only inches away, and Alex could feel the heat of his breath.

"Which of us should feel more responsible, Judge?" Alex asked. "Tell me that, will you?"

Steele's eyes flashed, and for a moment Alex thought he would lunge at him. But the siren of the arriving ambulance intervened, and Alex turned away, leaving behind a livid Emmett Steele standing near the lifeless form of Nathaniel Hodges.

Alex walked aimlessly, feeling helpless, and in spite of his words to Steele, smothering under an enormous sense of guilt. He could not erase from his mind the sound of the breaking glass and the sight of the twisted body. He knew he never would.

His steps finally took him to the hospital, to wait for Pat.

For almost an hour he sat in the hospital lobby after watching her walk in, surrounded and supported by three men dressed in long dark overcoats. Other judges, Alex guessed, although he did not recognize any of them.

She had not seen Alex then and would not have seen him now if he hadn't stepped forward to meet her. The three men in overcoats were still with her, and they paused, too, eyeing Alex curiously.

"Pat, may I speak to you, please?" Alex asked.

She hardly looked like the same woman. Her skin was devoid of any color and her eyes were unfocused. Her body seemed smaller and more fragile, ready to collapse under the weight of her winter coat.

"Not now, Alex."

"Pat, please."

He pulled her a few steps away from the three men. She would not look at him.

"Pat, I can't tell you how sorry I am—"

"What have we done, Alex? He's dead. Can you imagine the terror and shame he must have felt?"

She began to sob, and Alex could think of no words of comfort.

"I was with him, Pat," he finally said, "just before he did it. I had no idea he was so distraught."

"What did you say to him?" she asked sharply.

"I refused to back off the story," Alex said.

One of the men stepped closer to them. "Is there some problem, Patricia?" he asked.

She shook her head and waved him away. "I can't see you for a while, Alex. Please stay away from me. I've got to get through this somehow, to come to terms with what I've done."

"You didn't do anything, Pat."

"Who are you kidding, Alex? I started all of this, remember?"

She touched his hand and walked away.

Forty-two

The Hodges suicide became a major media event, and Alex found himself thrust into the middle of it all. Hodges's clerk told a newspaper reporter that Alex was the last person to see the judge, and he was soon besieged by the press.

Alex didn't want to lie to the reporters, but he couldn't be fully truthful, either. He simply said he'd been invited to the judge's chambers and that they'd discussed a subject he couldn't disclose. A private matter that would remain private.

"Was he despondent when you left?" one of the reporters asked.

"If you're asking me if I had any idea he was planning to kill himself, the answer is no," Alex replied.

"So what does this do to the story?" Barclay asked Alex later. "If he was going to jump, you'd think he would have done it *after* the story, not before. This fucks us up."

"For Christ's sake, George!" Alex said. "Show a little goddamned respect, will you? The man's dead."

"Listen, Alex. We didn't push him out the window. He did that by himself—with a little help from Steele. I feel bad for the guy, and especially for his wife. But the question is legitimate: What *does* it do to the story?"

"We've got to go ahead," Alex said. "Hodges's death doesn't

change the fact that Steele's about to become chief justice. We can't let that happen."

"So let's do it," Barclay said. "The funeral is on Thursday, the inauguration is next Tuesday. I hope to get Hawke out of town Wednesday . . . maybe through the weekend, if he decides to stay on in Vail to ski. So let's try to get the story on Friday night. I think that's the best we can do."

"Is Hawke leaving?"

"I think so. He's leaning that way."

"Have you seen my scripts?" Alex asked.

"Yeah, I like them. I've done some editing, but not much."

"God, I want this to be over," Alex said, putting his face in his hands.

Later that afternoon, John Knowles asked Alex to stop by his office. Alex found Linda Grabowski with John. Her face was drawn and her skin was pallid, and she had lost substantial weight. The weeks since Daniel's death had transformed her, and Alex suddenly saw what Knowles had tried to describe.

"Alex, Linda would like to ask a question," Knowles announced. He had warned Alex of her condition, but even that had not prepared him for the bitterness that spilled out of her.

"Was Judge Hodges part of Steele's dirty business?" Linda snarled. "Did he have anything to do with Daniel's death?"

"He may have, indirectly," Alex answered gently. "He owned the property where Steele built that house up near Daniel's grave, and he was in the car that took one of Steele's victims to his place in Golden Valley."

"Then I'm glad he's dead," Linda said.

"Linda—" Knowles said.

"No, I mean it!" she shouted. "Steele, too. They are evil, John. Don't you see?"

She was weeping now, and Knowles looked helplessly at Alex, slowly shaking his head as he tried to comfort her. She was still sobbing when Alex slipped quietly out of the office.

Hawke finally accepted the invitation to Vail, apparently convinced it demonstrated his growing stature as an industry leader. He complained to his secretary about the short notice, but said he was told it was an oversight by the conference planning committee.

The suicide of Judge Hodges, coming on the eve of his departure, gave Hawke pause. He called George Barclay to his office an hour before he was to leave for the airport.

"What do you know about this Hodges business?" Hawke asked.

"Only what we put on the news," Barclay replied. "He took a big leap, and nobody was there to catch him."

"No jokes, George, please. This is too serious a matter. I don't like the feel of it."

Barclay said nothing, but shifted uncomfortably in his chair.

"What was Collier doing over there with Hodges?" Hawke asked. "It seems more than a coincidence in light of our heated discussion about Judge Steele."

"Alex is an old college friend of Mrs. Hodges," Barclay said. "That may explain why he was there."

"I don't buy it," Hawke replied. "I find myself trusting Collier less and less. There's a recklessness about him, a tendency to defy authority. We were warned about him, George. He needs watching."

"He's a hell of an anchorman, Mr. Hawke. All you've got to do is glance at the ratings to know that."

"I don't care what the ratings say, I don't want a loose cannon rolling around the newsroom."

Barclay shrugged his shoulders and started to get up.

"George, I don't like to leave under the circumstances, but I've made a commitment. I'm trusting things will operate smoothly in my absence."

Barclay was on his feet. "We'll conduct ourselves in the best traditions of the station, Mr. Hawke. Be sure of that."

Hawke gave him a curious look as Barclay walked out of the room.

From his office, Barclay immediately placed another call to Anthony Logan. "Your buddy in Vail has got to do me one more favor," Barclay said.

"Are you shitting me?" Logan asked. "What now?"

"He's got to keep any messages away from Hawke. At least until after the last flight out of there on Friday."

"Forget it. You're asking too much."

"What else are old friends for?" Barclay laughed, and hung up.

Once he knew Hawke was on the plane to Colorado, Alex was on the phone to Jerry Caldwell in Steele's office. "I need an on-camera interview with Judge Steele," Alex said, "as soon as possible. It's very important."

"You're really going ahead with it?" Caldwell asked. "I thought Hawke had given his assurances that you wouldn't."

"That's for us to deal with," Alex said.

He thought he could trust Caldwell, but he chose his words carefully, aware that the phone conversation might be taped.

"We're preparing a story which contains serious allegations involving Judge Steele, and it is important that he be given the opportunity to respond to those allegations."

"Sounds very official," Caldwell said. "But I don't know how Judge Steele will react or when he'll have the time. There's the Hodges funeral tomorrow, then preparations for the transition."

"I'd think he'd want to find the time, Jerry. I'd hate to go on the air with a 'no comment' from the judge."

"When do you plan to broadcast the story?" Caldwell asked.

"Soon," Alex replied noncommittally. "Very soon."

"All right. I'll talk to the judge. But no promises."

"I just want to make sure he knows the offer has been extended," Alex said. "That he has the chance."

"He'll get the message," Caldwell assured him.

Pat was still numb. There was no denial of Nathaniel's death; she had come to accept that. What she could not accept was the way he had died, the horrible act of self-destruction. She wept at the desperation he must have felt before he threw himself through the glass.

There were no tears for what might have been, for Pat knew there had been no hope of a future with Nathaniel. Her tears were for the gentle and loving early years of their marriage, untroubled years, free of suspicion and doubt. How long ago that seemed.

Pat remembered wandering the house only a few days before, feeling the emptiness and solitude she imagined a new widow would feel. Now she knew firsthand. She wanted to be alone, but friends and relatives and the wives of the other judges threw up a shield around her, comforting her, protecting her from the press. They wanted to help her to prepare for the funeral and for a life without Nathaniel.

Pat told them she wanted no phone calls or visits until after the funeral, knowing full well the request would exclude Alex. She realized he would be hurt and confused, that it could threaten any possible future together, but she could not face him again at the moment.

Pat didn't blame Alex for her husband's death. If anyone besides Steele was to blame, she admitted, it was herself. But Alex embodied her own failings, her own role in the destruction of her marriage, and, finally, in the destruction of Nathaniel.

He was a mirror of her own sins, and she could not abide that reflection right now.

The funeral for Nathaniel Hodges was as big a media event as the suicide itself. Television cameras lined the front row of the church balcony, and the pews below were filled with all strata of the legal society—from the lowliest county court clerks to the mightiest justices of the Supreme Court.

Emmett Steele led the judicial delegation to a special section in the front of the church, across the aisle and slightly behind Pat and other grieving relatives.

Alex sat in the back, next to George Barclay, and listened as a succession of speakers eulogized the late Judge Hodges, recalling his selfless contributions to the community, his wisdom on the bench, and his unflagging dedication to the judicial system.

Judge Steele delivered the final eulogy.

"Which of us will ever understand the forces which would drive a man of Nathaniel's youth and vigor and vision to this senseless act? To deprive himself, and all of us, of his most productive years, to surrender the happiness of life?"

Alex could hear murmuring in the audience. *Would Steele really dare to talk about a man's suicide at his own funeral?* Alex rose slightly from the pew, trying to get a glimpse of Pat, but he could see only the back of her head, bowed, draped in black.

"The answer, of course," Steele continued, "is that none of us has that wisdom, that extraordinary power to fully understand the human mind and our human emotions in all of their complexities. Only God has those powers of understanding and forgiveness.

"But I can tell you this: There are sinister forces at work in our community, determined to destroy the reputations of respected, responsible citizens, particularly those who occupy high judicial office. I speak of sinister forces of enormous influence and persuasive power, whom I believe are dedicated to the ruination of the very judicial system we all hold so dear, and to which Judge Hodges devoted his life."

The murmurs in the church now turned to hushed conversations and restless stirring in the seats. Alex heard someone behind him whisper to his companion: "Is he crazy? What's he talking about?" Alex and Barclay exchanged a wary glance.

The cameras rolled on, and the print reporters scribbled Steele's words on their notepads.

"Was Nathaniel a victim of these forces? We will never know with certainty, but I would submit there is no other ready explanation for this ultimate act of self-sacrifice. May Judge Hodges rest in peace, and may those who have brought him to this end rest in the fiery depths of hell."

Steele strode from the lectern and returned to his seat, eyes straight ahead, ignoring the stares of the crowd, ignoring Pat. The reporters eased their way toward the doors, and the television photographers began to dismantle their equipment.

"Can you believe that?" Barclay said. "The guy's gone mad."

"You may be right," Alex said, "and if he has, it only makes him more dangerous."

Alex wasn't able to speak to Pat either at the church or the cemetery. She was always surrounded, but so alone; face veiled, eyes hidden. Alex was sure she never saw him.

As Alex walked from the grave to his car, he saw Steele staring after him, and he again heard his words: "*May those who brought him to this end rest in the fiery depths of hell.*"

Alex pulled his coat tighter and walked on.

Forty-three

Alex stood in the back of the darkened editing booth, watching as the images of the television monitors blurred with the swift back-and-forth motion of the videotapes. Cody sat in front of Alex and manipulated the controls of the editing machines to electronically wed the scenes from the separate tapes into one.

Alex heard his recorded narration—*"The pictures you see on your screen are not pretty"*—and he saw Cody's fingers cue the videotape to the scene of a nameless boy performing on the small stage at Steele's house. *"Although they've been carefully edited to conform ..."* The tape sped forward as the editor sought yet another scene to reinforce the words.

Alex had been there for an hour, hardly moving, hypnotized by the sight of the story coming together—words and pictures blended into a meaningful whole. He had seen the process hundreds of times, but it never lost its fascination for him. Especially now, as he watched the most important story of his career come alive on the screen.

"Pretty raw stuff," Cody said, fast-forwarding the machine in search of the next pictures. "Is this really going to get on the air?"

"Never know," Alex replied, vaguely, realizing there were still almost thirty-six hours before the broadcast.

The phone in the booth buzzed, and Alex picked it up.

"Jerry Caldwell for you," the newsroom secretary said. "Should I transfer it up there?"

"Go ahead," Alex said, and waited for Caldwell's voice.

"*Collier?*" It was not Jerry Caldwell, but Emmett Steele.

"Judge Steele?"

"Caldwell gave me your message," Steele said. "I can't believe you are persisting in this, not after what you did to Hodges. Nicholas Hawke gave his word. Does he know about this?"

Alex ignored the references to Hodges and Hawke. "Judge Steele, are you going to respond to these charges? I believe it would be in your best interest to do so."

"*What do you know about my best interests?*" Steele shouted. "I will not dignify your slander with any sort of a response. I will be speaking to Hawke and others shortly—to put an end to this nonsense, once and for all. Is that clear?"

"Perfectly," Alex said. "But, again, for the record, are you sure you do not wish to respond, on camera or off, to the charges of sexual and physical abuse of children? These are serious charges, Judge. Potential fel—"

The crash of the receiver resounded in Alex's ear.

Steele stared at the telephone, then dialed again.

"Mr. Hawke's office."

"This is Judge Emmett Steele again. I must reach Hawke immediately."

"I'm sorry, Judge Steele," Marie Stickney, Hawke's secretary, said, "I've left several messages for Mr. Hawke since your last call, but I've not heard from him."

"Well, try again. This is urgent!"

"Yes, Judge, I will."

"You don't understand what's at stake here! I could be ruined by your television station."

"Judge, please, I'll try—"

"I don't want you to try, goddamnit. I want you to *do* it. *Now!*"

Minutes later, Steele's phone rang back. It was not Hawke, but Russell, calling from Wisconsin.

"There's a sheriff and two deputies here," Russell said breathlessly. "They say they've got a warrant signed by some local judge. They want to search the place, and they want me to give them the keys to all the rooms."

"Search for what?" Steele demanded.

There was a pause on the other end of the line. "It's got something to do with that dead deputy."

Steele's mind churned. Unbelievable, he thought. The world was caving in around him.

"What do you want me to do, Judge?" Russell asked. "One of them is standing here, waiting for the keys."

"Listen carefully, Russell," he said, trying to master his emotions, "let them look, but remember, it's Hodges's house, and Hodges is dead. Just tell them we're using the place. Don't say anything else."

"I understand, Judge," he replied.

"What's the name of the judge who issued the warrant?" Steele asked.

There was another pause, then Russell's voice again.

"Holmes," he said. "Judge Harry Holmes, from Siren."

"I'll call him now," Steele said.

First he made another call to Channel Seven—not to Hawke, but to Derek Glover.

George Barclay looked up from his desk and found Marie Stickney at his door.

"Do you know why I can't get hold of Mr. Hawke?" she asked. "I've left messages at the hotel where he said he'd be, but he's not returning them."

"I'm not sure," Barclay said, uneasily. "Is there a problem?"

"He's gotten several calls from Judge Steele and the governor's office. They say it's urgent."

"Let me return the calls," Barclay offered. "Maybe I can handle them and we won't need to bother Mr. Hawke."

"I'd appreciate that," Marie said, "because I do have to catch the last bus home."

"No problem, Marie. Just leave it to me."

After he'd made his call to Steele, Russell was ordered to stay in the kitchen while Sheriff Tolliver and his deputies searched the rest of the lodge. One of the deputies finally returned and led him to a room in the basement.

"What's in these boxes, Russell?" Tolliver asked.

"Got me," Russell said. "We don't own the place, we just use it now and then."

"Really? Well, let's take a look." Tolliver and the deputies split open each of the boxes, pulling out the magazines and tapes. "What have we here?" Tolliver said, flipping through the pages as though he were seeing them for the first time. "My goodness, this is pretty racy stuff. Men and little boys all naked, doing nasty things. I'd say this is downright pornographic, Russell."

"I don't know nothin' about it," Russell said, the slightest quaver in his voice. "Never saw them before."

"Who'd you say owned the place?" Tolliver asked.

"Judge Hodges, I think. But he's dead. He died a few days ago."

"Took a jump or something, right?"

"Yeah. A big jump," Russell replied.

"And you work for Judge Steele?"

"Right. He's pretty pissed off about this. You and that local judge will be hearing from him."

"Good," Tolliver said. "Maybe he can tell me about these boxes."

The sheriff walked up the steps and into the garage, followed by the deputies and Russell.

"Do you folks own a chain saw?" Tolliver asked casually.

"Not that I know of," Russell said quickly.

Tolliver walked around the garage. "You've never seen one? I see there's a gas can here and some chain oil."

"What's this all about?" Russell asked.

"We checked with the Homelite factory to see if anybody from around here had returned a warranty card on a new chain saw. Lots of people did, Russell. And you were one of them."

Russell looked around. One deputy stood next to him, the other by the door. "I don't know what you're talking about," he said.

"The serial number on your warranty card matches the one on the saw that was dumped into the lake with that deputy," Tolliver said. "What do you say, Russell?"

"I'm not saying anything until I talk to Judge Steele again."

One of the deputies handed Tolliver a cloth bag. "While we're here, I wonder if you might try this on for size?" Tolliver pulled out a heavy snowmobile suit, still bearing the faint odor of gas. "How about it, Russell? Think it'll fit?"

Russell stared at Tolliver. "I want to talk to Judge Steele."

"That's fine, but for now, I think you'd better come along with us."

Alex stayed late at the station to watch Cody put the final touches to his taped report. It ran six minutes and twenty-five seconds, an almost unheard-of story length in television news; it would account for more than half of the available news time in Friday night's newscast. *If it got on.*

It was almost midnight when Alex said goodnight to Cody and climbed into his TR4. He was too exhausted to pay much attention to the traffic as he drove down the ramp and headed for home.

He was about six blocks from his house when he noticed the headlights in the mirror, coming up fast.

Alex slowed the car and drove as close to the curb as he could. The car behind did the same. Its headlights were set high, and flashed from dim to bright, Alex's rearview mirror reflecting the glare.

He slowed the car more, but this time the trailing car did the opposite. It slammed into his car, a grinding impact that made the steel frame shudder and threw Alex violently against the seat-belt harness.

Alex tried to control the car, to keep off the sidewalk and away from the cars parked along the curb. He twisted the steering wheel and tried to brake.

He could hear the engine behind him revving up seconds before he was thrown by the second jarring jolt. Alex's ears were fill with the sounds of breaking glass and dragging metal.

Alex had no time to respond before the car—no, not a car, a pickup truck with a snowplow on front—was next to him, the driver's face hidden in the shadows of the cab. The side of his car collapsed, the window next to Alex crumbling into a million pieces.

The collision pushed him over the curb and across the sidewalk, narrowly past a giant elm. The crumpled car came to rest halfway up the sloped lawn of a large house. Alex was stunned and shaken, and did not see the pickup speed away.

The yard lights of the house flashed on, and Alex saw people running from the front door and from neighboring homes. He could hear sirens in the distance as the people wrestled with the car doors. The one on Alex's side was crushed, but the other door finally came free.

"Don't move him!" a voice said. "Wait for the ambulance."

"Get some blankets." Another voice from the darkness.

"God! Look at the car." The first voice again. "What the hell happened, anyway?"

After that, it was a collage of flashing lights, blurred figures, and staring faces. Alex remembered moving his arms and hands, feeling for broken bones, but he was loaded on to a stretcher and pushed into an ambulance before he could complete the task.

Two attendants bent over him, examining him, and Alex was relieved when he heard one of them tell the driver to kill the siren and slow down as they neared the hospital.

"You're going to be okay," the attendant told Alex. "All your vital signs are fine, and I don't think anything's broken."

"Then why do I hurt so much?" Alex asked.

"From the looks of your car, you got tossed around pretty good. You're lucky to come out of this with cuts and bruises."

A doctor in the emergency room confirmed the attendant's findings: a possible slight concussion, bruises on several parts of his body, and a few cuts from the flying glass.

"We'd like to keep you under observation for an hour or so," the doctor said, "but then you can go home and get some rest. I'd suggest you take a day or two off from work."

"I'm afraid that won't be possible." George Barclay was standing a few feet away, just inside the curtained partition.

"How'd you get here?" Alex asked.

"The hospital called the newsroom, and they called me."

"Who are you?" the doctor asked.

"His boss," Barclay said. "He can rest all he wants to, but not until after tomorrow night."

Alex hurt too much to laugh.

The next morning, Marie Stickney was waiting by Barclay's office door when he came to work. Her expression was both worried and disapproving. "Mr. Hawke finally returned my calls," she said. "He's talked to Judge Steele. He's flying back immediately. He sounds quite angry, George."

"What times does he get in, Marie?" Barclay asked, casually.

"He didn't say, and I'm not sure he'd want me to tell you if he had. He sounds very upset, George."

It was Marie's understated way of telling him they were in deep shit.

Forty-four

Alex slept late that morning. He was stiff and sore when he finally hobbled into the station. He was immediately summoned to a hurried conference in Barclay's office.

"I've told everyone about your accident, Alex," Barclay said, "but we don't have much time for sympathy. We have more pressing business. Here's the deal: The story's done, Steele's on the warpath, and Hawke's on his way home. I checked. He should be on a plane that gets in here around eight-thirty. That'll give him an hour and a half to kill the story and fire all of us."

"Why don't we call in an anonymous bomb threat," Barbara offered, half seriously. "That'll delay the plane for a while."

"Jesus, Barbara," Knowles said. "Get real."

"Wait a second, though," Alex said. "She may have something."

"Alex! That's a fucking federal offense," Knowles said.

"I'm not talking about a bomb," Alex said. "I'm talking about a delay. Does Hawke park at the airport?"

"Usually," Barclay replied. "But not always."

"What does he drive?"

"A new silver Mercedes. It's hard to miss."

"Are you going to bomb it?" Knowles asked sarcastically.

"No," Alex said. "But it's no federal offense to let the air out of

347

a couple of tires, is it? That should hold him up for a little while, anyway."

"He'll just jump into a cab," Barbara said. "And he'll be even angrier when he finally gets here."

"Every few minutes may count," Alex insisted.

"Okay," Barclay said. "We'll do it. Cody, you find his car and deflate one of the tires. Then let us know when he gets a cab and leaves the airport."

"Why don't we try simple persuasion?" Knowles argued. "When Hawke sees Alex's story, there's no way he'll block it."

"We can't count on that, John, and there may not time," Alex replied, suddenly remembering Knowles's words of a few days before: "*Shit, he can't fire the whole staff.*"

"Let me toss another idea out," Alex said.

Pat found a different telegram waiting when she answered her doorbell. The man handed her another brightly colored holiday envelope.

DEAR PAT. TONIGHT MAY BE THE NIGHT. TUNE IN
AT TEN. I THANK YOU. AND I LOVE YOU. ALEX.

The lights in the studio came up, and the videotape of the Steele story faded to black. Alex rose to face the station's night staff. It was still an hour before the late newscast.

"I know I'm still pretty much of a stranger to many of you," he said, "but I'm going to ask you to trust me anyway. What you just saw on that videotape is true. Judge Steele is guilty of those crimes. We want to broadcast that story on tonight's ten o'clock news, but we may need your help to make it happen."

George Barclay stood up next to Alex. "Judge Steele has many friends and supporters in this community—people who respect him, or are indebted to him, people in high places who don't want to see that story on the air. Nicholas Hawke is one of those people, and he is determined to kill it. Collier and I, and maybe others, could be fired if we defy him and put it on the news."

"Hawke is flying back from Colorado at this very moment," Alex said, "and he may arrive here before the news begins. We know what he will try to do, and he'll succeed if you allow him to."

"What do you want from us?" one of the technicians asked.

"We want you to ignore him," Barclay said. "Pretend he's not here. Pretend you don't hear him. Be too busy. Find any excuse. Do anything, but don't let him kill the story."

"Sounds like a goddamned mutiny," the audio man said. "He could fire the whole fucking bunch of us."

"You're right," Alex agreed, again recalling Knowles's words. "But the chances of him firing the whole night crew are next to nil, especially when he doesn't know who most of you are or what you do. And he can't run a station alone."

"This is *crazy*," one of the directors said. "You're asking us to risk our jobs to get this story on? I've got a wife and kids. No story's that important."

"Wait a minute!" Scotty Hansen jumped up in the back of the studio. "Most of you don't know this, but Hawke would've dumped me without a second glance if it hadn't been for Collier. He saved my ass by risking his own. I don't know what the hell I can do, Alex, but if you want me to tackle the bastard in the hallway, I'll do it."

"Not that, Scotty," Alex laughed, "but you might engage him in a little lively conversation."

"Our union contract's up in a month," another of the techs said, "and Hawke hasn't even talked about negotiations yet. I'm not sure a little job action about now wouldn't jack him up a bit."

"Listen," Barclay said. "We know we don't have any right to ask any one of you to risk your job, and we don't have the time to try and persuade every one of you, anyway. You don't have the same stake in this story as we do, but you do have a stake in this station. You have pride in it, just as we do. I don't want to see a story like this killed because of one man, and I don't think you do, either. Don't let this story die."

"The decision will be up to you," Alex concluded. "Whatever you decide, thanks for listening to us."

As Alex was leaving the studio, Barbara intercepted him.

"Cody called," she said. "Hawke just left the airport in a cab."

Alex nodded and walked down the hall to the back security office.

"You want me to take Hawke's number out of the computer?" Norm Schmaeder was disbelieving. "Are you shitting me?"

All employees, from Hawke on down, were issued personalized

security cards, which allowed them electronic entry to the station. Without it they had to sign in with the guard and be buzzed through the door.

"No, Norm, I'm not shitting you," Alex said. "I'll take full responsibility. Just erase his number. Computer errors happen all the time. Then disappear a little before nine-thirty. Go make your rounds or something. I don't want you here when he arrives."

"This could get me canned," Norm protested.

"Listen, Norm. There's a hundred bucks in it for you, and Hawke doesn't even know your name. He didn't hire you, and he sure as hell won't fire you. Just play dumb. Honest mistake, you know."

Norm looked unconvinced, but Alex had no more time to spend with him. It was worth a try, he thought.

9:33 P.M. Alex was standing by the back door of the station when he saw the cab pull up. Hawke hurried up the sidewalk to the door, travel bag hanging on his shoulder, security card in hand. The card was in the slot. The door opened and Norm greeted him.

Fuck you, Norm, Alex breathed. Chicken-shit bastard.

Hawke threw his bag into the security office, and strode down the hallway, looking like a man with a purpose. He was heading directly toward George Barclay's office. Alex could see the eyes of other employees follow Hawke along his path.

Alex took another route in the same direction.

9:36 P.M. Hawke was at Barclay's door.

"Mr. Hawke! What a surprise."

"Don't fuck with me, George. I'm not in the mood. Are you planning to run a story on Judge Steele tonight? I want a straight answer. No more bullshit."

"I am." Barclay pulled himself out of his chair, standing as erect as his hefty body would allow.

"Against my direct orders? Didn't I make myself clear enough?"

"No, your orders were quite clear."

"Then why the fuck are you doing it?"

"Because it's the responsible thing to do," Barclay said, simply. "For this community and for this television station."

"Cut the shit!" Hawke shouted. *"Kill the story!"*

"Sorry," Barclay said. "I can't do that."

"Then pick up your stuff and get the hell out of here," Hawke said, his voice full of fury. "I should have fired your fat ass months ago."

Neither Hawke nor Barclay noticed Alex standing in the doorway of the office. "Mr. Hawke, nice to see you back," Alex said sociably. "Hope I'm not interrupting anything important."

Hawke turned and glared at him, but before he could speak, Alex stepped back and motioned to the newsroom. "Mr. Hawke, you remember Joel Petersen of the *Star-Trib*, don't you?" Petersen walked into sight. "I told Joel about the story we're breaking tonight and invited him over to see it in person. I'm glad you're here to give him your reaction."

"It won't work, Collier. I don't care if Jesus Christ himself is here. That story's not going to run."

"I trust you'll be willing to explain your decision to Mr. Petersen then."

"Listen, smartass. I don't have to explain my decisions to anybody," Hawke said, brushing past Alex and Petersen. "And if you want to follow Barclay out the door, it's all right with me."

Hawke found Scotty Hansen standing in the aisle.

"I never did get a chance to thank you, personally, for that new contract, Mr. Hawke. My wife and kids are grateful, too. It'll be a wonderful three years—"

"Not now, Scotty. I don't have the time."

"This'll just take a minute, Mr. Hawke," Hansen said, still blocking the aisle. "I just wanted to tell you what my wife—"

Hawke stood within an inch of Scotty's nose. "I know what you're up to, Hansen. Now get the hell out of my way."

"Catch you later then," Scotty said, backing away.

9:47:30 P.M. "Are you producing tonight's newscast?" Hawke demanded. The words were aimed at a slim young woman with short hair standing next to a director.

"Yes, sir, I am."

"What's your name?" Hawke asked.

"Sylvia. Sylvia Chesman. I'm new here."

"I want you to eliminate Collier's story on Judge Steele from the newscast. That's a direct order. Do you understand?"

"Yes, sir. But how do I fill the six-and-a-half-minute hole it will leave, sir? I have nothing else prepared."

"Figure it out. Get something off the network."

"I'm sorry, sir, but there's not enough time."

"Do you like your job?" Hawke asked.

"Until tonight, yes, sir."

"Then do it!"

Hawke turned and found Joel Petersen standing behind him, taking notes on a small pad. "If you print any of this, I'll sue your ass," Hawke said. "Now get out of my station."

John Knowles caught up with Hawke just outside the newsroom. "Mr. Hawke, I know if you'd seen Alex's piece, you wouldn't be trying to kill it. It's an important story, and it's true, whatever you might like to believe about Judge Steele."

Hawke barely paused. "I don't believe in this kind of personal attack journalism, Knowles. Judge Steele is a respected man and a good friend of mine. If he's guilty of something, he ought to be tried in a court of law, not on television."

Knowles was left standing in the hallway.

9:55 P.M. Hawke found the videotape room vacant. The tape machines stood idling, humming softly, but no operators were to be seen. Hawke walked around the equipment, searching the corners of the room. "Where is everybody?" he shouted. The only reply was the purr of the machinery.

He walked up to one of the playback tape decks. The cued tape bore the label "Steele/Collier," and he reached for the eject button.

"I wouldn't touch that if I were you," said a voice from behind him. Hawke turned and recognized Matt Ferguson, a technician who led the union's negotiating team.

"It's a violation of the contract for anybody but us to touch those machines," Ferguson said. "You should know that, Mr. Hawke."

"I want the tape out of there. That story will not air."

"Sorry, Mr. Hawke. This close to the newscast, I can only take orders from the director. He's my boss right now. Best talk to him."

"Fuck you," Hawke said as he pushed the eject button. The tape popped out of the machine and into Hawke's hand. "We'll see who runs this station," he said, stomping out of the room.

The tape operator followed him to the door and quietly locked it behind him. Then he pulled a backup tape from a shelf and reloaded the machine.

9:57:30 P.M. As Hawke walked into the studio, the final network program was ending. The director, producer, technical director, and graphics director were at their places in the control room, the news anchor team was on the set, and the studio lights came up.

"*Stand by!*" the floor director shouted. "*News tease coming up. Quiet in the studio!* Five, four, three . . . two . . . one . . . cue!"

Hawke was triumphant. He didn't know how the producer would fill the big hole left in the newscast by the absence of Collier's story, but at that moment he didn't care.

As he walked back to the door, he heard Alex Collier's voice. "*Next on Channel Seven News, the exclusive investigative report of a prominent local judge who has been sexually abusing children . . .*"

Hawke stopped and turned, disbelieving. *Why are they promoting the story? They must know the tape's not there.* He hurried back to the tape room. The door was locked. He pounded on it, but the operator's back was turned to him. He pounded again, then searched his pockets for the master keys.

From the anchor desk, Alex had seen Hawke rush out of the studio, and he now waited impatiently for the final break commercial to end. He heard the director's words in his earpiece: "The backup tape is cued, stand by everybody!"

Alex looked at Barbara, who smiled nervously and gave him a quick thumbs-up. Then he fastened his eyes on the red light above the camera. The final seconds seemed to pass more slowly than minutes.

He heard pounding from down the hall at the same time he heard the first bars of the opening music.

"We're rolling," the director shouted through the earpiece.

The red light came on. To Alex, it was a green light.

Hawke was still struggling to find the key when he heard the same music and the announcer's words: "*And now, live from the WCKT Television Newsroom. . . .*"

It was too late. Hawke's body slumped. Short of shutting off the station or hurling his body onto the set, there was nothing more he could do.

He'd lost.

9:59:45 P.M. *"This is NightWatch . . . with Alex Collier . . . Barbara Miller . . . Charlie Nichols with the weather . . . and Scotty Hansen on sports."*

The director dissolved from the opening tape to a two-shot of Alex and Barbara. There were no smiles now, and the camera zoomed slowly in on Alex.

"Good evening, everyone. Channel Seven News has learned that Hennepin County Chief Judge Emmett Steele, who is about to be sworn in as the new chief justice of the Minnesota Supreme Court, has been sexually abusing children for years. . . ."

Forty-five

Only the burning brightness of the television tube illuminated the living room. Emmett Steele sat alone, huddled in a corner of the couch, a throw pillow clutched tight to his chest.

It provided little comfort.

"Channel Seven News has learned that Judge Steele himself was the victim of violent sexual abuse as a child. He will not confirm that or any other element of this story. The judge has flatly refused to respond in any way, on camera, or off . . ."

Steele's skin was a pasty reflection of the gray glow from the screen. A thin bead of sweat, almost invisible in the dim light, spread across his forehead. His eyes never wavered, never blinked, never left the hated image of Alexander Collier.

"The question which remains, of course, is Judge Steele's fitness for public office, not only for the office he now holds as chief judge of Hennepin County, but for his pending appointment as chief justice of the Minnesota Supreme Court . . ."

Once the tears began, Steele was helpless to hold them back. They tumbled down his cheeks like a river in search of the sea, dripping from his chin to his neck, soaking his shirt collar.

"If these charges are substantiated in a court of law, Judge Steele could wind up in prison. So far, there's been no reaction from the governor's office, although an aide to the governor did attempt to

prevent this story from being broadcast. We do know that Min-
neapolis police are investigating many of these allegations, and that
a grand jury may be summoned."

Steele lifted himself from the couch and walked slowly to the
television set. He stood quietly, listening to the final words of the
report. Then his foot lashed out, and the image of Alex Collier
disintegrated in a shower of sparks and glass.

The house was left utterly still and dark. Steele had unplugged
the telephone, and the repeated calls from the governor's office,
and from Russell in a Wisconsin jail, went unanswered.

Linda Grabowski sat cross-legged on the floor of her tiny living
room, a small rosary clutched in her fingers. She thought she could
feel the waves of evil spilling from the television set. She watched
intently, her eyes moving from the vile image of Steele on the
screen to the serene portrait of Daniel on the wall above.

She twisted the string tighter, her fingers pinched bright red
from the pressure, until the rosary suddenly burst apart in her
hand—scattering the tiny beads across the floor.

Alex was swallowed up by the celebration in the studio.

Once the credits were over and the screen had faded to black,
Barbara was in his arms, twirling him around dizzily. Barclay was
by his side, pounding him on the back with his hamlike hands.
John Knowles was standing to the side, watching Cody pop open
a bottle of champagne.

When Alex could untangle himself, he stood on the edge of the
set and raised his glass in a toast to the night crew. The crowd
gradually quieted as Alex tried to find his words.

"I just want you to know that I've never felt more pride, more
respect, for any group of people than I feel for all of you at this
moment." Alex paused and looked down. "I've moved around a
lot in my life, and somewhere along the line I forgot why the hell
I ever got into this business. Well, now I know again—thanks to
George and Barbara and John and to all of you.

"I don't know what's going to happen next. That'll be up to Mr.
Hawke, to Steele, the governor, and a lot of other people. But
whatever happens, it can never erase what I'm feeling now. It can
never undo what we've done tonight."

The applause broke out again as Alex stepped off the set and tried to push his way through the crowd. Another glass of champagne was shoved into his hand, and he was surrounded by well-wishers clapping him on the back and shouting in his ear. Alex could not remember ever seeing news people so alive and excited.

One face he did not see in the crowd was Derek's.

Alex found himself next to Barbara and John Knowles. "C'mon, John, C'mon, Alex," Barbara said. "Come with us. We're heading for the bar."

Both Alex and Knowles declined. "Thanks, Barbara," John said, "but I'm going to stop and see Linda."

"How is she, anyway?" Barbara asked.

"Not that great," Knowles said. "She just saw Alex's story, and I think it rekindled the whole thing. She sounds hysterical."

"What are you going to do?"

"I'm going to get her checked into the hospital. The outpatient therapy isn't working, and I think she needs more intensive psychiatric treatment or she'll really go off the deep end. It's all I can think to do. We should have done it long ago."

When Alex finally managed to disentangle himself, he went in search of George Barclay. He found him in his office, staring out the window at the darkened street.

"What's next, George?"

"I'm leaving, what else? You heard the man."

"I wouldn't be too hasty. Everyone in the newsroom will stand behind you."

"Defying Hawke's orders to get the story on the air was one thing, Alex. Defying a dismissal is something else. You're going to have to face that, too. Shit, who wants to work for someone like that, anyway?"

Before Alex could respond, he heard a cough behind him. It was Nicholas Hawke, standing in the doorway.

"I'll see you later, George," Alex said and walked past Hawke without a word or a glance.

Barclay was standing behind his desk, slowly stacking files into two big boxes.

"I wouldn't do that yet," Hawke said. "It's Friday night. Let's take the weekend to think about this."

"I don't think so," Barclay replied. "I *have* thought about it. I've decided I don't want to fight to get every big story about one of your buddies on the air. Life's too short."

"Let's *both* think about it," Hawke replied. "We'll talk on Monday."

Barclay stared at him across the desk, the elephant facing the weasel.

"We'll see," Barclay said.

Alex drove his rental car into the driveway, feeling as exhausted as a runner after a marathon. He still tingled with the aftereffects of excitement, but knowing the race was over, he felt the inevitable letdown.

As Alex got out of the car, he saw the huddled figure on the step, wearing the familiar parka.

"How long have you been here?" he asked as he approached.

"I don't know," Pat said. "Since after the news."

"Will you come in?"

"No, I don't think so. I just wanted to see you. To say I'm sorry and that I'm proud of you."

"Are you okay?" he asked.

"I don't know, Alex. I hope I will be, but I just don't know."

"Can I do anything?"

"Did you mean what you said in the telegram? About being in love with me?"

"Yes."

"That helps, Alex. Thank you."

She reached up and touched her lips to his. Then she walked away.

The next morning's newspaper bore the five-column headline.

JUDGE STEELE ACCUSED
OF CHILD SEXUAL ABUSE
Television Report Claims Judge a Pedophile

Alex found little new information in the story. The newspaper had been unable to contact Steele, and the governor's office said only that it was "reviewing" Steele's appointment as chief justice in light of the Channel Seven allegations. The paper said the governor would hold a news conference later that day.

Joel Petersen's story, on the television page, told of Hawke's unsuccessful efforts to block Alex's report. It painted an unflattering picture of Hawke's threats and tirades, but ended with Hawke's later admission that he might have been wrong—including his strong endorsement of an independent, but responsible, news department.

"I have great respect for our newspeople," Hawke said, "but they also have to respect station management's final responsibility and authority. Perhaps we both learned something from all of this."

Not bad, Alex thought. Hawke had landed on his feet again.

Walking from the kitchen to the living room, Alex looked out into the darkness. It was an hour later in Philadelphia. Maybe things were stirring there. He reached for the phone.

Governor Hamel stood erect and alone behind the podium.

The reception room was filled to capacity with reporters and photographers, including a network crew from Chicago, all jockeying for position, making last-minute adjustments to the lights.

"And I thought it looked like a circus *last* time," Alex whispered to Barclay, as they stood on the edge of the crowd.

The governor cleared his throat, and the room fell silent.

"In light of the serious allegations regarding Judge Steele made public on a television newscast last night," said the governor, "I am temporarily rescinding my appointment of Judge Steele as the new chief justice of the Minnesota Supreme Court. While this decision is not intended to prejudge the guilt or innocence of Judge Steele, it seems clear that this appointment cannot go forward until the proper legal inquiry has taken place, and until and unless the judge is fully vindicated. In the meantime, I have asked Justice John McGregor to serve as acting chief justice until this matter has been resolved, or until another appointment is announced. Thank you, ladies and gentlemen, that is the end of the statement. I will have nothing further to say."

As the governor walked from the podium, shouted questions flew after him. "Have you talked to Judge Steele? Have you seen him? Did you conduct your own investigation?"

The questions fell off the governor's back, and in less than thirty seconds he was through the door and out of the room. The reporters then descended on his aide, the same ones who had confronted Alex and Barclay in Hawke's office.

"Is it true that you tried to block the story?" one reporter asked. "Did you know about this in advance?" asked another.

"I, I have no . . . comment . . . no response to that," the aide stammered, following the path of the governor's retreat. But as he was leaving, his eyes found Alex's face in the crowd.

He couldn't have missed the little smile.

Alex's mind was tumbling.

Steele must know he's had it, but don't underestimate him. He's too cunning, too clever, too powerful to take this without a whimper, without striking back. Keep your guard up, watch your backside, try to outguess him.

On his way back to the station, Alex made two stops, the first on Summit Avenue, to see therapist Duane Johnson again.

"Now you know who I was talking about," Alex said.

"Indeed," Johnson replied. "I watched it on the news."

"Do you know Steele?" Alex asked.

"Not personally, no, but I've watched his career over the years. From your report, he certainly seems to fit the profile."

"What do you think someone like him might do next?" Alex asked. "Now that he's been exposed?"

"Damned if I know," Johnson replied without hesitation. "It's impossible to predict. He must be facing that question this very moment, I suspect."

"Take your best guess," Alex urged.

"He could do anything: admit it and meekly resign, deny it and lash out, commit suicide, almost anything." Johnson paused and took a deep breath. "But with his apparent arrogance and compulsion for power and control, he could go crazy, or crazier, at this point. He could really become quite irrational and dangerous."

"That's what I thought," Alex said, with fresh visions of Daniel's grave and Seuss's body in his mind. "He doesn't seem the type to meekly step aside. He never has before."

"From what I know about people like him," Johnson said, "I'd be amazed if he gave in. He won't run away, he won't disappear. He'll be back . . . to reclaim what he thinks is his. The only question is when and where."

Alex's second stop was at Minneapolis City Hall, to see Phil.

"The sky is falling! The sky is falling!" Phil shouted, with a laugh, when he saw Alex.

"Little busy, are you?" Alex asked. "No pun intended."

"Christ, I've got everybody from the county attorney to the whole county board on my back. Everybody's demanding action now. They want me to be ready for the grand jury next week."

"Steele's not without friends," Alex said. "A lot of big-time lawyers and some of the judges are already attacking the 'trial by television' and are waiting for Steele to come out and fight."

"Did you hear about Tolliver?" Phil asked.

"No. What?"

"He was able to trace the chain saw to Russell and finally got a search warrant for Steele's lake place. He found Russell there, along with that whole stack of pornography you saw with Tolliver. Russell's in the jug for the weekend, at least. He can't get hold of Steele, either."

"Son of a bitch," Alex breathed.

"I've got another surprise for you," Phil said.

"What's that?"

"Your old friend, Derek. Seems like he got arrested the other night for speeding."

"So?"

"In a pickup with a snowplow on it, Alex. His uncle's. A half hour after your car got bounced around."

"That dirty bastard!" Alex said.

"Nobody connected things until this morning, when some bright young cop in traffic put the two reports together. They picked Derek up and are holding him until they see if the paint on the plow and the side of the truck matches that TR4 of yours."

"What's left of it, you mean," Alex said.

"So Derek's out of circulation for a while. We're going to talk plea bargain if he's willing to implicate Steele in the hit and run."

"Good luck," Alex said.

When he returned to the station, Alex's phone would not stop ringing. Everyone was calling with outspoken opinions on the Steele story. Alex was getting almost as much heat as the judge was, and he was ready to take the phone off the hook when he heard a familiar voice.

"Mr. Collier?"

"*Rick?* Is that you? Where are you?"

"Up north. But we read the paper. It sounds like you got him."

"I think we got him, Rick. Thanks to you and Roger."

"Do you need us?" Rick asked.

"I'd like to talk to Roger. Is he there?"

"I'll put him on," Rick said.

After speaking with Roger, Alex was finally able to get a phone call through to Jerry Caldwell at Steele's courthouse office. But before Alex could say anything, Caldwell cut him off. "No, I don't know where he is, Alex. I haven't been able to reach him. And you are the one-thousandth caller I've had."

"Hold on, Jerry," Alex said. "I wasn't calling about Steele; I was calling about you, to see how you're doing in the midst of all this."

"Horseshit, if you really want to know. I'm getting tarred with the same brush as the judge. People insult me on the phone. Friends won't talk to me. It's like I'm invisible in the hallways around here."

"I'm sorry, Jerry," Alex said. "I did try to warn you."

"I know, I know. In my worst nightmares, I never thought it would be as bad as you said. Then for Steele to go into hiding, leaving me to take the shit, is just too much."

"What are you going to do?"

"I'm going to resign and issue some kind of statement proclaiming my innocence, but I don't know if anybody will believe me. It's like I've wasted the last five years of my life."

"Then what?"

"I'll probably get out of town, try to start over somewhere else."

"And you truly don't know where Steele is?" Alex asked.

"Not a clue. I suspect he's holed up at home, trying to figure something out. I don't think you've heard the last of him."

"I don't, either," Alex said, remembering the words of Dr. Johnson.

Steele's house was like a fortress. The gate was locked, the doors were bolted, the drapes and shades were drawn in every room. The lights were out, and the phone remained disconnected.

The judge had not left the house since Alex's report. He'd spoken to no one and had seen no one.

Perhaps he knew there would be reporters and cameras by the gate, waiting for him.

So he had stayed locked away, pacing the house like a leopard in a cage.

The next morning's St. Paul *Pioneer Press* carried a banner head-line:

WHERE IS JUDGE STEELE?
Accused Jurist in Seclusion

The story described the unsuccessful efforts to contact Steele, and reported that he apparently had spoken to no one, including his own staff and members of the governor's staff.

"Officials are at a loss to explain Judge Steele's silence or his whereabouts," the newspaper said. "It is believed the judge may be closeted inside his Golden Valley home, which is protected by a fence and a locked gate. Efforts to reach him by telephone have failed."

If the reporters could have seen through the walls, they would have found Steele now spending most of his time in the darkness, sitting in his high-backed chair in front of the stage and screens, watching an endless number of tapes from his collection. He seemed determined to see them all, recalling vividly each of the boys. He called each of them by name, and talked to them quietly, endearingly, as they appeared on screen.

Steele seemed to have little interest in the storm which was swirling around him. His only contact with the outside world was the radio. His television set was a shattered heap, and he chose not to walk to the gate to retrieve his newspapers.

Three times a day he would leave the videos and walk to the kitchen to turn on the small radio atop the refrigerator. He listened attentively to the stories about himself, as if he were hearing about the predicament of some stranger in another part of the world.

Finally, on Sunday afternoon, he reconnected the telephone and dialed a number.

"Associated Press," the voice on the other end said.

"This is Judge Emmett M. Steele. Please make a note. I will reply to these preposterous, slanderous, and venomous reports about me on Tuesday—at a time and place to be designated later. Do you have that? Thank you."

Tuesday was to have been Judge Steele's inauguration day.

Forty-six

The word spread like a prairie fire whipped by late March winds.

The AP wire story ignited the flames. Judge Steele was coming out of hiding! He was going to respond. But where, and at what time?

Was it really Judge Steele who called?

The mystery only heightened the drama. Speculation abounded; the media were ripe with rumors.

All the while, Steele sat at home and watched his tapes. And listened to his radio.

Russell had not moved from the cell bunk except to make several unsuccessful calls to Judge Steele. He'd refused all meals, dozing off now and then as the hours passed. The grating of the key in the lock of the cell door awakened him with a start.

"C'mon, Russell," Tolliver said, opening the steel door. "You've got a visitor."

Russell breathed deeply and smiled, convinced Judge Steele would be waiting with bail money and reassuring words. He *knew* the judge wouldn't abandon him; freedom and fresh air awaited him at the end of the hall.

"I told you you couldn't keep me in here," Russell said.

"We'll see, Russell," Tolliver replied.

The sheriff stopped at a door outside the cellblock and opened it. Russell strode through, but stopped short, his mouth falling open.

Roger Anderson rose to greet him.

"Hello, Russell. Good to see you again."

Russell's legs felt weak, and there was a queasiness rising in his empty stomach.

"Sit down, Russell," Tolliver said. "Roger here has been telling us some very interesting things. About how he spent a few days with you and the judge."

The sheriff held up a pair of shackles, one in each hand, a severed chain hanging from each.

"Do you recognize these, Russell?" Tolliver asked.

"I want to talk to Judge Steele," Russell demanded. "I want to talk to a lawyer."

"You've had the chance to make your phone calls, Russell. I can't help it if the judge doesn't answer. You certainly have every right to an attorney. Just ask, and we'll provide you with some names, or with a public defender if you can't afford your own lawyer."

"Steele isn't going to talk to you, Russell," Roger said. "He's got enough problems without worrying about you."

"He'll have more problems if he doesn't worry about me," Russell muttered, remembering Steele's harsh words after the fire.

"What was that, Russell?" Tolliver asked.

"Never mind."

"Remember that snowmobile suit I showed you in the garage? The one that still smelled like gas? Roger says he saw you wearing it the night my deputy disappeared. Only Roger says the suit was all wet, and *really* smelled of gas. Remember that, Russell?"

Russell surprised Tolliver with his speed and strength, bolting for the door and ripping it open. But a deputy, even larger and stronger than Russell the Linebacker, was waiting calmly outside.

His bear hug made even Russell grunt.

Tolliver walked slowly out of the room, cuffing Russell's hands behind his back.

"Russell Tosier," the sheriff said, softly, "I charge you with the kidnapping and assault of Roger Anderson and with the murder of

Deputy Sheriff Fred Jensen. You have the right to remain silent . . ."

On Tuesday morning, a Golden Valley policeman, his fur earlaps
pulled tight around his chin, stood in front of Steele's house, directing local traffic through the parked news cars and Minicam
vans. The rival news teams took turns keeping watch on Steele's
driveway, forsaking their competitive urges for the warmth of their
heated cars.

The morning hours passed slowly. Exhaust from the idling cars
beclouded the street, and the news helicopters buzzed overhead,
doing their best to keep out of each other's way.

At precisely 12:30, the front door of Steele's house opened and
the judge emerged. He stood on the step for a moment, breathing
in the cold air, and then walked briskly to his parked Continental.

The lookout at the foot of the drive shouted, and the news cars
emptied out. Some of the reporters were still carrying their half-
eaten sandwiches as they ran, and the photographers struggled to
hoist their cameras on their shoulders without tripping over the
microphone cords.

Steele paused at the door of his car. He stood erect, clad in a
tailored black wool coat with felt lapels and a matching felt hat.
He watched the crowd gather at the gate, then got into the car
and backed down the driveway.

He stopped at the gate and unlocked the chain, ignoring the
shouted questions and the cameras poking through the bars. Finally, he held up his hand, and said simply: "Ladies and gentlemen, please follow me."

It was like a parade winding through the streets of Golden Valley
to Interstate 394. The black Continental was in the lead, moving
slowly, followed by a dozen news cars and vans, escorted overhead
by three helicopters.

Through the Lowry Tunnel, heading east on Interstate 94 for
St. Paul. Off at the Marion Street exit, moving directly toward the
State Capitol.

"He's going to see the governor," one of the reporters shouted
into his car radio. "He's got to be."

The caravan continued unimpeded, turning onto University
Avenue, then into the Capitol complex.

"Get somebody to the governor's office," the reporter said. "Get Steele coming in."

At 12:55, the Continental pulled up squarely in front of the Capitol steps. Judge Steele stepped out of the car, leaving the door open. He took the stairs two at a time, coat now open, flapping in the cold wind. The news people struggled to keep up, the photographers shooting on the fly, fighting for position.

The judge ignored them, moving without pause through the Capitol doors, across the rotunda, and up the broad marble stairway.

It was now one o'clock, exactly the time Steele was to have been sworn in as chief justice. He did not go to the governor's office, but walked directly to one of the two courtrooms used by the Supreme Court and pushed open the heavy, eight-foot-high oak doors.

And came face to face with Alex Collier.

Alex was standing just inside the door, a photographer by his side, the camera rolling as Steele came to an abrupt halt.

"Afternoon, Judge," Alex said. "I thought you might come here."

"You can go to hell, Collier," Steele said as he tried to block the lens of the camera. "You're a liar and a fool," he fumed, "just like all reporters. You're so obsessed by your romantic ideas of justice that you would undermine the very man who has devoted his life to preserving it. But you'll see that the law protects the truly innocent."

With that, Steele pushed past Alex, walking toward the high mahogany bench. Behind it, seven tall, brown leather chairs sat empty, and Steele moved quickly to the one in the center, the chair of the chief justice.

"You will have five minutes to set up your cameras and microphones," Steele told the milling crowd of news people. "My statement will begin at precisely one-oh-eight."

Steele sat calmly in the midst of the bedlam.

"What's going on in here?" a man who had just entered the chambers demanded. It was Justice John McGregor, the acting chief justice. "What is this madness?" A Capitol policeman stood by his side.

"Relax, John," Steele said amiably. "I'm going to hold a news conference in a moment. It shouldn't take too long."

"That's impossible," McGregor said. "This courtroom cannot be used for such a purpose. I must ask you to leave, Judge Steele. Take your news conference elsewhere."

By now, the courtroom had quieted. The cameras were recording the confrontation.

"I'm afraid that's not possible, Justice McGregor. It is imperative my statement be heard here, from this chair—which I was unfairly denied by the slanderous attacks of Alex Collier and the rest of the media."

Steele had grown agitated; he had risen halfway out of the chief justice's chair, his palms flat on the surface of the bench.

"It's a conspiracy, don't you see? A plot designed to deny me my rightful place on this bench, to prevent the fulfillment of my lifelong dream."

His eyes darted to Justice McGregor.

"I'm surprised to find you part of this, John. But perhaps I shouldn't be—since I understand you've inherited the position that has been stolen from me."

Everyone in the room now realized they were dealing with someone on the verge of hysteria. McGregor became sympathetically wary, climbing the steps of the bench, extending his arms. The Capitol cop followed closely behind.

"Come now, Judge Steele. Just relax. No one is out to get you. Why don't you come with us? You can speak to the press later."

"No!" Steele shouted, reaching into his pocket and pulling out a small-caliber pistol. "Stay back!" Everyone in the chamber scattered, diving for the doors or for cover behind the wooden seats.

But the pistol was not pointed in their direction; Steele held it firmly against the soft flesh beneath his chin.

Justice McGregor and the policeman stood stock-still.

"I was afraid it might come to this," Steele said, his voice barely audible. "But I will be heard by all you fools."

By now, a large crowd of spectators and more Capitol policemen had gathered outside the doors of the courtroom, opening them only wide enough to peek through. Inside, heads were slowly rising from behind the seats, and photographers were crawling back toward their cameras. Alex hadn't moved, sitting bolt upright on the hard wooden bench, staring at Steele, refusing to cower before him.

"You have all heard the charges against me," Steele began. "In fact, many of you helped to perpetuate them. You're idiots, all of you. You have no idea what you're doing, or who my accusers are. Whores, all of them. Amoral misfits, dregs of society, the scum of the streets, whose words have no more credence than the ravings of a lunatic."

Steele's eyes swept wildly across the room. His right arm was flailing in the air, but his left was steady, holding the pistol tight against his neck.

"Did I force myself on them?" he shouted. "Of course not! I am the one who has been violated. By them and by people like Alex Collier, who sits smugly among you today. Alex Collier, an itinerant mudslinger who has carried on a vicious vendetta against me since the day he arrived."

Alex watched, spellbound, as Steele raved on.

"Collier has already destroyed my trusted friend and colleague, Nathaniel Hodges, who leaped to his death rather than face what has befallen me. Well, I will not plunge from that same precipice. I will continue to do things my way, to make sure everyone is dealt with properly. I will fight these charges with all of the vigor at my command, until the end of time if necessary. And, one day, I will regain my rightful place in this most distinguished chair."

With that, Emmett Steele placed the pistol on the benchtop. But he continued too speak, his monologue growing more bizarre, his gestures more frenzied. "Can't you understand how proud my mother would have been to see me here in this chair . . ."

McGregor and the policeman began to edge toward him.

Steele was looking into the distance, arms uplifted, a strange smile on his face. "She was an angel, she understood me, nurtured me . . ."

As the officer reached for the pistol, McGregor wrapped his arms around Steele, gently but firmly.

Steele kept talking unintelligibly, but did not struggle as he was led through the side door of the courtroom.

The newspapers and the television newscasts were filled with the story and pictures of Steele's dramatic, crazed appearance in the Supreme Court.

Alex and his photographer had followed the police as they took Steele to the psychiatric ward of the St. Paul-Ramsey Medical Center, but the doctors there would say nothing to the press.

"Do you really think he would have shot himself?" Knowles asked Alex later.

"I doubt it, but who knows? He was determined to speak."

"This case could be in the courts for years," Knowles said. "With his money and moxie, Steele could stretch this out for a long time."

"An insanity defense could complicate things, all right," Alex admitted. "It could take months by the time they finish with the psychiatric exams and the conflicting opinions of all the shrinks."

"It may take even longer to get him officially off the bench," Knowles said. "Judges don't exactly like to defrock other judges, I don't care what they've done."

Alex nodded, remembering Pat's words of weeks before: *And who judges the judges? Other judges, that's who.*

"Is there a chance he'll be set free?" Knowles asked.

"Not if Tolliver can get Russell to talk. Phil says they've got him cold, that he's on the verge of breaking."

"How about Rick and Roger?"

"I've got to try and find them jobs," Alex replied. "But, shit, I'm not even sure I still have one."

When Alex returned home that night, he found the light blinking on his answering machine.

"Alex," Pat's voice was as hushed as it was the first night he had heard it in the newsroom. "I just called to say I'm sorry that I brought all this upon you. Can you ever forgive me? And can you forgive me for loving you, because even now I cannot help but be glad that we met again."

Forgive her? he thought. He wanted to race over to her and thank her for bringing all the meaning back into his life and showing him that he could love.

It was morning before Judge Steele realized where he was. He'd grown increasingly agitated in the police car on the way to the hospital and had been sedated immediately upon his arrival.

He had drifted in and out of sleep, but even in his waking moments, he'd been confused by his surroundings. His room was small, dimly lit, and starkly furnished. A small stand stood next to the bed, and a television set, dark now, was tilted toward him from a shelf high on the opposite wall.

Steele had tried to raise himself up and out of the bed, but he found that he didn't have the strength. The sidebars of the bed posed an insurmountable barrier.

The bed seemed to swallow up his body, sucking it into the sheets. He had grown old overnight; his skin sagged beneath his cheekbones, and the hands gripping the siderails were skeleton-thin. His breath came in short gasps, and his eyes were never still, blinking with the blur of a hummingbird's wings.

He closed his eyes again, recalling only fragments of the scene in the Supreme Court. He thought of it as a dream, but somehow knew it had been real.

He awoke to the sound of voices in the doorway of his room.

He tried to raise his head. Someone in white was talking to another man in uniform. *Who? A policeman?*

"We don't want him disturbed by anybody but staff. He's a sick man and needs his rest."

The policeman nodded and the man in white walked to Steele's bedside. "You're awake," he said. "I'm Doctor Spangler. I'll be taking care of you."

"Why am I here?" Steele growled. "I demand to be released immediately."

"I'm afraid that's not possible," the doctor said. "You're here under police guard and are not free to leave."

"Police guard? What's going on here?" he shouted, lifting his head from the pillow. "Who's responsible for this? I demand to know. This is outrageous!"

The doctor quieted him. "Relax, Judge Steele, relax. We'll take good care of you."

When Steele's eyes opened again, the room was dark except for the diffused light spilling in from the hallway. His television set was still off, and he could hear soft chatter and laughter from the nursing station.

He stared at the ceiling and walls, his eyes restlessly moving back and forth. In the gloom, he was sure he saw pictures etched into the ceiling tile—out-of-focus images of the boys from his tapes, intermingled with the mocking smile of Alex Collier, and the sprawled body of Nathaniel Hodges.

It must be the drugs, he thought as he shut his eyes to erase the pictures. When his eyelids lifted, a nurse he had not seen before walked to the door of his room. She stopped to speak to the policeman, then came in and shut the door behind her.

"Good evening, Judge," she said. "My name's Linda. I'll be taking care of you."

She lowered the siderail of his bed, and began to slip an elastic restraint around one of his wrists. "You're not going to like this," she said, "but the doctor says he'd like to keep you in hand and leg restraints tonight. He doesn't want you thrashing around so you can't sleep."

Steele started to protest, but she smiled and held her finger to her lips. "Shhhh," she whispered. "Doctor's orders. Don't wake up the other patients." By then she had completed putting the elastic bands on his wrists and ankles and tightened them.

She walked to the door and opened it a crack. "I'm going to give him his bath now," she told the officer, "so please don't let us be disturbed." Then she closed the door.

"Bath?" Steele said. "You didn't say anything about a—"

The fist-sized ball of cotton was in his mouth before he could finish the sentence. He tried to spit it out, but she pushed it in farther, gagging him.

"Do you remember Daniel Grabowski?" she asked, tears falling down her cheeks. "He was my brother. I loved him very much. You killed him, didn't you?"

Steele shook his head from side to side, eyes bulging.

Linda studied his thrashing body. She showed no agitation, but the grief and the hatred swirled inside her. Her heart pounded, her confused mind raced. Until now, she hadn't known what she would do, but as she looked into Steele's panicked face, she saw Daniel again. Then she decided.

What did the Bible say? An eye for an eye.

She took one of his fingers in her hands and, with a quick snap, bent it sharply toward his wrist. She heard the bone crack.

His scream was absorbed by the cotton, and by her hand firmly cupped over his mouth. His eyes moved wildly from side to side.

"But you didn't just kill him, did you? You tortured him first, broke his fingers, one by one. They didn't want me to know, but I found out. Poor Daniel."

The second finger snapped as easily as the first. She thought he'd pass out. His back arched off the bed, and his arms and legs pulled violently against the restraints.

"Then you left him where the animals could get at his body. There was almost nothing left to bury."

She heard no sound when the third finger broke. Steele tried to jar the bed, to move it with the jerks of his body, but it was no use. He was too weak, the pain too great.

"I never even had the chance to say goodbye to Daniel," she said, "to tell him how much I loved him. I'll never forgive you for that."

Her face above him became fuzzy, and Steele realized he was seeing her through tears. He tried to blink them away, and for a moment his vision cleared. Time enough to see her smile, the pillow raised above her head, slowly descending to cover his face.

When his body was still, Linda put the pillow back beneath his head and removed the restraints from his arms and legs. Then she walked out of the door, closing it quietly behind her.

"He should sleep well now," she told the policeman, who nodded absently as her footsteps echoed down the hall.

Back to her own room on the floor below.